MY PARIS ROMANCE

FALLING IN LOVE WITH A BILLIONAIRE...

OLIVIA SPRING

HARTLEY PUBLISHING

CHAPTER ONE

N*ew Year's resolutions.*
        I wasn't a fan of making them. I'd lost count of the times I'd vowed to get fitter, joined the gym, then only ended up going once (or maybe twice if I was really on fire). Or said I'd give up chocolate, but then got seduced by the sight of a Galaxy bar at the supermarket checkout.

My track record of sticking to resolutions wasn't great. But *this* year really *was* going to be different. Guaranteed. How could I be so sure? Because I was seconds away from following through on my resolution to resign from my personal assistant role: something I'd wanted to do for ages.

Today would be the day I finally bit the bullet and told Spencer, my arsehole of a boss, to stick his job where the sun didn't shine.

Well, not in those exact words, *obviously*. As much as I couldn't stand him, I had to stay professional. After all, I needed a reference.

My heart thudded as I read over the email once, twice,

then a third time. I'll admit, sending an email wasn't ideal. It would've been better to do it in person, but we didn't live in an ideal world. Sometimes a woman had to do what a woman had to do to preserve her sanity. Given the circumstances, this was the only option.

It was now or never.

I hovered the mouse over the send button, took a deep breath and…

Done.

My stomach fluttered with a mixture of nerves and excitement. I quickly picked up my handbag, hat and coat, rushed to the lift, then, once I'd reached the large glass revolving doors, stepped out of the building and inhaled the cold January air.

I'd resigned.

Finally.

I wanted to race down the street with a megaphone, announcing the great news to the world. If they knew Spencer and the crap I'd put up with over the years, they'd understand why.

But as much as I'd like to shout it from the rooftops, there was one person I wanted to tell first.

I plucked my phone from my bag. After several rings, he answered.

'I did it!' Elation swept through me.

'*Fantastique!*' Nico said in his gorgeous thick French accent. 'I am very happy to hear that. We should do a video call so I can see your face.'

'Okay!' My body fizzed with excitement. I'd love to see him too. 'Give me a sec. Let me find somewhere to sit.'

After ending the call, I quickly crossed the road and

walked towards a little park opposite our office, then sat down on a bench. It was freezing, but seeing Nico was worth staying out in the cold.

I pulled out my mirror, swiped on some lip gloss, straightened my green woolly hat, then pressed the video call button.

As Nico's face appeared on the screen, I nearly wet my pants. *Damn.* Did this man ever look bad? His rich chocolate-brown eyes sparkled and his face broke into a smile, flashing his perfect white teeth.

'*Chérie!* It is so nice to see you!'

'Same!' My stomach flipped as I watched his full lips move. God, I missed those lips. It was a good thing I'd decided to sit down; otherwise, my knees would've buckled.

As usual, his thick dark hair was perfectly styled. To be expected for a hairdresser and hair tools company CEO. His skin glowed and looked so smooth I wished I could reach into the screen and stroke his chiselled jaw. I wanted to tell him he looked hot, but decided to play it cool.

'So, Cassie'—I loved the way he said my name —*Cass-seee*—'tell me: you speak with your boss? He is back?'

'No…' I paused. 'I emailed him instead.'

'You still do not know when he will return to the office?' Nico frowned.

'Nope. The last email I received was two days ago and he's banned anyone from calling, which is a cheek considering he never thinks twice about ringing me when I'm on holiday.'

Spencer was in the Bahamas. When his wife had discovered he'd been having an affair on New Year's Day, he'd quickly suggested they go away so he could 'make it up to her'.

Bollocks. Spencer didn't give a toss about his wife's feelings. To him, the trip was just a damage limitation exercise. His way of avoiding a very expensive divorce.

They were only supposed to be gone for a week, so even though I'd vowed to hand in my notice as soon as I returned to the office after the Christmas holidays, I had a heart. I knew how much he relied on me, and if he was trying to avoid the breakdown of his marriage and working out how he'd still get to see his kids, me handing in my notice on the first day back might push him over the edge. I didn't want that on my conscience, so I'd reasoned that after holding on for so long, one week wasn't going to make a big difference.

But then he'd extended their holiday by a week. Two weeks were fast becoming three. Which was why today I'd decided that enough was enough.

Although Spencer was going through a difficult time, he'd brought the whole sorry mess on himself and I'd put up with his BS for too long.

Him insisting I find a sold-out gift for his mistress whilst I was on holiday, the day before Christmas Eve, and then calling me repeatedly on Christmas Day were the last straws. I had to think of myself for a change. My mental health was more important than Spencer's bank balance.

Every time I'd asked when he was coming back, he'd ignored me, so I'd had no option but to resign via email. I'd cc'd in HR too, so there was no way he could say he hadn't received it. It was done. There was no going back now.

'You do—*pardon*, you *did* the right thing. If he will not

speak to you or tell you when he will return, you have no choice.'

'Exactly!'

'I am so happy for you. How do you feel?'

'Amazing! It's hard to describe. I feel a bit like Mary Poppins.'

'Who?'

'You know, the film, where she comes and looks after the kids? She's like a magical nanny.'

'*Comment?*' His thick, dark eyebrows knitted together. 'You want to become a nanny?'

'No!' I laughed. '*She's* a nanny. Mary Poppins. In the film she has an umbrella and when she opens it, she can fly up to the sky. That's how I feel. Like, I'm so happy that if I lifted my feet off the ground I might take off and fly!'

'Oh, I see,' he chuckled. 'That is good!'

'I'm also bricking it, because I haven't got another job lined up yet.'

'Bricking?' Nico's face crumpled.

Oops. Another thing lost in translation. Nico was so easy to talk to that sometimes I forgot about the language barrier.

'Sorry. *Bricking it* means being scared or worried.'

'I see. But you do not need to worry. Let me help you.'

'Thanks'—I smiled—'but I can handle it.' Just because Nico had money, I wasn't about to start sponging off him. He'd already surprised me last week by delivering a new oven to my flat after mine had broken down on Christmas Day. It was top of the range too. Probably cost two months' salary or something crazy like that.

I didn't want to start relying on Nico to pay my bills. I'd find a new role. Even though I'd only just resigned, I'd been job-hunting religiously for the past month and had sent my CV to dozens of recruitment agencies, asking to be considered for any PA opportunities. Preferably something permanent, but I'd even consider temp work initially. Anything to get out of here.

'If you are sure.'

'I am. When I followed up with the recruitment agencies last week, a few sounded enthusiastic, so hopefully something will come up soon. Anyway, I'm not going to think about that. Right now I want to focus on the good things. I've resigned, and next week I'll be getting ready to come and see you in Paris!'

'*Oui!* This is very exciting!'

It was. Well... mostly. The seeing Nico part definitely was. It'd been more than three weeks since I'd laid eyes on him in the flesh, when he'd left a couple of days after Christmas, but sometimes it felt like three months.

We'd hoped to at least meet up for a weekend by now, but the first two weeks of January he'd been on a business trip in America. He could've come last weekend, but I'd already promised my cousin Bella that I'd look after my godson, Paul and I couldn't let her down. And this weekend it was my sister's birthday, so we were having a family get-together.

The thought of inviting Nico had crossed my mind, but then logic had quickly set in. I loved my family, but it was too soon for him to meet them. As much as I hoped this could develop into a relationship, it was best not to risk it. Five minutes with my mother or brother and he'd be running for the hills. *Nope*. Not a good idea.

Nico had offered to travel to London for the day, but as much as I wanted him to, after waiting almost a month, I reckoned seeing him for just a few hours might somehow be worse. As hard as it would be, it was better to wait until next Saturday. Then I'd be able to stay with Nico for a whole week.

My stomach tightened. It'd been more than a decade since I'd gone abroad, so I was a little apprehensive about travelling. Still, at least I didn't have to take the ferry like we had on that nightmare school trip to Calais twenty years ago. That had put me off boats for life.

So yeah, I was definitely looking forward to being reunited, but the other stuff, like meeting his friends, trying to communicate in another language and mixing in his fancy millionaire circles? Hmmm, not so much.

'I can't wait to see you!' I said, focusing on the part that was true.

'It will be great. You will love Paris. It is the perfect time for you to come, because after that week I will be very busy. I make sure I move some meetings until after you leave so we can spend more time together when you are here.'

'Wow, thank you!' I knew how hectic life was for Nico, so that meant a lot.

'*Chérie*, I have a meeting. I must go now, but *félicitations*—congratulations! We will talk soon, okay?'

'Okay.'

He kissed the screen, then hung up. The sight of his lips made my body tingle.

Nine more days. Just nine more days.

And if things went well after that, maybe I could spend another week there in a month's time, when I left this job and before I started the next one. *Yes*. Great idea.

I pulled a homemade cheese and pickle sandwich out

of my bag. A latte here, a muffin there, plus spending money on lunch every day quickly added up. That was why another New Year's resolution was bringing in food from home. Knowing I planned to resign meant I needed to be extra careful with money. Just in case.

I'd even contemplated whether I should go on this trip. Seeing as I didn't have another job lined up yet, maybe it was irresponsible to go gallivanting off to Paris. But it was too good an opportunity to miss. Nico had already paid for my ticket as a Christmas gift and I wouldn't have any accommodation costs.

Although I still wanted to pay my way whilst I was there and I needed to look the part, because I'd curbed my spending, I had enough to buy a few new outfits and to cover some excursions. Plus, I'd be getting paid soon, so that would take care of my bills for at least another month. *Yes*. There was no need to worry. As long as I didn't splash out too much and got a new job soon, I'd be fine.

After finishing my sandwich, I walked back to the office. A little boy in a pushchair ahead of me dropped his glove, so I quickly picked it up, handed it to his mum, then headed inside the tall glass building.

As I slipped back into the warmth, my mind buzzed as I thought about Nico again. I scrolled through some photos on my phone. The selfie we had taken on Christmas Day in the snow on the South Bank with the river Thames, Big Ben and the London Eye in the background was one of my favourites. Not long to go until we'd get to create more memories together.

As I strode towards my desk, I froze. Spencer's door was open. I peered inside.

OMG.

He's back.

Spencer looked up from his computer screen and raised his eyebrow. His thinning blond hair had lightened and his normally pale skin looked sunburnt. Knowing him, he was too lazy to wear sunscreen.

'Well, well, well…' He put his feet up on the dark wooden desk and rested his hands behind his head. 'If it isn't the little traitor! I got your *email*. After years of working for me, you resign with a poxy email? That's like dumping someone with a text. I expected better from you, Cassandra.'

Ouch.

That was what my ex had done to me. I'd never do something so cold.

'I know an email wasn't ideal…' My heart raced. His unexpected arrival had thrown me. 'But you've been gone for weeks and you didn't tell me when you were coming back.'

'Oh, *I'm* sorry,' he said sarcastically. 'Here I was thinking *I* was the boss and I could do whatever I wanted. I didn't realise I had to check in with *you* first.'

'That's not what I meant, I—'

'I don't care what you meant!' he hissed. 'I'm in the bloody doghouse with my girlfriend because I had to cancel our weekend in New York, my wife wants to leave me, and now you want to piss off too? Talk about kicking a guy when he's down.'

Seriously? Even though his wife had found out about his affair and he'd spent the last three weeks supposedly trying to make it up to her, he was still seeing his mistress? This man really was scum.

'Look…' I took a deep breath, hoping it would help to

slow my thumping heart rate. 'I know the timing isn't ideal for you, but I've made my decision, so I think it's best if we can find a way to be professional about this. I'll of course help to find my replacement and continue to work hard whilst I serve my month's notice.'

'*Month's* notice?' he laughed.

Why was that funny?

'Someone hasn't checked their contract.' He smirked. 'I think you'll find that you'll be serving your notice for much longer than that.'

WTF?

Admittedly, I didn't have my contract with me. It was in a box at my parents' house somewhere in the loft. I'd put it there when I was decorating last year, but I was pretty sure it *was* a month's notice. I'd checked that contract religiously not long after I'd signed it, because I'd contemplated leaving so many times.

'What do you mean? The contract I signed said I needed to give one month's notice.'

'You're mistaken. See for yourself.'

Spencer swivelled his computer screen around and opened a document. It was a contract with my name at the top. He then highlighted a section which stated…

'Wait, *what*? A month's notice, plus an extra week for every year of service? But that would mean…' I did the maths in my head. Nine weeks. Nine weeks' notice? I didn't have a calendar with me, but we were already in the third week of January, so by my mental calculations, I was pretty sure that would mean I couldn't leave until… towards the end of March. That was a week before the start of April. 'That's practically April!'

My mouth dropped open and my stomach plummeted.

April.

No way.

'That's too long! I can't wait until then.'

'I'm afraid you'll have to. Otherwise, you'll be in breach of contract. And that won't be good if you're looking for another job.'

'Can't you just get a temp to fill in for me? Wendy's covering my holiday from the Monday after next, so I'm sure she could fill in once I left if we gave her enough notice.'

'Your *holiday*? What holiday?'

'My annual leave. I'm off from next Friday evening for a week.' I swallowed hard. I didn't like the sound of where this conversation was going.

'Annual leave? Pff! No can do, sweetheart. I need you here.'

'But you said!' My chest tightened. 'When we spoke on the phone last week. On Monday morning. Remember? I even emailed you to confirm the dates.' I always followed everything up in writing with Spencer, just in case.

'I have no recollection of that conversation. And even if I did, the year has barely started, so you haven't even accrued two days' holiday yet. And seeing as you're leaving, you'd probably have to work for at least a couple of months to earn enough time off for a week's break.'

'But...'

'Don't worry. Time flies when you're having fun, eh? April will be here before you know it, so you can save your holiday until then. If you're a good girl, maybe I'll let you use some of it to leave a few days earlier. Close the door on your way out.' He grinned.

I stormed out of the office and slammed the door.

Classic Spencer. It was clearly his way of getting back at me for resigning. This was why I needed to get away from his toxicity. Just when I thought I'd finally be free, he'd pulled the rug out from under me again.

And what about Nico? Like me, he was excited that we'd get to spend a whole week together. Now what? I'd only be able to see him at the weekends, so for no more than two days at a time until I left my job? That would never work. A rich, powerful, gorgeous man like him would have women falling at his feet every day.

With both of us living in different countries and coming from two different worlds, the chances of our fling developing into something more long-term were already slim enough without throwing this kind of spanner in the works.

Shit.

I'd waited so long to find a great guy. And now I was about to lose him before our relationship even had a chance to get off the ground.

CHAPTER TWO

I dropped my keys on the hallway table, then shut the front door. I was glad I'd forced myself out of the house.

For the past couple of days I'd had an annoying, tight feeling in my chest. I'd noticed it had started after Spencer had gleefully told me that not only would I be stuck working for him for at least two more miserable months, but that the holiday he'd approved (and trust me, he *had*) was also a no-go.

Today I'd intended to buy some outfits for Paris, but as those plans had gone south, I'd contemplated spending the day moping on the sofa with my adult colouring books. But then I'd given myself a pep talk and decided to do some voluntary work at the local retirement home instead.

I'd only been going for a couple of weeks, but I really enjoyed it. One of the residents, Doris, who was eighty-seven, always put a smile on my face. And I knew that if I visited her, I'd feel better.

I tried to do little things to help others. I often donated flowers to the nearby hospital and asked the nurses to give them to whoever they thought needed cheering up. I'd also leave colouring books and crayons at the paediatric wing. But somehow, that hadn't seemed like enough. That was why I decided to start giving my time instead.

I knew a lot of elderly people felt lonely or isolated—especially if they didn't have family to visit them. So when the retirement home had advertised for volunteers to sit and chat with the residents, I'd jumped at the chance. If taking a few hours out of my weekend could help lift the spirits of others, I was happy to do it.

I especially loved listening to Doris's stories. Today she told me she'd been married seven times and joked that her one regret in life was that she hadn't found an eighth husband to match Elizabeth Taylor's record. But then she'd winked at one of the male workers and said there was still time. *Yeah*. At least being there this afternoon had brought a smile to my face.

Doris's conversation about her multiple husbands reminded me that I really needed to speak to Nico. I hadn't told him that I wouldn't be able to come next week yet and I really needed to. ASAP. The tight feeling returned to my chest. The idea of disappointing him made my stomach sink.

Maybe it wasn't a big deal. After all, we still had the weekends. Although I'd said before that I preferred us to spend a longer amount of time together, it was better than nothing, right?

One of the advantages of Nico being loaded was that he wasn't concerned about the cost of travel in the same way that normal people like me would be. I mean, before we'd arranged for me to come over next week, Nico had even suggested that he could come to London for a few hours tonight. But that clashed with my family dinner. It'd been planned for ages, so I couldn't let my little sister down.

I knew he had plans tomorrow, so seeing him then would be out. But he'd have to be free next weekend, because that was when I was supposed to be in Paris.

Problem solved. I'd call him tomorrow and do a 'good news, bad news' scenario. Bad news is, I can't come for a week, but the good news is, I can come for a weekend. Forty-eight hours with just the two of us would have to do for now.

I changed into a fresh pair of jeans and my comfy red jumper, buttoned up my coat and slid on my favourite green leather gloves. Nico had bought them for me just a few hours after we'd met. It was the day before Christmas Eve and he'd offered to help me find a sold-out hairdryer that Spencer had demanded I track down for his mistress, and in return I'd agreed to give Nico a festive tour of London.

Although I'd first thought he was an arrogant dickhead, I'd gradually realised he was a sweetheart. And later I'd discovered that the reason he was able to source the hairdryer was because he owned Icon: the mega-successful company that made luxury straightening irons and hair tools used by the rich and famous. Nico was worth millions. *Crikey.* I still couldn't quite get my head around it.

Bloody Spencer. If it wasn't for him, next week I'd be

reunited with Nico properly. I wished Reg, Spencer's dad and owner of the company, hadn't retired and left his stupid son to run it.

I walked to the high street and jumped on a bus. We were gathering at my parents' house to celebrate my little sister Lily's thirty-second birthday. Even though there were only four years between us, we'd always seen her as the baby of the family.

It'd been ages since we'd all been together. Normally we celebrated Christmas at my parents', but last month we'd all decided to do our own thing, which, to be honest, I'd been *very* relieved about.

Family get-togethers always involved some scrutiny, especially from my mum, who'd fire more questions at me than a lawyer cross-examining a murder suspect. Still, maybe everyone was feeling more relaxed after the holidays and wouldn't give me such a hard time.

A girl can dream.

'Hey!' I threw my arms around Lily. 'Happy birthday, little sis!'

'Thanks!' She squeezed me tight. Like my older sister Floella and me, Lily had thick, curly hair. Mine was past my shoulders, but Lily's was a little shorter, just like her really. She'd always been the smallest in the family. At the last count, she was a few inches shorter than me at five foot four, although she was adamant she was five foot six.

'Can't believe I'm so old!' she groaned.

'Old?' I folded my arms. 'What does that make me, then? I'm thirty-five. Thirty-bloody-six this year!' I handed Lily a gift bag, which had a birthday balloon wrapped around the handle.

'Try being thirty-eight!' Nate stood in front of us and

opened his arms. 'Come on, Cass, bring it in. Give your big brother a hug.' At six foot three, Nate towered over me. His short curly hair looked like it had been freshly shaved at the sides and as always, his beard was shaped to perfection.

He lifted me up in the air, put me down, then squeezed my cheeks.

'Really?' I folded my arms in mock protest. 'We're still doing *that*?'

'C'mon. You know you'll always be my sweet little Cassie-Cheeks!'

When I was a baby, I used to have big cheeks, which apparently Nate was obsessed with. Throughout my childhood, he'd greeted me with a squeeze of the cheeks, so Cheeks had quickly become my nickname. As annoying as I found it, I was used to it now. It was just one of Nate's things.

'Hello, sweetheart!' Dad said in his Cockney accent. He rushed over to give me a hug.

'Dad!' I tiptoed so I could rest my head on his broad shoulder. Both Nate and Dad were the tall ones in the family. 'You're looking well.'

'Thanks, love. Must be all that lovely sun we got on holiday.' They'd not long got back from visiting Mum's family in St Lucia. At first, they'd contemplated visiting Dad's maternal family in Scotland for Christmas, but the temptation of winter sunshine had won out. 'Go and say hello to your mother. She's cooking up a storm in the kitchen.'

After removing my coat and shoes, I headed to the kitchen. Mum was examining the chicken, which looked like it'd just come out of the oven, and my elder sister,

Floella, was taking some wine glasses from the cupboard.

'Hi, Mum.'

'Hello, Cassie dear.' She switched off the oven. 'Well, come on, then. Don't you have a hug for your mother?'

I walked over and wrapped my arms around her. Mum was smartly dressed in a dark purple dress and the scent of her sweet perfume flooded my nostrils. She'd worn the same one since I was a child. She patted down my body like a security guard frisking a drug mule at an airport.

'Are you eating properly?' She pulled away and narrowed her eyes. 'You've lost weight. Floella, pass the girl some bread before she wastes away.'

Mum had always been a feeder. To her, food was the answer to everything. Feeling under the weather? A spicy curry with plenty of rice was the answer. Broken heart? Yep, you guessed it. More food. I couldn't disagree with her on that one.

She was a great cook, though. I used to love our sessions in the kitchen, where she'd teach me how to whip up one of her many tasty Caribbean dishes.

'Shouldn't we wait until we're all around the table, Mum?' Floella frowned. 'And where's *my* hug?'

'Coming right up!' I added as I headed over to her in the corner.

It wasn't long before we had all sat down and inhaled dinner, which was promptly followed by singing 'Happy Birthday' and cutting the cake.

The wine and Prosecco were flowing, and so far we were having a good evening. There'd been no Spanish inquisition about the state of my life. *Result.*

'This is lovely, isn't it, George?' Mum leant forward and smiled at Dad. 'All our babies here together with us.'

'It is, love.' He squeezed her hand.

'So, what's new with you, dear?' Everyone turned to face me. I'd spoken too soon. That was Mum's way of asking if there was a man on the scene, but I wasn't biting.

'Well, I finally resigned.' Saying that out loud still felt so good.

'What?' Mum gasped. 'But you have a good, steady job! Why would you leave? What are you going to do now? Remember, beggars can't be choosers.'

There went Mum's favourite phrase. She'd said *beggars can't be choosers* at least once a day when we were growing up. That and *you get what you're given*.

I swallowed hard as I felt the beads of sweat pool on my forehead. Even though I'd planned to leave and was confident that my job-hunting would pay off, hearing those familiar words instantly sowed a seed of doubt.

'I-I've already had some interest from some recruitment agencies, so I've got a good chance of finding another job.' I took a serviette from the table and dabbed it across my forehead. 'I hate it there, Mum, and Spencer treats me like crap. I have to get out.'

'That's just what bosses do.' She shook her head with disapproval. 'You're not supposed to *like* your job. You work to pay the bills and to put a roof over your head, not for enjoyment. Do you think I liked cleaning toilets? George,' she turned to Dad, 'did you enjoy waking up at the crack of dawn and working on a cold building site every day?'

'Not particularly, but I had to provide for my family.

You have to be careful, love. You might not find another job so easily.'

I wasn't surprised at their reaction. My parents were old-school and still believed a job was for life. In their eyes, the idea of resigning without having another role lined up was about as logical as wearing a bikini to trek through Antarctica.

I reached for my glass and took a large gulp of Prosecco, then inhaled and exhaled slowly to calm my breathing. I knew it was a risk. That was why I'd been careful to start saving and job-hunting *before* I'd resigned, and why I continued searching every single day.

'But if Cheeks isn't happy and her boss disrespects her, she should get out,' said Nate. 'It's not healthy.'

'Exactly!' My shoulders loosened a little. At least Nate understood.

'Well,' she huffed. 'I'm hoping that things are more positive on the romantic side of things?' Mum raised her eyebrow. 'I'm happy that most of my children are settled. Lily with her young man, River, and Flo with Darren. The only one who needs a partner now is you, Cassie.'

'Excuse me?' I straightened up in my seat. 'What about Nate?

'That's different.'

'Why?' I folded my arms. So much for my life not being scrutinised.

'Well, he's a man.'

'What the hell?' I snapped.

'Language, darling,' Mum added.

'That's so sexist! What is this? The 1950s?'

'It's not sexist, sweetie. It's biology. I had four children by the time I was your age. You can't be a mum if you haven't even found a man. It's different for my Nathan. He has more time to become a dad. Although I wouldn't say no to a grandchild now…' The corner of her mouth twitched.

I couldn't see that happening anytime soon. Nate definitely took advantage of his good looks. I'd never known him to be with a woman for longer than a few weeks.

'You won't be getting one from me for a while, Mum,' Nate laughed. 'I'm having *way* too much fun to settle down. Barcelona at Christmas was *lit*. Then we partied at another club in Spain for New Year's.'

'Was that with Carlos?' Lily perked up.

'Yeah. He's been DJing at some really cool places.'

'Wow! I bet you guys had fun.'

Lily had now gone into her own little world. She'd always fancied Carlos. He was Spanish, but had come to London to study. He and Nate had been as thick as thieves throughout uni. I'd always sensed that Carlos liked Lily too, but I knew there was no way Nate would be happy with his sister hooking up with his bestie.

'How was your Christmas with River?' I added quickly, to break her out of her daydream before anyone else noticed.

'It was okay. I was hoping to meet his parents, but River said they'd come down with a bug and he didn't want us to catch it. So he just came round to mine. He really wanted to meet you guys tonight, but had to work late. I'm going to see him after dinner.'

Flo's husband was also working, so he hadn't made it tonight either.

'See? That's what you need too, Cassie. Someone to come home to. You really shouldn't leave it so long. We thought you were finally going to settle down with that nice Jasper, but somehow you managed to let him slip through your fingers, like they always do.'

'Sorry, *what*?' My nostrils flared. 'Did you just call him *nice*? The bastard cheated on me, Mum!'

'Well, everyone makes mistakes, darling. I just want you to meet someone.'

Unbelievable.

This was one of the reasons I dreaded these family gatherings. For some reason, I always seemed to be the disappointment of the family.

Nate was the only son, so he'd always be the golden boy. Flo was the brainbox, with a high-flying job and a husband, which in Mum's eyes made her perfect. Lily was the baby of the family and for the last three months had been dating a guy that Mum thought sounded like Mr Right personified, even though she'd never even met him. And then there was me.

Mum had made it clear on multiple occasions that I was a failure. It wasn't so much that I hadn't done well at school or didn't have a successful career—it was more my personal shortcomings.

To her, family was everything, and the fact that I'd reached the grand old age of thirty-five without being able to hold on to a man long enough for him to even consider proposing or impregnating me was my greatest sin.

Flo was actively trying to have children. Lily had a couple of years before Mum was on her case. And she had a boyfriend, so as far as Mum was concerned, at least marriage and kids were possible. I, on the other hand, was considered a lost cause.

Even though most of the time it wasn't my fault that

the relationships had ended, somehow she always made me feel like I was the one who'd done something wrong. Like I wasn't worthy of being loved or keeping a guy.

It wasn't like I didn't want to settle down. I really did. It just hadn't happened for me yet. But maybe I had a chance. Now I'd met Nico, maybe things might change.

'Actually, I *have* met someone!' The words flew out of my mouth before I could stop them.

'You have?'

Dammit. I wasn't ready to tell them about Nico yet. It was way too soon, and knowing my track record, things between us wouldn't work out—especially considering the trouble I was having getting Spencer to give me time off. But I was tired of being the only single woman in my family. And fed up of Mum being disappointed in me and my inability to hold down a relationship.

'Yes. At Christmas. And *he's* actually a decent guy. Unlike Jasper.'

'That's wonderful! You should've brought him along tonight. Who is he? What's his name?'

'His name is Nico—Nicolas.'

'How lovely! Where did you meet him?'

'Yeah, sis!' Flo's eyes widened. 'This is so exciting!'

My heart fluttered and relief washed over me. It was so nice to see the joy in their eyes and not feel like such an outcast for a change.

'We met in town, after I'd taken Paul to see Father Christmas.'

'That's so sweet. Is he handsome? Does he have a good job?'

Classic Mum.

'Yes, and yes.'

'Wonderful! Why don't you call him now and invite him over? We'd love to meet him.'

Shit. I should've thought this through before opening my big mouth. Everyone's eyes were fixed on me. Waiting for me to answer.

'I can't,' I muttered, wishing I could rewind the last few minutes.

'Why not?'

'He… he lives in… Paris,' I stuttered. 'We met whilst he was in London. For Christmas…' My voice trailed off as I realised how pathetic it sounded.

'Oh…' Mum's shoulders sank and she blew out a breath, yet more disappointment written all over her face. 'So it was just a holiday romance.'

'No!' I shouted. 'It's… it's not just a fling.'

'Oh darling,' she sighed. '*So gullible*. If he lives in another country and you just courted during the holidays, then it's a *holiday* romance. It's not real.'

'You don't know that!'

My cheeks burned. She'd struck a nerve. As much as I hated to admit it, I'd been thinking the same thing, but was trying to stay positive. We'd both said we'd wanted to explore things and see where it went, so there was hope. I mean, yeah, the odds were stacked against us, but even if we had a ten percent chance of overcoming the obstacles, there was still a chance of us making a go of things, right? *Right?*

Why hadn't I just said Nico was busy, or working like Flo's husband? This conversation was opening up a can of worms and playing on the doubts that had been plaguing my mind for weeks, and I didn't like it.

'Cheeks…' Nate took a gulp of his rum and Coke. 'I

hate to break it to you, but Mum's right. Take it from me. I've seen what my friends and other guys do whilst they're on holiday. Men will say anything to get a woman into bed.'

'Oh dear! You didn't have intercourse with this man, did you, Cassie? If you jump into bed with a man a few days after you've just met, he won't respect you.'

If only I'd been able to hold out for days…

If Mum knew it had only been a matter of hours before Nico and I had got jiggy, she'd faint on the spot, then hide in the house for weeks from the shame. Even though I was a grown woman, in her eyes we were all still sweet, innocent kids.

'Jesus, Mum!' I snapped, angry at the thoughts racing through my mind about the fading feasibility of a long-term future with Nico. 'I'm not a teenager. You don't have to give me the whole sex lecture.'

'She's not wrong,' Nate added. 'The thing is, sis, on holiday everyone is happy. They've escaped their real life. They can pretend to be whoever they want. They're in a new country. Being in a city like London is exciting. Especially at Christmas. I bet he swept you off your feet and turned on the charm with his sexy accent and you melted faster than ice cream under a blow torch!'

'It wasn't like that…' My cheeks warmed again, as I attempted to hide the fact that once I'd overcome my initial dislike of Nico, he *had* made me melt. I'd never even contemplated sleeping with a guy on the first night before then.

'I bet it was. When you have a foreign accent, women love that shit. I'm telling you, when I travel, women go crazy for the British accent. And you should see the way

British girls fall over Carlos. Especially when they're partying in Spain. Their knickers come off so quickly, you'd think they were on fire. Carlos gets more chicks than a rock star.'

'Chicks?' I hissed. '*Seriously?*'

'Look, sis, don't get caught up with my terminology. I have three sisters. You know I have the utmost respect for women. Which is why I'm looking out for you by telling you how it is.'

'What does this Nicolas do for a living?' Mum chimed in.

'He runs a business,' I said proudly. They didn't need to know the extent of his success and that he was absolutely loaded.

'Ooh, fancy!' Lily smiled enthusiastically.

'Red flag.' Nate shook his head.

'How is running a business a red flag?' I frowned.

'He'll never have time for you. Plus, if he's really successful, he'll also have money and be drunk with power. And you said he's good looking, right?'

'Yeah. So?' I huffed.

'Good looking, successful, minted *and* a French accent? My man is living the dream! That means he'll be surrounded by women, like, *all* the time.'

It was like Nate was crawling around inside my head with a magnifying glass. Zooming in on every insecurity I had about the whole Nico situation. I'd be lying if those thoughts hadn't crossed my mind on more than one occasion.

I hated to admit it, but I *was* worried that Nico's success and money would get in the way. I *was* concerned that this was just a holiday romance. I *was* worried about the distance and how on earth it'd be possible to have any kind of relationship when we lived in different countries. And if we *did* decide to get serious, I was worried about how Nico would be able to stay strong when temptation was all around him. The truth was, I thought about all of the many obstacles at least once a day.

Naturally, I wanted to believe that I would go to Paris and fall madly in love with Nico and that we'd live happily ever after.

I'd love to think that a hot, sexy millionaire like him, who had women begging to jump into his pants every day would turn them all down. The optimistic part of me imagined him saying: *'It does not matter if we do not see each other very often. Of course I will be happy to wait for you and your golden pussy, chérie.'* But the realistic part reminded me that this was real life, not a fairy tale, and if I believed that, I was living in cloud cuckoo land.

Jasper had lived in the same city as me and he'd still managed to cheat, and we'd been together for two years, not just a few days. And as I'd discovered during the time we'd spent together, Nico had a very big sexual appetite. In fact, as much as I hoped he was a decent guy, it wouldn't surprise me if he had already jumped into bed with another woman. After all, he'd said when we first met that he wasn't looking for a relationship.

No, no, no. He'd said that *before* we'd got together. When we'd grown closer, he'd explained that was because he'd had a bad experience with his money-grabbing, superficial ex. Since then, he'd said he wanted to see where things between us could go. He *wanted* to take things further.

Nico isn't like the other men I've dated. He's different.

This isn't just about sex for him. This has the potential to turn into a real relationship.

Didn't it?

'Not all men are the same.' I pushed the toxic thoughts out of my mind. That was what I'd told myself when we were together at Christmas. I'd believed it then, and I wanted to believe it now too. I really did.

'Maybe.' Nate shrugged his shoulders. 'Sometimes there are exceptions. But not when it comes to guys like that. *Nah*. As tempting as he might seem, Cheeks, best to forget that one. If you're looking for the whole long-term thing, you need to find someone less appealing. You know, more normal and boring. Like Flo's other half.'

'What?' Flo protested. 'Darren's not boring!'

'If you say so, Flo. Anyway, bottom line is, guys like this Nico bloke aren't relationship material.'

'You don't even know him!' I shouted a little too loudly.

Nate's words were clearly getting to me. I felt like a thousand-watt spotlight was shining down on me. I swept my clammy hands across my damp forehead, then wiped them on my jeans.

Since meeting Nico, it was like I'd existed in a dreamy bubble of happiness. I'd been living in a balloon filled with hopes that a relationship with him *could* be possible. But now Nate had come along with a giant pin, determined to burst my bubble and give me a big reality check.

'Don't need to. I know how men think. You should be thanking me for keeping it real and sharing this kind of classified info. Trust me, sis, he'll break your heart. And this River bloke sounds like bad news too, Lil-Lil.' He turned to face Lily. 'All that stuff about his parents coming down with a bug is just bull. He straight up doesn't want you to meet them. And I doubt he's working late tonight either. It's your birthday, for Christ's sake. He should be taking you out. Not just coming round to yours later. That's got *booty call* written all over it.'

Lily's mouth fell open.

'That's not true,' she blurted out. 'Talk about being a negative Nigel!'

'I hope it's not, but I'm just saying...' Nate shrugged his shoulders. 'If he's just a fuck buddy, then cool. But if you're looking for commitment, he ain't the one. And tell him from me, that if he hurts my little sis, I'll make him cry a bloody *river*. And, Cheeks, you can tell your Nicolas guy the same thing. If he strings you along with promises of romantic trips to Paris and a stupid happily ever after and doesn't come through, tell him he'll have me to answer to.'

The whole table fell silent.

The reason Lily, Flo and I were lost for words was because, when it came to advice about men, Nate had an annoying quality of always being right.

From the get-go he'd predicted that things wouldn't work with me and Jasper because his family was too rich and stuck-up. And when I'd protested that Jasper wasn't like that, he'd patted me on the back and said, 'If you say so, Cheeks. But you're wrong.' And I was.

He'd predicted that my relationship before Jasper wouldn't last more than a few months and he'd been right about that too. His accuracy about our love lives was scarily always on point.

And he was right about Flo's husband. Darren really was duller than dishwater.

Nate had had a good run of predicting the crappy outcome of my previous relationships, but things with Nico would be different, right?

It was clear what I had to do. I needed to find a way to get to Paris ASAP to find out. One way or the other.

CHAPTER THREE

It was Sunday afternoon and Nate's comments were still running through my head.

As much as I'd tried to convince myself otherwise, he was right. I'd allowed myself to get carried away. Just because I'd got lucky once and enjoyed a fun fling with Nico at Christmas, it didn't mean it could work long-term and lead to a lifetime of happiness.

My best friend and cousin, Bella, and her husband, Mike, who'd reunited at their ten-year university reunion and ended up getting married, were the exception, not the rule. Most people were like me and my other bestie, Melody. Serial daters. Women that had been hurt by men so many times in the past, but still persevered. Hoping that the next one could be *the one*. We were stuck on a hamster wheel. Enduring a constant cycle of getting our hopes up only to have every relationship repeatedly crash and burn.

That was why it was better to be realistic. Keep my expectations low.

I needed to rein in my emotions. Fast. Before I got hurt again.

Part of me thought maybe it was safer not to go to Paris at all. But that would be like never venturing out of your front door, just in case you got run over whilst crossing the road. No. That was too extreme. I just needed to be more pragmatic about the whole thing.

I'd been given an opportunity to visit Nico in Paris, which I'd be crazy to pass up. The plan was to just go and enjoy myself. Soak up the experience. But I was under no illusions. No matter how much I might want it, there would be no falling in love and riding off into the sunset together.

I had to accept it for what it was: just an extension of our fling. Some extended, temporary fun. Two single, consenting adults enjoying each other's company for a limited amount of time. Nothing more. Nothing less. End of. And I could handle that.

I'd survived after we'd enjoyed our time in London, so I just had to do the same again. It would just be a few more days together in Paris. Yeah, we had a connection, but I'd find a way to suppress it. I'd keep it under control. How hard could it be?

My phone pinged.

My first thought was that it was Nico, but then I saw it was an email. I read the subject line:

Hello Cassie! It's time for your daily French lesson!

I'd forgotten about that. It was the language app I'd signed up for in the New Year as another resolution.

After Nico had left, I had been filled with enthusiasm about learning the lingo to make things easier when I went to Paris.

So far, my attempts to try and *parler français* hadn't been great, but I'd have another go at the app later. First, I needed to do some more job-hunting.

Maybe today was the day I'd find my ideal job advertised online. Not that I knew what that was. Being a PA was a good career, though. In my opinion, people didn't give the role the credit it deserved. It had just never been my dream. I'd love to do something more meaningful that would help dozens of people in need, rather than just one CEO or company director. But being a PA was all I knew, so that was that.

I sat on the sofa with my laptop and started scanning the pages of more recruitment websites to see if anything new had come up since I'd last checked yesterday morning. The doorbell rang. I put the laptop on the coffee table, went into the hallway and picked up the intercom receiver.

'Hello?'

'Amazon delivery.'

'Okay. First floor.' I pressed the buzzer to let him in.

I took the package and ripped it open. *Oh yeah.* I'd ordered a Paris travel guide and a *French for Dummies* book.

Dammit.

My thoughts turned to Nico. I needed to tell him I couldn't make it next week.

I went into the bedroom, put on a fresh top, checked my hair and face in the mirror, quickly swiped on some mascara and gloss, then returned to the sofa. Nico and I mainly video called, because he said he didn't like typing out texts and preferred to see me, so I always tried to make an effort to look decent.

He was busy today, so might not answer, but it was best to be prepared.

After leaving the phone to ring for almost a minute, I was about to hang up when he answered.

'Cassie!' Nico beamed. The way he looked at me with such happiness in his eyes made me melt.

'Hey, you!' I said casually. I couldn't stop grinning and my stomach felt like it had millions of butterflies fluttering around inside. '*Ça va?*'

'*Très bien!* I love it when you speak French.'

'*Merci!*' I joked.

'Someone has been studying.' He smiled.

'Not as much as I should, but *you know...*'

'It is a beginning. The important thing is that you try.'

I loved how encouraging Nico was. I'd hardly said anything groundbreaking, yet he still praised my efforts. Which made me want to try harder. As soon as I got off the phone, I'd log onto the language app.

'Are you on your way out?' I noticed Nico was wearing a jacket.

'*Oui.* I will go to meet Lucien.' Nico often spoke of his best friend. They always went out for drinks after work or for early morning runs together. 'How was your dinner with your family?'

'It was fine.' I pushed Nate's comments out of my head for the hundredth time.

'*Bien.* So, is everything okay? Ready for Saturday?'

As soon as those words tumbled from his lips, the fluttering in my stomach turned into churning cramps. For a moment I'd forgotten why I was calling him. Oh yeah. To give him the bad news. Shit.

'Erm, not really. There's a bit of a spanner in the works.'

'Spanner?' Nico frowned.

'Sorry.' I slapped my forehead, reminding myself to keep my language simple. 'I mean, about Saturday. There's a bit of a problem. Spencer said I can't have the time off…'

'He just tell you this today? He is calling you again on a Sunday?'

'No…' My voice trailed off. 'He told me at the end of the week…'

'So why do you just tell me this now?'

My throat went dry. It was bad, I know. I had tried on Friday evening, but I hadn't let the phone ring for very long. The truth was, I'd hoped some kind of miracle would happen and that things would work themselves out. But, nope.

'I'm sorry,' I sighed. 'I wanted to think of a solution first.'

'You should tell me sooner.' Nico ground his jaw. I knew he was annoyed but was trying to suppress it. My stomach twisted. I hated the fact that I'd let him down. 'So, you think of a solution?'

'I could come for the weekend instead? It'll still be lovely. Just the two of us. Like at Christmas.'

'Ah.' He paused. 'I was going to tell you when you come here, but next weekend I plan for us to go to Monaco. My friend will have a party so we can go and celebrate.'

Party. Friends. Monaco.

A chill ran through me.

I'd booked hotels and flights to Monaco for Spencer

many times. He'd been there for the Formula 1 Grand Prix and for other trips to see his fancy friends on their yachts.

I hoped it wasn't on a boat…

'Will it be *all* weekend?'

'*Oui*. We will leave on Saturday afternoon to join his boat.'

'You mean *yacht*?' I added as a guess, praying he'd say no.

'*Oui, voilà, c'est ça*. That is right. We will spend the weekend on his yacht with his friends.'

To a lot of people, that would sound like a dream. Sailing on a fancy yacht with a load of rich people. It was the definition of glamour, right? Well, not for me.

As much as I loved looking at sea views, I hated boats. Every time I went on them I got seasick. When it had happened on that school trip to France, my vomit had gone all over my clothes and smelt so bad, everyone had called me *stinky puke* for weeks. The last thing I wanted was to spend the weekend with my head down a toilet or to throw up in front of Nico. That'd put him off me for life.

And a party. With his friends. A roomful of people I didn't know. Speaking French. A language I didn't understand. Somehow I doubted knowing how to say *bonjour*, *ça va* and *merci* was going to cut the mustard. I wouldn't be able to communicate.

Although I was sure Nico would do his best to check I was okay, sooner or later he'd want to socialise and I'd get left alone.

And they would all be loaded. Not to stereotype, but with the exception of Nico, my experience of mixing with the upper classes hadn't gone well.

When I was younger, on top of her full-time nursing

job, Mum used to clean for a rich family, the Grosvenors. She'd been a loyal employee for years. Then one day, the husband had accused Mum of stealing his wife's diamond necklace and fired her.

We all knew Mum would never do that—no matter how tight things were financially. She'd tried to put on a front, but she was devastated.

Then a week later, the toffee-nosed tossers had asked her to return. They'd found the necklace in their daughter's bedroom—draped over her favourite dolly. She'd been playing dress-up.

Nate had been pissed that Mum went back, but Mum always said *beggars can't be choosers*. It was like rich people could do whatever they wanted and people like us just had to suck it up and nod politely. We needed the money, so that was that.

Then there was my ex, Jasper. We'd met at a work event. He was handsome, charming, and from a mega-wealthy background. I'd fallen for him hook, line and sinker.

We'd dated for two years and now that I looked back, I shouldn't have got involved. I'd been feeling vulnerable from a break-up a few months earlier and stupidly I'd been flattered that a guy like him would be interested in me.

He was Oxford-educated and worked in the city. Jasper had charmed my family with his plummy accent, his good job and his flattery. Well, everyone except Nate, but he'd never been a fan of any of my boyfriends, so that wasn't a surprise.

I hadn't realised it at the time, but being with Jasper had fuelled my insecurities. When we were out with his friends, their talks about the 'good old uni days' were a constant reminder of my limited education. My grades hadn't even been good enough to go to college, let alone university. I still remembered the look of horror on his friends' faces when I confessed I'd left school at sixteen. You'd think I'd just eaten a live tarantula in front of them.

And don't even get me started on his parents. They'd made it very clear what they thought of us being together. His mum always looked me up and down, grimacing as if her son had just dragged a flea-infested rat through the door rather than his girlfriend.

I always had stomach cramps on the way to meet them and my heart raced constantly whilst I was there because I was worried that I'd do or say something stupid.

Whenever we went to visit, I always committed some sort of faux pas. Like using the wrong fork or glass. It was an easy mistake to make. There was always more cutlery and glassware on their dining table than the homeware section of a department store.

Oh, and the fact that, when we met for the first time, I accidentally gave her a vibrator for Christmas that was meant for Melody probably didn't help either. It was an honest mistake. The size of the box was similar to the flask I'd bought her and they were wrapped in the same paper. *Oops*. I could laugh about it now, but at the time, I'd been mortified.

Then of course Spencer and the other snooty people at work who always looked down on me didn't help matters.

So, yeah. My track record with the well-off wasn't great. They tended not to have a lot in common with a PA like me who didn't speak English like the queen and had barely travelled or done anything particularly interesting with her life. And that was just in the UK. I'd imagine our differences would be magnified in France.

My stomach plummeted.

I was coming to Paris to spend the weekend with Nico. *Alone.* Not with his friends. If I came for a week and we spent a few days together first, then went to see his mates, it'd be better. *Slightly.* But just the thought of being launched straight into seeing them and being stuck on a boat for two days with nowhere else to go made me feel about as comfortable as an elephant charging across a tightrope.

'Cassie? Are you there?'

'Um, yeah. Erm. Listen, Nico. I'm going to find a way to come over. Not just for a weekend. For longer. Hopefully for four or five days.'

'You do not want to come next weekend?'

Now I had to lie.

'Of *course* I want to see you. But *properly*. It's been so long that I want to make it worthwhile. Not that next weekend wouldn't be worthwhile.' I needed to stop rambling. 'I mean, I want us to spend *proper* time together.'

This was crazy. I shouldn't even be in this position. I was entitled to bloody time off. If I could make Spencer see sense and let me go to Paris using my annual leave, I could avoid the fancy yacht party—or at least spend a few days with Nico beforehand, and have more time to mentally prepare myself for a weekend filled with French strangers and the inevitable seasickness.

'Leave it with me. Just give me a couple of days and I'll talk to my boss again. See what I can arrange.'

'If you are not able to come, I will need to know so I can change plans. Let me know tomorrow, okay?'

Tomorrow? A day was reasonable and would be totally fine if I was dealing with someone reasonable. But unfortunately, I wasn't. Spencer was quite possibly the most awkward man on the planet.

'Okay,' I sighed. 'I'll get straight on it in the morning and will call tomorrow to confirm.'

I didn't rate my chances, but I had to try.

CHAPTER FOUR

It was 10 a.m. Surprisingly, Spencer had already been locked in his office when I'd arrived just before nine and I hadn't heard a peep from him since.

I'd been researching online and, just as I thought, I was entitled to holiday, even if I was leaving.

I hated the fact that Nico had moved a load of meetings around for me and I had to tell him I wasn't coming as planned. I *had* to fix this.

I got up, knocked on Spencer's door, then entered.

'Jesus!' Spencer jumped, red in the face with his hands between his legs. 'You're supposed to wait for someone to tell you to come in. You can't just barge into my office like that!'

Was he…?

No. He wouldn't…

'Were you…? Did I just see you…? At your *desk*?'

My mouth dropped open.

I knew Spencer was a depraved dickhead, but was he seriously wanking at his desk at ten in the morning? He had a wife *and* a mistress for God's sake. How much bloody sex did this man need? Actually, scrap that. I didn't want to know. *Gross.*

'You saw *nothing*!' He quickly zipped up his flies. 'I was just... anyway, what do you want?'

Hmmm. If Spencer was sexually frustrated, maybe now wasn't the best time to ask about my holiday. I needed him to be in a good mood. Perhaps a few minutes *after* he'd finished would be better. *Ugh.*

'Don't worry about it.' I turned and walked towards the door.

Then again, this was Spencer we were talking about, so would there ever be a good time? Today it was one thing, but tomorrow it'd be another. There was no time like the present. I had to try.

'Actually...' I walked back to his desk. 'I'd like to talk to you again about my annual leave next week. I've just resent the email I sent you straight after we'd had a conversation and you'd said it was fine, so that should jog your memory. Could you reconsider? *Please?* Wendy is still free to cover for me.'

I was tempted to ask if he could shorten my notice period too, but one battle at a time.

I'd already asked HR for a copy of my contract to double-check it and they said they were snowed under, but would get back to me ASAP. If not, I'd get my copy from my parents' loft at the weekend. As there was nothing more I could do on that front, right now, going to Paris was the priority.

'No.' Spencer crossed his arms and leant back in his chair. No elaboration as to why. No apology for wanting to, but his hands being tied. *Nothing*. I swear he even tried to stifle a smile. The man was plain evil.

'But *why*? For five years, I've worked hard for you. Done everything you've asked, even when I've had to compromise my morals in the process.' I cringed, thinking of all the times I had to organise hotel or dinner reservations and gifts for his mistress, Sally. *So wrong*. 'I've never asked you for anything in return. *Please*. Can you just be reasonable for a change?'

'Working hard for me is your *job*. That's what you're paid to do, so don't act like you're some kind of saint for just doing what you're told. This has nothing to do with being reasonable.'

What. An. Arse.

I had to fight the temptation to jump over his desk and shake him. He was deliberately being difficult.

'All I'm asking for is a week off. I've got legal advice and I'm entitled to holiday. It's my legal right as an employee.'

Hopefully the use of the word 'legal' would make him see sense. He didn't need to know that my legal consultant was Google.

'I am well aware of an employee's right to annual leave. But holidays may only be taken at times convenient to the company, so whether you sent me an email or not is irrelevant.'

'But it's *really* important.' I was running out of arguments. The only option I had left was to appeal to his emotional side and hope there was a heart buried in his chest. Somewhere.

Spencer leant forward on his desk.

'Important, you say? Are you dying?'

'No.' I frowned. 'Not as far as I know.'

'Are you sick?'

'No, but...'

'Well, in that case, it's still a no. Now if you'll excuse me, I've got important business to attend to.'

'Yeah. Tossing yourself off,' I muttered under my breath. Note to self to disinfect my hands after touching anything in Spencer's office. I had no idea he masturbated at work. God knows what else he did in here.

'What did you say?' Spencer hissed.

'Nothing!' I slammed the door behind me.

So that was that, then. I'd tried and it had gone just as abysmally as I'd expected.

Spencer was such a dick.

I plonked myself back down at my desk and unlocked my phone.

Time to prepare myself for breaking the bad news to Nico. I typed out a message.

Me

Hey. Let me know when's a good time to call. Lunchtime (around 1 p.m. UK time) or after I finish work is good for me.

I knew Nico was busy during working hours, so asking in advance was usually best.

Once I'd answered my emails and typed up a report, I checked my phone to see if he'd replied, but there was nothing so far. It had only been an hour since I'd messaged. Sometimes if things were hectic, he couldn't reply until the next day.

I walked to the kitchen and put the kettle on. I needed a break with a nice cup of tea and some biscuits.

I clicked on Bella's name in WhatsApp. She taught English to foreign business professionals, but I'd remembered her saying yesterday that she had this morning off.

Me

Tried asking Spencer and he won't budge. Still says it's a no to holiday.

Me

Thought about going to HR, but if he doesn't give it the green light, they won't either.

Me

Maybe handing in my notice was a bad idea. If I hadn't, he wouldn't have changed his mind about giving me the time off. He's deliberately punishing me because I'm leaving.

I looked at the string of messages I'd sent, remembering that Bella always asked why I sent multiple texts instead of putting it all in one. It was just a habit. Our friend Melody also did the same.

I glanced at the screen and saw Bella typing.

Bella

So sorry, hon. At least you tried. You seriously have the worst boss!

Me

Tell me about it! He's such a wanker!

Me

Speaking of which, can you believe I caught him bashing the bishop at his desk earlier!

Bella

What? He hit a bishop? What was a bishop doing at your office?

I chuckled to myself as I realised she wasn't used to the terminology. I supposed I wouldn't have been either if I didn't have an older brother with a bunch of potty-mouth friends who often hung out at our house when I was growing up. I could fill a dictionary with the amount of words and phrases I'd heard them use over the years for masturbation.

As well as the American terms like jerking or whacking off, there was a load of British slang they used too, like *cleaning the pipes*, *rounding up the tadpoles*, *jackin' the Beanstalk*, *teasing the weasel*, *tickling the pickle*, and *stroking the salami*. Oh, and how could I forget: *shaking hands with the milkman*.

Crude? Definitely. Although it used to make me laugh, there was nothing fun about walking in on your boss *buffing his banana*.

Me

To put it delicately, I think he was pleasuring himself.

Bella

No way!

Me

Yes, way!

Bella

Nothing wrong with a bit of self-care. We all do it, but there's a time and a place! He should've waited until he got home.

Me

Exactly!

. . .

I added the green vomit face emoji.

Me

Anyway, I've messaged Nico to see if we can talk later. Looks like we'll just have to see each other at weekends for now.

Bella

That's something at least. It's a shame about your seasickness. I wouldn't say no to spending a weekend on a yacht in Monaco!

I'd told Bella all about it when we spoke on the phone last night.

Me

I know. Gutted about my seasickness.

Me

Anyway, Better get back to it. Hope your lessons go well this afternoon. Speak soon xxx

Bella sent me a row of blowing kisses emojis, then went offline.

There was no reply from Nico yet, which was to be expected. Probably for the best. Hopefully by the time we did speak, a miracle would've happened or I would've thought of a Plan B.

CHAPTER FIVE

I jumped out of bed. It was half seven. I should've been up twenty minutes ago, but I'd slept badly, so I couldn't resist hitting the snooze button. But I must've hit it a few times too many.

The tight feeling in my chest had returned. I'd been worrying about work. Not just about going to Paris. It was also the prospect of being stuck working for Spencer for another two months. I wasn't joking yesterday when I'd said to Bella that the whole holiday refusal thing was his revenge.

Spencer was a control freak. He liked to call the shots. So the fact that *I'd* had the audacity to resign and leave *him* was unacceptable. I had a feeling that he planned to make the next eight weeks a living hell. I wished I didn't have to go to work today.

As I approached the office, my phone chimed. I fished it out of my bag. Nico had replied! My stomach flipped with anticipation. As always, it was a voice message. I clicked play.

'*Salut*! Sorry I could not message yesterday. I travel to Germany. Tell me: do you have the holiday time from your boss? My secretary, she needs to confirm my meetings, so I must know quickly, *s'il te plaît. Bisous*.'

God, I could listen to that man speak all day. His accent always made my heart race. When I'd met him, I remembered thinking he could read the instruction leaflet for constipation tablets and still make it sound sexy.

Nico's tone of voice was official, but I felt a little relieved that he'd added the *bisous*, which I knew meant *kisses*, at the end.

I pushed the large glass office doors open, stepped inside and moved to the right of the entrance, then pressed the call button. Nico would probably be busy, but I wanted to at least try to get back to him quickly.

After only two rings he answered. '*Salut!*'

My heart thudded with a mixture of excitement at hearing his voice and fear of how he'd react when I broke the news. My body tensed. This was going to be hard. He sounded so happy and now I was about to ruin his morning. '*Ça va, chérie?*'

'I'm okay, thanks.' I attempted to sound upbeat. 'You?'

'*Oui, oui. Tout va bien.*'

'I know you're busy, so I'll be quick…' There was no way I was having this conversation upstairs. I'd just wait here. 'The thing is… er, about me coming over. I…'

'Cassie?' I heard someone call my name and looked up.

'Reg?' I held the phone to my chest.

'How are you, my dear?'

I smiled and mouthed *one second please* to Reg, then put the phone back against my ear.

'I-I actually… sorry, Nico. Something's just come up at work. Can I call you back? I'll make sure I do it this morning.'

Talk about bad timing. I didn't have a choice, though. Standing in front of me was Reg Pattison: the founder of the real estate company I worked for, RJP Associates. I couldn't exactly say 'sorry, big cheese, but I can't chat to you now, I'm talking to my lover.'

'Of course.' Nico sounded disappointed. *Dammit.* Little did he know me needing to speak later was only the tip of the disappointment iceberg.

'Thanks.'

I hung up, then walked towards Reg. As always, he was dressed in a smart suit that was clearly custom made. His silver hair was perfectly groomed. Even though he was in his seventies, it was still so thick and shiny. Maybe that was the by-product of having so much money.

'Sorry about that! I'm fine, thank you!' I stifled a grin. My mind raced. I hated ending the call so abruptly. For about the hundredth time this morning, I wished I could storm up to the office and scream at Spencer until he saw sense and gave me the bloody holiday I'd asked for. It was so frustrating.

'Forgive me, dear, but your eyes are telling a different story. Why don't we grab a quick coffee and you can tell me all about it?'

I glanced at my watch. It was 8.56 and I started at nine.

'That's really kind, but I start in four minutes, so…'

'Oh, don't worry about that. My son might be running the company, but until I kick the bucket, it's still mine. *Come.* It's been far too long since we had one of our chats.'

It was amazing how a father and son could be so different. When Reg had worked at the company, the atmosphere had been so much better. It was when Reg had retired and Spencer had taken over that things had gone down the toilet. For me anyway.

Spencer loved the power of running a business and it had expanded his already huge ego to horrific proportions.

I knew Reg had built the company from scratch in his early twenties and worked his arse off to make it a success, so his retirement was a long time coming and well deserved. But there wasn't a day that went by where I didn't wish that he was back in charge.

We went to the coffee shop next door to the office and sat down at a little red table by the window.

'So how are you?' I asked quickly.

'I'm very well, thank you for asking. Very well indeed.'

'What brings you back to the office?' I couldn't remember the last time I'd seen him here. Must have been at least six months ago. Maybe longer. He was clearly enjoying his retirement. Didn't blame him.

'Today is my fiftieth wedding anniversary, so I've treated my lovely wife to a morning at the spa not too far from here, so whilst she gets pampered, I thought I'd pop in and say hello to everyone.'

'Fifty years! Congratulations!' I said as the waiter brought over our drinks.

'Thank you. It feels like only yesterday since we met.' As he spoke, his eyes twinkled.

'What's your secret?'

'Ah! Good question. I'm not sure if there's any magic formula. Yes, all the things you hear people say, like the importance of communication and honesty, are true. But I believe it's because we get on so well. We always laugh together and love each other deeply. Sounds a little simplistic, but it's true. Even after all these years, she's the love of my life. When we met, I just knew we had something special.'

'That's so lovely.'

My heart practically melted into a puddle. That was how I felt when I was with Nico. I pushed the thought out of my mind. I was supposed to be reining in my feelings. This wasn't about me. This was about Reg and his wife. They sounded like the poster couple for true love.

I believed every word Reg said. He was genuine. I bet he'd never cheated on his wife like Spencer. That wanker could learn a lot from his dad.

'And how about you, dear? Are you courting anyone special?'

My warm heart suddenly froze and my stomach plummeted. I took a sip of my coffee whilst I worked out how to respond.

'Oh dear, did I touch a nerve?'

'No, no. You didn't say anything wrong. I've actually met someone amazing, but things are... difficult.'

'How so? If you don't mind me asking? Tell me to keep my nose out of your business if you prefer.'

'No, it's fine.' Reg had always been easy to talk to. Even though he was a big boss, he always made time to speak with his employees.

It was because of him that I'd got this job. As well as being a nurse, my mum used to have an evening cleaning job at the company and often bumped into Reg when he was working late, so they used to talk.

At the time, the small insurance firm I'd worked for had folded, so I'd been unemployed and it was Reg that had suggested that I come in to interview for an admin assistant role in their accounts department. I'd been up against a lot of candidates and hadn't got the job that time. But HR had kept my details on file, and when a PA position had come up a few months later, I'd been interviewed again and they'd given me the job.

I had been a PA for a couple of different directors over the years before working for Spencer.

Reg was like a mentor to me and, despite his position in the company, had always been on hand to lend an ear. I'd been so sad when he'd retired.

I gave him an ABC version of what had happened. How I'd met Nico, how much we'd enjoyed our time together and how it was now proving difficult to see each other for longer than a couple of days.

'That's very unfortunate,' Reg sighed. 'Sounds like he's a nice young chap. I hate the idea of two soul mates being kept apart. But if weekends are proving difficult, why don't you just book some annual leave?'

I paused. I wanted to shout, 'Because your arse of a son is an evil bastard,' but I had to remain professional.

'That was what we planned. I booked the time off and even had a ticket for Paris booked for this Saturday, but unfortunately Spencer said that now he needs me here.'

'Nonsense!' Reg said. 'I know you're great at your job, but I'm sure someone else can fill in for a week. You've been very good to him, and a happy worker is a motivated worker. He needs to remember that if he wants to keep you.'

Amen. At least *someone* valued me. As for keeping me, Reg didn't know that ship had already sailed.

'Thing is, I handed in my notice last week.'

'Oh no!' His face fell. That's very unfortunate news. Our company needs good, loyal people like you. And I might be going a bit soft in my old age, but I reckon we need more love in the world. You and your young French chap need to be reunited. I've heard enough.' Reg downed the rest of his coffee, then stood up. 'Come on, dear. Follow me. I think I need to have a few strong words with my son.'

CHAPTER SIX

O MG.

My heart had been racing before, but now it had gone into overdrive. Half an hour ago, my prospects of going to Paris had been looking grim. But now I had an ally. And not just any ally—the bloody founder of the company.

Like Reg had said earlier, Spencer might be the muppet running the business, but Reg still owned it (admittedly he hadn't called his son a muppet, but even he must know it was true…). So if Reg pulled rank, Spencer would have no choice but to agree. Right?

This was exciting. I had a chance! Best not to count my chickens just yet, though…

Reg hit the button for the fifth floor, where our office was based, and the doors closed.

'How's your new dog?' I asked. I wanted to keep the conversation going but preferred not to talk about Paris. I was already brimming with excitement that there might just be hope and wanted to at least attempt to play it a bit cool. 'It was Vinnie, wasn't it?'

'Well remembered! Vinnie's doing fine, thank you. He's got his own very special personality. We still miss Betsy terribly, but having Vinnie has been a real comfort.'

The last time Reg had come to the office, he'd mentioned that his beloved dog had passed away. I knew how much she meant to him, so at lunchtime I'd bought a sympathy card and some flowers. When I'd given them to Reg, I thought he was going to burst into tears. He must have thanked me a dozen times.

'So glad to hear that.' I stepped out of the lift doors and into the main office.

'Dad?' Spencer bolted up from his desk. Thank God the door was already open. Could you imagine if his dad had walked in on him whacking off his little soldier like I did the other day? *Cringe*. Although something told me Spencer was the kind of idiot who must've got caught up to no good by his parents when he was a teenager. Probably had a pile of sticky porn magazines under his bed and a soiled sock in his drawer. Gross.

'Spencer,' Reg said firmly.

'Wh-what are you doing here?' Blood drained from his face.

'Cassie, dear.' His voice softened. 'Could you give me a moment alone with my son, please?'

'Course! I'll hold his calls. Would either of you like a drink? Tea? Coffee?'

'We're fine, thank you,' Reg answered on their behalf. He was in business mode. That was what made him so unique. Reg was no pushover. He could be serious and in control when he wanted to close a deal, but he was soft and charming too.

'No problem.'

I was tempted to stand by the door and eavesdrop, but I knew I'd get rumbled, so I quickly returned to my desk.

I had to speak to someone, though. I'd try Melody to see if she was free. I pulled out my phone.

Me

Hey, are you there?

After a few minutes, *typing...* flashed up.

Melody

Hello, you! Just back from the loo. How's it going? Have you tied up your evil boss and demanded he let you go to Paris?

Me

I've been tempted, but no!

Me

I might be in with a chance, though... bumped into his dad, aka the big boss, earlier and spilled my guts to him about how hard it is being away from Nico etc. and not being able to take any holiday and now he's having a word with Spencer!!!!

Melody

That's ace!

Me

I know, right! Trying not to get excited, but... fingers crossed.

Melody

Is Spencer's dad that silver fox that I saw when I came to meet you for lunch years ago?

Me

He's got grey hair, yes. Well-dressed. Polite and charming.

Melody

Yup! That's the one! He kissed my hand when we met and it gave me serious fanny flutters!

Me

OMG Melody! You're terrible! Not to be ageist, but you do realise he's old enough to be your granddad, right…?

Melody

Nothing wrong with a bit of vintage. Plenty of pensioners still love getting frisky. These days there's Viagra and all sorts.

Melody

The way my love life is going, I can't be too choosy. Got to keep my options open. I'll consider anyone between the ages of 21 and 81!

Me

Each to their own!

Melody

Yep! Some older guys are hot! Hello? Keanu Reeves? Still got it. Richard Gere must be in his seventies and he's still a fox. I wouldn't kick Denzel Washington out of bed either.

Me

Well, as far as I know, they're all attached. Just like Reg is. In fact, he's celebrating his fiftieth wedding anniversary today, so he's well and truly off the market.

Melody

Shame. Let me know if you find any other contenders.

My romantic prospects are so grim right now I even swiped right on your brother on Tinder.

Me

What??? I thought you didn't like Nate?

Me

I love my brother dearly, but he's a total player. He only does hook-ups.

Melody

I know. He's definitely NOT my type. And his profile had so many bloody topless photos of him flexing his enormous muscles, which normally makes my eyes roll faster than a washing machine.

Melody

He might be an arrogant twat, but I have to admit he is HOT. Maybe some angry sex is just what I need!

Melody

I need to get my leg over, pronto, before my vag closes up.

Me

Thanks for that mental image!

Suddenly the door to Spencer's office opened.

Me

Better go. They're coming out of the office! Keep your fingers crossed for me! Let's meet up soon. Want to hear how things are with you.

Melody

Will do. Let me know how it goes. xoxo

. . .

I looked up and saw Spencer walking towards me, scowling.

Oh dear. This doesn't look good...

'Cassandra.' He stopped at my desk, arms folded. 'About the annual leave you requested...' Spencer paused, looked up at his dad, then back at me. His tone was forced and robotic. Like he was a call centre worker reading from a script. 'I am *thrilled* to confirm that it will now be possible for you to take some time off. Three days was sufficient, wasn't it?'

Holy shit.

He just said I could go on holiday!

I wanted to jump on the table and start dancing, then jump down again and do cartwheels and backflips around the office.

This was *major*.

My eyes widened and I bit my lip as I tried to compose myself.

Both he and Reg were waiting for a reply. He'd said three days. That would be brilliant. If I timed it right, by including a weekend, that would give me five days in Paris. Not as much as I'd had planned before, but close enough to a week.

Truth be told, at this point, I was so grateful I'd probably accept two days. That would give me a long weekend. Leave London on Thursday night and return on Monday night. At least I'd have a whole day with Nico before we went to Monaco at the weekend.

Reg winked at me. It felt like a secret signal. As if he was encouraging me to seize the opportunity and ask for more. My first thought was that it was risky and I should just accept the three days. Like Mum always said, *beggars can't be choosers.* But with Reg in my corner, backing me up, I felt stronger.

This was my chance.

'I'm so glad to hear that, Spencer, and although I really appreciate your offer of three days' leave, I was thinking more like… *eight*?'

I let my words hang in the air and put on my best poker face. I knew I was pushing it, but what the hell.

Reg gave a smile of approval. Spencer, on the other hand, wasn't looking so pleased. His face grew redder by the second. If he opened his mouth again, I wouldn't be surprised if he started spitting fire.

'Four,' he hissed.

'Six,' I fired back.

'Fine.'

Yes.

Six days! That was bloody brilliant. With two weekends, that would give me ten days in Paris. Which was more than the few days I'd just hoped for. *Result.* My whole body fizzed with happiness.

'Excellent!' Reg clapped his hands. 'Let's get it all confirmed in an email straight away, shall we, Spencer? Anyway, I best be off. Tell your mother I said hello.'

I had no idea what he'd said to Spencer, but I was beyond grateful.

'Bloody snitch!' Spencer sneered, then slammed his office door.

I knew he wouldn't be happy, but I didn't care. It wasn't as if I'd tracked Reg down and told on Spencer like a child in the playground. Reg had asked me how things were and I'd just answered. The thought of getting him to speak to Spencer hadn't even crossed my mind. But I was glad it'd happened.

To think that when I'd first bumped into Reg, I'd thought it was bad timing because I'd had to cut the call short with Nico. Little did I know that Reg was about to be my angel in disguise.

I had to let him know how much I appreciated his actions. I raced out to the lifts, where Reg was standing, then threw my arms around him.

'Thank you! Oops.' I pulled away quickly. 'Sorry about the hug. Probably not appropriate in the workplace, but seriously, you don't know how much this means to me!'

'Oh, I think I do, dear.' Reg smiled and stepped into the lift. 'No thanks necessary. You were always so helpful and considerate to me. I'm simply paying your kindness forward. Here.' He reached into the inside pocket of his suit and pulled out a business card. 'This has my personal email. If ever you need anything in the future, get in touch.'

'Thanks.'

'You're welcome. Just promise me that you'll have a fantastic time with your French chap.'

'I will!'

As the doors closed, I let out a squeal of excitement. I couldn't help it.

I was finally going to Paris!

CHAPTER SEVEN

A s soon as the curt email came through from Spencer, confirming my annual leave, I jumped straight on the phone to the temp agency we used to check Wendy's availability.

Wendy filled in for me on the rare occasions that I took holiday from work. She had loads of experience and, most importantly, knew how to handle Spencer. With her standing in for me, I wouldn't have to worry.

The only snag was that I couldn't go to Paris this Saturday as planned. Spencer said it was too short notice. He'd just acquired a new building in central London and needed help with that. Plus Wendy had been snapped up for another assignment until next Thursday. So we'd agreed that I'd be off from next Friday.

Given all the ups and downs and what it had taken to get to this point, it wasn't worth rocking the boat by trying to push to go this week. Especially as I'd got more holiday than I'd hoped for.

I'd had to agree to work beyond my notice period to

cover the time off, but I didn't care. I'd worry about that when I returned.

I was itching to speak to Nico to tell him the good news. I was glad that I hadn't spoken to him properly earlier. I would've upset him unnecessarily. Instead of ruining his day, now hopefully I'd be making it. We'd be reunited in just ten days' time.

I tried Nico's phone again. It just rang out. He was probably in a meeting.

It still hadn't quite sunk in yet that I was going. And although it was daunting, I was excited. Now that the time off was a hundred percent confirmed, it made sense to start thinking about the places I'd like to see.

I tabbed to my internet browser and typed 'romantic places to visit in Paris' into Google.

As I suspected, the Eiffel Tower came top of the list. *Of course* I had to go there.

Going for a cruise on the river Seine popped up next. *Hmm.* Not sure about the boat thing…

There were suggestions of places that Nico had mentioned during our many telephone conversations, like visiting the Temple of Love and the Luxembourg Gardens. And I *had* to see the Louvre. Even though I wasn't that cultured, it looked so pretty. Nico would know a million more sights to see. My stomach fluttered with anticipation.

I scrolled down the page, scanning through the millions of search results. I chuckled when I stumbled onto the 'People also ask' section. Second on the list was 'Where can I make love in Paris?' I couldn't resist taking a look. If you'd asked me that question a month ago, my answer would've been 'duh, in a bed of course,' but after my Christmas experience with Nico, I knew that there were plenty more places to get down and dirty...

My mind flashed back to when things had first started to get heated between us in the lift on the way up to a rooftop bar. Then there was the time we'd done it on the floor in front of the fireplace at the Ritz, on the sofa on Christmas Eve, as well as Christmas Day and Boxing Day...

Heat flooded my cheeks. I clicked on the link to the article. Something told me that it was going to reveal some suggestions that didn't take place within the four walls of a hotel or bedroom. I reckoned they were talking about some al fresco outdoor fun.

I skimmed through the suggestions:

At the top of the Eiffel Tower...

Really? How the hell would we manage that without anyone seeing? Even though I wasn't a fan of heights, being that high up might be a thrill.

In a Latin Quarter café...

I reckoned the customers might have something to say about that whilst they were sipping on their coffee and eating their buttery croissants.

In front of Oscar Wilde's grave.

That was a bit weird...

While dangling your legs off the banks of the Seine.

Could you imagine? Knowing my luck, one of us would fall in. Still, probably less embarrassing than throwing up on a boat.

I read it more carefully and the article actually had the headline *The 20 Most Romantic Places to Kiss in Paris. Aha.* Now *kissing* in those places made a lot more sense. Still wasn't sure about the graveyard suggestion, though.

I had to admit that the original question had piqued my curiosity and brought out my naughty side. It would be pretty cool to somehow make love with Nico under the stars with the Eiffel Tower as a backdrop.

My mind drifted as I pictured the scene. Nico peeling off his clothes, revealing his rock-solid chest, me wrapped just in a blanket, climbing on top of his solid thighs, him touching my...

My phone rang, breaking me away from my fantasies. Probably just as well. I was venturing into very saucy territory. I quickly closed the tabs on my computer, then reached for my phone.

'Hi!' I said excitedly, rising from my desk and rushing out to the loos.

'*Salut!* I am sorry I could not answer before. I am out with a customer. When I saw that you had called many times, I thought it must be urgent. Is everything okay?'

'Sorry! Sorry, I didn't mean to hound you. I know you must be busy, but I promised I'd get back to you ASAP and I was just so excited to share the news.'

'I am guessing that it must be good, because you sound much happier than when we speak before.'

'Yep! I'm coming to Paris!'

'*Fantastique!*' Nico shouted with delight. '*Pardon, excusez-moi,*' Nico muttered. 'Sorry, I just apologise to everyone in the restaurant. They think I am madman for shouting. I am very excited!' The happiness radiated from his voice.

'I was the same,' I laughed. 'I literally had to go in the toilets after it was confirmed and let out a huge squeal!'

'You will come this Saturday?'

'Not exactly...' My voice trailed off. 'Okay, so this is a

good news, bad news scenario... the bad news is, I'm not coming this weekend. But the *good* news is, I'm coming *next* Friday. For ten days! Isn't that amazing?'

'Next Friday?' The phone line went silent.

'Hello? Nico? Are you there?' I frowned.

'*Oui, oui.*'

'Did you hear what I said? I'm coming for ten days! I'll arrive next Friday.'

'Ah, *chérie*...' Nico sighed. 'I am not sure if these dates will be good for me.' My shoulders slumped.

'Oh God! I'm so sorry. I should've checked with you first.' I'd got so excited about finally getting the time off that I'd forgotten to consider the fact that Nico was mega busy.

'Because I think you will come this weekend, I moved many meetings to the week when you will be back in London. Remember I say to you that it will be calmer for me the week that you come, but after that it will be a busy time?'

Shit. He had said that. During the video call when I'd told him I'd resigned. Big, fat giant bollocks.

'So what does this mean? I shouldn't come anymore?' I held my breath, waiting for a response. It'd taken so much to get to this point. Imagine if, after all of the hassle, I couldn't go. The line was silent for what felt like an eternity.

'No... come. I will make it work.'

'Okay, thanks.' I blew out a breath. I'd hoped this would be a joyous moment, but now I was worried that Nico felt pressured to fit me in when he was busy. Bloody hell. This long-distance stuff was so complicated.

'I must go now *chérie*, but *ne t'inquiète pas*—please

do not worry. Even if I am busy, I will do my best to spend time with you. I cannot wait to see you, Cassie.'

This man. I didn't know if it was the accent, the way he said my name, *Cass-seee*, or just the warmth that radiated from him when he spoke, but he instantly knew how to make me feel better.

'I can't wait to see you either! Next Friday will be here before we know it!'

'*Oui.* Speak later. *Bisous.*'

'*Bisous,*' I repeated.

I ended the call, beaming from ear to ear. It was going to be fine.

There was so much to do. As well as rearranging the Eurostar ticket, I had to organise my clothes. The shopping trip I'd cancelled last Saturday was back on. What did a woman wear when she was going to meet her hot lover in one of the chicest cities in the world?

And I needed a new suitcase to put everything in. On the rare occasions I went on weekend breaks in the UK, I'd just chucked everything in Nate's old suitcase. But that was battered from his many travels abroad. I wanted something nicer.

I'd also need stuff to keep my curly hair under control, and of course I hoped Nico and I would have lots of sex, so a jumbo pack of condoms would definitely be required too. Just the thought of us getting intimate sent a tingle between my legs.

It wasn't just about the physical things, though. I really enjoyed spending time with him. Extended holiday romance or not, I planned to go and have lots of fun.

Next Friday morning couldn't come quick enough.

CHAPTER EIGHT

I pushed my shoulder against the big glass door and hauled myself into the restaurant.

I was meeting Bella and Melody for dinner at a French restaurant in St Christopher's Place, which was hidden behind Oxford Street, so it was super convenient. Bella reckoned that it would be good preparation for my trip, which was now less than forty-eight hours away. Whoop!

Just as I was about to give my name, I spotted Bella and Melody, who were already seated on the comfy green banquette sofas, so I headed over.

'Hey!' Bella came out from behind the table to give me a hug. At five foot eleven, she was four inches taller than me. Her dark curly hair was tied in a bun, and as always, she looked naturally beautiful with just a flick of black eyeliner and clear gloss. 'Mike's putting Paul to bed, so I came early.'

'And I've got a moody teenager at home, so thought I'd escape and get the party started early!' Melody squeezed me tightly and the dozens of colourful bangles she always wore jangled loudly behind my back. She'd scooped her reddish-brown hair into a beehive, which made her big orange hoop earrings stand out.

After we'd ordered, we started to catch up. Bella told us that Paul was growing up fast, teaching was going well and she and Mike were still like a pair of loved-up teenagers.

Melody was working at the council and making jewellery in her spare time, but things weren't going as well as she hoped on the romantic front.

'So, I'm back on the dating sites.' Melody sighed before taking a large gulp of her vodka and Coke. 'If I had a pound for every dick pic I received, I'd be rich. What is it with guys? Why are they so obsessed with sending photos of their cocks? And they're not exactly pretty, are they? I mean, if you're going to send one, at least put a bow or some glitter on it to make it look nice!'

I almost choked on my salmon. Classic Melody.

'I suppose it's the guys looking for a hook-up that do that. Maybe they see it as a kind of preview, which they think will get you excited? No idea!'

'God knows.' She shook her head. 'Anyway. Enough about me and Bella. Let's talk about you and your exciting trip to *Pa-reeh*! Looking forward to seeing your sexy French fuck buddy?' Melody smirked.

'He's not my *fuck buddy*.' I rolled my eyes.

'So what is he, then?'

Good question. We hadn't had the define-the-relation-ship talk, so with my friends, I just referred to him by his name. Maybe I'd start calling him my *lover*. That sounded more exciting.

'I don't know.' I shrugged my shoulders. 'We just had

a connection. I like being with him. We had a great time at Christmas and I'd be crazy not to take him up on his invite to Paris. I'm just going for the experience, though,' I said, remembering my pep talk and decision to not get carried away. 'It probably won't work long-term, but it'll be a cool story to share when I'm older. I can tell all my pensioner friends at my retirement home that when I was young, I had a wild ten days with a hot Frenchman.'

'Ha! I can see it now. You and the old biddies gathering in a circle in rocking chairs with blankets over your dodgy knees, knitting needles in hand, and you telling them you got fucked at the Eiffel Tower. "What did you say, dear?"' Melody did a terrible impersonation of an elderly woman. '"You had nookie on an electric tower? That must have given you a shock!"'

'That was a *terrible* joke, and so ageist too. The residents at the retirement home that I volunteer at aren't all stereotypical, frail old people. They're smart, wise and funny.' I smiled as Doris and the stories she'd told me about her life and her many husbands came to mind. 'Doing it on the Eiffel Tower would be pretty thrilling, though…'

I pictured the research I'd done last week, when I'd stumbled on an article which I'd thought was about where to do it outdoors in Paris. A tingle of excitement rushed through me.

'Why don't you think it can work long-term?' Bella asked.

'Where do you want me to start?' I blew out a breath. 'He lives in Paris, I live in London. He's rich, I'm always broke. He moves in fancy circles, my friends are—'

'Careful…' Melody raised an eyebrow.

'I was about to say down to earth, genuine and normal.'

'I'm not normal! What a bloody insult!' Melody cackled.

'You know what I mean. Nico may be down to earth and he says he's not into the glam lifestyle, but I mean, *come on*. If you're a millionaire, you're not exactly going to live in a one-bedroom flat, eat beans on toast and take the bus everywhere, are you? I know I wouldn't. I'd live in a mansion, stuff my face with M&S food every night and get Ubers everywhere.'

'Nah. You'd have a chef and a driver. And *staff*. Yes! If I was minted, I'd deffo have a nanny and a cleaner. Jeeves, my butler-slash-driver, would take me everywhere in a fancy Rolls-Royce. Oh my God, Cass, you are *so* lucky! You're going to be like Julia Roberts in *Pretty Woman*. Going shopping with his credit card, being showered with diamonds. You're living the dream!'

It was exciting. Not the shopping and diamonds bit. I didn't need a man to buy clothes or jewellery for me. I meant in terms of having the chance to go to Paris like this. It wasn't every day that someone like me had the opportunity to experience how the other half lived. Yep. That was the keyword—this was an *experience*.

I really liked Nico. A *lot*. But I had to be careful when I went to see him. It was unlikely that it was going to turn into something serious, so I couldn't risk catching feelings and falling in love. It would only lead to heartbreak.

'Yeah, hopefully it'll be fun.'

'I think you should keep yourself open for something long-term. Be ready for everything, hon,' Bella said. 'Even if it means moving there.'

'Whoa!' I raised my hand. 'Hold your horses! I've barely known the guy a month. I'm going for a holiday. It's just ten days in Paris, that's all.'

'You never know. Look what happened to Sophia.'

'Oh yeah!' said Melody. 'She's living in Italy now, isn't she?'

I'd met Sophia a few times over the years. She was one of Bella's closest friends. I really liked her.

'Yeah. She met her boyfriend, Lorenzo, in Italy on a cookery holiday. She had an amazing house and successful PR business in London, but decided to go and live in Italy to be with him.'

'Well, I guess it can happen, but it's rare. Probably like a one-in-a-billion chance. Anyway, this is different. Lorenzo is a chef, right? Not a millionaire running a global empire. I think *that's* what adds to the obstacles.'

'Ooh… reminds me of *Sex in the City*. Do you remember, Cass, when Carrie moved to Paris to be with that guy in the last season?'

When Melody and I lived together in Bella's flat when Bella went to work in Vietnam, we used to binge-watch the *Sex in the City* box sets. We were both single girls living in London, so on Saturday nights after we'd put her daughter, Andrea, to bed, we'd make cocktails and watch two or three episodes in a row. Those days were so fun.

'Ugh, I think he should've been called *arsehole*. I hated that guy.'

'Yeah, that Aleksandr was a right tit.' Melody shook her head. 'He was rich too and he never had time for the poor girl. He was always busy with his exhibition and left Carrie alone in her five-star hotel room. She was so lonely.'

I remembered those episodes. Carrie was miserable, wandering the streets of Paris alone all day whilst her boyfriend was always working. Then when they *did* go out to parties together, he'd either leave her by herself or sit there speaking French all night and Carrie didn't understand a word.

My stomach plummeted. I was visiting Nico when he'd be busy, so I'd probably have a similar experience.

'Ladies, come on. Yeah, I'm not saying it's guaranteed to be all hearts and roses.' Bella sipped on her Chardonnay. 'You could go there and it might not be what you were hoping for. *But* it could also be amazing!'

'True. You *could* have the fairy tale, Cass. Give me something to believe in. God knows I need it with the way my love life is going.'

I might have been lucky at Christmas, but I wasn't going to be one of those delusional women who went on holiday and fell head over heels for a local after a few days of hot sex, then uprooted their whole lives to go there believing that they'd get married, have babies and live happily ever after. Like I said, Sophia was the exception. That didn't happen to people like me.

Of course, I'd thought about it. Dreamt that it could happen. Especially during those magical days I'd shared with Nico over Christmas. I really hoped that we could have a future together. But now I was thinking more clearly, that wasn't realistic. I mean, look how complicated it was just to arrange meeting up for ten days. If it'd taken over a month to do that, what chance did we have of making a long-term relationship work?

Nah. Like I'd said to myself after Nate's lecture-slash-prophecy, best to just go there with no expectations other than to enjoy myself. That way I wouldn't get hurt.

'If you want relationship goals, you're better off looking at Bella and Mike, not me. Anyway, enough speculation about my future. I'm already an overthinker—I don't need any encouragement. In less than two days, I'll be in Paris, so let's just see what happens then.'

'Are you all set? Got everything you need?'

'As I'll ever be. I've got my passport, money, phone, new clothes, sexy lingerie and enough condoms to open a chemist!'

It was true. Well, slight exaggeration about the condoms, but not as far as the clothes were concerned.

I'd bought a new pair of jeans, different jumpers, a sparkly dress in case we went somewhere fancy, new boots, perfume, make-up…

I swallowed hard as I reminded myself that I'd gone a bit over budget. Given that I needed to watch every penny I spent, it wasn't wise, but if I had to, I'd cut back on other stuff when I got back to balance it out.

I'd crammed packs of chocolate Hobnobs and custard creams into my suitcase too. Nico had tried those biscuits when he'd stayed at mine and liked them, so I thought I'd bring some over for him. Yep. I was good to go.

'Sounds like you've got all bases covered,' said Bella.

'Promise me you'll have an amazing time! And lots of sex!' Melody shouted, causing the waitress passing our table to raise an eyebrow. 'And don't wait until we're in our rocking chairs at the retirement home to share your saucy escapades. I'll be waiting to hear your stories, so make sure they're good!'

CHAPTER NINE

I came out of the tube station exit and looked for directions to the Eurostar concourse.

There it is.

My heart fluttered. Today was the day. After five and a half long weeks, I was finally going to be reunited with Nico.

As much as I'd told myself not to get carried away, my brain had insisted on playing a romantic montage of our Paris reunion. I'd see him at Gare du Nord train station from a distance and run into his arms, and he'd give me the most amazing, passionate kiss. I'd clearly watched too many romcoms.

I pushed the soppy thoughts out of my head and pulled my suitcase along to the Eurostar entrance whilst going through my mental checklist for what felt like the hundredth time. I had my passport, the e-ticket on my phone and euros. My charger was safely packed away in my new suitcase along with an EU converter plug, just in case. Nico knew the time I was arriving. Everything was sorted.

God, I was hot. Even though it was a chilly February morning, I was burning up. Must be the adrenaline and excitement. Being on a packed tube on the way here didn't help.

I took off my coat, unzipped my case and squeezed it inside. The zip got halfway, then stopped. Bloody hell. I'd packed way too much. Carrying it around would be annoying, though.

I quickly wheeled my case around a corner, then sat on top. It was the only way to get it shut. After a few bum wiggles, the zip went all the way round. *That's better.* Now I only had my case and handbag to carry.

I headed back to the ticket gates. There was a section dedicated to Business Premier—the class I'd be travelling in. *Fancy.* I took my phone out of my handbag and pulled up the ticket. After I scanned the barcode at the gate, the barrier opened.

I was in. This was real. I was actually going to Paris.

I could count the places I'd been outside of the UK on one hand. St Lucia to see Mum's family when I was a kid, a school trip to France when I was a teenager, a trip to Tenerife in my twenties… erm… yeah. That was about it. Pretty sad.

After going through security and passport control, I was directed to the Business Premier lounge. I walked through the entrance.

Whoa. Normally when I took a train somewhere, the closest I got to a *lounge* was a crowded waiting room. But this was on a different level.

I stepped across the dark glossy wooden floor and

marvelled at the sleek and stylish blue-and-grey decor, with glass and exposed-brick walls and big, bright lamp-shades hanging from the white ceiling.

The hum of people chatting filled the air. Some were walking around the lounge and others were seated at the desks, tapping away on iPads and laptops or chatting on the phone.

I scanned the room. There was a cabinet with a selection of newspapers and a stylish gold bookcase with stacks of glossy magazines on display. I wondered if you had to read them here or if you could take them away on the Eurostar? I'd pick up a few on the way out for the journey.

Next, I spotted the food. My mouth watered as I took in the display. There were huge silver bowls filled with crackers and savoury snacks, yogurts, bread, fresh fruit and the pastries—*oh my days*. I'd definitely be trying one of the buttery croissants or pains au chocolat. Actually, I'd have both. I was on holiday, so might as well make the most of it.

My eyes darted to the silver-and-glass fridges, which were filled to the brim with soft drinks, juices and—wait, bottles of wine too? Wow. And I didn't have to pay extra for any of it. This was so cool. That was clearly why the tickets had cost Nico hundreds of pounds.

Just when I thought I'd seen it all, I clocked an impressive metallic spiral staircase and just had to take a look. As I reached the next floor, I noticed it was much quieter up here than downstairs. There were more comfy-looking chairs and tables too. After I'd had something to eat, I might come up here to read a magazine.

Holy macaroni. My eyes widened as I saw the cocktail bar. It looked very plush with a circular design and red velvet chairs. I couldn't believe that they gave you free cocktails too. Good thing the bar wasn't open yet. Otherwise they might need to carry me to the train.

I hadn't even got on the Eurostar yet and my head was already spinning as I tried to take everything in. This was another world.

As I walked through the lounge, a few people stared. They must think I shouldn't be here. They were right. *Let's face it*. If Nico hadn't bought my ticket, I'd be in the normal waiting area like most people.

I headed back downstairs, grabbed some food, and before I knew it, there was only thirty-five minutes before the train was due to leave. Thankfully, because this was fancy-class, they let you board right at the last minute, so I still had time to go to the loo.

Would it be sad to take photos? *Sod it*. I'd probably get a few stares, but who knew if I'd get the chance to come to a place like this again? I needed to document it.

As I pulled out my phone, I saw that a few messages had come through.

There was one from Nico. He'd had a breakfast meeting in Nice, but would be leaving soon so that he could fly back to Paris in time to meet me at the station. My heart fluttered again at the thought of seeing him. Being wrapped in his arms. Feeling his lips on mine. Oh God. It was pointless trying to contain it. I was beyond excited. Nervous, but excited.

I quickly texted back.

Me

See you in a few hours! Can't wait xxx

. . .

There were also messages from Melody and Bella in our group chat, asking if I'd checked in okay.

I took a few photos of the lounge, then held the phone up for a quick selfie. Yeah, it was probably a tacky thing to do in a posh lounge, but I did it anyway.

Me

Just half an hour until we board!

Melody texted back first. She always had her phone glued to her hip. Even when she was working.

Melody

Yay! Send us loads of pics.

Me

Will do! This Business Premier lounge is amazing, daaaarling!!

Me

Can you believe they give you free champagne, food and magazines??!! There's even a free cocktail bar too. Good thing it doesn't open until later, or I'd be pissed by now!

I fired off some photos of the cocktail bar and a few others I'd taken. Bella came online and started typing. She must be on a break.

Bella

So excited for you, hon! It all looks très fancy! Glad you're enjoying. And it's great to see that you're calmer about the outfit thing too.

.   .   .

I frowned and then remembered that when we had spoken last night, I'd been debating what to wear, and in my selfie, she'd seen what I had on.

Me

No! I'm not wearing *this*! This is just for the journey.

I was dressed in a light pink tracksuit and my favourite white trainers. I'd had them for years, so they'd seen better days, but they were so comfy. I also liked the design and the fact that they had multicoloured laces.

I wanted my hair to be extra curly, so after I'd washed it last night, I'd twisted it, then covered it with a colourful headscarf. Just as well, really, because when I'd walked to the station it was raining. It was that annoying type of rain too. The kind that isn't heavy enough for an umbrella, but still has the ability to turn your hair into a ball of frizz. At least under the headscarf it was protected.

Right now, I definitely looked more casual than chic, which was probably why I'd had a few looks from some other travellers. I was doing my best not to let it get to me. I'd told myself before Christmas that I was going to try not to worry so much about what other people thought of me. They were strangers. It was how I looked when I arrived in Paris that was the important thing.

Me

I've packed that gorgeous silk shirt dress I showed you and my new boots that I'll change into before the train pulls into the station.

. . .

That was definitely the most sensible option. I knew that we'd get served food and wine during the trip. If I wore my dress on the train, I was guaranteed to spill something down it before I arrived.

I was already glad that I'd worn a travel outfit, because when I'd got the tube earlier, the escalator and the lift hadn't been working, so I'd had to lug my suitcase up the stairs, which was no picnic. If I'd worn my lovely dress, it would've had pit stains already or sweat dripping down it by now.

Nico had offered to pay for a taxi from my house to St Pancras, but I'd said I couldn't accept. He'd already paid for my ticket. I wasn't going to get all la-di-da just because he was rich. As much as it wasn't my favourite thing in the world, I was fine taking public transport.

I planned to do my hair and make-up and transform myself in the loos about an hour before we arrived. I was sure we would've eaten by then. I'd be like Superman going into a phone box to change into his superhero outfit. It'd be my modern-day Cinderella moment. I'll whip off my headscarf to reveal a head of nicely defined curls, take off my tracksuit, freshen up, slip into my nice dress, then step off the Eurostar feeling as fresh as a daisy and *hopefully* looking super polished like a Parisian.

Melody

Good idea.

Melody

Bit like if I wear heels for a meeting. I always have some flats to wear beforehand and then put the heels on at the last minute.

Melody

No point torturing your tootsies sooner than you need to.

Melody

And silk is a bugger. If you sit down in it for too long it gets super creased.

Me

Good point.

Best to leave putting that on until the very last minute. I'd heard everyone was so chic in Paris. I was already nervous about how I'd fit into Nico's lifestyle, meeting his friends and maybe his family. I wanted to look good and feel confident.

Bella

And try not to be too nervous. It's going to be great! Better go, hon. Got a lesson starting in ten. Enjoy first class and message us later to let us know you've arrived safely.

Melody

That's if you're not too busy sitting on his Eiffel Tower!

I snorted as I looked at the row of aubergine emojis Melody had added to her message.

Me

Laters, ladies! xxx

Oops. I hadn't meant to stay on the phone so long. There were now only twenty-five minutes until the train left. I'd better go to the loo quickly. Just in case. All the nerves of my journey were affecting my bladder. That, and probably the glass of champers that I'd had with my croissant.

After I came out of the toilet, I headed to the platform. This was it!

As I pulled my suitcase along, scanning the coach numbers, I smiled at the Eurostar staff standing outside each of the Premier class carriages. I'd never travelled in anything other than standard class, so I was looking forward to the experience.

This was my coach. How exciting.

'Welcome to Eurostar,' the lady said with a French accent. 'May I see your ticket, please?' I pulled out my phone and showed her my screen. 'Thank you. Your seat will be on the left-hand side. Enjoy your journey.'

'Thank you!'

I stepped up onto the train, where another member of staff greeted me with a smile. The carriage was already pretty full. To be expected, considering the train was almost about to leave.

I found my seat quickly. It was much wider than the ones I'd seen in standard class and it had plenty of legroom. Perfect.

First things first: put my suitcase away. I glanced up at the luggage racks near my seat and they were already taken up with fancy leather designer cases. I recognised the logo. I'd had to order them for Spencer's wife and had nearly fallen off my chair when I'd seen the price. It cost more than an actual holiday. They probably belonged to the group of four sitting on the other side of the carriage. The Eurostar luggage allowance was generous, and they'd clearly decided to make the most of it.

I walked down the aisle and spotted a few empty spaces in the large rack at the end.

I popped my case up onto it. It looked quite smart. I'd been tempted to get a simple one from one of the discount stores, but in the end had gone for a decent brand. The lady in the department store had said it was a popular design because it was stylish and hard-wearing. She reckoned it would last for years, so I'd decided to go for it.

Not long afterwards, the train departed. I scanned the menu. We got a three-course meal? *Nice.*

The beetroot salad sounded lovely for the starter. I bet the chicken with cinnamon and plum ketchup was divine too. And I was definitely having the pear and almond tart for dessert.

Yes, I said to myself as I reclined in the comfy chair. *I could get used to travelling like this.*

Whilst I waited for the food to arrive, I scrolled through my phone, looking at the websites I'd bookmarked for places to visit. I put my headphones in and watched some funny videos that Nate had sent.

The Eurostar hostess brought my food to the table. It looked so good. It was a tray with multiple cute rectangular white plates and bowls—each one with a different course. Apparently, a Michelin-star chef had created the menu. That was another first for me. Definitely different to grabbing a sandwich and a bag of crisps, which was what I normally did if I was feeling peckish on a long train journey.

After snapping some photos, ignoring the raised eyebrow of the well-dressed woman in her sixties sat adjacent to me, I sent them to Bella and Melody. I knew they always appreciated a good food pic.

I tucked into the salad. It had pistachios, capers and different grains and was very tasty. Just as I lifted another forkful of beetroot towards my mouth, my phone chimed. I turned my head to look at the screen and... shit. The food landed right in my lap. *Great*. Should've put my napkin over my tracksuit.

I quickly grabbed the serviette and attempted to pick the food off my clothes, but the beetroot had already left a mark right in the crotch area. *Bollocks*. I poured a few drops of water onto a serviette and started tackling the stain. So glad I hadn't worn my dress.

As I rubbed vigorously, I heard a loud tut. The snooty woman looked disgusted. I frowned, then glanced back down at my hand poised between my legs. *Oh*. Yeah. Me rubbing at my crotch under the table probably wasn't a good look.

I knew I was trying to get the beetroot out, but she probably thought I was doing something entirely different. *Point taken*. Didn't want to look like I was getting my rocks off on the train.

The man sitting beside her winked and licked his lips. I hoped he was appreciating his starter, rather than enjoying the sight of me cleaning myself. I tossed the serviette onto the table. I'd get the stain out in the toilets later once I got changed.

After finishing the salad, I wolfed down the chicken and thankfully avoided getting plum ketchup on my clothes because this time I had the good sense to put the napkin on my lap.

Once I'd polished off dessert, I checked my messages and fired off more images to Bella and Melody.

The journey time in the tunnel went quickly and before

I knew it, we were out in the open again with acres of French countryside in view.

Now that we were in France, I should probably change my clothes. My battery was running low, so I should get my charger out of my suitcase soon too. The train made a stop at Calais. As I watched some passengers get off, my phone rang. It was Lily.

'Hey, sis.'

'Hey, Cassie. Are you in Paris now?'

'Not yet. We've just arrived at Calais, though.'

'Cool. You're so lucky to be going abroad. I've always wanted to travel.'

'You should, Lil!'

'I know. I keep suggesting to River that we go some-where, but something always comes up…' Her voice trailed off. 'River's actually the reason I'm calling. Do you have a sec to talk?'

'Course! What's up?'

'Do you think it's still weird that I haven't met his family and we've been together for almost four months?'

Lily then went on to tell me the whole backstory of how every time she'd asked River about it, he'd changed the subject. And the two occasions that he'd said they would, either his parents had become mysteriously ill or something else had come up.

'It's hard to say, Lil. I haven't met him, so…'

'And that's the other thing. He's always busy when I suggest he meets you guys. Do you think Nate was right? When he said River wasn't serious? It's so difficult. When we're together, he's really attentive.'

The more Lily spoke, talking about how they usually met up at her house and rarely went out in public, the more

I couldn't help but think Nate might have a point about River's reasons for avoiding family introductions.

As Lily continued to vent, I glanced at the phone. We'd been speaking now for almost forty-five minutes and my battery was dangerously low. How was it that when I was at home, it would stay fully charged, but whenever I left the house, it depleted so quickly? Admittedly, I had used it a lot. Probably didn't help that my phone needed upgrading too.

'I'd say, just ask him outright about it and see what he says. Sis, I'm really sorry, but I'm going to have to go. I'll be in Paris soon and I need to get changed and charge my phone a bit. Can we speak later?'

'Okay.' She sounded so upset. I wished I could stay on the line, but I was already cutting it fine.

'Love you!' I hung up.

There was a message from Nico. He'd probably arrived early. I'd listen to it once I got changed. I rushed to the end of the aisle and looked down the rack for my black hard-shell suitcase. I thought I'd put it in the middle section, but that was empty. I bent down to the bottom. *There it is*. Maybe the Eurostar people had shuffled them around to make more room. Like they did on planes when they got busy.

I wheeled it back to my seat and rested it on the edge of the table. As I opened it, it slipped off onto the floor and...

OMG.

Several big boxes of condoms, a French maid's outfit, a red PVC catsuit with what looked like devil horns and a tail, a leather whip, a bright pink vibrator, and several pairs of lacy thongs all tumbled onto the floor.

WTF.

The snooty woman gasped so loudly everyone turned around and stared.

I know I'd joked to Bella and Melody that I'd bought enough condoms to open a chemist and I'd got some new underwear too, but this was taking the sexy holiday in Paris stuff to a whole other level.

'Do you need some help, madam?' A staff member rushed over. I felt the passengers' eyes burning into me.

'This isn't my case!' My heart thudded.

'*Sure…,*' I heard the businessman mutter under his breath. He licked his lips again. Gross. The lady beside him shook her head with disgust.

I supposed I couldn't blame them. First they saw me rubbing my crotch under the table and now the X-rated contents of a suitcase that I'd opened were all over the aisle. I looked like I was on my way to an orgy.

I shoved everything back inside, zipped up the case, then rushed back over to the rack. I didn't understand. This case was the only plain black one here. Everything else was another colour or covered in designer logos.

The Eurostar lady came to help.

'My case isn't here!' My heart thumped from my chest. I raced down the aisle, glancing at the racks above the seats. I knew it wouldn't be there, but I wanted to check anyway. Just in case it had been moved. But it hadn't.

It was gone.

Which meant so were my change of clothes, my coat. *Everything*.

'Um, madam,' a French lady who'd just come from the toilets whispered in my ear. 'Do you need a pad? Or a tampon? I have one…'

'Sorry, what?' I frowned. What was she on about?

'You need, yes? It has happened to all of us before… please do not be embarrassed.' The woman glanced between my legs.

I looked down and… *oh fuck*. There was a big beetroot stain between my legs, which looked like I'd started my period and leaked onto my clothes.

I couldn't change into my dress, so I'd have to cover up with my coat.

Shit. My coat. I'd packed that into my case too.

I'd had big plans of arriving in Paris in style. Looking glamorous. And now I was minutes away from meeting Nico, the hot French guy I'd been waiting to see for so long, in Paris. In a tracksuit. With the crotch covered in red stains. *Jesus.*

This wasn't what I had planned.

At all.

CHAPTER TEN

'Ladies and gentlemen. Welcome to Paris Gare du Nord: our final destination…'

Already? No, no, no!

As the announcement boomed over the speakers, beads of sweat pooled on my forehead. What the hell was I going to do now?

'Please.' I turned to the Eurostar hostess. 'I really need your help. I put my case here when I got on the train at St Pancras, but it's not here.'

'That is strange. Are you sure that you did not put it somewhere else, madam?'

'No! It was definitely here. There was no room on the racks above my seat, so I put it here.'

'How does your case look?' she replied in a thick French accent.

'It's exactly like this one. Same colour, same brand,' I shouted. *That'll teach me not to buy popular things.* 'Just not filled with sex toys, condoms and kinky outfits!' Her eyes widened. I'd probably said that last part a bit too loudly, but I wasn't thinking straight.

'Ah, I see.' She nodded. 'If it look the same, then it is possible that another passenger take it by mistake when they leave the train at Calais. Do not worry. I am sure that they will return it. When they see that what is inside their case is not...' She stifled a smile. 'When they realise that the contents are not what they expect.'

Yeah. I imagined that when they rocked up to their sex orgy and popped open my case to slip into their French maid's outfit or don their devil catsuit, they might be a bit disappointed to find my coat, some very vanilla clothes and several packets of biscuits. Maybe I'd be able to laugh about this in a few months, but right now, it wasn't funny.

The train was now in the station and the passengers had already started to get off. Nico would be on the platform waiting for me and I couldn't meet him like this. I was a mess.

'Where should I go? To find out if someone has reported the mix-up?'

'If you ask one of my colleagues on the platform for lost property, they will help you.'

'Okay, thank you.'

I rushed back to my seat to get my handbag.

'Welcome to Paris,' said the friendly hostess as I stepped off the train.

'Thanks. Erm, where's the lost property office, please?'

'It is on level minus one. But madam'—she glanced at her watch—'I am afraid it is closed for lunch. It will open again in one hour.'

Oh. I'd read about French places closing for lunch.

That was unheard of in England. We just staggered our lunch breaks instead. In my office, we mostly ate at our desks. I couldn't wait an hour.

I looked ahead at the passengers exiting the platform and being reunited with their loved ones. I hadn't realised that you just walked straight through like a normal train station. I thought there'd be security and passport checks like at an airport. That meant that right now, Nico was out there waiting for me.

Think, think, think.

I took off my tracksuit top, then wrapped it around my waist. Although I would freeze in this short-sleeved T-shirt, at least I'd be spared the embarrassment of walking around with a red stain between my legs.

A sharp pain shot through my bladder. I needed the loo. I'd drunk champagne, wine and water on the train and hadn't been to the toilet at all during the journey. I could see they were already preparing the Eurostar for the next wave of passengers, so I wouldn't be able to get back on the train.

I tensed my pelvic muscles to hold it in, but that wouldn't work for long. I desperately needed to go and there was no way I could meet Nico until then. I'd end up pissing myself on the spot. I was already looking like the complete opposite of sexy, so I didn't need to make things even worse.

It was busy, so he wouldn't see me. Probably wouldn't recognise me either with my headscarf on. I slipped through the platform exit, then followed the signs to the toilets. When I arrived, I realised I had to pay. I reached in my handbag for the little coin purse of euros I'd found in

Nate's old suitcase. He'd said I should take it because it would come in handy. He was right.

My phone chimed. I quickly pulled it out of my pocket. My battery was at four percent. I needed to find a way to charge it before it died completely.

It was a voice note from Nico. I quickly pressed the play button.

'I am so sorry, *chérie*, but I cannot meet you. There is a delay with the plane, but I will send someone to the station to meet you…'

Oh no! I was really looking forward to seeing him.

The message cut off abruptly. There was another longer message below, but I needed the loo. Right now.

I pushed my phone into the pocket of my tracksuit bottoms, paid the lady, then flew into the nearest vacant cubicle.

I didn't even bother to shut the door properly. There was no time. I yanked down my tracksuit bottoms and squatted above the seat.

Finally.

Relief washed over me. A second later and I wouldn't have made it.

That's better.

As much as I'd dreamt of running into Nico's arms at the station, it was clear that wasn't going to happen now that he was running late. There was a silver lining, though. If he wasn't meeting me at the station, he wouldn't see me looking a complete mess.

He'd probably send an assistant to get me, and hopefully he or she could recommend where I could go to buy a decent outfit quickly. It wouldn't be what I had planned, but it'd be better than what I was wearing now.

Then by the time I met him, I'd at least look more presentable. *Good plan.* I wouldn't let a setback like losing a suitcase with every item of decent clothing I owned get me down.

God, I really did drink a lot. This wee was going on forever.

I sighed as I ran through all the things that were in that case. The brand-new clothes I'd spent a fortune on. Lingerie. The biscuits I'd bought for Nico. The jewellery Melody had made for me. *Oh God.*

But at least I still had my phone and my purse, so all wasn't lost.

Wait.

My purse.

Now that I thought about it, I was pretty sure that I'd put my purse in the inside pocket of my coat after I'd topped up my Oyster card at the tube station. Nate had warned me about pickpockets and said not to put too much stuff in my handbag.

Yes. I'd put my purse in my coat. The coat that I'd then put in my suitcase. Which was now lost.

Fuck.

My heart was now pounding so much it could burst from my chest at any second.

No. No. No. Why was this happening to me?

Keep calm. Think of a solution. There must be a way to get through this. Think.

Was this wee ever going to end?

Eventually, the flow stopped.

I still couldn't think of what to do right now, but I would. *Somehow.*

First things first, I needed to get back to the concourse.

I'd work everything else out once I'd seen whoever Nico sent to meet me.

I wiped myself, then, just as I pulled up my tracksuit bottoms, I heard a loud plop.

No... don't tell me...

I glanced down and yep. Sure enough, there it was. My phone. Swimming around in the toilet bowl. Covered in piss.

Just when I thought the day couldn't get any worse.

CHAPTER ELEVEN

I had a theory: the universe had clearly decided to save all the bad luck they normally gave me at Christmas for this trip to Paris instead. It was the only explanation.

The powers that be clearly thought I was far too happy meeting Nico and having a wonderful time with him over the holidays and so decided to throw a load of crap at me today. *Bastards*.

After fishing my phone out of the toilet and frantically trying to wipe, then dry it, I attempted to turn it on, but it was dead. It hadn't been in the bowl for too long, so if I had a charger, I could at least go to one of the charging points they often had at train stations try and see if I could rescue it. But, *nope*.

I headed to the bustling concourse. The sharp sounds of the trains stopping on the iron tracks and the loud announcements filled the air.

I scanned the area to see if anyone seemed like they were waiting for me. There was no one holding up a sign, and I'd imagine that whoever he sent wouldn't know what

I looked like. There was only one thing for it. *I* had to approach *them*.

'Hello, I mean, *bonjour*!' I said to a man dressed in a suit. 'My name is Cassie…'

'I am not interested,' he snapped and turned away. Oh crap. He thought I was trying to chat him up. Cringe.

I approached a woman and she clutched her handbag tighter, then shuffled away.

Okay. This wasn't proving to be the best idea. Time to think of something else.

As the minutes ticked by, the concourse emptied a little. There was no one here for me. My heart sank. *So much for a romantic reunion.*

I was trying to stay positive, but it was hard. With my phone being out of action, I didn't know what Nico had said in his message. Apart from the loose change that Nate had given me, I had no money, so I couldn't buy a cheap mobile to call him. I couldn't even call him from a phone box because I didn't know his number off by heart.

I was screwed.

I sat on the station floor, shivering from the cold. At least I didn't have to worry about getting my clothes dirty. They were already soiled.

There *must* be a way.

Yeah, I'd had some crazy setbacks, but I wanted to see Nico. No. I *needed* to see him. I wasn't going to give up.

Then it came to me: like a flash of lightning. I had a brainwave. I didn't know Nico's *number* off by heart, but I remembered the name of the street where his company was based. Rue Marcel Baptiste. I remembered it because it reminded me of Marcel the monkey in *Friends*.

Yes. That's right.

I didn't remember the number, but that wasn't important right now.

I reached in my handbag and pulled out the coins. I had a few euros. That would be enough for the Metro.

I'd look up the road and ask for the nearest tube stop. I'd get the Metro there, find the street and walk down it until I found Nico's office. It'd be a challenge, but I'd faced a lot of those already today and I was still standing.

I'd come too far to give up now.

I'd come to see Nico and that was exactly what I planned to do.

CHAPTER TWELVE

I glanced up at the pretty blue-and-green street sign. This was the road.

Despite feeling like screaming after all the crap the universe had thrown at me today, I'd dragged my arse off the Gare du Nord station floor and found the sign to the Metro, which was only down a couple of flights of stairs.

Luckily, I'd found a map of Paris on the station floor, so after scanning the street index, I'd been able to find the street name and then the nearest tube. Result.

After that, I'd joined the queue at the ticket office, and thankfully the man behind the counter had spoken English and I'd been able to buy a ticket and get instructions on which Metro lines to take.

I'd had to change tubes twice and almost missed my stop, but it hadn't taken too long to get here. I'd survived my first trip on the Metro. After the day I'd had, that was an achievement.

Now I was here, I had to work out where the Icon HQ building was. Should be straightforward enough.

I reached in my bag for my phone to check the notes I'd made on how to ask for things.

Oh yeah. I forgot.

My phone was out of action. Nothing like not having a working mobile to make you realise how much you relied on it.

Asking passers-by in the street probably wasn't the best idea. They might be tourists just like me. Going into a shop would be best.

I pushed the door of a little boutique open and stepped inside.

'*Bonjour…*' That was one French word in the bag. '*Parlez* English? Do you speak English?'

'*Non.*'

Okay, then…

The woman folded her arms. She wasn't impressed with my poor attempt at French. Everything I'd learnt on the language app had evaporated from my brain just when I needed it.

Maybe sign language would help?

'I'm looking for…' I curved the thumb and fore-finger on each hand into circle-like shapes and put each one in front of my eyes to make what I hoped looked like binoculars. 'Icon. The company that makes hair straighteners and hairdryers.' I now started waving my hands over my head like I was holding a hairdryer. The woman's frown grew more intense. Something told me that she didn't have a clue what I was going on about.

Hmmm. Think.

Aha. A picture! If I showed her a photo of Nico, I was sure she'd recognise him. If he worked on this street, she must be familiar with him. A hot man like him couldn't go unnoticed. I reached for my phone…

Dammit.

'Erm… internet? Can I use your computer?' This time the woman glared at me as if to say, *get out of my shop, you weirdo, before I call the police*. Point taken. 'Okay. *Merci*.'

I quickly made my exit, then continued walking down the street. A man stepped out of a fromagerie and the strong scent of cheese flooded my nostrils. Yum.

There was no sign of Nico's office. I'd just have to keep looking at every building until I found it.

After a few minutes, there was still no joy. Then in the distance, I noticed a huge, shiny black executive car pull up. A tall, handsome man dressed in a smart dark suit stepped out. I squinted, as if the action allowed my eyes to zoom in.

Was that…?

He looked like Nico.

Before I got a closer look, he darted into the building.

I was sure that was him. I quickened my pace and before I knew it, I was jogging down the street, eager to see if I'd found the building.

When I got outside, I glanced upwards.

Yes! This was it.

A big silver Icon logo hung above the grand art deco limestone building. I stepped through the huge black double doors. *Wow*. I walked across the immaculately polished white tiled flooring, scanning the reception area. There was no sign of Nico, just two stunningly beautiful women sat on the glossy black leather sofa to my left and a man waiting at the reception desk in front of me.

The receptionist babbled something in French to him and he went to sit on another sofa.

'*Oui? Puis-je vous aider?*' The woman looked me up and down, with her lip curled in disgust like she'd just smelt an eggy fart. '*Si vous êtes ici pour le travail de nettoyage, vous êtes trop tard.*'

'*Bonjour.* Sorry, I mean, *pardon*. I don't understand. Do you speak English?'

'I say, if you are here for the cleaning job, you are too late.' She scowled. 'The interviews finish.'

What the hell? She thought I was here for a cleaning job? Why would she think...

She folded her arms and looked me up and down again, this time fixating on my head.

Oh God. I forgot.

I was still wearing my headscarf and my tracksuit with my top wrapped around my waist. I hadn't even looked in the mirror before I'd stepped inside. And now here I was in this fancy building, with two twenty-something supermodels to my left and this pristine-looking receptionist glaring at me like I was a monster with five heads.

Maybe I should go to the toilets before she called Nico down and at least take my scarf off and untwist my hair so I looked more decent.

Out of order of her to make assumptions just based on my clothes. And she'd said cleaning job in such a demeaning way. My mum used to clean part-time. It was hard work and it helped put food on the table. This woman didn't have to be so snooty about it.

'No, I'm not here for the cleaning job. I'm here to see Nico.'

'*Comment?*' She laughed. 'What reason could *you* possibly have to see Mr Chevalier?'

Wow. This woman was such a stuck-up bitch.

'It's personal. Could you call him and tell him that Cassie is here, *s'il vous plaît?*' I put on my best fake smile. Yes. I even threw in some French too. Take that, *biatch*!

'He is a very busy man, so it is unlikely that he will be able to see unexpected visitors,' she huffed, picking up the phone.

'If you call him, I'm sure you'll find that he is expecting me. *Merci.*' She might be rude, but I wasn't going to be.

She babbled some stuff in French in a disinterested tone. The only words I understood were Nico's name—Mr Chevalier, as she called him—and then I heard mine. Suddenly, she sat up straighter, surprise filling her voice, then hung up.

'Wait here,' she hissed.

Boom.

You weren't expecting that, were you?

That'd teach her to jump to conclusions.

I wasn't sure if his assistant or someone would be coming down to get me. Whilst I was waiting, I could go to the loo quickly to try and sort myself out.

'Can you tell me where the—'

'Cassie!' I heard someone shout my name. As I spun around, I saw Nico racing towards me.

Oh. My. God.

He'd looked good from afar when I'd seen him on the street, but close up, it was on a whole different level.

He was dressed in a dark grey suit, which looked like it had been sewn by angels. It fit every inch of his body perfectly. Underneath he had a crisp white shirt that had the top few buttons undone, showing a glimpse of his toned muscular chest.

His dark eyes sparkled, and as always, his hair looked like he was about to shoot a shampoo commercial. Perfectly glossy and styled. His skin was glowing and his smile—if the whole of Paris suddenly lost electricity, that smile had enough power to light the whole city.

Nico threw his arms around me and lifted me into the air. *What a welcome.*

I felt like a dozen bottles of champagne had just been opened in my stomach. The bubbles of excitement fizzed through my body.

I breathed in his gorgeous woody scent. His hair smelt just as fresh as I remembered. If I hadn't just seen him get out of the car, I would've sworn he'd just stepped out of the shower. *So delicious.*

'I am so glad you are here! I try to call you. What happened?'

'You won't believe the day I've had…'

As Nico put me back down, I caught the eye of the receptionist, whose jaw was on the floor. She certainly hadn't been expecting the woman she'd thought was a cleaner to get a passionate hug from the CEO. I was so tempted to stick my middle finger up at her to teach her a lesson, but I just smiled instead. *Kill them with kindness.* I hoped she'd learned a lesson today.

'Come.' Nico took my hand and squeezed it. 'Let us go upstairs. Then you can tell me all about it.'

CHAPTER THIRTEEN

As we climbed the stairs, I tried to take in my surroundings, but I was finding it hard to concentrate.

Nico was still holding my hand and the heat from his palms was sending shock waves through me.

I still couldn't believe I was finally here. I wasn't just speaking to him. I wasn't just staring at his gorgeous face on a screen. He was right beside me. I didn't have to wish that I could reach through the phone to touch his smooth, chiselled jaw. Now it was just inches away from me. One movement and my hand would be on his skin. This was amazing.

'I cannot believe you are here.' Nico turned to face me as we climbed another flight of stairs. His eyes sparkled.

'I was just thinking the same thing. Hold on...' I squeezed his hand tighter, released it, then pinched his bicep, which was even firmer than I remembered. I took his hand again. 'I just needed to make sure you're real!'

'And?'

'Hmmm… I'm still not sure. I think I'll need to carry out a more detailed inspection later, just to double-check,' I chuckled.

'I will be happy to help you perform a very thorough investigation.' Nico smiled. *God, that smile*. Even if I used all the whitening toothpaste in France, I couldn't get my teeth as perfect as his. And his skin looked softer than a baby's bottom. If he hadn't told me, I would've thought he was a lot younger than thirty-seven. I wondered what face cream he used.

'Welcome!' He stepped through huge light-grey double doors into a large white room with tall ceilings.

Beautiful black-and-white images of striking models with gorgeous hair adorned the walls, which I recognised from their advertising campaigns.

Straight ahead of us, a petite brunette sat at a desk.

'Miriam, this is Cassie. You speak on the phone. Cassie, this is my secretary, Miriam.'

'*Enchantée*.' Miriam nodded. 'It is very nice to meet you. We were all very worried when you were not at the station and we could not contact you. I am glad you find us.'

'Thanks, I mean, *merci*. I had a bit of a nightmare…'

'Miriam, hold my calls. Cassie, you would like something to drink or eat?'

'Just some water would be great.'

'I will bring it now.' Miriam got up.

'Come.' Nico took my hand and led me into a grand office.

'This is nice! Look at the views!' I rushed towards the floor-to-ceiling windows and took in the Paris skyline. I could even see the Eiffel Tower in the distance.

'*Merci.* I am glad you like it.' He pressed a button by his desk, which automatically shut the blinds draped over the tall glass walls that overlooked Miriam's desk. 'But it is not those views that I am interested in. It is the beautiful view right in front of me…'

Nico strode forwards, his eyes molten with heat, and pulled me into him. Before I'd even had time to catch my breath, he crushed his lips onto mine, his mouth hot and hungry with desire.

Jesus.

I'd remembered that Nico was an amazing kisser, but my imagination had underestimated the intensity by at least a million percent.

As his tongue hungrily flicked against mine, arousal charged through me and my knees buckled. I wrapped my hands around his waist to steady myself.

His lips were so soft, yet powerful, and the more he kissed me, the more I wanted him. But then I reminded myself that we were in his office, told myself to calm down and allowed my hands to just roam underneath his suit jacket and across his arse.

Holy shit. Nico's arse. I'd forgotten how good it felt. So firm, so solid, so, *oh*…

Nico's kisses grew more passionate. It was as if we hadn't seen each other for five years rather than five weeks. Like he'd been stranded in a desert for days, dying of thirst, and I was water. He kissed me as if his life depended on it and I enjoyed every second.

Sod it. I didn't care that we were in his office anymore. There was a time for common sense and logic and now wasn't it. I'd dreamt about this moment for too long. I felt like an animal, wild with lust and desire, and nothing was going to stop me.

I clawed at his crisp shirt, undoing one button, then the next, allowing my hands to roam across his glorious muscular chest. If I had my way, I'd rip this expensive suit off him right here too.

There was a knock at the door, but neither of us flinched. We were in our own world and nothing else existed.

Nico's hand moved downwards to my bum. He tugged at the top tied around my waist until it dropped on the floor, then pulled me in even closer. *Oh God.* I felt his hard-on rub against me and the floodgates opened in my knickers.

All those weeks of wanting to see him, every moment of longing, every sexual craving flooded to the surface like a giant wave. Before, I'd said I wanted him. But I was wrong. It was more than that.

I *needed* him.

Now.

It was probably Miriam with the water. Ten minutes ago I would've gulped it down, but Nico had more than satisfied my thirst.

'Ignore it,' Nico said, his mouth now trailing along my neck. 'I have not finished kissing you yet…' He slammed his lips onto mine again, then lifted me onto the edge of his huge glass desk.

I'd never done it on a desk before, and having the Parisian skyline as a backdrop was an even bigger thrill. All the obstacles I'd encountered earlier today melted away. If this pleasure was the reward for the pain, then it was more than worth it.

Just as he slipped his hand under my T-shirt, the door flew open.

'Nico?' a male voice boomed from the door. I quickly jumped down from the desk and Nico spun around.

'*Lucien? Mais qu'est-ce tu fous là?*'

As the two of them launched into a heated discussion in French, I quickly picked my top off the floor and tied it back around my waist.

Nico pressed the button by his desk again to reopen the blinds. They were still talking and I didn't have a clue what they were yabbering on about.

'*Pardon.*' Nico turned to me. 'This is Lucien, one of our directors and…'

'And his best friend.' He finished Nico's sentence. Lucien was noticeably shorter than Nico. My guess was he was around five foot six, maybe five foot seven at a push. He had dark hair, which had started to recede a little at the front, and wore a navy shirt with black trousers.

'Lucien, this is Cassie. Her phone does not work. That is why you could not contact her at the station.'

Aha. So that was who he'd sent to meet me.

'*This* is Cassie?' Lucien frowned, looking me up and down. If I had a pound for every time someone had done that today, *I'd* be a bloody millionaire by now.

I knew I should try and brush it off, but it still hurt. Knowing I was being judged by all these people. I knew exactly what he was thinking: what was someone like me doing with someone like him? Nico could have his pick of women, so what was he doing frolicking in his office with a girl in a dirty pink tracksuit and trainers, when he could have an elegant supermodel by his side. I wasn't going to lie. It was a good question.

'*Oui. Écoute*. We will speak later. Cassie has just arrived and I want to get her settled.'

Lucien launched into more French. I got the impression that he was pissed off and whatever he wanted couldn't wait. But Nico's tone remained firm. The next thing I knew, Lucien was out the door.

Okay. Bye, then.

He was Nico's best friend? The one he talked so much about? If I was judging him on first impressions, like he'd just done with me, then I couldn't say I was impressed by his manners.

'Is everything okay?'

'*Oui*, fine. There is something he needs, but it will have to wait. First, tell me, Cassie.' Nico patted a seat on the leather sofa. 'What happened?'

I told him all about the suitcase mix-up, my clothes debacle, dropping my phone down the toilet, not having my money and how I'd remembered the name of the street and had found my way here.

'And so, yeah, that's why I'm dressed like this. In hindsight, maybe I should've changed into the red PVC catsuit or the French maid's outfit. I probably would've got less stares wearing that than this tracksuit.' Nico laughed. 'It's true! You'd think I was walking around naked or something.'

'Mmm. Now *that* I would like to see.' Nico smirked. 'It does not matter. You still look beautiful.'

My heart fluttered. Then my guard flew back up.

'*Come on!* I'm wearing a headscarf and everyone in this building looks like they're about to go onto the catwalk.'

'You are on holiday. You come to see me. That is what

is important.'

The look in his eyes was genuine. Now that I thought about it, Nico hadn't flinched when he saw me. There hadn't been even a hint of disappointment. The way he'd welcomed me, taken me in his arms, and the kiss we'd just shared. Everything about that said that he was still attracted to me. Even dressed like this. Relief washed over me. This was why I was here. Why I'd come to see him. This guy really was special.

'You're so sweet.'

'Sweet?' Nico grimaced. 'Like that disgusting wine you make me drink at Christmas?'

'Ha!' I smiled as I remembered how much he'd hated mulled wine. 'Okay, you're so… lovely. Like, er, pure French wine, with absolutely no fruit pieces or spices added. How's that?'

'Better. You have only just arrived, so try not to insult me. *Mademoiselle Fraise*…' Nico smirked and my stomach flipped as I remembered the nickname he'd given me when we'd first met. I'd been wearing a red coat and a green hat and he'd said I looked like a strawberry. I'd thought he was being rude, but later he'd told me it was one of his favourite fruits, so he'd meant it as a compliment.

'Oi, behave yourself, *dickhead*!' I poked at his solid chest. 'Two can play at that game.' Dickhead was the nickname I'd given him because at the time, I really had thought he was one. I was glad he'd proved me wrong.

'*Mon Dieu*,' Nico groaned. 'When I hear you call me that, it bring back memories of London… if you know what I would like to do to you right now… but I must go and discuss something with Lucien first.'

'Oh.' My heart sank a little, but Nico had warned me it was a busy time, so it was to be expected.

'Maurice, my driver, is downstairs. Instead of waiting for me here, he can take you to my apartment. Miriam will contact Eurostar about your case. If you give her your phone, she will order a new one. And tell her your size so she can arrange some clothes for you.'

'I can call about my case and try and sort out the phone and stuff myself…'

'*Non.* I insist. You are on holiday. Miriam will take care of everything. Just go home and relax and I will be there as soon as I can. *Je te promets.* I promise. Okay?'

I had to admit, it would be nice to have a shower and relax for a bit. And I might as well give her my phone. It was no use to me anyway.

'Okay.' I nodded. 'I'd better make some calls to check my bank accounts and cancel my cards first, though, just in case.' Now more than ever, I couldn't afford to have someone cloning my cards or racking up a load of debt.

'*Bien.*' Nico kissed me gently on the lips. 'See you soon, *chérie.*'

CHAPTER FOURTEEN

After I'd called my bank, Miriam took my phone and my measurements, then walked me downstairs.

As we passed through reception, the rude receptionist looked me up and down again and frowned. I could tell her head was still spinning with a million questions, wondering who the hell I was. *Cow*.

We slipped through the front door and Miriam approached the huge executive car. The electric window lowered and Miriam spoke to the chauffeur in French, then gestured for me to come over.

'Cassie, this is Maurice. He will take you to the apartment of Nicolas. I will call the concierge to let them know you will arrive.'

Chauffeur? Concierge? Bloody hell. So bougie.

'Sounds great, thank you.'

As Miriam returned inside, Maurice jumped out of the driver's seat and rushed around to the pavement.

'*Enchanté*, Cassie!' He held out his hand and flashed a wide smile. He was dressed in a suit and tie. I'd half expected him to wear a chauffeur's hat, but instead he just had short-cropped dark hair.

'Lovely to meet you, Maurice.' I shook his hand firmly.

'My English is not good, but I do my best.' He opened the door to the passenger seat and gestured for me to climb inside.

'No worries!' I slid onto the black leather seat. This was so plush. 'I'm sure your English is better than my French.'

Maurice flashed his smile again and closed the door.

'I will take a special route, so you can see some sights.'

'*Merci!*'

He started the engine, then pulled away from the pavement. As we drove through Paris, I was in danger of developing whiplash as my neck jerked from left to right, trying take everything in.

Maurice turned down a narrow side street and I lowered the window to get a closer look. My eyes were drawn to a couple sitting outside a little café. We were so close that I could even smell the strong scent of coffee mixed with their cigarette smoke.

Further along, I spotted a pretty patisserie with a colourful window display of sweet treats. The scent of butter flooded my nostrils and made me want to dive out of the car to grab a golden croissant.

Soon afterwards, I caught a glimpse of the iconic monuments Maurice had promised. First, I spotted the grand Opéra Garnier, which I recognised from my tour guide, and then the Eiffel Tower. *Wow.*

I knew it was big. Practically my whole life I'd seen

pictures of it, but seeing it in real life was different. It was *huge*. My heart raced with excitement. I still couldn't quite believe I was really here.

As we travelled along the Champs-Élysées, I ignored the thick exhaust fumes coming from the car in front of us and stuck my head out the window again to watch hundreds of tourists strolling down the busy road, clutching multiple shopping bags.

In the distance I saw the Arc de Triomphe. The giant stone archway was so grand. I couldn't wait to walk around this city and take a closer look at *everything*.

It wasn't long before Maurice pulled up to a gorgeous tree-lined street. I took in the beautiful grand limestone buildings. They were just like the ones I'd seen on TV.

He came round to open my door. I was tempted to let him know that I was fine to get out of the car myself, but I had to admit it was kind of nice having him doing it for me.

Jesus. I'd only been in Paris five minutes and already I was getting sucked into this five-star lifestyle. Shameless. I needed to hotfoot it down to McDonald's sharpish to bring me back down to earth.

Maurice swiped a card to gain entry and we walked into the courtyard and through to another building. When we arrived at the concierge, Maurice said something to the smartly dressed woman at the desk who nodded.

'Prudence will take you up to the apartment now. I will see you soon.'

'*Merci*, Maurice.' Prudence stepped out from behind her desk.

'Please. Follow me.' She walked towards a lift. 'Did you have a pleasant journey?'

'It was fine, thank you.' I was sure she didn't really want to hear the ins and outs of my journey. She was just being polite.

'This building is one of the most prestigious in Paris.' She pressed the button to the seventh floor. I was surprised there was even a lift here because I'd heard a lot of buildings in Paris were old and didn't have one, so I was half expecting I'd need to lug my suitcase up the stairs. Not that I had any luggage, of course. God only knew where it was right now.

'It looks very nice.'

'The penthouse that Mr Chevalier has is the largest in the building. A duplex on the seventh and last floor.' Whoa: a duplex penthouse. I couldn't wait to see it.

'Here we are.' The doors opened directly into his apartment. 'If you need anything, please press the concierge button on one of the telephones located inside.'

'Will do, thanks.'

I stepped inside the grand entrance, and wow. I knew it was going to be impressive, but I wasn't expecting *this*.

A sweet fragrance filled the air. It smelt like fresh laundry or the scent of newly picked flowers.

I walked down the hallway, poking my head into the different rooms. The huge living room was bathed in light, thanks to the large French windows, and the ceilings were so high.

I literally skipped along to the grand dining room, then the modern chrome-and-white kitchen.

A gym? So cool. I gawped at the state-of-the-art treadmill, bike, weights and other equipment. That was why Nico was in such good shape.

I climbed the stairs. Now *this* was what you called a

bedroom. Right in the centre, opposite the large windows and balcony, was a ginormous bed. As I walked through, I saw a dressing room which was like the men's section in a department store. Various suits and clothing were hung neatly and colour-coordinated. Underneath there were rows of shoes and trainers which looked fresh from the box.

I continued through to an en suite bathroom, which was probably half the size of my entire flat, my jaw trailing on the floor. There was a fancy walk-in rainfall shower and one of those smart toilets that, judging from the icons on the remote control, looked like it did everything for you: heated your bum, washed and dried it. Bloody hell. I was surprised there wasn't a button to kiss your arse afterwards too.

And, oh wow. I glanced over at the bath, which was half-filled with a sprinkling of pretty pink petals. The sweet scent of rose bath oil filled the room.

Across the tub was a large tray, which had a champagne flute and a plate of colourful macarons. Beside the bath was a stand with an ice bucket and a bottle of... *no way*. Dom Pérignon? That was the super expensive champagne Spencer always insisted on ordering for his parties. Some of the bottles cost hundreds of pounds. And now there was a whole bottle for me to drink. In the bath. I pinched myself twice to check this was real.

I heard a phone ringing and looked around to locate where the sound was coming from. *Crikey.* There was even a phone built into the wall.

Should I answer it? I hesitated for a moment, but it kept ringing, so I leant forward and lifted the receiver.

'Hello? I mean, *bonjour*?'

'*Salut, chérie.*' It was Nico.

'Hey! How did you know I'd be in here?'

'Prudence tell me you are in the apartment, so I thought I would try. Is the bath ready?'

'Yes! How did you arrange this? It's amazing!'

'I ask Odette, my housekeeper, to prepare it for you.' Of course he had a housekeeper. 'If you turn the TV on, there is a film I am sure you will like.'

'TV?'

'*Oui.* In the wall. You see it?'

OMG. Yes. Opposite the bath, embedded in the wall, was a large black flat-screen. I'd been so blown away looking at the bath and tray of goodies that I'd completely missed it.

'I see it.'

'*Bien.* You can watch the film or command the room to play music.'

'Command the room?'

'Yes. If you say "play music", then music will play.'

'Oh… like Siri or Alexa?'

'*Oui, exactement.* It has been programmed to under-stand English too, so you will be fine. There should be fresh towels and a… how you say? Bath gown on the back of the door. Some clothes will come soon. If you need something, just say "Odette" loudly and she will come. Okay?'

'Wow. Thank you. And by the way, you have a beau-tiful flat.' Calling it a flat seemed inaccurate somehow. Palatial mansion flat or mega-cool apartment still didn't do it justice. 'I haven't seen it all yet, but it's incredible.'

'*Merci.* I am glad you like it. I must go now, but I hope

to be there soon. *À toute à l'heure*. It means—see you later.'

'Laters! And thanks again.'

'*De rien.*'

Nico hung up.

A fancy bath, champagne… *a girl could get used to this*.

As much as I was dying to sink beneath the bubbles, I wanted to check out the rest of the apartment first. I know. *So nosy*.

There were more bedrooms and even a mini hair salon. As I returned to the main bedroom, I saw that there was a balcony. I stepped outside and I nearly keeled over. And OMG, the views.

In the distance I saw the Eiffel Tower. It was so close that if I ran across the rooftops in front of me, I'd be able to touch it. I'd imagine it wouldn't take long to walk there from here.

And below this balcony, coming off Nico's living room, there was a big terrace with a garden. It was like a secret oasis in the centre of the city. I'd definitely need to check that out later.

I was lost for words. When I'd first seen the suite Nico stayed in at the Ritz on the night we'd met, I'd been blown away, but this was on a whole different level. I couldn't even begin to imagine how many millions a place like this would cost.

My head spun as I tried to take it all in. How had I ended up here? It was baffling. I had to just push all of my thoughts and insecurities out of my head and try to enjoy it.

I headed back to the bathroom, closed the door, turned

on the hot water tap and whipped off my clothes. I poured the champagne into the flute, slid inside the bath, then called out, 'Play film.'

The Holiday flashed up on the screen. My favourite! I'd watched it with Nico over Christmas and told him how much I loved it and how I watched it all year round and he'd remembered.

I plucked a cute pink macaron from the tray and looked at all the sweet things he'd arranged to cheer me up, and a picture of his gorgeous face flashed through my mind. This guy was a keeper.

Oops. There I went getting carried away. I quickly reminded myself that this was only temporary. I was a novelty to Nico. In a world full of rich or fake people, I made him feel a little bit normal. He'd get bored of me soon, so I needed to just enjoy it whilst it lasted and not get too attached. And I absolutely couldn't fall in love with him.

It'd be no problem. I could totally avoid doing that. Once, I'd had a whole box of chocolates in my kitchen cupboard during the Christmas holidays and lasted three whole days without eating a single one.

Okay, that might have had something to do with the fact that I'd had food poisoning and couldn't keep anything down, but still. I was sure my willpower could be strong if I really wanted it to be.

Yep. I had my heart handled. It was all under control.

CHAPTER FIFTEEN

That was divine. I'd stayed in the bath and watched the entire film, which was over two hours. I couldn't remember the last time I'd had an actual bath, never mind being in a tub for that long. I was surprised my skin didn't look like a shrivelled prune. Must be all the lovely oils the housekeeper had poured in the water.

I'd polished off all the macarons, which were out of this world, and guzzled down at least three glasses of champagne. You know, just to keep myself hydrated.

Normally, I wasn't a huge fan of champers—I preferred Prosecco—but after drinking a lot of the good stuff today, I was starting to understand what all the fuss was about. It was pretty tasty.

It was a good thing I was only staying here for ten days. I was getting far too comfortable with these nice things. Could you imagine if I stayed any longer? I'd go to my parents and say, 'Prosecco? Where's the Dom P?' If I did that, they'd boot me out of the house faster than you could say *bubbly*. *No way*. The last thing I wanted to do was become one of the snooty people I hated.

I stepped out of the bath and wrapped myself in a fluffy towel.

There were a selection of luxury body creams and oils on a shelf, so I helped myself, slathered them all over, then put on the big bathrobe. Next, I unlocked the door and walked into the dressing room.

Wow. When had these arrived? There were two rails in the middle of the floor. The first had an assortment of different clothes and the second a selection of lingerie and nightwear. When Nico had said Miriam was going to arrange something for me to wear, I thought she'd just go and get me a new jumper and pair of leggings, not this.

I went through the rack. There were some simple things, like a pair of blue jeans and a casual top, but most of it was all designer and very glam. Sparkly tops and dresses and teeny-tiny skirts. All very nice, but not really me. Was this the kind of stuff that Nico wanted me to wear? I thought he'd said earlier that what I wore didn't matter.

Maybe he'd arranged for us to go to fancy places this weekend and these were the kind of outfits that people expected. My heart sank. I'd spent all that time buying clothes that I liked in London and now I couldn't even wear them. I wondered if I'd ever get my suitcase back.

There were shoeboxes on the floor too. As I opened them, I saw there were various pairs of high heels. They looked pretty, but extremely uncomfortable. Ten seconds in those and Nico would be picking me off the floor. I sometimes wore small heels to work, but most days I was more of a flat boots or trainers kind of girl.

I moved over to the lingerie rack. Everything here was so sexy. There were low-cut lace teddies, frilly G-strings and whoa… I plucked the hanger off the rail and held it up in the air to inspect it. It was a pair of lacy black crotchless knickers. I stuck my hand through the huge hole in the fabric and chuckled to myself.

I'd never worn anything like that before. Still, I'd imagine that crotchless knickers would be more comfortable than wearing G-strings all day. Thongs might be good for hiding visible panty lines, but they were uncomfortable as hell. I didn't want a skinny string chafing between my bum cheeks whilst I was visiting tourist attractions. I'd prefer a pair of big comfy knickers any day of the week.

Was this the payoff for dating a rich man? If they paid for your clothes, did they then expect to have a say over what you wore? If that was the case, I wasn't down for that. It was really kind of Nico to help by arranging these clothes for me until I hopefully got my own case back, but I'd never had a man pick out clothes for me and I wasn't about to start now.

I opted for a lovely cashmere jumper along with a T-shirt, jeans, and some underwear (with the crotch intact) and got changed.

I also finally removed my headscarf and untwisted my hair. The heat from the bath had really helped my hair set so it was extra curly. I felt a million times better than I had a few hours ago. Much more like me.

When I went through to the bedroom, there was a small box on the bed with a Post-it note resting on top.

Cassie,

Here is your new phone. It has your SIM card inside. I could not set it up because I do not have your password,

but it should be simple. Call me if there is a problem or
you need something more and I will send someone to
help you.

Miriam

When I peeled the note off the top, my eyes nearly popped out of their sockets. A brand-new top-of-the-range iPhone! I'd wanted to upgrade my mobile for ages, but had never been able to afford it.

I switched it on, and after following the easy set-up instructions, I was ready to go.

A flurry of messages flashed up on the screen: several voice notes from Nico earlier, as well as some brief texts asking if I was at the station and saying he was worried and to call him.

There were multiple messages from Bella and Melody too, asking if I'd arrived safely. Mum had also messaged to ask the same.

I sat on the bed and fired off some replies. Firstly to Nico, to let him know that I'd got the phone and clothes and to thank him profusely. Then to my mum and the group chat with Bella and Melody.

I'd barely finished typing out the message before Melody replied. I looked at the time. It was just gone six in the evening in London, so she must be home from work.

Melody

Glad you're safe. Bella was worried because we hadn't heard from you.

Melody

But I said you were probably too busy enjoying Nico's big baguette!

                    .   .   .

I chuckled as I typed out my reply.

Me

If only. I had a few mishaps on the way here…

Bella

Oh no! What happened?

Melody

Bella, are you at home?

Bella

Yeah, why?

Melody

Can you video call us, Cass? Much easier than typing.
Plus I want to see what Nico's place looks like!

Bella

Oooh, good idea!

I'd be the same. I pressed the video call button.

'Hello, ladies!'

'Hey you!' said Melody. 'Oooh. Is that where the
magic happened? Have you guys been at it all afternoon?'

'No magic has happened in the bedroom yet, I'm
afraid. Nico's still at work.'

'Oh no.' Melody's face creased with concern. 'I know
he said he'd be busy, but I hope he's still making some
time for you.'

'Nico's been amazing. Especially with all the stuff that
happened today.' I filled them in on everything and then
explained what he'd arranged with the bath, champagne,
clothes and my phone.

'That's so sweet,' said Bella.

'Cassie, love, you are seriously living the dream. If I were you, I'd never come back to London. Told you he'd have a driver and a housekeeper! Will she clean the bath out for you too? God, I hate scrubbing the bath. It's such a pain in the arse.' I hadn't thought of that. I'd better look for a sponge and bathroom cleaner. Didn't want to leave it dirty.

'Of course I'm coming back to London. That's my home. That's reality. I'm only here for ten days.'

'You never know…,' said Bella. 'This could become your life. *Permanently*.'

'Come off it.' I rolled my eyes. 'It's not like that. We're just having fun. This is just a little fantasy holiday. That's all.'

'Whatever you say, sweetie,' Melody added. 'So! Are you going to give us a tour of the rest of the mansion?'

'It's not a mansion, it's a flat, or apartment as they call it.'

'Cass, you and I live in *flats*. His place is a bloody castle in comparison.' She wasn't wrong. I heard a male voice downstairs. Sounded like Nico.

'Ladies, I think Nico's back, so I'm going to love you and leave you.'

'Nooo!' Melody cried out. 'Leave the phone line open so we can hear Nico. Better still, prop it up on a dressing table or somewhere opposite the bed so I can watch you two at it!'

'Melody!' My eyes widened. 'I'm not giving you a live sex show!'

'Spoilsport,' she cackled. 'I told you. I *seriously* need some action.'

'If you want to watch people doing it, there are plenty

of respectable porn sites out there. I was reading about one the other day that's run by a woman who makes sure all the actors and actresses get treated fairly and aren't exploited. I'll send you a link to the article to have a look.'

'Oooh! Andrea's staying over at her friend's house tonight, so sounds like that's my Friday night sorted. An ethical porno and a bottle of vino. Or should I say *vin*. I'll let you know how it goes. Orgasmland, here I come! Ha, ha! *Come*. Quite literally, I hope!'

'And on that note…' Bella laughed. 'Have fun, Cass.'

'Will do.'

Just as I ended the call, Nico walked in.

'*Salut*.' He leant down to kiss me, took off his suit jacket and then started unbuttoning his shirt. I caught a glimpse of his firm chest and my body instantly started sparking. 'Sorry I am so late. I will just have a shower and then I will be yours for the night.'

Mmm. Finally, a night alone with Nico. That sounded like music to my ears.

CHAPTER SIXTEEN

Nico came out of the bathroom with the towel wrapped around his toned waist. His six-pack glistened as he massaged some cream into his skin. Should've asked me. I would've definitely enjoyed running my hands all over his body. And a whole lot more.

He stopped in the dressing room and looked over the rack of clothes that Miriam had sent for me.

'See something you like?' I teased. 'I was thinking the sparkly silver miniskirt might suit you. You've definitely got the legs for it.'

'I thought I would try this.' He picked up the crotchless knickers, putting his hand through the gap.

'Maybe…' I rested my finger on my chin. 'From what I can remember, that huge hole *might* be big enough to accommodate you.' My gaze dropped between his legs and lust flooded my veins.

'I will take that as a compliment,' Nico said with a wicked grin.

'That's how it was intended.' I licked my lips and

Nico's eyes darkened. 'Although, my memory isn't the best, so I think I need a reminder.'

'That can be arranged...' Nico strode towards me. He sat down on the bed, took my face in his hands, planted his lips on mine, then kissed me, hungrily.

Oh God. That felt incredible.

As his hot tongue slid over mine, I ran my hands over his chest. It was so firm, yet his skin was so soft. And his scent. *Damn.* It was all woody and spicy. So manly. I just wanted to bury my head into his shoulder, then sniff and lick every inch of him. Was that weird? I didn't care. I wanted to do it anyway.

Nico gently pushed me back onto the bed and straddled me. I could feel his hard-on pressing between my thighs. I couldn't wait to finish what we'd started earlier in his office.

'Cassie, *j'ai envie de toi,*' Nico whispered in my ear.

My French vocab was rubbish, but I remembered that phrase. He'd said it to me at Christmas. It meant that he wanted me. And the feeling was mutual.

'Take me,' I replied like a horny character in a romance novel.

Nico slid his hand up my thigh and started undoing my jeans. Just as he reached for the zip, the phone rang loudly. Nico jumped and I hit my head on the headboard. Ouch.

'*Merde!*' he sighed as he pulled away and reached for the receiver. '*Oui?*' I heard a male voice speaking quickly on the other end of the line. '*J'arrive.*'

'Everything okay?' I sat up.

'Lucien is downstairs. He needs me to sign something.'

'*Now?*'

'*Oui.* We have a lot of things happening with the

company. It should not take long. What would you like to do this evening? I plan for us to go out to dinner, but perhaps it is better to stay in. Fabien will make us something.'

'Fabien?'

'My chef.'

Bloody hell. Melody was right. Nico had a chef.

Just imagine. After a long day at work, you didn't have to worry about having to trudge to the supermarket, carry the shopping home, then stand in front of the stove slaving away. You just walked through the front door and *voilà*. There was a top-notch meal ready and waiting and you didn't have to lift a finger to make it. Or do the washing up. Sounded like heaven.

Even though technically I hadn't done anything intensive today, I was feeling a bit tired, so a night in was appealing. I wouldn't have to work out what to wear and most importantly, after his friend left, Nico and I could finally spend some time alone together. After two false starts today, I was chomping at the bit for some sexy time.

'I'm happy to stay in if you are.'

'*Bien*.' Nico picked up the phone and I think confirmed that we would be staying for dinner. 'Come. It is all arranged.' He put on a fresh T-shirt, boxers and jeans. 'Let us go downstairs.'

As we walked in the living room, Lucien was sprawled across the sofa, clutching some papers.

He greeted Nico and handed the documents to him. Nico sat on the sofa and skimmed them.

'This is for the order of the new products?'

'*Oui*.' Lucien nodded before saying more stuff in French. Nico ran his finger across the page, turned it over and moved on to the next one. He then took out a pen and signed the paperwork.

Wow. He was a speedy reader. Whenever I had to read over an important email or sign something, it took me ages because I always had to go through it multiple times to double-check. I knew it was OTT, but I couldn't help it. I supposed when you got to Nico's level, if you always did that, you'd never get anything done. You needed to be decisive.

'*Voilà.*' Nico handed it back to him.

'*Parfait. Tu veux aller boire un verre?*'

'*Non*, not tonight.'

'*Mais on boit toujours ensemble le vendredi soir!*'

'Please,' Nico added. 'Speak English when Cassie is here. She has just started to learn French.' *Awww*. So sweet of him. I had no idea what Lucien was saying before, so it was nice that Nico recognised that and thought of me. 'It is her first night in Paris, so we will stay at home. Fabien will make dinner.'

'Smells good. I have not eaten, so I can join you.'

'I will have dinner with Cassie,' Nico said firmly.

'Oh.' Lucien's face fell.

'It's okay!' I jumped in without realising. 'You can join us.'

What was I doing? I wanted to spend the evening with Nico. *Alone*. But this was his bestie. It felt bad to ask him to leave. If the shoe was on the other foot and it was Bella or Melody, I wouldn't kick them out of my flat because of a man. Then again, they wouldn't gatecrash our first night alone in ages. They'd thank me for the offer and make a swift exit so that we could enjoy a proper reunion. Hopefully Lucien would do the same.

'*Genial!*' Lucien jumped up. 'I will tell Fabien to make dinner for three.'

Great.

At least he spoke English, so it shouldn't be too awkward.

'Are you sure you are okay with this, *chérie*?' Nico stroked my cheek. 'Normally I drink with Lucien every Friday night, but tonight is different. I will tell him to leave if you prefer.'

'It's fine.' I kissed him quickly on the lips. 'Any friend of yours is a friend of mine. It will be good for me to get to know him.'

'Did I tell you that you are amazing?'

'No, I don't think you did.' I smiled.

'Well, you are.' He took my hand and pulled me closer. 'Tell me: the clothes Miriam send for you upstairs, do you like?'

'Well…' I paused, thinking of the best way to be truthful without sounding ungrateful. 'Some of them. Like, this jumper is gorgeous and the jeans are so comfy, but the rest are…'

'It is too much for you, *non*? I will get something else.'

'No, no! Honestly, it's fine. You've done enough. I have something to wear for now, so I can just go shopping myself. Don't worry about it.'

There must be a Zara or H&M in Paris. Even though I had to curb my spending, I should be okay to buy one or two things.

Except that I didn't have my credit card. *Shit*. I'd have to borrow some money from Nico. My chest tightened. I hated borrowing money.

'Okay. This weekend you must go shopping.'

'*Oui!*' Lucien returned to the room and squeezed up next to Nico on the sofa. 'You speak about the weekend? Will be very difficult to do something better than last weekend. Guillaume's yacht was *fantastique*, *non*?' Lucien beamed. 'Champagne, beautiful women… of course they all wanted to speak to Nico.' Lucien looked at me and rolled his eyes. 'Actually, I want to ask you, where did you go?'

'*Pardon?*' Nico frowned.

'I saw you with Adrianna—you know, one of the beautiful models—and after that I could not find you for hours…'

Nico disappeared with a model on the yacht? My blood ran cold.

Pull yourself together, Cassie, my inner voice commanded. *It's none of your business. You haven't agreed to be exclusive. You haven't had the DTR: the define-the-relationship talk. Did you really expect him to just cross his legs and wait for you? You and Nico are just having fun together.*

'*Mais qu'est-ce tu fous?*' Nico's nostrils flared. Maybe he was annoyed that Lucien had dropped him in it.

'I thought we were talking English?' Lucien raised his eyebrow. That was true. Did Nico not want me to understand what he was saying?

'I was there with everyone all night.' Nico clenched his jaw.

'*Oui…*' Lucien paused. 'Of course. I must be mistaken.'

'*Pardon, excusez-moi.*' A softly-spoken young man entered the room and looked over at Nico. Must be Fabien.

Nico excused himself and followed him into the kitchen, leaving me alone with Lucien.

'I could not find you at the station.' Lucien turned to face me. 'I look around, but I could not see you. Well, I did not know how you look, so when I arrive, I search for someone tall and beautiful like supermodel or actress—the kind of woman that Nico normally date. I did not expect someone… like *you*. You are, you…' Lucien paused. 'I guess Nico want to try someone more exotic. Maybe he like your hair. It is… interesting.'

Exotic?

Interesting?

WTF.

There were so many things I hated about what Lucien had just said, I didn't even know where to start.

I knew this was Nico's friend, but after that comment, it was clear that this guy was a twat.

So he couldn't find me at the station because I didn't look like a supermodel?

The implication that Nico was only interested in me because I had curly hair was plain rude.

And I *hated* being called *exotic*. I wasn't a piece of imported bloody fruit. I used to get that a lot on the dating apps. Creepy men messaging me, commenting on my brown skin and saying they'd always wanted to try some *chocolate*.

Just because I was mixed-race, it didn't mean I was some sort of object that could be used to indulge some kind of fetish or fantasy. *Ugh*. To think I'd suggested that Lucien stay for dinner too.

Nico returned to the room.

'Dinner is ready.' Nico reached for my hand to help me

up off the sofa. I took it, eager to get as far away from Lucien as possible.

We headed to the dining room, where a large quiche and a colourful salad were laid out on the table. It smelt divine, and as soon as my teeth sank into the crumbly pastry, I realised it tasted divine too.

I tried to focus on the food and push Lucien's comments out of my head, but they continued swirling around.

For much of dinner, Lucien dominated the conversation. Continuously reverting to French, even when Nico asked him to speak English. After a while, I kind of zoned out. It wasn't realistic for Nico to keep trying to translate everything for me. Just like I'd feared before I'd arrived, I felt out of place.

'Did you enjoy?' Nico popped the last forkful of food into his mouth.

'I loved it, thank you.'

'You would like dessert?'

'Actually'—I stretched my arms up in the air—'I'm feeling a bit tired. I'm going to just head upstairs.' Nico's face fell.

'You want me to come with you?'

'No, no. You guys carry on down here. I'll see you upstairs,' I said, wishing it would be sooner rather than later.

So far this hadn't been the romantic evening I'd hoped for. But the night was still young.

CHAPTER SEVENTEEN

'Good morning!'

    I squinted, then strained my eyes open. For a moment, I forgot where I was. I looked up and Nico towered over the bed. He was already dressed and, of course, looking gorgeous. He raked his hand through his hair and my stomach flipped.

'Morning,' I croaked. 'What time is it?'

'Almost eight.'

I'd slept like a baby. I knew I'd come upstairs about eleven, washed my face, and brushed my teeth, but I didn't remember getting into bed.

'What time did you go to sleep?'

'I come upstairs about half an hour after you, but you are already sleeping. On the toilet.' Nico grinned.

'No way!' *How embarrassing*. I hoped I hadn't had my knickers around my ankles and that I'd already wiped myself. I cringed as I imagined Nico lifting me off the toilet seat, wee dribbling down my leg.

When I'd pictured my first night in Paris, I'd had

visions of us going at it like rabbits, not him helping me off the loo. What a way to look sexy.

'*Ne t'inquiète pas.* Do not worry. You close the toilet and you had on underwear.'

'Thank God for that.'

Ah. I remembered now. I'd sent Melody the ethical porn weblink, then a long message had come through from Lily. And after my phone had fallen down the toilet before, I'd decided it was safer to sit on it with the lid closed to read it. But then I must have fallen asleep. I blamed the underfloor heating. And the heated toilet seat. Everything was so warm and soothing. 'And my phone?'

'You have it on your lap.' It was a miracle it hadn't dropped and smashed on the tiles. 'I carry the two of you to bed.'

'Thanks. And sorry I passed out. That wasn't how I wanted to spend our first night together.'

'It is okay. Last night I am—*pardon*, I *was* also tired. This morning, I must go to the salon. You want to go shopping and buy some clothes you like?'

'Yes!' I was going to ask if he knew where the nearest Zara was, but if they had those shops in Paris, they wouldn't be on Nico's radar. I'd just Google it.

My excitement levels plummeted when I remembered I'd need to borrow some money.

Before I'd even had a chance to open my mouth, Nico reached in his wallet and pulled out a black credit card. 'Here. Take this. Buy whatever you want. Maurice will take you so you will not get lost or have to carry the bags home.'

'Huh?' My eyes popped open. I definitely wasn't comfortable taking Nico's card, especially one like that. I glanced at the logo. He was holding a black American Express card. Pretty sure it was invite-only and was just available to the mega-rich. I couldn't take it. 'Thanks, but all I need is maybe seventy euros, a hundred max, to get a few bits. I'll pay you back as soon as they return my suitcase.'

I couldn't spend too much. I had to be responsible. Plus, the idea of asking a man for money made my stomach sink. I'd always been taught to pay my own way and never to depend on anyone.

When we were kids, money had been tight. Even with Mum and Dad working multiple jobs, there was rarely any cash for treats. They'd always made sure we received a present at birthdays or Christmas, but that was about it. With four kids who quickly outgrew their clothes and a house which always had something that needed repairing, they'd just made enough to cover essentials. So if we wanted anything extra, we had to earn it.

I'd offer to wash our neighbour's car or do Nate's chores. Sometimes I'd walked the few miles to and from school so I could use my bus fare to buy something I wanted or fund a trip to the cinema.

I'd started working as soon as I could. I'd got a paper round when I was fourteen and I'd worked ever since. I'd never expected handouts.

Whenever I *had* let my guard down and allowed someone to pay for me, I'd always regretted it.

My ex had always wanted to go to expensive places, which I couldn't afford. Whilst he'd order pricey bottles of wine and extravagant dishes, I'd opt for the cheapest thing on the menu. Even then, each time I'd offer to contribute something to at least cover my share, he'd throw his credit card on the table in front of the serving staff and say loudly, 'Don't worry, I'll pay.' But afterwards he'd ram it down my throat with reminders about the fact that he 'always had to pay' when we went out—or he'd suggest that it was time I got a 'decent job' so that he wouldn't have to keep 'supporting me'. *Ugh*. He made it sound like he was paying my bloody mortgage. The last thing I needed was another rich guy acting like my saviour.

'*S'il te plaît, chérie*. Take it. And of course you do not have to pay me back.' He shook his head. 'Fabien made breakfast, but tell him if there is something else you need. I will be back at one to take you out, so be ready, okay?'

'Okay.' My eyes fixated on the card, trying to take it all in. I could tell he wouldn't take no for an answer. Plus, without my purse, my financial options were limited. I'd accept, but just this once. 'Thanks…'

Nico leant forward, kissed me on the lips, then left.

The smell of freshly baked bread and sweet pastries wafted up into the room and my stomach rumbled.

I wrapped a dressing gown around me and headed down to the dining room.

On the grand stone table was a spread that looked like it was fit for a king, queen and the entire royal family. There were croissants, pains au chocolat, pains aux raisins, some other pretty pastries, a big bowl of fresh fruit salad, eggs, bread… was this all for me? It couldn't be. There was about a week's worth of breakfast here.

'*Bonjour*, Cassie. Did you sleep well?'

'*Bonjour*, Fabien. Like a baby, *merci*.'

'I am not sure what you like to eat, so I make a few things.' Fabien signalled to the sumptuous spread on the table. 'If you prefer, I make something else?'

'No, no, this is all more than enough, thank you. It's perfect. I don't think I'll be able to eat even half of this.'

'It is okay. Eat what you can. It will not go to waste. *Bon appétit*.'

I sat at the head of the table and I swear I felt like royalty. As I bit into the croissant, I let out a loud groan of pleasure. *Oh God*. That tasted amazing. It was nothing like the ones I bought in the bakeries or supermarkets in London. It was so soft, yet flaky. And the scent of butter was divine.

If I was feeling motivated on a Saturday morning, I might make myself a bacon butty or fried eggs and baked beans with some toast and cereal. But this. *This*. I'd died and gone to breakfast heaven.

It didn't take me long to devour multiple pastries (I knew Fabien had said nothing would go to waste, but you know, I thought it best to try as many as possible, to show my appreciation). I was sure I'd walk off all the extra calories going around the shops.

I got changed into my new jeans and jumper, slid on my trainers, tucked Nico's card safely in my handbag and headed downstairs. Maurice was waiting by the car with the passenger door already open. I had no idea how he knew I was coming down at that moment. I hoped he hadn't been standing here long.

'*Bonjour!*' I beamed. '*Ça va*, Maurice?'

'*Bonjour!* You speak French very well!'

'Ha! Hardly, but thank you.' I climbed into the passenger seat, then Maurice shut the door.

'So, Nicolas tell me you want to go shopping, yes?'

'Yes.' I winced. I hoped Maurice didn't think I'd demanded to go shopping like a kept woman. 'My suitcase was taken by mistake on my way to Paris, so I don't have any clothes to wear. I don't need anything fancy. I haven't had a chance to look up where to go, but if you can take me to normal shops, that'd be great.'

'*Pas de problème*. I know where to go.'

I sat back on the heated leather seats. I hadn't noticed yesterday because I was taking everything in, but there was a TV at the back and a selection of drinks and snacks. There were even adult colouring books and pencils. I'd heard there was a lot of traffic in Paris, so Nico must like to have something to keep him entertained.

I pulled out my phone. I'd never got to read Lily's message. Looked like she still hadn't had a chance to speak to River.

Melody had messaged in the group chat about half an hour ago.

Melody

Sooo… how was your night of passion in Paris? Hope you had fun with Nico's giant baguette!

I snorted, then winced. God. So far this trip hadn't been the romantic sex fest I'd hoped it would be, but it was still early days.

Me

Not quite. I fell asleep…

It wasn't long until she replied. She was probably having a lie-in.

Melody

WTF? You finally had the chance to enjoy a nice bit of

French cock and you chose to get some shut-eye?

Me

I didn't plan it that way. But I was so tired that I passed out. On the toilet. Nico had to carry me to bed. Sigh.

Me

PS Nico said I was fully clothed, thankfully.

Melody

OMG! That's hilarious. And also tragic. Get on his Eiffel Tower pronto, woman. You need to make the most of this trip. Enjoy every second.

Me

I know, I know.

Melody

BTW, thanks for recommending that ethical porn site. I had a LOT of fun last night! Might even log on again this afternoon. Not all of us are lucky enough to have the real thing!

Me

Glad you enjoyed! Just going shopping now. Nico's given me his card. I hate the idea of a man paying for my clothes.

Melody

WTF is wrong with you? He's a millionaire. Go and spend his money. He won't miss it!

Melody

God knows when you'll get your suitcase back. And if you're going to fancy places, you'll need some decent clothes.

Me

Yeah, I know. I just hate feeling so dependent. Like I'm one of those women who just goes after a man for his money.

Melody

But you're not a gold digger. You know that, Nico knows that, so just enjoy it!

Melody

Anyway, luv, better get to the supermarket. Happy shopping! Xoxo

Me

Thanks. Speak later xxx

I quickly put my phone back in my bag. I wanted to take in the sights. As I looked out of the window, I instantly recognised that we were driving down the Champs-Élysées again.

Even though it was barely eleven in the morning, there were plenty of people strolling along the wide tree-lined street. The sounds of impatient drivers beeping their horns and a loud siren filled the air.

I was itching to jump out of the car to explore. I probably wouldn't have time to walk all the way down here and go to loads of shops this morning, but I'd definitely make time to during the week.

Maurice turned down a road. My mouth dropped open as I took in the shops. There was designer boutique after boutique. It was like the French equivalent of New Bond Street in London. This was clearly where all the rich people went. Suddenly Maurice pulled over.

'We are here. This is FSH: Rue du Faubourg Saint-Honoré.'

'Oh no, sorry, Maurice.' I frowned. 'This isn't where I need to be. I just wanted to go to the normal shops.'

'*Oui*. This is the normal shops. When Nicolas take

women shopping'—Maurice paused, as if considering his words carefully—'this is where they go. Here and also Avenue Montaigne, Avenue George-V and Rue François 1er, which is the Triangle d'Or—in English I think you say the triangle of gold.'

My brain couldn't take in all the different streets Maurice had mentioned. It was too busy focusing on a specific part of what he'd said instead: *when Nicolas takes women shopping...*

Hearing that out loud made me wince. Obviously I knew I wasn't the first, but just how many women did he take exactly?

Maybe there was some truth in what Lucien had said last night. I wondered whether this was Nico's thing. Plucking paupers like me from their normal lives and giving them his card. I hated the idea of just being another number.

'I am sorry,' Maurice added, clearly realising how what he'd said sounded and that he'd ratted Nicolas out.

'It's okay.' I didn't want him to feel bad. Nico's past was his past, so I had to accept that. I got out of the car. 'I'll try not to be too long.'

'I will wait for you.'

'Thanks.'

Hmm. Where to start? Talk about feeling like a fish out of water. After hesitating for several seconds, I walked towards a designer boutique and a stern-looking man dressed in a suit opened the door.

As I stepped inside, the shop assistant looked me up and down before squeezing out a curt *bonjour*. They probably didn't have many customers dressed in jeans and trainers, but I hadn't known I was coming to a shop like this. I'd thought I'd be trudging up and down the streets, so I was hardly going to wear heels, was I?

Everything was so immaculately laid out. All colour-coordinated and hung in small batches on fancy wooden hangers. There were no flimsy plastic ones here.

I flicked through the clothes on the racks. A white T-shirt with a small cute pink design in the centre caught my eye. I searched for the price tag. *Bloody hell.* Two hundred euros? That was ridiculous. I could buy about a hundred T-shirts in Primark for that.

I quickly put it down and went over to a rack with colourful trousers. A purple pair caught my eye. I pulled the price tag out from the back. *Jesus.* That was a week's wages.

'Can I help you?' said the shop assistant. How did she know I was English?

'No, I'm just looking, thank you.'

'We have a small selection of sale items at the back that may be better for you.' She flashed a fake smile. 'Or perhaps our diffusion line of casual wear may be more affordable.'

Bloody cheek.

'It's okay. I was just leaving.' I knew when I wasn't wanted. I crept out of the shop into the cold morning air.

This was exactly what I'd been afraid of. I didn't belong here. On this fancy road. In these fancy shops. One look at me and the shop assistant knew I wasn't part of this world.

I walked back to the car and climbed inside. I'd ask Maurice to take me somewhere where I'd fit in better.

'You are back?' Maurice spun around. 'Where are your bags?'

'I didn't get anything.'

'Nicolas give me instructions to take you shopping. You do not want to cause me trouble, do you?' He raised an eyebrow.

'No, no. Course not.'

'There are many shops here. Perhaps you can find something in another store? If you continue along this road, there is another part where it becomes Rue Saint-Honoré, which has more nice shops.'

'Oh. Okay.'

'Nicolas is a generous man. If he has offered, you should accept. It will make him happy. I cannot say where, but you will go somewhere special today. It will be nice to have a new outfit, no?'

There was no escaping it. I needed something decent to wear. We were bound to be going places this weekend, so I wouldn't get another chance.

Sod it. I couldn't let a shop assistant intimidate me. I wouldn't think twice about walking into a shop on the high street, so I just had to pretend it was exactly the same.

'You're right. I'll be back.' I strolled along the street. Another designer shop caught my eye. This time I walked in confidently, my head held high.

I immediately spotted a stunning floor-length royal-blue gown draped elegantly over a mannequin in the centre of the store. It was gorgeous. I hated to think how much that would cost. Probably thousands. I couldn't take my eyes off it.

Anyway, it was an evening gown—something that you wore to a super posh event. I reckoned that today Nico and I would go out for lunch and maybe dinner, so I had to focus on finding something for that.

After scrolling through various rails, I spotted a pair of vibrant red flared trousers. They were beautiful. Sophisticated. Then I saw a green skirt with a massive slit up one leg. It looked so sexy.

I plucked a silk blouse and a few other items from a rack, then walked up to the shop assistant.

'Hi. Do you speak English?'

'Yes. You would like to try these on?'

'Yes, please.' I hadn't checked the prices. It'd be better to do it inside the changing room, so they wouldn't see the look of horror on my face.

She showed me to a room with multiple mirrors and even an armchair. They didn't do things by halves in these stores.

After hanging up the clothes, I quickly shut the door and looked at the prices. Crikey. It was hard to justify spending a month's salary on a handful of items. Granted, it was Nico's money and not mine, but still.

I'd try them on anyway. I was sure some of them wouldn't look great.

But as I slipped into one item and then another, I loved them all. Dammit.

Nico had said to buy whatever I wanted, but how much was too much? I didn't want to sponge off him like he'd said his ex did, or be accused of spending his money recklessly.

I looked at my reflection in the mirror, debating which items to choose. In the end, I decided on the trousers, skirt, blouse and one top. That might be pushing it, but if Nico thought I'd overspent, I'd bring something straight back.

I got dressed, took the clothes to the counter, reluctantly handed over Nico's card, then tucked the receipt safely away in my bag, just in case I needed to return the items.

As I walked past the first store I'd gone in, I saw the rude shop assistant hovering by the door and a flash of annoyance filled me.

I remembered the scene in *Pretty Woman* where Julia Roberts' character went back to the store and I was tempted to do the same. But that would be petty, right? *So what*? She needed to learn a lesson. It was wrong of her to make me feel bad.

Yeah, on the one hand she was right. I wasn't rich personally and I didn't look like I belonged in a store like this. *But* I had the means to pay for the clothes and *that* was what mattered. Rather than waiting to see if I could afford them or giving me the benefit of the doubt, she'd immediately judged and dismissed me. Not cool.

Everyone deserved to be treated with respect. I was sure I wasn't the first person she'd turned her nose up at, but maybe if I said something, she might think twice about doing it to someone else in the future.

I headed towards the door and the surly man opened it.

'Remember me?' I walked up to the shop assistant, who just stood there, arms folded. She glared at me like I was a decaying mouse that a stray cat had just dragged in. My blood boiled. 'When I was here earlier, you judged me and assumed I wasn't able to buy anything here. See this?' I reached inside my bag. 'It's a black card. And I used it to get these.' I lifted up the bag and her eyes almost flew from their sockets. 'You shouldn't judge a book by its cover. *Big mistake. Huge.* Have a nice day!'

I strutted out the door.

That'll teach her.

CHAPTER EIGHTEEN

'Ready to see Paris?' Nico peeked his head into the dressing room.

'Do French people like cheese?' I smirked. I was sure there must be some who didn't, but like wine, I knew it was part of the culture.

'Some people say there may be one thousand six hundred different types of cheese in France, so I think we can agree that the answer is *oui*! So this means you are ready?' A glint of amusement danced in his eyes.

'Well... when I say I'm *ready*, all I have to do is finish getting dressed.' I'd just been trying to decide what top to wear.

'Where is your shopping?' Nico glanced around the room.

'Here.' I pointed to the bag. He walked over, peeked inside and frowned.

'And the rest?'

'What do you mean *the rest*?' Now it was my turn to frown.

'If I say a woman can go shopping with my card, normally I cannot get into my apartment because there are so many bags,' Nico laughed. 'But you, you go shopping and you buy just a pair of trousers?'

'No. I got a skirt and a couple of tops too.'

My stomach sank as I realised he'd basically just confirmed that he *did* give his card to other women to shop, and fairly frequently by the sounds of it. Anyway. I couldn't get hung up on stuff he'd done in the past. It didn't matter. He'd done a kind thing and treated me to some lovely clothes. That was the important thing.

'And that is all?'

'Well, yeah. Everything was just so expensive. I didn't want to take the piss.'

'*Chérie.*' Nico rubbed my shoulder. 'You do not take the piss. If I give you my card, it is because I *want* you to spend money. Next time, do not look at the price. Close your eyes. Buy what you want. Perhaps not a house or car.' He smiled. 'But just clothes is okay. I trust you.'

'Thanks.' Relief washed over me. That was kind of him. 'I need to decide what to wear. If we're sightseeing this afternoon, we'll be doing a lot of walking, right? So will it be okay to wear trainers?'

'Hmmm.' Nico rested his hand on his chin. 'We will go somewhere nice with a dress code, so perhaps not sneakers.'

'Got it.' I nodded. I'd noticed that French people did tend to dress a lot smarter. I supposed it was nice to get glammed up a bit sometimes.

I picked out a blue blazer and the white jumper Miriam had sent over, the nice flared trousers I'd just bought and a pair of boots.

'I will be downstairs. Come when you are ready.'

'Will do.'

After quickly getting dressed, Nico and I headed down to the car. We drove through the busy streets, and soon the Eiffel Tower was in sight. Maurice pulled over.

'Yay! We're going to the Eiffel Tower!' I gushed as Maurice opened my door.

'*Oui.*' Nico followed me out of the car. 'It is the place that all tourists want to visit when they come to Paris, so I make a guess that you will want to come here first.'

'You guessed right.' It looked even more impressive close up. I hadn't realised how striking the iron looked until now. But *whoa*... I gulped as I took in the view of the queue snaking at the bottom of the monument. Looked like it would take hours. 'Isn't it better to book online? I heard that's the best way to avoid the queues.'

'*Ne t'inquiète pas.* It is not a problem.'

Nico reached for my hand and led me past the long lines to a security gate by one of the pillars.

After we went through security checks, an attendant guided us to a private lift. It was quite small; there were only a few other people in there with us. I smiled to myself as I remembered the last time Nico and I had been huddled together in a lift in London. We'd got stuck and let's just say that was the first time Nico and I had *felt* each other's bodies. *Oh, sweet memories.*

There were windows on both sides of the lift so we could see inside the tower as well as the stunning views of Paris. *So cool.* The lift even had a display telling us how far above the ground we were.

Fifty metres... a hundred. My heart pounded as I

watched the numbers climb. At one hundred and twenty-three metres the lift stopped and the doors slid open.

'Welcome to Le Jules Verne,' said the man, who greeted us warmly. 'Let me escort you to your table.'

Holy macaroni. I'd thought we were just going to the Eiffel Tower to look at the views of Paris. I hadn't realised we'd be eating here too.

The restaurant had a light, airy decor with lots of steel, white and gold accents. The hum of people chatting at their tables and the clinking of the waiters collecting empty plates and glasses filled the air.

I swallowed hard and my body tensed. I'd never been to a place like this before. I couldn't stop my head from spinning, taking in the breathtaking views of Paris. My palms started to sweat as I struggled to keep my jaw off the floor. As if sensing my nerves, Nico placed his hand on the small of my back. My shoulders instantly loosened and my heart rate began to stabilise.

Our waiter took us to a room, then pulled out a chair. He explained that we'd be eating a seven-course set menu. *Seven courses.* They'd need to wheel me out of here afterwards.

'So... you like?'

'Er, *yeah*!' My eyes widened. 'It—it's incredible!'

'Because we do not choose what to eat, I think it is better, *non*? It will give us more time to talk and enjoy the views instead of reading the menu.'

'Definitely.' Especially in my case. It always took me ages to decide. I often struggled to choose between the chicken, fish or veggie option. And when the menu was huge, it was even harder. Plus, I hadn't eaten a lot of

French food, so I wouldn't have a clue what to pick. Yep, this was easier all round.

As the waiter poured us both a glass of champers, I looked through the large bay windows once again. It really was stunning.

'You okay?' Nico frowned.

'Yeah, it's just… I know I'm supposed to be cool about all this, but, seriously, your life is mad! I'm trying to take it all in. I mean, you have a driver, a chef, a housekeeper… and now we're at a Michelin-starred restaurant in the Eiffel Tower. *Bloody hell.* Don't you ever pinch yourself to check that it's real?'

'Sometimes. It is true. I have a nice life, but because I work hard, many of these things are necessary.'

'What do you mean?'

'For a long time I try to do everything. Work, cook, clean—but it was impossible. After a long day it is best if I do not have to wait for taxi or take the Metro and cook if I am tired. Fabien makes sure I eat healthy, Odette give me clean house and prepare my clothes. Maurice takes care to get me to meetings on time. So I do not have to worry. And now that I have the money, it is important to enjoy it. That is why it is nice to have you here. I like to have someone to share this with.'

My stomach fluttered. That was lovely of him to say, but I was sure a man like Nico wouldn't be short of company.

Could you imagine saying to someone: 'I know it's a big ask, but I need a favour. Would you mind coming with me to a fancy restaurant in the Eiffel Tower for lunch? As it's such a pain in the arse for you, I'll pay for everything to sweeten the deal.'

Oh, the complaints I'd get! *Not.* I couldn't imagine anyone saying, 'What? You want me to come and sit in one of the most iconic buildings in the world and eat nice food and drink expensive champagne? For free? No way. That sounds like torture. How could you suggest something so awful, you evil, wicked woman?'

Ha. As if. Everyone I knew would bite my hand off faster than you could say 'frogs' legs'. Nico's friends must love him.

'You must have *loads* of people who would want to come to places like this with you.'

'*Oui*, I could ask many people, but there are not many people that I would *choose* to do this with. It is very different.' He leant across the table and gently stroked my cheek, sending shock waves around my body.

I was just about to lean in to peck him on the lips when the waiter approached our table. He placed a white dome-shaped dish in front of me which was apparently a savoury crab meringue, lightly perfumed with curry. I took a mouthful and closed my eyes with delight. *Yum.* I never would've ordered something like this, but it tasted amazing.

'What about your family? You don't talk about them much.' I'd raised it a couple of times when Nico was in London at Christmas, but he'd cut the conversation short.

'My sister is in America, my brother is in Canada.'

'Do you see them often?'

'I see my sister for a few hours last month, when I went to the US for business. My brother, well—he has his own family in Canada. I think I see him last year. We are not very close.'

'And your parents?' Nico wasn't making this easy.

Perhaps he preferred not to talk about them, so maybe it was better I took the hint. 'You don't have to tell me if you don't want to.'

'My mother is in the South of France. She enjoys my money. My father, well—we do not speak.' Nico fell silent.

That must be so hard. I couldn't imagine not speaking to my dad. I adored him. Even though my mum and I clashed sometimes, I knew she still had my best interests at heart. Although he hadn't gone into detail, reading between the lines, it seemed like Nico's mum was only interested in sponging off him.

'Sorry to hear that.'

'Do not be. I am fine. It is not that I sit at home at night and drink alone. I have friends.'

The waiter brought the next course, which looked like a frothy soup with big bubbles and some black circular stuff in the middle. He explained it was a cauliflower soup with leek and caviar. *Aha.* I'd never tried caviar before.

'They say friends are the family you choose, right? I'm lucky, but my friend Melody's so-called family are pretty awful. She says that Bella and I are her real family. We're all more like sisters.'

'It is similar with Lucien. Not the sister thing, obvious-ly.' Nico smiled. 'He is like my brother. We work together but also see each other almost every day outside of work. We socialise together, run together, many things.'

I was intrigued by this. Lucien wasn't the kind of guy I would've placed as Nico's bestie. Nico was so kind, caring and genuine, whereas from what I'd seen of Lucien so far, he seemed like the total opposite. Then again, when I'd first met Nico I'd thought he was a rude dickhead, so maybe I'd got Lucien all wrong. Maybe he hadn't meant to be so offensive last night. Perhaps the language barrier had made him come across as being rude and it wasn't intentional.

'How long have you known Lucien?'

'A long time. We meet at school and become best friends. We lose touch for a while. But we become friends again last year and he offered to help me with the company.'

Questions raced through my mind. I wondered why they'd lost touch. And it was interesting that they'd become friends again last year. Was Nico's money a motivation? You know how they say when people get rich, all their old friends crawl out of the woodwork, wanting to know them. Well, that's what I'd heard people say in films and on TV. None of my friends were millionaires. Then again, for all I knew, Lucien could be rich in his own right.

'How come you didn't speak for a while?'

Nico's face tensed. He paused before replying.

'It was stupid. Just a misunderstanding.' He waved his hand dismissively. 'We were kids, but now things are good. I do not know how I would run the business without him.'

A misunderstanding, eh? I wanted to know more, but if Nico wanted to tell me, he would. I was glad that he felt supported.

'Good to know you've got someone you can trust. Your job sounds so overwhelming.'

'It can be. But I enjoy it. But let us not talk about work. It is the weekend. In France, weekends are time to enjoy and relax. How is your food?'

'Incredible!'

It really was. I loved food, so having the opportunity to try so many different dishes was heavenly.

After we polished off the soup, we had some sort of prawn ravioli with truffles, parmesan cream and a beetroot gelée. I cringed a little when I saw the beetroot. But it was fine. I had the napkin on my lap this time, so there would be no more incidents.

Before I knew it, we'd inhaled the final few courses, which included some delicious desserts. Even though the portion sizes looked small and dainty on the plate, I was full. The multiple glasses of wine must have helped fill my belly too. Honestly, I think I'd drunk more bubbly and French wine in the past couple of days than I had in my whole life.

'I'm stuffed.' I leant back on the chair, patting my stomach. Thank goodness these trousers had an elasticated waistband.

'*Bien*. If you eat well, I am happy. You want to go to the top of the tower now?'

'Of course!' I said.

The waiter brought over the bill and when I caught a glimpse of it, I almost fell off my chair. If I read that correctly, the lunch bill cost more than what I earned in a whole week. Wowsers. This really was another world.

'Should we split the bill, somehow?' I asked. Even though I couldn't afford it, I wanted to ask. After all, we'd come to the Eiffel Tower because of me, so it was only right that I contributed something. 'I don't have my card right now, but when I get my purse, I can—'

'*Non*,' Nico jumped in. '*Merci*, but it is not necessary. I invite you.'

I had to admit I was a little relieved, but asking was the

right thing to do. Not having my card was a pain in the arse. If I'd had it, I definitely would have paid for the tickets to go to the top of the tower. Then again, maybe they were included in the price of lunch.

'Thank you.' I squeezed Nico's hand. 'That's really kind. It was amazing. So do we need to go downstairs and buy the tickets to go to the top or does it come with lunch?'

'It is not included, but I have the tickets already, so we can go now.'

After Nico paid, we took the glass-walled lift to the summit. As I stood out on the platform, the cold wind biting my face, my jaw fell open.

I'd always dreamt of coming to the Eiffel Tower and now I was finally here. I walked up to the edge and took in the views. I spotted the river Seine. The people down on the grassy Champ-de-Mars area beneath us looked like miniature dolls, and the cars driving along Trocadéro resembled little toys.

'You like?' Nico wrapped his arms around my waist. The warmth from his body was divine.

'I don't like it, I *love* it!' As he squeezed me tighter, I breathed in his woody scent and instantly wanted to kiss him. I spun around and placed my lips on his.

I should have been bothered that we were kissing passionately at the top of the Eiffel Tower with God knows how many people around us, but I wasn't. I let Nico's tongue flick against mine and the rest of the world melted away.

This trip was already amazing. To think I'd been nervous about coming here. If I hadn't, I would've missed this. The experience of the Eiffel Tower, and most importantly, the chance to be reunited with Nico and his delicious lips.

It was only when my hands started to roam past his back down to his bum and I felt him hardening against me that I came to my senses and realised that maybe our public display of affection was going a bit too far. And if I was in any doubt, it was definitely confirmed when I saw a mother covering her son's eyes to shield him from our snogging session.

'This way, Kenneth,' she called out. Ah, she was a Brit. Yeah, we weren't so big on PDA. Understandable when there were kids around, but I couldn't help myself.

'Got a bit carried away.' I smiled.

'I like.' Nico pecked me on the lips again.

'As much as I'd like to push you on the ground and jump you, maybe we should save it until later.'

'Mmm, that is a shame.'

'It is…' Now that would be a story. I thought back to the dinner I'd had before coming to Paris where Melody had joked about me telling my fellow residents in a retirement home about the time I'd screwed a hot Frenchman on the Eiffel Tower.

Now that I was here, though, I definitely couldn't see how that would be remotely possible. There were so many people. Shame. I probably wouldn't ever be brave enough to do anything naughty out in the open, though. Al fresco sex was way out of my comfort zone. Nice to fantasise about it, though.

'So, do you come to the Eiffel Tower all the time, then, to check out the views of Paris?'

'Not at all.' Nico shook his head. 'If you are from Paris, it is not common to come to the top of *La Tour*

Eiffel. There are a lot of people. And there are many other places to see beautiful views of Paris. Sacré-Coeur, Tour Montparnasse... I will show you. But this is your first time, so it is important that you come here.'

'Thank you. I'm glad I did. So where to next?'

'We will walk in the gardens at the bottom of the tower and then I will take you home. I must take care of something, so you can relax until later, when Maurice will take you to meet me.'

'Where?'

'It is a surprise.'

'Another one?'

'*Oui*.' Nico pulled me into him and kissed me softly. 'And this is only the beginning, *chérie*.'

CHAPTER NINETEEN

W *hat to wear?*
      I had no idea where we were going. Despite texting a few times to ask if he could give me a clue, Nico hadn't revealed our destination. He insisted he wanted it to be a surprise.

My guess was that we'd be going somewhere posh for dinner. After that slap-up meal at the Eiffel Tower (still couldn't quite get my head around the fact that it had happened) I was still pretty full, but Nico had revealed that we'd be out for a few hours, so I was certain we'd be going somewhere to eat.

I hopped off the bed and headed to the dressing room. It still didn't feel like the clothes hanging on this rack were for me. It was like I'd gone to sleep and woken up in the middle of a fairy tale.

As much as I wanted to be comfortable, I also wanted to make an effort and look nice. I plucked the long skirt with a slit and a sheer white blouse off their hangers. I might even wear some heels. From what I could gather,

Nico's driver took him everywhere, so it wasn't as if I'd have to worry about hobbling to the tube or walking miles. Boots and flats were my normal preference, but even *I* could manage walking from a car to a building.

Underwear... hmm. I ran my hands over the lingerie, which Odette had neatly arranged inside a drawer, and stopped at the crotchless knickers Miriam had sent over. I was drawn to them. Maybe because they were so different to the comfy undies I normally wore.

On the rare occasion that I knew I was going to have a 'night in' with a boyfriend, I might put on some lace undies and a matching bra, but I never would've considered wearing something like *this*. It was so naughty. Not to mention impractical. But yet... now that I was here in another country, something had shifted. I was intrigued. Perhaps it was good to try something new.

Maybe after our dinner at some swanky restaurant, Nico and I would be so horny that we'd stumble into his apartment and end up doing it on the sofa, and wearing crotchless knickers would help us save valuable seconds so we could get down to business quicker.

Okay. That was a bit of a stretch. It wasn't like a few seconds would make a big difference. If I felt like trying something new, I should. It was only a piece of underwear. I didn't need to make silly excuses to justify it.

Sod it. I plucked the knickers from the drawer and rested them on the chair. I'd decided: I was wearing them tonight.

After a quick shower, I got changed, did my make-up and hair using some products Miriam had sent over and was ready with a few minutes to spare.

My phone rang.

'*Salut*. It is Maurice. I want to let you know that I am downstairs. Please come when you are ready. We will meet Nicolas at our destination.'

'*Bonjour!* Okay, thanks. I'll be right down.'

I sat on the chaise longue in the dressing room. The slit in the skirt was pretty racy. It went all the way up to the top of my thigh and revealed even more skin when I sat down, which I hadn't realised when I'd tried it on in the boutique. I liked it, though. It was sexy, but still elegant.

I slid my feet into the heels. They looked so pretty, but I felt like someone had put my foot in a vice and was squeezing it tighter. I was glad I wouldn't have to walk far.

Once I was downstairs, Maurice jumped out of the driver's seat and rushed round to open the door.

'Maurice, it's really kind of you, but you know you don't have to do that for me, right? I can just open it myself.'

'*S'il vous plaît*, Cassie. I like. It is my job. And is what gentlemen do, *non*?'

'That's very sweet. *Merci.*' I slid onto the back seat. 'As long as you're sure you don't mind.'

As we drove along, I took in the views of the beautiful buildings whilst chatting to Maurice about his day. He also asked me how lunch at the Eiffel Tower had been.

Maurice pulled over, and I glanced at the surroundings. *Uh-oh.* We were by the river. That could only mean one thing: we were going on a boat. My throat went dry.

After looking through dozens of Paris tourist guides, I knew that going on a river cruise was one of the top things to do when visiting the city, so I completely understood why Nico would think I'd want to do this. He didn't know about my aversion to boats.

I'd read all about Les Bateaux Mouches—the big boats that give amazing views of the city from the river. They even did dinner cruises, so I imagined this was what Nico had booked. Just the thought of eating on a boat made me want to be sick. Throwing up in front of Nico and hundreds of other people was going to be so embarrassing.

No. It'd be fine. I'd ask someone on board for a sick bag. Better to use that if I couldn't get to the toilets in time, rather than puking on the floor or all over my nice clothes.

The car door opened, and this time it wasn't Maurice.

'Good evening, *chérie*.'

I looked up and saw Nico. God, he was a vision. He was dressed in a pair of smart charcoal trousers and a white shirt that was so crisp, it was like it'd just been ironed directly onto his skin. As his smile widened, my stomach did multiple backflips.

'Well, hello there,' I beamed, my fears melting away. I stepped out of the car.

A gust of wind hit me and my skirt blew open. I gasped as the cold breeze hit me between my thighs. If I'd known we'd be outdoors, I would've chosen underwear with all the fabric intact.

'Mmm, nice skirt.' Nico's eyes fixated on my legs before he leant forward, kissing me gently on the lips.

'Thank you.' A bolt of electricity shot through my body.

'So, this evening, we will take a cruise on the Seine. We will watch the sunset, eat and see Paris at night. It will be beautiful.'

'Great!' I said as enthusiastically as I could. Seeing the sunset and Paris at night would be so romantic. Although I was still apprehensive about travelling by boat, I was sure

Nico had gone to a lot of trouble to arrange this, so I wanted to make the most of it.

Anyway, it'd been years since I'd been on a boat, so maybe I'd be okay now. Maybe it was just a childhood thing.

I looked around, but I couldn't see the large boat that I'd seen in all the Paris articles. We must be early. It was strange that there was no one else around, though.

'Come.' Nico offered his arm. I put my arm in the crook of his elbow and walked along with him. 'Here we are.'

We stopped in front of a boat which looked nothing like the ones I'd seen. A captain and one other man, who I guessed was a waiter, stood on the deck.

'*Bienvenue*. Welcome!' They beamed.

My face contorted in all different directions as I followed Nico on board.

'I thought we were going on the tourist boat?'

'*Non*.' Nico smiled and shook his head. 'It is nice, of course, and is something that is very traditional to do when you visit Paris. But it is big public boat with lot of people. I prefer something more private. More intimate. Tonight, there are no crowds, no tourists, just us.'

Bloody hell. He'd hired a private boat. Just when I'd thought I couldn't be amazed by anything else on this trip, Nico had pulled something new out of the bag to blow me away.

'Champagne?' said the waiter.

'*Merci*.' I plucked the flute from his hand and took a gulp. Oops. That was bad etiquette. I knew I was supposed to sip it, but I needed something to help steady my nerves ASAP.

The waiter showed us around. There were comfy sofa banquettes on the deck for us to relax on whilst taking in the city views, or we could sit inside. As well as a bathroom and kitchen, the interior had a circular sofa with a dining table that was set for two with a fancy white tablecloth and napkins.

Food.

Oh gosh. The boat moved on the water and my stomach churned with it. I really wished I didn't suffer from seasickness. In hindsight, that glass of champagne probably wasn't a good idea.

'Are you okay?' Nico frowned as we both sat at the table.

'Yes, yes! I'm fine! This is… it's amazing! Thanks so much for organising this. It's going to be *great*!' I gushed, hoping I'd convinced him.

It would be fine. Like he said, we'd be watching the sunset from our own private boat, cruising along the Seine, taking in the sights. That was what romantic dreams were made of. I just hoped I could keep my head away from the toilet long enough to enjoy it.

A few minutes later, we set sail. Nico explained that the area we were passing through was called the Île Saint-Germain, then we passed by Île aux Cygnes and the Statue of Liberty. I hadn't even realised that there was one in Paris, so I was even more surprised when he told me that there were more Statues of Liberty in France than in the US.

'Really? How many?' I asked.

'There are ten in France. Four of them are in Paris. The Statue of Liberty you see there on the island is the biggest and most famous. There is also one in Jardin du Luxembourg.'

'Well, now I know! Thank you, Monsieur Tour Guide.'

'*De rien.*'

As we cruised along, I felt a bit dizzy. I hoped this wasn't the start of the sickness. I got up and felt a bit wobbly.

'I just need to go to the loo.'

I hobbled along the deck, ducked inside the toilet and shut the door. Deep breaths. Deep breaths.

When I returned, Nico patted the sofa, signalling for me to sit beside him.

'What is wrong? You do not like?'

'Of course!' I forced a smile. 'It's great!

'Cassie.' Nico softened his voice, took my hand in his and looked me straight in the eyes. 'Tell me the truth. It is okay.'

'Well…' I sucked in a breath. 'It's just, I'm not very good with boats. I went on a couple when I was younger and always ended up spending the whole journey feeling sick, so I'm just a bit worried about throwing up.'

'Throwing up?' He frowned.

'Sorry, slang for being sick.'

'*Chérie*, you should tell me.' He squeezed my hand. 'Wait.' He got up and went to speak to the captain and the waiter, Hubert. A few minutes later he returned. 'I ask him to go more slow for you, okay? The captain say that it is rare for someone to become ill from a river cruise because there is less movement on the water. There are not a lot of waves like the sea, so you should be fine. But if you want, we can go back.'

'No, no. I'm sure I'll be fine.' The last thing I wanted

to do was ruin the evening. 'It's probably just all in my head. I just need to relax and stop worrying, that's all.'

'Okay. Well, if you do not feel good, you tell me. This boat is for us, so if you want to stop, we stop. If you think we go too fast, I ask for him to go more slow. Whatever you want.' Nico kissed me gently on my forehead.

'That's really sweet, thanks.' My heart melted.

'I will ask them to make a special ginger tea for you. It is what we used to give my sister when she get travel sick. I think it will help.'

Nico jumped up and went out to speak to the captain and Hubert again.

'It is done. They do not have ginger on the boat, but we will make a stop and get some.'

'Stop? I don't want to put them out.'

'Do not worry. This is the advantage of having this boat just for us. I want you to enjoy. It is better to have it to make sure.'

I didn't know where we were, but shortly afterwards, the boat pulled over.

About half an hour later, I saw Maurice heading towards the boat, clutching a huge bag.

I watched from the window as Maurice stepped on board and handed the bag to Hubert, then left the boat again. Hubert then returned inside the cabin.

'I have the ginger, I will make the tea now.'

'*Bien.*' Nico nodded. 'And the other things?'

'They are all inside.' He handed the bag to Nico, who rested it on the seat beside him.

'I have some extra blankets.' He started unpacking the contents. 'And some travel medication and a coat. It may be cold later.' He plucked a huge fur coat from the bag. 'Do not worry, it is faux fur.'

'Oh my God, I can't believe you arranged all of this for me, I... *merci*.'

'*De rien.*'

Hubert returned to the table clutching a bowl. The spicy scent of fresh ginger hit my nostrils. I thanked him and, after it had cooled a little, gulped the whole lot down. I felt better almost instantly.

'How are you feeling?' Nico rubbed my back.

'Much better, thanks.' The heat from his hand was so soothing.

'Are you hungry?'

'A little.'

'*Bien.* I will ask the captain to restart the boat and Hubert will bring something to eat.'

Minutes later, we set off once more, gently cruising along. Hubert laid some light snacks on the table. Whilst I was hungry, I didn't want to risk upsetting my stomach, so I stuck to nibbling on some bread.

I glanced out of the window at the orange-and-yellow sky, which was so pretty it took my breath away.

'The sky looks gorgeous! As nice as it is in here, now I'm feeling okay, I'd like to try and see it from outside.'

'*Parfait!*' Nico's eyes brightened.

I thought back to when we'd met at Christmas. I'd taken Nico to Winter Wonderland and whilst I'd gone to the loo, he'd surprised me with ice skating tickets. But because I'd had bad memories of when I'd last skated, I'd been apprehensive about joining him. Nico had encouraged me to face my fears and he was right. I'd been fine and ended up really enjoying it. I wanted to try and do the same again.

I reckoned he was right. Gently cruising down a river was a lot different to being on a big boat on the sea. It was the fear that had made me feel queasy. I'd be fine. And the best way to prove it would be to get my bum outside, sit on the deck and enjoy the views like a normal person.

I was lucky that Nico had taken the time and trouble to organise this private boat tour for me, so I wanted to do my best to enjoy it.

I picked up the faux fur coat and slid my arms through the sleeves. It was lovely and warm. Then I scooped up the pile of soft blankets and headed up the steps onto the deck. Nico followed behind me.

'*Ça va mieux?*' the captain shouted out. I understood the *ça va* part of what he'd said but not the other part. 'You feel better?' He clarified.

'Ah! Yes. *Oui. Bien. Merci!*' I replied, exhausting all of my French vocab.

Nico and I cozied up on the comfy seat and wrapped the blanket over our legs.

Soft classical music played in the background and I breathed in the fresh evening air.

'This is beautiful.' I smiled. 'The colours of the sky. The views. *Everything.*' Even the river seemed calmer. I was glad I'd come outside.

'So I was right?'

'Right? Right about what?'

'When I tell you that Paris is the most beautiful city in the world.' He smirked.

'Don't get carried away,' I laughed. 'I've only been here for just over twenty-four hours, so it's too soon for me to decide that. But so far, your city is looking pretty great to me.' The light was fading fast. I was excited that we'd get to see Paris illuminated soon.

'You will see. By the end of the trip, you will fall in love.'

If he kept doing lovely things like stopping a boat to bring fresh ginger on board and arranging lovely bubble baths to make me feel better, I just might. And that was a problem.

Oh.

Hold on. He meant that I'd fall in love with *Paris*. Not with him. I didn't know why I was even thinking of something so ridiculous. *Of course* I wasn't going to fall in love with Nico. I was going back to London next weekend, so that would be stupid.

'Yeah, your city is pretty cool.'

'Like you.' He smiled.

'So cheesy!' I laughed.

'Cheese?'

'It means sappy.' No. He wouldn't understand that word either. 'Mushy, you know, romantic.'

'And romantic is bad? We are in the city of love.' He traced his thumb over my cheek. 'Or perhaps you prefer romantic action rather than words…' He leant forward and gently pressed his lips on mine.

'Mmm.' My pulse quickened. 'Maybe. You should try that again.'

Nico planted one kiss on my neck. Then another. Each time his lips connected with my skin, my body fizzed with desire.

'How is that?'

'Nice… but I need more.'

'To help you feel more relaxed?'

'Yes,' I added as he continued gently kissing my neck, then my ear. 'If I'm more relaxed, then I won't think about the fact that we're on a boat.'

'*Entendu*,' Nico added, now kissing the other side of my neck. 'That is important.'

Before I could catch my breath, Nico started kissing me, passionately. His lips were hot and hungry, and as he slid his tongue into my mouth, excitement rippled through me.

He pulled the blanket up just below our chins and his hand dipped underneath. After pushing the coat to one side, Nico undid my blouse, his fingers slipping inside, trailing across my shoulders, then towards my breasts. He stroked my hard nipples through the fabric of my bra and I whimpered. I'd give anything right now for him to rip off my clothes and take them in his mouth.

God, I wanted this man. Right here. Right now. But we couldn't. We were outside. On a boat. In public.

As the kisses became more frenzied, I raked my hand through his thick, dark hair. I cracked one eye open. The captain was facing forward at the front of the boat and Hubert must be downstairs in the kitchen.

Although the light was fading, it wasn't quite dark yet, so the passers-by, not to mention the passengers on the huge tourist boat approaching in the distance, would be able to see us kissing. Thankfully, because I was wrapped in the thick coat, with the blanket over us, there was no way they'd be able to see where Nico's hands were roaming.

Just as well, because...

OMG.

Nico's hand trailed past my stomach, down my thigh, and then slipped under the slit in my skirt. His fingers reversed their direction, travelling upwards, higher and higher, until…

'Oh, God.' A moan escaped my lips.

Nico paused and looked at me, his dark eyes burning with desire. 'These are the special panties?' he licked his lips.

'Yes,' I panted. 'They're the crotchless knickers.' He hadn't even touched me there yet, but my blood was already on fire and I could feel the dampness pooling between my legs. The anticipation was too much.

'Mmm, I like. I am happy that we will not have the same problem that we have before in the lift.' He smirked.

When we'd been stuck in the lift in London, Nico had touched me, but because I'd been wearing jeans, his access had been limited. That wouldn't be a problem tonight.

'This time you have an all-access pass.' My heart pounded.

That was all he needed to hear. Nico dipped his fingers between my legs and the chill from his fingertips making contact struck me like a bolt of lightning.

As he moved his fingers back and forth slowly, in long, teasing strokes, my clit throbbed. I threw my head back and groaned with pleasure.

A few minutes ago, I'd been worried about who might see us, but right now, I didn't care.

'Open wider,' Nico commanded. I spread my legs without hesitation and gasped as he slid two fingers inside me.

'Fuck,' I moaned. This man was so good with his hands. Arousal ripped through me as I felt the sensation of

Nico thrusting his fingers in and out with one hand whilst circling my clit with the other.

Damn.

I couldn't believe this was really happening. I was on the deck of a private boat, cruising down the Seine, with Nico's fingers fucking me so good that I was already on the verge of orgasm.

'The lights will come on at any second,' the captain shouted out. I didn't even bother to check whether he was still facing forward or not. I was so close and nothing was going to ruin my high.

'*Bien,*' Nico shouted back.

'Don't stop,' I panted. I vaguely heard what the captain said about the lights, but the only lights I cared about right now were the ones that seemed to be switching on in every part of my body.

That's it. Right there.

Nico picked up the pace, his fingers plunging harder and faster. As his strokes became firmer, I felt the wave building. And it wasn't a wave of seasickness. It was the most exquisite wave of ecstasy.

I arched my back and my toes curled as the flurry of fireworks exploded within me.

'Ah, *oui*!' I cried out. '*Oui!*'

I was done.

I collapsed on Nico's shoulder, my chest heaving.

'Open your eyes, *chérie,*' Nico whispered.

I squinted them open, just in time to catch the lights of the Eiffel Tower springing to life.

The large boat I'd seen before in the distance sailed right past us, filled with tourists out on the deck, with their phones taking pictures of the iconic monument.

Wow. That was close. A minute earlier and they would've got an eyeful of a more X-rated show.

'It is *magnifique, oui*?' The captain spun around. 'I timed everything so that we sail past just when the lights turn on. I am happy you like.' He turned back to face the river again.

Nico and I looked at each other, then burst out laughing.

'Oops. He thought my screams of joy were because I was excited about the Eiffel Tower lights!'

Of course it was amazing to see it illuminated, but that wasn't the only thing that had been turned on...

'Why?' Nico said with a devilish grin. 'There is something else that make you excited?'

'Oh, nothing much,' I said, my heart rate stabilising. 'Just the orgasm you gave me.'

'So, you feel relaxed now?' He slowly slid his fingers out of me.

'Definitely. I feel *really good*.'

'I am happy to hear that.'

We looked up and Hubert was approaching.

'Would you like something to eat? Perhaps something sweet?'

'Nothing for me, thanks.' I smiled mischievously. As Hubert walked away, I whispered in Nico's ear, 'I'm already feeling *more* than satisfied.'

CHAPTER TWENTY

As the boat continued down the sparkling river with the reflection of a thousand lights, I took in the views. I was still wrapped in the blanket, sitting on Nico's lap, with his arms around me.

I didn't know if I was still on a high from that incredible orgasm or if it was the magic of seeing Paris illuminated as we sailed under the stars, but right now I felt like I was living in a fairy tale.

Nico pointed out so many sights that I'd seen in my Paris tour guides and online. The Grand Palais, Pont Alexandre III, Musée d'Orsay and the Louvre. It felt so surreal that I was here, seeing them all in real life.

We passed Notre Dame. Because of the fire, it still had scaffolding over various parts of the cathedral. Such a shame that we wouldn't be able to visit it this week. Maybe next time.

Not that I was presuming there would be a next time with Nico. Coming here again would be verging on proper relationship territory and I was sure this wouldn't last long enough for a second visit. I was just speaking generally. There was no reason I couldn't return at some point. Melody had always wanted to see Paris, so we could have a girly weekend.

The boat turned around and we were able to view all the different bridges and monuments again from the other side of the river. Which was handy, as there were a few things I'd missed when I was, *ahem*, otherwise engaged…

'I will never get tired of these views.' Nico squeezed me tighter.

'I can see why. It's so beautiful.'

'I still remember when my grandmother take me, my brother and sister here when we were younger. She take us on *un bateau mouche* and after we have ice cream or crêpes.'

'Sounds amazing.'

'I will take you for a crêpe too this week. Perhaps it is too cold for ice cream.'

'It's *never* too cold for ice cream! I can eat it in summer or when there's snow on the ground.'

'You are joking, yes?'

'No way! Ice cream can be enjoyed all year round. Just like tea. You can have it when it's five degrees outside or twenty-five. Some things aren't seasonal.'

'I cannot agree with you on this.'

'We'll see.' I smirked. 'I'll make it my mission to let you try ice cream in winter and hot tea in summer…' My voice trailed off. There I went again, thinking too far ahead. It was February now. It wouldn't get properly hot until June or July. And like I'd said earlier, I might not still be speaking to Nico then. I reminded myself for the hundredth time to focus on the moment. 'Anyway,' I said, keen to change the subject, 'thanks again for bringing me here.'

'You are welcome. The tour has nearly finished, but if you want to stay longer, I will let the captain know.'

'No, no. It's fine.' As much as I'd enjoyed seeing the sights this evening, after the little taster Nico had given me under the blankets, I wanted to see more of his bedroom ceiling or, putting it bluntly, his naked body on top of mine. It was a bit too crude to say that out loud, though. 'I'm sure Hubert and the captain want to go home.'

'Okay.' Nico went to talk to the captain and then I heard him on the phone. Sounded like he was calling Maurice.

Not long afterwards, the boat docked. We said our thanks and goodbyes, then I spotted Maurice standing outside by the car.

'Good evening, Cassie. You like the boat?'

'I loved it, thanks.'

He opened the door and I slid across the seat. Nico followed and squeezed up beside me.

Once Maurice had set off, Nico pressed a button and a privacy screen rose up. *Very cool.*

It was hot in here. I took off the coat and laid it on the seat.

'So.' Nico turned to face me. 'You say that you enjoy the cruise—which part was your favourite?' He traced his thumb over my cheek.

'Mmm, that's a tough question. There was so much beauty—the Louvre, seeing the whole city lit up so brightly—but I think the orgasm as we passed the Eiffel Tower was the highlight for me.'

'Really?' Nico began kissing my neck, oh so slowly… 'And you would like another *petite mort*?'

'*Petite* what?' I tried and failed to concentrate on what he said. The sensation of his warm, sweet breath on my neck made it hard to focus.

'*Petite mort*.' He continued kissing me, moving his attention towards my chest. 'It is how we say orgasm in French. The translation is *little death*.'

'*Oh*…,' I said, partly because now I understood, but mainly because of how he was making me feel. '*Oui*. I would definitely like another *petite mort*.'

'Understood.' Nico undid the top button of my blouse, followed by another button and another, his kisses getting lower and lower until my bra was completely exposed.

My blouse fell around my waist. Nico pushed my bra straps down so they hung below my shoulders, then gently lowered the front of my bra, causing my breasts to pop out.

'This is okay?' he paused.

'Yes.' I nodded, the warm air from the car heater hitting my bare skin.

Nico cupped my breasts, squeezing them passionately before flicking his thumbs over my nipples, which instantly hardened against his touch.

Before I'd had a chance to catch my breath, he leant forward, dipped his head, took my nipple in his mouth and started sucking, slowly.

'Oh God,' I groaned, throwing my head back. My whole body pulsed as lust flooded my veins.

What had happened on the boat was hot, and now this impromptu back-seat encounter was shattering the thermometer.

A loud car horn sounded, reminding me of our

surroundings. Here we were sitting in traffic, with cars on either side, just inches away, and Nico was sucking my boobs. Because the windows were tinted, nobody else knew what we were doing. And knowing that gave me such a thrill.

Goddamn.

As Nico licked and flicked my nipples with his tongue, his hand traced up my legs through the slit of my skirt and climbed along my thighs. Before I'd even realised it, my legs flopped open. It was a natural response. I wanted him so badly.

Nico's fingers continued upwards, until he reached between my legs.

'Oh God, *yes*,' I groaned, flashbacks of the pleasure he'd given me on the boat racing through my mind. 'Right *there*.'

As Nico started stroking my clit whilst sucking on my nipples, I knew I was already close. How did he do it? How did he know exactly where to touch me? And how did he bring me so close to the edge so quickly?

'Suck me harder,' I moaned, breathless. Nico moved his mouth to my other breast, his teeth tugging at my nipple. Excitement rippled through me.

'*J'ai envie de toi*,' I panted, remembering Nico's words.

'*Très bien.*' Nico lifted his head from my chest and smiled. 'You are very sexy when you tell me this in French. I also want you, Cassie. But first I give you another orgasm.'

Nico picked up the pace and I started rocking myself against him, rubbing against his fingers as he continued stroking my throbbing clit. Harder. Faster.

It was happening.

Again.

My heart pounded against my chest, my body trembled and my head went fuzzy as the wave tore through me.

It was like Nico had taken a match and set my blood on fire.

Oh. My. God.

'Fuuuuuuckkkk!' I screamed before collapsing beneath him.

Holy shit. Two orgasms in less than two hours. And neither of them in a bedroom. I'd never done anything naughty in a car before. Never mind on a boat. I'd definitely upgraded from vanilla sex. If this was ice cream, it would be something a lot spicier, like rich chocolate and chilli.

'That was… that was amazing.' I tried to catch my breath. 'I wasn't sure about these knickers at first, but they're actually quite handy.' Miriam had definitely known what she was doing sending these over. I could hug her.

'Yes, they are very convenient. *Chérie*, I do not want to rush you'—Nico pressed his face to the window—'but we are almost home, so although I prefer that you stay like this, perhaps it is better if you get dressed. Only for a few minutes. I would like to continue this upstairs…' The corner of his mouth twitched.

Seconds later, the car pulled over.

Shit. Here I was with my tits out and my top off and Maurice was about to open the door any minute.

I quickly pulled up my bra, slipped my blouse back on and started doing it up.

Nico pressed a button on a control panel in front of

him and said something in French to Maurice, then leant back in the seat.

'Do not worry. I ask Maurice to give us a few minutes.'

Phew.

My heart rate slowed as I finished buttoning up my blouse and threw the coat on. Thank God this would cover my arse too. Nico had turned me on so much that I was soaked through. Crotchless knickers were good for easy access, but not for containing *things*, shall we say. I hoped I hadn't ruined this skirt. I'd hand-wash it in the morning. There was no way I could leave this for Odette to clean.

I nodded at Nico to let him know I was ready. We slipped out of the car, then made fast work of getting the lift upstairs.

As soon as we crashed into the apartment, our clothes flew through the air.

First my coat, then my skirt and my blouse, until I was just in my underwear. Nico quickly shed his trousers and shirt in a heap on the floor, pushed me up against the wall, then kissed me hungrily.

I felt his hard-on pressing into me and couldn't wait a second longer.

'I need you.' I rubbed my hand against him. Nico paused, stood back, his eyes burning into me, then scooped me into his arms, carrying me up the stairs.

I buried my head into his muscular chest and inhaled his gorgeous woody scent. I wanted to lick every inch of him.

After switching on the bedroom light, Nico placed me carefully down at the edge of the bed, pushed me back then straddled me.

'*Mon Dieu.*' He traced his tongue across my neck. 'You are so beautiful.' He reached behind my back, unclasped my bra, then buried his head into my chest once more. Even though he'd been sucking my breasts mere minutes ago, it still felt like the first time. So raw and exhilarating. My body sparked all over again. I couldn't get enough of him.

His tongue trailed around my nipples, then down my stomach until he reached in between my legs. He tugged at my knickers with his teeth. *Oh God.* Just the thought of him peeling them off was enough to make me explode again.

Nico groaned as he buried his head between my thighs and started licking my clit hungrily. 'Cassie, you are so wet.'

He wasn't joking. I don't think I'd been so turned on in my life.

Fuck. Every flick of his tongue sent me closer to the edge. I desperately wanted him to continue because I loved how he was making me feel, but at the same time, I wanted him inside me.

'Wait,' I panted. Nico's head bolted up and his eyes widened.

'I am sorry, did I go too far? You want me to stop?'

'No, no. I want to carry on… I can't believe I'm saying this, but if you continue going down on me, I'm going to come.'

'And this is a problem?' he frowned.

'No, of course I want to, but I'd like my third orgasm of the night to *come* from you being inside me. It's been five long weeks and I want you. *Now*. And seeing as they're crotchless, let's leave the knickers on.'

'*Comme tu veux, chérie.* As you wish.'

Nico jumped up, pulled open his bedside drawer, took out a condom, then rolled it down his solid length. He climbed back on top of me and we started kissing. Deep, hard, fast, urgent kisses. My hands roamed along his back, across his firm chest, trailing all the way down between his legs.

I wrapped my hand around him. God, it was so good to feel him again. He was just as long and thick as I remembered. But touching wasn't enough. I needed to feel *all* of him.

I guided Nico between my legs, then he plunged inside.

Normally if a man this big entered me, it would be uncomfortable. But tonight, with all the foreplay, my body was already primed and ready for action.

As he slid in and out of me, I felt overcome with pleasure. I'd remembered that the sex was amazing in London, but this. *This.* Holy fuck. Quite literally. I felt every sensation.

I gripped his backside and pushed him deeper. I wanted it all. I wanted him to fill me. I wanted him to fuck me so hard that I would still feel the aftermath between my legs tomorrow morning.

I lifted my legs up and wrapped them around Nico's neck, giving me a glorious view of his chest. Delicious beads of sweat trickled down his pecs, and I wanted to lick them off. I couldn't get enough of this man.

If Nico touched my clit now, this joyous moment would be over in seconds and I definitely didn't want that. I wanted to savour this for as long as possible.

'I want you from behind,' Nico panted. My eyes widened.

'Behind as in…?' I left the words hanging in the air.

'Doggy,' he said.

'Yes!'

Nico pulled out quickly. I got on my knees and gasped as he entered me again. God, that felt good.

He gripped my hips, slamming in and out. It didn't take him long to find the right angle. With every thrust, I was sure my body temperature rose several degrees.

I looked up, and *wow*. I'd just realised that when we'd crashed into the bedroom, we'd turned the lights on but hadn't drawn the curtains. Which meant as well as seeing the wonderful reflection of Nico thrusting in and out of my wet, red-hot centre, through the window, I also saw Paris lit up in front of me.

Nico caressed my breasts, then reached in between my legs to stroke my pulsing clit, and I swear for a second I stopped breathing. I'd been on fire before, but now my whole body lit up like a volcano. There was no way I'd be able to hold out for much longer.

I arched my back, pushing my bum into him. 'Oh my God,' I screamed as Nico picked up speed. He pumped faster and faster whilst the wave ripped through me. I felt it in my toes, racing through my bloodstream, between my legs, in my nipples, and my head went fuzzy as I flopped forward onto the bed.

Nico tightened his grip around my waist, continuing to thrust in and out until he groaned loudly, then collapsed on top of me.

We both lay in silence for a few minutes, our chests heaving.

Wow. That was definitely going in the experience archives.

'So, you have another *petite mort*, *non*?'

'Could you tell?' I grinned.

'A little…'

'Although less, *petite mort* and more, what's big again? *Grande*?'

'*Oui*.' Nico stroked my face.

'Yep. That was definitely a big death. I feel like I've died and gone to orgasm heaven.'

I wasn't joking. If I died now, I'd want it written on my death certificate. Cassie Williams: cause of death: multiple orgasms including the biggest, most mind-blowing climax of her life.

A big grin spread across Nico's face.

'That makes me very happy.'

'Well, you've made me very, very, *very* happy tonight.' I smiled.

I was so glad that I'd come. Both sexually and geographically—to Paris. Right here, right now, I didn't care whether this would only be a holiday romance or fling. If it meant I got to feel like this, I'd take it. Maybe I'd regret it when I got back to London, but I wasn't going to think about that. I was enjoying myself way too much.

Eight more days of this pleasure? Even if it came at the cost of getting my heart broken?

Count me in.

CHAPTER TWENTY-ONE

I stretched my arms into the air. I'd slept like a baby again.

I swear this mattress was handcrafted by angels. The pillow, the duvet, the sheets, everything just felt so heavenly. It was as if I'd spent the night sleeping on clouds. Nico making sure I was on cloud nine last night had probably helped me doze off too.

I'd set a new personal record for pleasure. I'd always believed that women having multiple orgasms in films or books was exaggerated BS. Then when Nico had stayed at my place over Christmas and we'd done it three times in one night, I'd become a believer. But now, I was evangelical. I'd come *four times*. Four bloody times in one night. I wasn't even sure I'd had that many orgasms during my two-year relationship with my ex.

About an hour after we'd finished in the bedroom, I'd gone to get some water and Nico had followed; he'd pulled me into the living room and we'd done it again. Oh, sweet memories. I was *loving* this trip.

After I showered, I headed downstairs to find Nico. He'd got up at half-six this morning to go for a run. I had no idea how he'd found the energy.

'So, what's on the agenda for today?'

'First we will go out for breakfast, then we will *flâner* in Paris. This means we will walk around and how do you say? *Go with the flow*. So far you visit most places by car, but it is important to experience the city by foot.'

'Sounds good! I'll get dressed.'

Once I'd put on my jeans, trainers and coat, we set off.

As nice as it was to be chauffeured around the city, Nico was right. It was good to walk.

'Do you drive?' I asked as we weaved through various cobbled streets, where people sat outside little cafés, drinking their coffees. I caught sight of a woman biting into a pastry and my stomach rumbled. I'd love a croissant right now.

'*Oui*.'

'I mean, I know you have the car that Maurice drives you around in, but do you have other cars? Like, a hundred Ferraris or something?'

Nico smiled, then shook his head.

'*Non*, just two cars: Tesla and Mercedes.'

'Just?' I laughed.

'I do not mean *just* because I think it is not a lot. I mean *just* because of course I could have more. In the beginning, when I first have money, I buy different cars.'

'Let me guess: a Ferrari?' I raised my eyebrow.

'*Oui*.' Nico cracked another smile.

'*So* predictable.'

'Well, it is the dream for many people. But I did not keep it for very long. It did not feel right for me. I use the car only if I want to drive somewhere by myself, so to have something so fancy is not necessary. And a car like this brings a lot of attention, which I prefer to avoid.'

'That's true.'

'Here we are.' Nico stopped outside a patisserie. As I glanced at the display of colourful cakes, glistening tarts and pretty pastries in the window, I almost started dribbling. 'Come.' He ushered me inside.

There was already a queue. I wasn't surprised. The smell of butter, sugar and freshly baked bread flooded the air. I scanned the delights behind the glass counter. Of course I instantly recognised the croissants and pains au chocolat, but there were so many other things I'd never seen before.

'You know what you would like?'

'I wouldn't even know where to start!' My eyes bulged.

'Okay. Find a table. I will choose.'

The hum of French conversation surrounded me as I sat back on the red-and-white chair. Minutes later, Nico arrived with a tray. There was a baguette, croissants, some pastries and what looked like coffee, but in bowls. Similar to the one I'd drunk from on the boat.

Nico spread some butter over his bread.

'We call this *tartine*,' he said.

'So basically buttered toast.'

Nico took his bread and…

'What the hell?' I gasped as he dipped it in the bowl of coffee. 'What are you doing?'

'There is something wrong with your eyes?' Nico frowned. 'You can see what I do, *non*? I put the bread in my coffee.'

'Eurgh!' I winced. 'You dip *bread* in *coffee*? What's wrong with you?'

'There is nothing wrong with me.' He shook his head. 'It is normal. I also do this sometimes with croissants.'

'Oh my God!' Maybe that was why they drank coffee from bowls. It was much easier to fit a baguette in a bowl rather than a mug. 'I thought you'd be all refined with your food. Surely this must be some sort of crime against breakfast?' I winced again as I imagined all the sludgy bits of bread at the bottom of the cup. And the butter too. Gross.

'You put biscuits in your tea, *non*?'

'Yeah, but that's different. *That* is *completely* acceptable.'

'That is what all the British people say.' Nico smirked.

'What is *this*?' I picked up a pretty pastry. As I took a bite, I closed my eyes and groaned with pleasure. I felt like I'd died and gone to cake heaven.

'*Chausson aux pommes*. I think in English it is like apple turnover, *non*? But better.'

I wanted to give him stick about the fact he'd said it was better than what we have in the UK, but I couldn't argue. It was true.

The flaky pastry was delicate and buttery. The apples were firm, yet soft. Somehow they melted like caramel in my mouth. And the design was like art. It had been decorated like a leaf and was a beautiful golden-brown colour. Utter perfection.

'Move over, croissants.' I took another bite. 'There's a new breakfast pastry in town.'

After we'd wolfed down our breakfast and I'd tried to recover from the trauma of seeing Nico enjoy soggy bread, we headed over to the centre of Paris to an area Nico said was the first arrondissement. It wasn't long before I spotted an iconic landmark.

'Welcome to the Louvre.' Nico held out his hand. 'The world's most beautiful and largest museum.'

As we approached the huge glass pyramid, my mouth fell open. The closer we got, the more beautiful I found it. I'd seen it in books, on TV, and online—and we'd even sailed past it on the river last night—but being here allowed me to see the triangular and diamond-shaped glass panels much more clearly. As the light reflected off them, it gave the effect of sparkling jewels.

It wasn't just the monument itself that made me gasp; it was also the queues. But I imagined Nico had some sort of all-access VIP pass to get in here too. I wondered, though, whether we'd have time to go to the Louvre and see the rest of Paris.

'Are we going in there now?'

'*Non*. As you can see, it is very popular. Perhaps we can come during the week. Even then, it is impossible to see everything in one visit. There is so much inside. Today, I want just to show you the building.'

'Thanks—you're right. It's really pretty.' I pulled out my mobile. 'Can you take some photos?'

'*Bien sûr*.' Nico took my phone as I posed in front of the pyramid, just like dozens of other tourists. What could I say? It had to be done.

Next, Nico took us to the Tuileries Garden, which was a short walk away.

'This is one of the largest parks in Paris. Come.' Nico took my hand and my body instantly sparked. His hand was so big, soft and warm. 'Let me show you.'

We strolled hand in hand down the tree-lined paths, pausing only so I could take photos of the beautiful green landscape, pretty fountains, ponds and statues we passed.

After walking around for over an hour, Nico suggested we continue our tour elsewhere. Next, we stopped at the Place de la Concorde, a square which was actually in the shape of an octagon (yep, I was confused at first too). It had monuments representing eight French cities around it, and in the centre of the square was an obelisk, which apparently was the oldest monument in Paris.

I spotted the Champs-Élysées and Arc de Triomphe in the distance. I was surprised at how quickly we got to places.

'I didn't realise we were so close. I thought it would take ages to get everywhere.'

'Paris is not as big as people think,' Nico said. 'To walk from the north to the south of Paris takes only two hours.'

'No way?'

'Yes. It is not so big. Especially when you compare it to a city like New York, which is several times larger. Parisians often walk to many places, as they are sometimes just a few minutes away. You have seen the Champs-Élysées already, yes?'

'In the car when I went shopping. From what I saw, it's mainly big shops and restaurants for tourists, isn't it?'

'*Oui*. There is of course *L'Arc de Triomphe* at the top.'

'It's up to you, but I can go there tomorrow whilst you're at work. Maybe today you can take me to some different places.'

'*Bien sûr.*' Nico nodded.

After having lunch, we continued walking.

'We are now in Montmartre,' said Nico. 'Remember I tell you that there are different places with beautiful views of Paris, not just the Eiffel Tower?'

'Yeah.'

'Now I will take you to see Sacré-Coeur Basilica—one of the most spectacular churches in the world. It has fantastic views.'

'Have you noticed that everywhere we've gone so far, everything you've described is either the oldest, the biggest or the best?' I smirked. 'Like, "this church is *the most spectacular in the world…* this museum is *the most popular in the world.*"'

'But it is true!'

'I'm sure it is!'

'You will see.'

'Even if it is, I'm not sure that you'll ever convince me that Paris is better than London.' I chuckled.

Nico and I always bantered about which of our cities was the best. It was just a bit of fun. I couldn't deny that I was *loving* Paris. What I'd seen so far was beautiful. *Stunning.* And even though I was teasing Nico, I didn't doubt it when he said the places were known to be the biggest. But London was my home.

As pretty as Paris was, everything was so different. I mean, *duh*, of course—it was another country. But despite Nico saying the city was small compared to others, everything still felt so big. So unfamiliar. So daunting.

I couldn't imagine leaving London to come and live here. It would be too scary.

Back home I had a job (albeit a shitty and temporary

one), my flat, my friends and family. It would be too much to leave behind.

Anyway, I didn't even know why I was thinking about that. It was a crazy idea. As attached as I could feel myself becoming to Nico, I had to remind myself that this was short-term. I'd promised myself that I wouldn't get carried away with making future plans and how we could make it work beyond this trip.

'Welcome to Sacré-Coeur.'

'Wow!' I said, as we approached the huge Roman-style domed church, which had a striking white limestone exterior. I'd seen it in the distance and I remembered the photos from tour guides, but being here, with it right in front of me, was extra special.

'I tell you it is spectacular, *non*?' He said. 'After *La Tour Eiffel*, the dome is the highest point of the city.'

'This time, I actually believe you. There's a lot of steps to climb…' I glanced at the huge staircase in front of us.

The area was swarming with tourists. I quickly moved to the left to avoid bumping into a large group of shrieking children eagerly heading towards the colourful carousel at the base of Sacré-Coeur.

I'd noticed there were a lot of carousels in Paris. I spotted one at the bottom of the Eiffel Tower yesterday, another at the Jardin des Tuileries earlier, and now this one, which was decorated with a pretty Venetian theme. I used to love going on merry-go-rounds as a child.

'Yes, there are almost three hundred steps.' Nico nodded.

'Isn't there a little funicular cable car thingy that takes you to the top?' I asked, remembering what I'd read online.

'*Oui*. It is possible to take the Funiculaire, but is better to walk. It is good exercise, *non*?'

I preferred the kind of exercise we'd had last night in the bedroom, but after indulging with that delicious *chausson aux pommes* earlier, followed by lunch, burning off some extra calories wouldn't be a bad idea.

Once we reached the top and walked to the edge of the large terrace, I saw why Nico wanted to bring me here. He was right. The sweeping panoramic views really were incredible.

'It is beautiful, *non*?'

'It really is!'

He slipped his arm around my waist, then pointed out the various landmarks: the opera house, the Pantheon, Notre Dame and, of course, the Eiffel Tower.

'You want to go inside the basilica?'

'What would you recommend?'

'Many people just enjoy the views from the terrace. We can go inside or we can sit here for a while and then I can take you somewhere else.'

After trudging up that staircase, I was quite happy to have a breather.

'Okay, let's sit for a bit.'

I sat on the steps and Nico squeezed up beside me. Before I'd even realised, I rested my head on his shoulder like it was the most natural thing to do. It was as if that was where my head was supposed to be. Somehow it felt like home.

Nico stroked my back, then gently kissed the top of my head, and my body buzzed with warmth and happiness. I knew we were supposed to be sightseeing, but I wished I could just sit here, with him beside me, forever.

I closed my eyes as I breathed in his woody scent. I loved the smell of Nico more than the delicious aroma of sweet French pastries and buttery croissants. If only I could bottle it and take it back to London with me…

After taking some pictures, Nico took my hand and we weaved through the cobbled streets until we reached a busy square called the Place du Tertre.

'Do not laugh, but this is the highest square in Paris.'

'Of course it is!' I rolled my eyes. 'Because we could never go to an *ordinary* square!' I chuckled.

The square was packed with artists. Nico said it was popular with many painters, including Pablo Picasso and Vincent Van Gogh, back in the day. He went on to explain that apparently the waiting list to work here was about ten years. Crikey.

As I looked more closely, I saw that some of the artists were selling colourful paintings of the Parisian scenery and others were in front of their easels, drawing portraits of the tourists sat opposite them.

'Oooh, shall we get one?' My eyes widened. 'It'd be fun to have a portrait done!'

'It is better for you to have one by yourself, *non*?'

'Why? Are you too cool to have one? Is it too touristy for you?

'A little.' He smirked. 'And I think it is more typical for them to draw just one person.'

'Come on…' I squeezed his arm and gave him my best puppy dog eyes. '*Please*. It will be a nice souvenir.' I knew I'd taken some photos of us earlier, but I'd love a portrait of us together to remember this trip. Not that I could ever be in danger of forgetting it anytime this century, but you know.

'Okay. If it will make you happy, I will do it.'

'Yes!' I jumped in the air, then gave him a peck on the lips.

We walked around looking for an artist. Nico said it was important to watch them working first to see who was the best because apparently, some tourists ended up with portraits that looked nothing like them.

We found one we liked and agreed on a price. Whilst we waited for them to be free, I took in the surroundings. All four sides of the bustling square were lined with restaurants, cafés, bars, and shops which Nico said sold souvenirs and more art.

I went to take a closer look whilst Nico got us some hot chocolate. Eventually, we took a seat and let the artist get to work.

It was weird having to sit still without doing anything else. I was so used to scrolling through my phone, colouring, watching TV or doing *something*. I was itching to know how the portrait looked. It was like going to the hairdressers and not having a mirror to see the transformation.

At various intervals, people walked past to watch the artist work. A few gave me the thumbs up, which made me feel better.

The artist said something to Nico in French, which he then translated. The portrait was finished.

I jumped up, eager to take a look, and it was actually pretty cool. He'd captured lots of little details, like the shape of my curls. Of course, Nico looked stunning. The artist had drawn his beautiful dark brown eyes and chiselled jaw perfectly.

As the artist signed and dated the portrait, I looked at

the time on my phone. It had barely taken an hour. Much faster than I'd thought it'd be.

'Are you tired?'

'A little, but don't worry. I'm here to soak up everything you're ready to show me.'

'*Parfait*. There is somewhere else I would like to take you. It is not far. After that, we will go home. It has been a long day for you. I hope I can show you more of Paris this week.'

Soon we arrived at another square, which was right by the Abbesses Metro station. It looked familiar. Pretty sure I'd seen it on TV. I was about to ask Nico, but he led me into a garden, then pointed at a large wall which was covered in dark blue tiles with white writing and splashes of red. 'We call this the I Love You Wall because it has the words *I love you*, written three hundred and eleven times in two hundred and fifty languages. The red represents pieces of a broken heart.'

I hurried past the tourists and what were probably some Instagrammers or influencers filming and posing in front of the wall, eager to see if I could recognise some of the languages.

Languages weren't my forte, but I was confident I'd spotted something in German and maybe Italian. My eyes scanned the wall from left to right and from right to left until I eventually found it written in English.

'How do you say *I love you* in French?' I asked. As soon as the words slipped out of my mouth, I regretted it. 'Just out of curiosity, of course…'

Hearing those three words out loud stung. Over the years, they'd become increasingly difficult for me to say.

In my twenties, I'd found it easier, but the less I'd

heard it in return, the more nervous I'd become about voicing my feelings.

I remembered first saying it to a guy I'd dated for almost a year. When I'd declared my love for him, he'd looked at me like I was a little kitten, tilted his head and said, 'Awww, that's so sweet.' He'd broken up with me soon afterwards because he was concerned that things were getting *too serious*.

I'd also said it to another boyfriend, who'd looked so horrified you'd think I'd just threatened to chop his balls off.

And then there was my last relationship. Whenever I'd mentioned those three words, he'd just say 'that's nice' or 'thank you'. I mean, who says bloody *thank you* when someone declares their deepest feelings for you? Thinking about how weak I was made me cringe.

I pulled him up on it a few times. Especially towards what I later realised was the end of our relationship and whenever I asked him if he loved me (which in hindsight I know should have set alarm bells ringing—after all, you shouldn't have to ask), he'd say 'of course!' but he'd never actually said the words.

So yeah, after making a fool of myself so many times before, there was no way I'd be declaring my love for someone again. Clearly Nico was hot, kind, intelligent, funny and amazing in bed. And even though I always felt so light and happy whenever he was around, it didn't mean I was falling in love with him. I'd only been here for forty-eight hours, for goodness' sake. It was *way* too soon for that.

And even if I did fall in love with him by accident— which, just to clarify one last time, I would *not* because this was just temporary—there was no way I'd ever tell him how I felt. It'd only end in embarrassment and tears.

Nope. I was never making that mistake again.

'*Je t'aime*,' Nico said.

'Huh?' I pulled myself out of my thoughts.

'*Je t'aime*,' Nico repeated. 'It means *I love you* in French.'

My heart fluttered and I instantly commanded it to behave.

He's just answering your question. He's not actually saying that he loves you for real.

If my subconscious was a person, it'd be rolling its eyes so hard right now.

'It is here.' Nico pointed to the left-hand side of the wall. 'Do you see? Look close to the centre.'

I squinted and then I spotted it. 'Yeah, I see it now.'

'That is why in French we call this wall *Le mur des je t'aime*. You would like a picture?'

'Uh…' I hesitated. 'Yeah, okay.'

'Come.' Nico pulled his phone from his pocket, wrapped his arm around my waist, then held the phone up in the air. 'We take a photo together.'

After snapping away a few times, Nico showed me the screen. God, I loved how we looked together. Nico's eyes were so bright. I adored the little laughter lines he had in the corners. And that smile. I looked so happy too. My stomach flipped.

If only things could be different.

If only we lived in the same country and came from a similar background. Maybe we'd have a chance.

Oh well. It is what it is.

I reminded myself for the millionth time not to think

beyond next Sunday. We still had a week together, so I needed to stop wishing and hoping and just enjoy it.

Even though I didn't know what would happen after that, at least I could be sure of one thing. I would always have these photos, the portrait, and of course my memories. And no one could ever take those away from me.

CHAPTER TWENTY-TWO

Nico and I stepped through the front door and kicked off our shoes. My feet throbbed. We'd walked a *lot* today.

'So.' Nico took his phone from his pocket and rested it on the hallway table. 'What would you like to do now? You want to colour together?'

'I'd love to!' A minute ago, I'd thought about relaxing on the sofa to rest my achy limbs, but I could do that later. There was no way I wanted to miss the chance to do my favourite hobby with Nico.

'Come.' He took my hand, led me into the dining room, then opened a big solid oak cupboard.

'Wow!' I gasped. There were at least a dozen colouring books that had been carefully displayed like a showcase in an upmarket bookstore. 'You have so many!'

'I have more here.' He pointed to a large chest beside the cupboard. 'But these are, how do you say? My short-list. The ones I want to colour first. You choose.'

I didn't know where to start. There were books with

cities, animals, flowers, rural landscapes… Nico rolled his sleeves up to his elbows, took out a set of fresh colouring pencils, then pulled out a chair at the table for me.

'How about this one?' I held up a summer scenes book which had lovely illustrations of beaches and tropical resorts. 'It's a double-page spread, so we could do it together?'

'*Parfait!*'

We both sat down and got to work. I picked up a green pencil and started with a palm tree on the left-hand side. I coloured around the edges of the leaves first, as it always helped me stay in the lines much better.

As I readjusted myself in the chair, my knee brushed against Nico's and my body sparked. Rather than move it away, I left it right there. Heat radiated from his leg and I loved the sensation. It was like sinking into a warm bath after spending hours out in the cold. I could happily stay like this all night.

I glanced to my right and saw Nico deep in concentration. He was lost in the page, focused on shading some seashells. I knew the feeling. Normally I was exactly the same when I coloured. It was like the rest of the world didn't exist.

Except this evening, it was different. Nico was here. Right beside me. The room was silent, but I could hear him breathing. The rate and the rhythm were perfectly uniform and I found it incredibly soothing. So much so that I swear my breathing pattern began to fall in line with his.

My gaze shifted, first to his toned bare forearms, which had the most exquisite dusting of dark hair, then down to his big hand. I was almost hypnotised as I watched it move back and forth, building up the colour. You could tell he was a perfectionist. I loved his attention to detail.

After finishing the palm tree, I picked up a light blue pencil and made a start on the sea. I felt Nico's eyes on me. I looked up again and saw him smiling. As our eyes locked, his smile widened and my stomach fluttered. A giggle almost escaped my lips. I was like a lust-drunk teenager. All giddy and tingly. I wondered if Nico felt the same crackle of electricity? We held each other's gaze for a few more seconds, then returned to the page.

As I continued colouring the different shades of the sea, my shoulders loosened. When we'd first got back to the apartment, my limbs had been heavy. But now, warmth flooded my body and I felt so much lighter.

To some people, the perfect evening would be going out to dinner or somewhere extravagant. And although I'd probably enjoy that, to me, being here alone with Nico, doing something we both loved, together, was even better. *This* was pure bliss. Even without words, by just being in each other's company, I still felt connected. I wished every night could be like this.

I didn't know how much time had passed. It could've been one hour, two or more, but Nico had finished. He put his pencil on the table and exhaled. I looked at his side of the illustration.

'If I hadn't seen you do this from scratch, I would've thought that was coloured digitally. It's flawless!' I pushed my pencil to one side, then held up the book to admire his handiwork.

'And so is yours. You are very good, Cassie.' Nico stroked my arm gently. 'The colour and shading are *fantastique.*'

'Thanks.' My cheeks warmed with pride. I'd never met anyone who'd been interested in adult colouring books. In fact, almost everyone at work laughed whenever they saw me colouring during my breaks, so for Nico to compliment me meant a lot.

'I enjoy colour with you.'

'Me too,' I beamed. 'I'm almost finished, but maybe we can have something to eat and then do another one?'

'*Absolument, chérie.* I was just thinking the same thing.'

CHAPTER TWENTY-THREE

I shut the bedroom door and headed downstairs to join Nico for breakfast. When I got to the table, he wasn't there, but Fabien was pouring coffee into the bowls. I still couldn't get over the fact that they drank from bowls instead of mugs. And don't even get me started on the whole dunking bread in coffee thing.

'Nico is in the bathroom. I have not had the chance to speak to you. How was your weekend in Paris?'

'It was amazing. On Saturday we went to *La Tour Eiffel*,' I said, pleased I'd said it in French. I remembered reading it was good to make an effort with speaking the language. 'Then we saw *le Seine*.'

Fabien's eyes widened and he let out a little chuckle.

'*Pardon, excusez-moi*.' He shook his head. 'I do not mean to laugh.'

'Was it my accent?'

'No… it is just that you say it like *le sein* instead of *la Seine*. *Le sein* mean…' He looked at my chest nervously.

'It mean… the breast. So you say that you saw the breast, but I think you mean the river, *non*?'

'Yes!' I slapped my forehead. 'Sorry! Of course I meant the river!'

Although truth be told, it wasn't completely inaccurate. There *was* nudity under that blanket as we'd sailed down the river and a lot of naked breast action going on in the back seat of the car afterwards, but Fabien didn't need to know that.

'And then yesterday we did a lot of sightseeing. It was great!' I added.

'I am glad you like.' Fabien put a fresh set of napkins on the table. 'Did you see the article?'

'What article?'

He hurried out of the room and returned clutching a glossy magazine. 'This.' He placed it in front of me, then walked towards the door. 'I will leave you to read it with your breakfast. Enjoy.'

OMG.

A close-up of Nico's gorgeous face was all over the front cover with the headline:

Le célibataire milliardaire le plus éligible de France

Wow.

I had no idea what the headline said. *Célibataire* perhaps meant celebrity? *Milliardaire* maybe meant millionaire. It probably said: *the most eligible celebrity millionaire in France*? I reached for my phone and quickly typed the sentence into my translation app.

What? My stomach plummeted. *Célibataire* meant bachelor and—hold on. *Milliardaire* meant *billionaire*?

Nico was a *billionaire*? Bloody hell. Knowing that made me even more nervous about our future. Not that we had a future because the words *eligible bachelor* clearly meant that he was single. On the market. Totally up for grabs.

Judging by what I'd found on Google (of course I'd googled him—purely out of curiosity, of course) and what Lucien had so gleefully told me, Nico had dated a lot of high-profile women.

As much as I'd love to tell myself I was worthy and say he was lucky to have me, at the end of the day, I had to face facts. I was just a PA. A normal woman from South London earning a basic salary. And in my experience, men always wanted the brightest, shiniest woman on their arm. What could little old me offer some hot French billionaire?

When I'd thought he was a millionaire, that had been daunting enough. But a *billionaire*? FFS. That was on a whole different level.

I didn't know why I was so bothered. I'd known this was always going to be a fling, so *whatever*. When I was older I could look back and say that I'd once dated France's most eligible bachelor.

I turned to the contents to see where the main article was. After quickly flicking through the pages, I came to a massive spread on Nico. There were photos of him in a suit with the buttons of the shirt undone and the tie flung over his shoulder. He looked so hot. There was another photo of him looking more casual on a sofa and shots of him styling supermodels backstage at what looked like Paris Fashion Week. Although I had no idea what the article actually said, I could tell this was *huge*.

Nico strolled into the room and kissed me gently on the lips.

'*Ça va, chérie?*'

'Yeah, I'm good, I'm just looking at your article. This is bloody amazing!'

'*Merci.*' Nico winced a little and sat down beside me.

'Don't you like it?' I frowned.

'I did not know it would be like this—with my face on the cover.' The magazine knew *exactly* what they were doing. Nico looked like a model. His face was going to sell them a shitload of copies. 'I do not really like the attention, but it will be good for business.'

'I bet! I have no idea what this magazine is or what the article says, but I'm guessing it's positive, so your sales are going to rocket after this.'

'That would be nice. How is your breakfast?'

I was amazed at Nico's humility. He was on the front cover of what looked like a big magazine, but acted like he'd had a name check in a small local paper. He genuinely didn't seem fussed about the article and the enormity of it. If this was someone like Spencer, he would've ordered me to buy copies for everyone in the office and take out billboard ads to show off. But Nico? He was more interested in talking about my breakfast.

I desperately wanted to ask about the whole billionaire thing. I'd known he was loaded, but I hadn't realised he was crazy rich. Maybe he owned other companies or had loads of investments? Asking him outright how he earned his money would be crass, though.

And even though I knew I shouldn't, I wanted to talk about the whole bachelor thing. I mean, did he really consider himself completely single and ready to mingle? Were things between us really so temporary? I suspected the answer was yes, so it was best not to mention it. I'd promised I would just come here and enjoy my holiday in

Paris, so that's what I had to do. Push this article and all serious, heavy relationship thoughts out of my head.

'It's delicious. I'm surprised you're not the size of a house, getting to eat food like this every day.'

'Fabien does not cook this much normally. It is just because you are here. I want to make it special for you.'

'*Awww*, thanks.'

'I must go.' Nico kissed me again on the lips. 'Enjoy your sightseeing today. *À toute à l'heure.*'

CHAPTER TWENTY-FOUR

I put my feet up on the sofa and massaged them. Today I'd walked all along the Champs-Élysées.

There were a lot of cafés, restaurants and tourist shops. I couldn't resist popping into some of the chain stores that we had in London to see if they had the same stuff.

I also queued up to visit the Arc de Triomphe. As I climbed the steps, it was weird to think that I'd walked in the same footsteps as people like Napoleon and Winston Churchill.

When I got to the top, the views of the Champs-Élysées were spectacular. Of course I took lots of pics. In a way, it was a blessing that my phone had dropped down the toilet and Nico had been kind enough to get me a new one. There wouldn't have been enough space on my old mobile to fit all the photos I'd taken.

For lunch, I stopped off at a café and did some people watching whilst sipping a glass of wine and eating a delicious grilled cheese and ham sandwich (or I should say a *croque-monsieur*). *Très* French.

On the subject of the language stuff, apart from my *breast* screw-up this morning with Fabien—*cringe*—so far it hadn't been as bad as I'd feared. I still tried to make a bit of an effort, but I'd found that because I'd been in mainly tourist areas, most people spoke English.

I walked to a pretty bridge called Pont Alexandre too, which was close to the Champs-Élysées, and I *had* to take a selfie with the Eiffel Tower in the background.

As much as I'd enjoyed exploring Paris today, it was also a little bit lonely wandering the streets by myself. It wasn't what I'd imagined when I'd thought about coming here, but there was nothing I could do about it. At least Nico and I were in the same country, and we'd spent a lot of time together at the weekend. I just had to get used to the fact that for the rest of the week we'd only be able to see each other in the evenings.

I'd returned just before six, had a shower, chatted to Fabien for a bit whilst he chopped some veg for tonight's dinner, which he said was a surprise, and now was just chilling in the living room with a colouring book until Nico got home.

Just as I'd finished shading some flowers in a garden landscape, I heard Nico's voice. I jumped up and went out into the hallway to greet him.

'Hey! How was your day?' I kissed him on the lips.

'*Bien, et toi?*'

'Erm… you're asking how my day was?'

'*Exactement.*'

'It was good.' It was. Overall. I didn't want to make him feel bad by telling him how much I'd missed him.

'I want to hear all about it. I will take a shower and then join you.'

After Nico's shower, we had an *apéro*, which was like pre-dinner nibbles and drinks, whilst we shared stories about our day. Fabien then announced that dinner was about to be served.

'So, I think tonight we should have some fun with our food.' Nico pulled a black tie from his pocket.

'Oh yeah?' I raised my eyebrow. 'What kind of fun are you talking about?'

'I will put this over your eyes and feed you two delicious things and you must guess what it is.'

'Hmmm.' I paused. 'I'm not sure. For all I know, you could feed me kangaroo testicles!'

I had visions of all the disgusting things they ate on challenge TV shows like *I'm a Celebrity… Get Me Out of Here!*, where the contestants had to do bush tucker trials and eat fish eyes or a cockroach milkshake to win a prize.

'*Come on!*' Nico rolled his eyes. 'This is France. My country is known for gastronomy. Everything was cooked by Fabien. I promise it is delicious. I would not give you something that I would not eat myself. Trust me.'

'Okay…' My pulse raced.

Nico got up from the table and stood behind me. His fresh scent flooded my nostrils as he wrapped the tie around my head, then gently tied it at the back.

'Ready for the first dish?' Nico asked.

I nodded. I heard footsteps pad into the room, followed by the sound of plates being placed on the table.

'Open wide,' he said. That made me smirk, as the last time he'd asked me to do that I'd been spread-eagled on the bed, waiting for him to enter me.

He slid a fork into my mouth. I started chewing. It was soft and garlicky.

'It tastes like chicken.'

'You like?'

'Yeah. It's nice.'

'Okay. Take some water.' He handed me the glass and I took a sip. 'We will have the next dish now.'

He slid it into my mouth.

'This is… it tastes of butter and garlic. With herbs, like parsley. I think it's seafood or some sort of fish? No, maybe it's chicken? I'm not sure. But it's soft. Chewy and also slimy. Like mushrooms?'

'You like?'

'It's okay.'

'*Très bien*.' I heard Nico get up and then he untied the blindfold.

I squinted as my eyes readjusted to the light. I looked down at the table and gasped.

'What the hell! Are those snails? Did I just…? I thought you said I could trust you!'

'You can!'

'But you just tricked me into eating snails. They crawl on the ground and are all slimy. *Gross*.'

'They are not gross. *Escargots* are a French delicacy. And you like them, *non*? But I know that you would not try if I suggest it. It is good to try new things.'

'And what's the other thing on that plate?'

'*Grenouilles*—frogs' legs.'

'Shit!' I wanted to run to the bathroom and stick my fingers down my throat. Just the thought of eating little green things made me want to hurl.

Annoyingly, Nico was right. I wouldn't have tried them if I'd known what they were.

'*Pardon, excuse-moi*, Nicolas.' Fabien came into the

room. He was clutching his phone, and he wasn't wearing his normal bright smile. He spoke in French to Nico at a million miles an hour and I had no idea what he said.

'Go, now,' Nico said. 'We will be fine. Please let me know she is okay.'

'*Merci*.' Fabien's shoulders instantly relaxed. He nodded at me in acknowledgement, then left the room.

'Fabien's wife is not well. She is pregnant, so he is worried. I tell him to go home.'

'Of course,' I said. 'I didn't realise. I hope she'll be okay.'

'It is not serious, but I still think it is better that he stay with her. That is more important than cook for us.'

'Definitely. I can make something for the main course instead that doesn't involve slimy frogs or snails,' I chuckled.

'But you like it!'

'Maybe.' I smirked. I didn't want to give him the satisfaction.

'I will cook.'

'But you've been working all day!'

'It is fine. I would not suggest it if I do not want to do it. Come.' He took my hand and led me to the kitchen.

He commanded the room and music sounded from the speakers.

'You like soul music?' I said, recognising the Marvin Gaye track, 'I Heard It Through the Grapevine.'

'*Oui*. My mother used to play it. She like music.'

'Same!' I said.

'It is relaxing. I like to listen to music if I cook. And sometimes when I colour.'

'Yeah, Mum used to always have music playing in the

house. Especially when she made Sunday dinner. I usually helped her or just played in my room or in the garden if the weather was good.'

'You were lucky to have a garden.' Nico chopped the potatoes. It looked like Fabien had started, but had stopped part way. 'I used to always wish that I could have one. We lived in very tall flats. It was not very nice.'

'Oh,' I said. 'Sorry.' I didn't know what to say.

We hadn't had much money growing up either, but we'd always had a house with a garden. That was a life-line. It was a three-bedroom house, but with four kids, it meant I'd had to share a room with my two sisters. Nate, being the only boy and the eldest, had been given his own, and Mum and Dad had obviously had one to themselves.

'So how did you spend your free time? Playing video games in your room or reading?'

'Not reading...' His voice trailed off. 'And we do not have money for video games. I play football in the street with friends, I draw, or at home I play with bottle lid on the floor.'

'Bottle lids?'

'My father, he drink a lot of beer. There were many to play with.'

Sounded like his dad had a drinking problem. Maybe that was why they didn't get on.

'I've never played with bottle caps before. I think my brother used to, though. There was never much time after school for playing games. I had to do my homework.'

'I did not like homework. Or school.'

'Bet you must have been good at it, though,' I said. 'You were probably top of the class in maths and English.

Or, no, I mean French. That's why you're such a successful businessman now.'

'Not at all.' He shook his head.

Nico was just being modest again. I knew he was smart. I bet he was a straight-A student.

'One of my regrets in life is not doing better at school.' My voice dimmed. 'I only got a few qualifications and my grades were embarrassing.' I winced, thinking about the nauseous, sinking feeling I'd got when I'd seen my results. 'My elder sister, Floella, my brother, Nate, and my cousin, Bella, all did well with As and Bs, but I struggled just to get Cs and Ds.'

It wasn't that I hadn't tried. I really had, but I just wasn't good at it. I was terrible at exams too. Everything that was in my head just seemed to evaporate the moment that I sat down in the daunting school hall and the teacher thrust the test paper in front of me. I was convinced sometimes that the only thing I got right in exams was my name.

'School and exams are not everything,' Nico said quietly as he walked to the fridge.

'Yeah. I try and tell myself that, but who knows how much further I could've got in life and how much more I would've achieved by now if I'd done better at school? And although you're being all modest, I can guarantee that you did better than me.' I sighed. *Oh well*. Nothing I could do about it now.

'So tonight we will have steak frites.' Nico pulled a frying pan out of the cupboard and avoided eye contact.

Oh. Looked like the topic of our childhoods was shut down. *Again*. Whenever I raised it, Nico would close up.

Just like he had when we were having lunch at the Eiffel Tower.

I sensed a shift in his mood. His shoulders seemed heavier somehow and the expression on his face appeared strained.

I didn't know what I'd said, but I'd touched a nerve. There was something he wasn't telling me. Something painful.

It was a shame that he didn't feel comfortable about opening up to me. He trusted me with his credit card, but not with his emotions.

Sharing your innermost thoughts and feelings was something you did in a proper relationship. Not with someone you weren't serious with.

Hopefully Nico would open up when he felt a bit closer to me. When and if that would ever happen, was impossible to predict.

CHAPTER TWENTY-FIVE

I'd been sitting outside a café I'd found for about an hour and it'd been fun people watching, taking in the sights of passers-by walking their dogs and people going out for lunch.

I smiled at a woman who was holding a baby on her lap. The lady smiled back and I swear the baby girl did too. Looked like I'd just made two new French friends.

The waiter brought over my cup of coffee and rested it on the bistro table with my *chausson aux pommes*. Ever since Nico had introduced them to me on Sunday, I'd become addicted. I didn't know whether it was the rich pastry I loved the most or the sweet apple filling. Either way, they were definitely better than the apple turnovers we had back home. In fact, I'd order a few more to take back to the apartment and get an extra one for Maurice. He must get hungry waiting around in the car all day.

I glanced at my watch. It was almost three. I wasn't sure what I wanted to do next. I'd already been to Boulevard Haussmann before lunch to visit the two big department stores: Printemps and Galeries Lafayette. I hadn't bought anything, but it was worth visiting Galeries Lafayette just to see the gilded central foyer and breath-taking stained-glass domed roof.

I wondered what Nico was doing. I knew he'd said he was extra busy today with internal meetings. Although I was on holiday, it felt wrong that I was swanning around Paris whilst he was hard at work in the office.

I fished my phone out of my bag and called Nico. He always said he preferred calls to texts.

The phone rang several times and I was about to resign myself to the fact that he was too busy to answer when I heard background noise. There was a pause before he spoke.

'Everything okay?'

'Yep, all good. Just sitting outside a café. I was think-ing, can I help with something? You said you guys are really busy at the office, so maybe there's something I can do?'

'But you are on holiday, *chérie*. Do you not want to explore Paris?'

'Of course, but I've still got five days to do that. You showed me a lot over the weekend and I've been to a few places myself, so it's fine. I'd love to come to your office and see what you do or help out somehow.'

The phone line went silent. Maybe I'd been too forward. For all I knew, Nico liked to keep his personal and professional life separate. Visiting the office on Friday was different. That was an emergency.

'I am sorry,' said Nico. *I knew I shouldn't have suggested it.* 'Did you say you want to come to the office to see what I do for work?'

'Yeah…,' I said cautiously, trying to gauge his tone.

'You are serious?'

'Yes,' I repeated. 'If it's a problem, don't worry about it. Just forget I mentioned it.'

'*Non!*' His voice brightened. 'You just surprise me, that is all.'

'Why?'

'I never have a woman who want to do this. Most women prefer to spend my money, not see how I make it.'

Oh. So he liked the suggestion. *Phew.* My shoulders loosened.

'I can't speak for most women, but I'm genuinely interested. I want to get to know all of you. Not just the fun parts.'

'Okay!' I could hear the happiness in his voice. 'Come. We will have brainstorm this afternoon. Perhaps you can join us?'

That sounded so cool. I'd never done a brainstorming session in an office before. No one ever cared enough to listen to my ideas.

'I'd love that! See you soon.'

'Good afternoon, Cassie, how are you?' The receptionist at Nico's office greeted me with a smile. It was a different woman to the one that had been here on Friday, so I had no idea how she knew who I was, but it was nice to receive such a warm welcome.

'*Bonjour!*'

'Do you know the way to Mr Chevalier's office or

would you like me to call Miriam?' Her English was flaw-less too. Very impressive.

'I can find it, *merci*.'

I climbed the stairs. At first I went through the wrong set of doors, but I got it right the second time around when I saw Miriam at her desk. I looked into Nico's office. He was sat next to a woman with tousled shoulder-length blonde hair. She threw her head back with laughter.

Miriam looked up and caught my gaze.

'Nico is in a meeting, but he will finish soon. How was your welcome at reception?'

'Good! It was *très bien*. Better than Friday. What happened to the other receptionist?' Maybe it was her day off. *Can't say I missed her.*

'Nico tell her to leave.'

Shit. I wasn't expecting that.

'Because of me?'

I knew she was rude, but I felt bad about someone losing their job over me. Unless it was Spencer, of course. If Reg gave him the boot, I'd gladly throw Spencer a *delighted you're leaving* party.

'Nico expects a certain level of excellence for his busi-nesses and it is clear that she does not deliver that,' Miriam said diplomatically.

Damn.

'But I thought you couldn't fire people in France?' Couldn't remember where I'd heard this, so I wasn't sure if it was true.

'She is not here for long. I do not know how it happen, but Nico has good lawyers and with money, everything is possible…'

Nico and the woman both got up. When he saw that I was outside, he waved me into the office.

'Cassie, this is Lucy. She is a make-up artist that I use for our photoshoot.'

'Hi, I mean, *bonjour*!' I went to kiss her cheeks, then paused. I couldn't remember if it was left or right cheek first or how many I needed to do.

'Hello!' she said.

'You're English?' My eyes widened.

'Yes. I moved to Paris about six years ago.'

'Oh, wow.' I smiled. That was interesting.

'Anyway, I better run. It was nice to meet you. I know what it's like to be the English girl in a new city, so get my number from Miriam and message me if you need anything whilst you're here, okay?'

'Thanks!' I'd love to do that and hear more about her story.

Lucy dashed out of the room.

'She seems nice.'

'*Oui*,' said Nico.

'I was just speaking to Miriam about the receptionist that was here on Friday. Is it true that you fired her because of me?'

'It is business. A company is only as strong as the weakest link. If she is bad, it make everyone look bad. Her job is to make every visitor feel welcome and she did not do that. It is very simple.'

'Well, when you put it like that…'

It made sense. I'd just got used to nice Nico, not hard businessman Nico. But he was right—when you were running a big company, you had to make those decisions.

'Anyway, I want to ask you, do you know a website called OnTheDaily.co.uk?'

'Yes!' I said excitedly. 'It's one of my favourite sites. They do news stories, but also fashion and beauty and life-style stuff. Why?'

'They want to do interview with me. The PR agency say they are good and that they feature our products before, but this will be a profile article, so I want to ask you because it is a London website.'

'Awww, thanks.' I was flattered he was interested in my opinion. 'I say go for it. It's really popular. All my friends and everyone at work reads their articles. It's a reputable website. If you're on there, I reckon it'll be good for business.'

'Okay. I will tell them yes. I must make a call before the meeting. Miriam will take you to the room and I will be there soon, okay?'

'Course.'

I sat in the large white meeting room and watched several people file in and take their seats at the grand table. As they glared at me, then started chatting amongst them-selves, I began to question whether this was a good idea after all. I'd completely forgotten about the fact that I was in Paris at the HQ of a French company, so obviously this brainstorm was going to be conducted in French.

Now that I was here, I wondered what I'd actually be able to contribute to this session. Everyone was probably university-educated, with oodles of business and marketing experience, and here I was an English PA with zero experience in this industry. I'd been so focused on helping Nico that I hadn't thought this through properly.

As soon as Nico entered, the room fell silent and

everyone sat up straighter. It was clear it was a mark of respect rather than fear. It was as if God himself had graced them with his presence.

Nico sat at the head of the table and Lucien, who'd also just entered, quickly positioned himself in the seat nearest to him, opposite me. I smiled, but he looked at me like I was a giant cockroach that had crawled into his coffee. *Arsehole.*

'I will introduce you to everyone in a moment,' Nico whispered to me.

He launched into speaking French for a few minutes. I caught about every tenth word, but had no idea what he was saying. I think the word *article* was mentioned a few times. There were multiple copies spread out across the table. I could be wrong, but I think maybe they were talking about the positive impact it was having? That was just a guess, though, based around the fact that I'd heard the word *positif.* But it could've been a million other things.

'*Je vous présente Cassie,*' Nico said. I smiled, hoping it would conceal my nerves. Nico went around the table and told me the names of several people, all of which went in one ear and out the other. I was terrible at memorising names. Especially when I had to meet multiple people.

'Nice to meet you—I mean *enchantée,*' I added.

'So, today we will discuss the direction of the marketing campaign for the new cordless copper irons,' Nico said.

I was glad he'd reverted to speaking English and impressed that everyone seemed to understand him. That would never happen in my office. I could count on one hand the people I knew who spoke or understood another language at a standard that was high enough to sit in a meeting. I supposed that knowing that most of the world spoke English didn't give people much motivation to try.

'The PR and advertising agencies will present ideas next week,' Lucien said, 'but I think we should continue the discussions with Hélène.'

I frowned. Who the hell was Hélène?

'Hélène is a supermodel,' Lucien added, looking directly at me as he clicked a remote control and glanced up to the wall.

A huge screen illuminated and a close-up image of a stunning woman appeared. Well, he was right. She was gorgeous. Thick, dark, glossy, straight hair. She was flaw-less. And kind of intimidating.

'She is beautiful, *non*?' Lucien glared at me.

'Well, of course,' I replied. 'She's a supermodel after all, so…' It was a stupid question.

The whole room filled with excitement. There were choruses of *oui* and I listened as everyone cooed and gushed about how *belle* she was, which was to be expected.

'Well, that is settled.' Lucien beamed, sitting up proudly. 'I will tell the agency to set up a meeting with her agent.'

'Wait.' Nico held up his hand. 'What do you think, Cassie?'

'Me?' My eyes widened. He really wanted *my* opinion? I know the point of a brainstorm was to share ideas, but the majority had already spoken and they were on board with using a supermodel, so I was pretty sure they didn't need to hear my two cents. Especially seeing as I disagreed.

'*Oui*. I want your opinion.'

Uh-oh. If I'd felt uncomfortable before, right now it was like I was sitting in a hundred-degree sunshine wearing a Puffa jacket. He might *think* he wanted my opinion, but I had a feeling that if I shared my thoughts, they'd be about as popular as a politician outlining his manifestos at a relaxed dinner party.

The easy option would be to lie and just agree with everyone else, but that wouldn't be right. I had to be truthful. *Here goes nothing…*

'Well, I think obviously it's great to have stunningly beautiful women represent your brand, but personally, I don't buy into that whole celebrity or supermodel stuff.'

The gasps around the room were audible. Anyone would think I'd just run through the streets of Paris screaming about how much I hated croissants, baguettes, cheese and red wine.

'*Pourquoi?* Tell me why.'

'Well, it's kind of fake, isn't it…?' I glanced around the room and saw the looks of horror on everyone's faces.

'This is stupid,' snapped Lucien. 'All successful brands use celebrity endorsements. It is a marketing method that is successful for years.'

'Yes, I know. And I'm sure if another huge celeb started endorsing your products tomorrow, your sales would explode even more. But I also think these days, women relate to people who are more real. Y'know, less intimidating.'

Lucien looked at me like I had five heads.

'Maybe this is not the case for you, *Cassie*, but most women want to aspire. Everyone likes to look at something beautiful.' Lucien raised his eyebrow. He was being a twat again.

'Yes, yes, I understand that,' I added, wishing I hadn't opened my mouth, 'but surely the beauty needs to be attainable and realistic. I mean, this woman is flawless. I bet this Hélène already had beautiful hair. She was born with those good genes, so it's not like using this new iron is going to help me look like her, is it?' Lucien smirked as if to say I'd need a lot more than that. *Arsehole.* 'Wouldn't it be better to show how your products can make normal people enhance their natural beauty?'

'With respect, Cassie, *normal people* like *you* are not our target audience,' Lucien hissed.

'Lucien,' Nico said firmly, grinding his jaw.

'It's okay,' I interrupted. It was sweet of Nico to step in, but I could handle this myself. 'Why?' I folded my arms. I'd had enough of his crap. 'Because I'm not rich?' Lucien didn't confirm or deny, but his raised eyebrow said it all. 'I know Icon is all about high-end luxury and aspiration and I might not be your primary audience, but I reckon every luxury brand has a lot of normal customers. Plenty of women who aren't rich still buy or want to buy designer handbags and clothes, and I'm sure it must be similar for hair tools.'

'This is true.' Nico nodded in support. 'Many of our customers save money to buy our tools or ask for it as a gift.'

I wasn't surprised. Their straighteners and hairdryers cost hundreds of pounds. Easily three or four times more than the ones I'd had before Nico had kindly given me some of his tools to use.

'Exactly. I mean, take my hair. It's super curly and can get really frizzy. If I wanted to wear my hair straight for a change and was looking for new irons, I'd be more likely to buy your brand if I saw an ad with someone with hair like mine that I could relate to, rather than a flawless supermodel.'

'So now you suggest that we use women from the street instead of models?'

Heat flooded my cheeks. This guy was really pushing my buttons. Nico went to speak, but I jumped in again before he had a chance.

'I'm saying it would be good to incorporate some everyday women into your campaign. They could be clients from the salon that fit the brand, or maybe social media influencers would be good. Or just models that are more accessible—that more women can relate to.'

There. I'd said it. Dampness pooled under my arms. Damn. This brainstorming stuff was nerve-racking. Especially when you were put on the spot and going against the consensus. Nico's face remained neutral whilst Lucien glared at me, shaking his head.

'And what are your qualifications to make these statements?' Lucien snapped.

Ouch. My stomach plummeted. I knew I was out of my depth. Yet again I was reminded that I didn't belong here. In this room. I'd barely left school with basic qualifications, let alone anything to do with marketing. And I had the feeling that everyone in the room knew that. But I couldn't sit there and admit that.

'I was asked my opinion, so I gave it,' I fired back. 'I'm talking from a woman's perspective about what I know would appeal to me and my friends. Also, I reckon putting all the focus for your campaign on a model like Hélène reflects quite a narrow image of beauty, don't you think?'

Fuck it. If I was going to go down, I might as well go down fighting and get everything off my chest.

'What do you mean?' Lucien snapped.

'Well, why just have one face for the new irons? Why not have multiple women with different hair types? Your last campaign only had models with long, straight hair. But what about representing curly hair textures too—you know, women with hair like mine? I don't know how it is in France, but in the UK, the mixed-race population is one of the fastest-growing ethnic groups. I'm guessing it's pretty similar in other big countries like the US too, so I think it's important to reflect that by showing more diversity in your campaigns. Otherwise, you'll be ignoring a whole audience who could be interested in buying Icon's products.'

The room was so silent, you could hear a pin drop. For a second, I wondered if I'd gone too far. Overstepped the mark. But then I pushed those thoughts out of my head. It had to be said.

'*Oui*.' Nico nodded. 'Our tools should be something that every woman would wish to use. And it is true. In the beginning, when I manage the campaigns and choose the models, we have women with different textures and lengths. Straight, Afro, curly, short, long hair—everything. We also have a man.'

'That's right!' I perked up. 'I remember seeing those campaigns—I think it was a couple of years ago. It was what first caught my attention. It made me feel like it was a brand I could aspire to use. But it seems like recently the direction had changed.'

The silence returned. Something told me I'd hit a nerve. Based on what Nico said, he'd handed the responsibility for the last campaign to someone else—that was why things had changed. And from the way Lucien's nostrils flared, it didn't take a genius to work out who that was.

'Thank you, Cassie.' Nico nodded again. I remembered hearing that in brainstorms there weren't supposed to be any good or bad ideas, so I guessed he had to remain neutral.

Lucien scowled at me for the rest of the meeting. He was such an arse. I honestly didn't know how Nico could be friends with him. Maybe he had qualities that I didn't see. Nico had said he'd really supported him with the business, so I supposed there was that. He wasn't my cup of tea, though.

When the brainstorm ended, Nico said he had another meeting with his accountants and suggested that, rather than wait, it would be best to head home or see more of Paris.

I opted for going back to the apartment. After the intensity of that session, the idea of relaxing with my colouring books for a couple of hours sounded like just what I needed.

When I got downstairs and stepped out onto the pavement, Maurice was there waiting. It was so cool having a driver. I definitely didn't miss trekking on the tube in rush hour.

'Thank you again, Cassie, for the *chausson aux pommes*. I just eat it now,' said Maurice as he pulled out into the traffic.

'Pleasure! Did you like it?'

'Very much. It has been a long time since I have one. How was the brainstorm?'

'Um, it was okay. I'm not sure if everyone agreed with

my ideas, but I had to be truthful,' I said, picturing Lucien's scowling face.

'That is important.' He nodded. 'I like that you are genuine. Nicolas is the same. I can see that you have a good heart.'

'Thanks.' Considering we'd only known each other a few days, that was sweet of him to say.

'So how long have you known Nico?' I asked, readjusting myself on the leather seats. It had just started raining and the traffic was thick, so it looked like it would take us a while to get back.

'Four years. He cut my hair when I live on the street.' I hadn't realised Maurice had been homeless. I'd love to hear his story, but he might not be comfortable talking about it. Best to let him lead the conversation. 'Nico help me change my life.'

'That's amazing!'

'I used to have a job. At a factory. I live with my mother. But suddenly she become sick and she die.'

'God, I'm so sorry.'

'I was very close to my mother. So I grieve badly. I could not find the strength to work. So I lose my job and the landlord, he—how you say when they tell you that you must leave?'

'Evict?'

'*Oui*. He evict me. In two months, I lose everything. My mother, my home, my job and I end up on the street. I have no other family here, so it was difficult time. For years I struggle to find a job and to leave the street. But no one help me. Until I meet Nico. He help me find somewhere to live and a job. First as taxi driver. Then he introduce me to a chauffeur and ask him to train me. After, he offer me a job as his driver. I am very happy.'

'I can imagine.' I smiled. Wow. That was so kind of Nico. 'But I'm sure your hard work had a lot to do with you turning your life around too. Nico obviously saw something in you. He knew you had potential.'

'*Merci*. Nico is a good man. He also help Fabien and Odette. They also live on the street, but Nico give them both a new life.'

I didn't know if it was possible to adore Nico any more than I already did, but hearing this warmed my soul more than a bowl of hot chicken soup on a cold winter's night. What a kind and selfless human.

When I got back to Nico's apartment, Fabien was cooking. Although I didn't want to disturb him, I wanted to find out how his wife was, so I went into the kitchen to ask. Thankfully, she was okay.

As Fabien seemed to welcome having company, I sat and chatted with him for a while. I couldn't resist asking how long he'd known Nico too. Just like Maurice, he openly spoke about his life on the streets and how Nico had helped him.

He'd paid for Fabien to train as a chef and helped him get work in some top restaurants before hiring him. He even still provided accommodation for Fabien, his wife and young daughter. Now they also had a baby on the way, Nico was understanding when he needed time to go with his wife to doctor's appointments.

Nico also covered the cost of providing food for a homeless shelter and asked Fabien to take any food that wasn't used at home to those in need. So that was what Fabien had meant when I'd said I wouldn't be able to finish my breakfast and he'd said nothing would go to waste.

Wow. *This man*. Good looks and a heart of gold were a powerful combination. I'd told myself I couldn't fall for Nico, but something told me it was going to be a lot more challenging than I'd thought…

CHAPTER TWENTY-SIX

All finished.

I held up the illustration and admired my handiwork. I'd just finished colouring a Parisian sunrise from a book that I'd found in the dining room cupboard. Although I felt relaxed, colouring on my own wasn't as enjoyable as on Sunday night, when Nico and I had done it together.

There was a big illustration in my own colouring book that I'd love us to try. It was in my suitcase, which Miriam had said should arrive any day now, so hopefully I'd get time to do it with Nico before I left.

I'd noticed that although Nico had loads of colouring books and some hairdressing coffee table hardbacks, there weren't any other books. I'd never known anyone not to have at least a few novels around the house. Maybe they were stored away in another cupboard. It was probably part of the whole sleek minimalist design of this apartment. I knew he was into technology, so he might have a Kindle filled with ebooks.

The front door closed, then Nico walked into the living room.

'*Salut!*' He smiled.

'Hi!' I put the colouring book on the coffee table and got up to give him a hug. As I wrapped my arms around his muscular back, I wondered how it was possible for him to smell so fresh and delicious after he'd been at work all day. 'How are you? Did you get everything done at the office?'

'More or less. Would you like to join me on the terrace for *l'apéro*? We can watch the sunset and relax.'

'Love to!'

Nico went to the kitchen, and after a few minutes, he returned with two glasses of wine.

'If you take these outside, I will prepare some snacks.' I was surprised he was going to do it himself rather than just ask Fabien.

I stepped out onto the terrace. It was almost six, so the sky was already a pretty reddish-orange shade.

It was the first time I'd come out here to sit down properly and I instantly regretted not doing it more. The views were stunning. Even though the Eiffel Tower was in the distance, it still felt like I could reach out and touch it.

To me, this was just as good as the views I'd seen from Sacré-Coeur. Because it was a private space, it was more intimate. Plus, there was lots of lovely greenery—tall plants in cute colourful ceramic pots dotted around the edges of the terrace to create privacy and a canopy with pretty fairy lights. It was like a little oasis in the centre of Paris. Beautiful.

I rested the glasses on the teak-and-glass table, then sank into the plush outdoor sofa. It had a chaise longue, which was like lying on an actual bed, and several seats with huge, comfy grey cushions. Nothing like the hard plastic furniture I was used to sitting on in my parents' garden.

Nico approached, clutching a tray. There were small plates of different cheeses, some dried meat and olives. He put it next to the wine, then sat beside me.

'Thank you for today. This means a lot to me.'

'It was nothing.' I waved my hand. 'I hope I didn't overstep—you know, with my ideas.'

'Not at all. I like your ideas. They are refreshing. And you are right. I tell the team that we should have different looks in our campaigns. Like before.'

'Glad to hear it.' That was a relief. I'd thought I might have rocked the boat by disagreeing with Lucien. 'If you need any other thoughts from a normal woman, just shout!'

'Shout?' He frowned.

'Ah—just another English saying. It just means *let me know*.'

'I will. And you are definitely not normal.'

'Erm, excuse me?' I folded my arms in mock protest. 'Are you being rude again?'

'*Moi?*' Nico smirked. 'Of course not. I compliment you. What is normal? If normal means to be the same as everyone, then it is not something good. It is better to be unique, *non*?'

'Well, when you put it like that, I suppose.' Melody had said something similar when we'd gone out to dinner. 'I meant normal as in not rich, like your customers.'

'I understand. Anyway, no more talk about work. What

did you do after you leave the office? You see more of Paris?'

'No. I just came back to the apartment, chatted with Fabien, had a shower and then did some colouring. You have such a great selection of colouring books.'

'*Merci.*'

'Do you read too? I noticed there weren't any books in the apartment.'

Nico's face fell. I wondered if I'd said something wrong. 'I... I would like, but I prefer to colour. I am more visual.'

'I hear you. As you know, I love colouring, but Bella got me into reading again recently and it's pretty great too. You should try it! Maybe audiobooks might be better for you. You could listen to them in traffic or when you're doing the housework...'

My voice trailed off as I remembered that Nico didn't do chores. As if to serve as another reminder that we were from two different worlds, Fabien appeared on the terrace with the bottle of wine in case we needed a top-up.

After we watched the sunset, Nico and I chatted about the places I'd visited earlier, then we started dinner. Fabien had whipped up a boeuf bourguignon and it was absolutely amazing.

It was criminal to think that if Nico hadn't given him a chance, his talents in the kitchen would have stayed undiscovered. I thought about mentioning the fact that I knew what Nico had done for Fabien, Maurice and Odette, but decided against it. I knew how humble he was, so it might make him uncomfortable.

Fabien appeared on the terrace again before we'd finished eating to ask if we wanted dessert, but I was stuffed. He was going to take the plates away, but I still had a few forkfuls left and I couldn't waste something that tasted that good. I'd have a break and come back to it later. Fabien left, closing the patio doors behind him.

'You are cold?' Nico's face creased with concern. He must have seen me shiver. Up until now, the weather had been mild, but I was starting to feel the cold. I should've brought a blanket up.

'Yeah, a bit.'

He opened a drawer from underneath the table, pulled out a remote control, and pointed it towards the outdoor heaters, which burst into bright orange flames. Nico pressed another button and soft music played. I had no idea where the speakers were, though. Could be in the floor, built into the furniture, or maybe they were suspended from the sky. Seemed like anything was possible when you were a billionaire.

It was another Marvin Gaye song. I chuckled as I realised which one.

'*Seriously?*' I laughed. '"Sexual Healing"? That's a bit presumptuous, isn't it? Is this one of your moves? What's next on the playlist? That "Voulez-Vous Couchez Avec Moi?" Lady Marmalade song? Or "Let's Get It On"?'

'What?' Nico frowned, then threw his head back with laughter as he realised what I meant. '*Non*, not at all! It is just a coincidence. I promise you!' A devilish smile spread across his face as he pulled out two big blankets and passed one to me.

'Yeah, yeah.' I grinned. 'I believe you!' Truth was, I did. He'd mentioned before that he liked old soul and Motown music and he'd played Marvin Gaye the other night at dinner. Plus, Nico didn't need to use any *moves*.

At least not with me. I was willing and ready to *get it on* with him whenever he wanted.

I wrapped the blanket around me. It smelt like it had been washed, then scented with rose petals.

'You have room for me?'

'Of course!' I lifted up the blanket and Nico snuggled underneath.

'This is so cosy,' I said. I could already feel the warmth from the heaters, and having Nico's body right beside me also raised the temperature.

'You know that earlier I say that I like your ideas?'

'Yeah?'

'Well'—he turned to face me—'I also want to say that when I see you in the meeting and you are so passionate about sharing your opinions, even when Lucien try to challenge you, I find it very sexy.' Nico's eyes darkened.

'Yeah?' I raised my eyebrow. 'How sexy?'

'Very, *very* sexy.' He moved his face towards me and I felt his sweet warm breath on my neck. 'It make me have very bad thoughts.'

'Tell me more about these *thoughts…*' I shifted closer, my breasts pressing against his chest.

'If I did not have another meeting, I would like to take you on my desk.'

'*Mmm*. That would've been great.' I licked my lips as I pictured myself spread-eagled with Nico on top of me. 'Well, you're not the only one who's been having bad thoughts.'

'Tell me…'

'Well, I can't stop thinking about the boat. The feeling of being outside and having the cold air on my skin and knowing people might be watching…' I paused, wondering whether that made me sound a bit kinky.

By my standards, it did. Before meeting Nico, I'd been so vanilla. Rarely having sex in anything other than the missionary position. And always doing it on a bed. Never anywhere else in the house, never mind in the places Nico and I had got frisky since I'd been here. Just thinking about it made my body tingle. With him I lost all my inhibitions and was up for anything.

Well, not *anything*. I still had my limits. I wasn't up for going to an orgy. I had nothing against people who did, but I knew I wouldn't have the guts. It was just the idea of doing something a *little* bit naughty. Knowing that I was doing something slightly risqué gave me a thrill.

'I've also been thinking about when we came back from the river and had sex on the bed facing the window. Doing it and seeing Paris right in front of me was *hot*.'

'I see,' Nico said. I couldn't read the expression on his face or tell what he was thinking. Maybe he thought I was an exhibitionist nympho. I was just being honest, though. 'Well, if you like that, tonight we should do something better.' He moved closer. Our lips were now just inches apart.

'Better?'

'*Oui*. Why have sex and watch the views of Paris from the window when you can be part of the views?' Before I had a chance to respond, Nico crushed his mouth onto mine. A whimper escaped my lips. I couldn't help it. Every time he kissed me, it was like I'd been struck by lightning.

His mouth trailed across my neck, then his hands slipped under my jumper and another shot of electricity raced through me.

'*Mmm*,' Nico murmured as his hands touched the lace bodysuit I'd slipped into after my shower.

Watching Nico in the meeting room earlier—the way he sat at the head of the table, all strong and powerful with everyone hanging on his every word, plus the way he wanted to step in and defend me—was hot. And then hearing about all the things he'd done to help people like Maurice rebuild their lives was even hotter. I was hoping we'd get some sexy time tonight, so thought I'd be prepared and dress for the occasion.

Nico's hands travelled further up towards my chest. *Any minute now...* I smiled to myself.

'*Mon Dieu...*'

He'd found it. He lifted up my jumper, revealing the seductive slits in the fabric of the bodysuit. My solid nipples peeked through the gaps. I'd picked out some lingerie at a store I'd stumbled upon earlier, and after the fun we'd had with the crotchless knickers, I thought I'd use some of the cash Nico had given me to buy it.

Nico wasted no time in taking advantage, slowly sucking and licking my nipples like they were sweet lollipops.

I lay back across the sofa and Nico climbed on top. As he continued sucking, his hands moved downwards, underneath the band of my long skirt. He glanced up at me and his eyes widened as his hands reached between my legs. He'd found the poppers. *More easy access*. He popped the buttons open, then trailed his tongue from my nipples down along the fabric on my stomach.

Nico pushed my skirt up around my waist, then flipped up the top flap of the bodysuit's snap crotch to clear his path.

'Open your legs wider,' he commanded. 'I need to taste you.'

Suddenly I came to my senses.

'You want to... here?'

'*Oui*. You say you like the feeling of outside, *non*?'

I did but... maybe this was *too* risqué? There were buildings across the road. His neighbours might see. Then again, the plants and greenery did provide some level of privacy. But what about Fabien? There was a chance that he could return at any minute to collect the plates.

I paused.

Screw it. Adrenaline was already coursing through my veins. For all I knew, now that we'd finished dinner and didn't want dessert, Fabien might have left for the night. This trip was all about enjoying the experience and creating memories. And when was I ever going to get a chance to have a hot guy go down on me on a rooftop terrace?

Exactly.

'I want it.' I spread my legs, my body sparking with anticipation.

Within seconds, Nico had buried his head between my thighs. My hips jerked up and I gasped loudly. I swear that after a few flicks of his tongue against my clit I could've fallen apart right there and then, but I had to enjoy this. Savour the moment.

I opened my eyes and watched as he licked my opening, with the sights of the illuminated Eiffel Tower in front of me.

Before I'd arrived, I'd fantasised about doing it at the Eiffel Tower, but this was even better. I had the whole of Paris as my backdrop, my legs spread and the most eligible man in France with his head in between them. What a thrill. The sensation of Nico's teasing tongue over my hot, molten core and the cool air was a powerful combination.

When we'd got frisky on the boat, I thought my arousal levels were off the chart. But then there was the car journey, and after doing it doggy style in front of the window I thought I couldn't feel more turned on. But now, thanks to his talented tongue, my body was on fire.

'*Oui*,' I moaned. '*Encore…*'

I raked my hands through his hair, pushing his head deeper and deeper into me. I couldn't get enough of him.

Nico built the pressure and my clit continued pulsing as I felt his warm wet tongue circling me. Round and round and *oh, fuck…*

The intense sensations struck me like a thunderbolt.

I'd held out for as long as I could, but I couldn't any more.

'Oh God.' I lifted my hips off the sofa. 'I'm about to enjoy another *petite mort. Encore!* Don't stop!' I cried out. 'For God's sake, don't you fucking stop!'

My whole body vibrated like a washing machine on the most powerful spin cycle.

I felt the sensations from the tips of my toes all the way up through every inch of my body. I squeezed my eyes shut. My head felt fuzzy as the sensation of complete satisfaction engulfed me like a giant wave, crashing against the rocks.

'*Mon Dieu!*' I screamed, probably alerting the whole of Paris to the fact that I'd just experienced the most mind-blowing orgasm. My general French vocabulary was terrible, but thanks to Nico, I knew how to say the important words.

I opened my eyes slowly, my heart still racing. Nico lifted his head and licked his damp lips.

'You enjoy?'

'*Oui*,' I panted. He covered me with a blanket, then lay down beside me. 'If you give me a few minutes to recover, I'd like to return the favour.' I reached out and stroked him. He was rock-hard. I loved the fact that pleasing me turned him on too.

'I enjoy too.' He licked his lips again. 'And you like it outside?'

'Yes, it was amazing.'

'So perhaps you want to stay here? To enjoy *encore*?'

'*Oui, oui, oui!*'

Nico sat up, unbuttoned his shirt slowly, then tossed it onto the sofa, revealing his muscular chest. It glistened, illuminated by the fairy lights entwined in the greenery. It was bright enough to see him in his glory but dark enough to create a little mystery, and of course prevent his neighbours from getting a full show.

He unbuckled his trousers, slid them down past his ankles, then crawled under the blanket.

Mmm. Come to Mama. This man was sex on legs. I slid my hands across his bare chest. 'Won't you get cold with your shirt off?' Although I was enjoying full access, I didn't want fulfilling my fantasies to make him ill.

Nico didn't say a word. He reached for the remote control, still keeping eye contact, and pointed it towards the heater again. The flames fired up a notch and I felt the temperature rise once more.

I pulled him on top of me, then tugged at his boxers, pulling them down past his solid thighs. He sat up, causing the blanket to fall onto the floor, and I watched his rod spring free. It was standing to full attention and ready for action.

I raked my eyes up and down his toned body. Nico was completely naked on his rooftop, right in front of me. *Jesus Christ*. This was what fantasies were made of.

I pushed the table out of the way, then kneeled down on the blanket on the floor.

'Sit here,' I commanded, patting the sofa. Nico moved towards the edge. 'Your turn to open your legs.' He did as instructed immediately and I positioned myself between them.

I wrapped my hands around him, opened my mouth and slid his solid rod inside, slowly.

I looked up and Nico's eyes rolled with pleasure.

'*Mon Dieu*,' he gasped.

I licked him slowly from the base right the way up, savouring the warm salty taste at the tip. After wrapping my lips around him I pushed his length deeper into my mouth, bobbing my head up and down as Nico's hips jerked beneath me.

In the past, I hadn't been a huge fan of giving blowjobs, but knowing that I was turning him on made my body tingle and I wanted to do it even more. I could lick and suck on Nico's dick all day long.

As I picked up the pace, his breathing became ragged.

'Cassie,' Nico cried out, gently grabbing my hair. '*J'ai envie de toi*. I want to be inside you.'

'You already are...,' I mumbled, making eye contact again before sliding him out slowly. 'Sorry, I was always told never to speak with my mouth full.' A devilish grin spread across my face. 'Seriously, though, you don't want me to finish?'

'*Oui*…,' Nico said. I wasted no time in wrapping my mouth around his throbbing head once more. 'But, *oh*…,' he groaned, as if finding it difficult to speak. 'I want to come inside you. Like you say that night after we come back from the boat. You say you want to orgasm with sex. I want this too.'

I slid him out again. 'Okay.'

Nico reached for his trousers and pulled out his wallet and then a condom.

If he was going all out naked on the rooftop, then I'd shed some clothes too. I quickly whipped off my skirt, tossing it in the air, so I was just wearing the lace bodysuit.

It was risky. Fabien might come back at any second, but I was overcome with desire. The need to have Nico inside me overruled all other logical thoughts. I climbed back onto the sofa, this time across the chaise longue, then lay down, spreading my legs wide.

Nico positioned himself between my thighs, rubbing his length against me, back and forth.

'You want this?'

'Yes,' I panted.

'You are sure?' he said, teasing his tip at my entrance. This was too much. I wanted him so badly that if I had to wait a second longer, I might pass out.

'Yes! *Please*. Stop torturing me and fuck me already!'

Nico smirked, then slammed inside my burning hot, wet centre. A sharp cry escaped my lips.

Goddamn. My body had been on fire before when he'd gone down on me, but now it felt like I'd been dropped into a volcano. Every inch of my skin fizzed with heat.

'Welcome back.' I rocked beneath him.

'*Merci.*' Nico leant forward, taking my nipple in his mouth as he continued to pump in and out of me.

How was it possible that he could make me feel so good? Every thrust of his hips was like a shot of adrenaline charging through my bloodstream. I wanted more. I wanted him to do this to me forever.

I grabbed Nico's bum cheeks, pushing him further inside.

'You want to go on top?' Nico asked. 'You will get a better view.'

From where I was lying, the view of Nico's chest and his thick rod sliding in and out of me was pretty damn great.

'I can see you just fine.' I smirked.

'*Non*, I mean of Paris.'

I'd been so focused on the sensations that for a moment, I'd forgotten about the surroundings.

'Okay, quickly.' I didn't want to be without the glorious feeling of him filling me up for a second longer than necessary.

Nico quickly pulled out, then lay on his back. I made fast work of straddling him, then easing him back where he belonged.

That's better.

He was right. I gasped as I saw the glorious views of Paris lit up in front of me. I could see why they called it the City of Light.

Behind Nico, the Eiffel Tower and the stars sparkled. Was this really happening?

A gust of wind struck me and my nipples hardened. My bum cheeks also felt a bit of the chill, but I didn't care.

The heat our bodies were generating was enough to keep me warm.

I looked down at Nico, desire burning in his eyes, and started riding him like I was a jockey racing towards the Grand National finishing line, my body rising up and down in perfect sync with his hips beneath me.

Nico began circling my clit and I almost lost my mind. I dug my nails into his chest. I could feel the wave building again, like it always did whenever Nico and I made love.

Did I just say *love*? These sensations were messing with my head.

This was supposed to be just *sex*. We were just screwing. Having fun. I was almost butt naked on a rooftop terrace, being fucked. I was fulfilling a fantasy. That was all. It wasn't supposed to be *love*—yet, somehow, it felt like it.

No. I was getting carried away again.

The emotions I felt, the desire to kiss every inch of his body, to give myself to him fully and do this again and again until the end of time, were just fuelled by lust, pure and simple. It was just animal attraction.

Nico's warm fingers rubbed against me as I continued grinding my hips into him. Harder. Faster. Watching his dark eyes roll with pleasure and hearing his deep groans was so hot.

As his strokes became firmer, I knew that was it. My clit throbbed like a heavy bassline. I was coming. I gripped his shoulders, throwing my head back as the sensations flooded my bloodstream. It was like my soul was floating out of my body. Calling orgasms a *little death* was pretty accurate.

I was done, but Nico wasn't. As much as I wanted to just fall on top of him, I carried on rocking my hips. I wanted Nico to come apart, just like I had.

A guttural sound escaped his lips as he squeezed his eyes shut. Nico grabbed my bum cheeks, pushing himself deeper, then thrust once, twice, three times and a fourth before his body stilled.

Mission accomplished.

I collapsed on top of him. His heart raced, just like mine.

Our chests heaved against one another, slicked with sweat. Neither of us had the energy to speak. Our bodies had done all the talking.

From the corner of my eye, I saw the light flick on in the apartment opposite the terrace. A neighbour opened the window and stuck her head outside. I froze. There was no way she could see us, right?

She turned to the left, then the right, then closed the window again.

That was close.

I wanted to reach for the blanket, but I didn't have the energy. I needed a few more minutes.

'So.' Nico eventually broke the silence. 'That was incredible.'

'You took the words out my mouth.' Well, *incredible* was just one of probably at least a hundred adjectives I could've used.

Amazing, earth-shattering, mind-blowing, out-of-this-world…

There weren't enough words in the dictionary to describe it.

'Is better to be part of the view, *non*?'

'Yeah, definitely. As long as it's only us enjoying it. Your neighbour just opened the window and looked around. Probably heard noises and wondered where they came from.' A mischievous smile crept onto my lips.

'We are fine. No one can see us from here.' That was a relief. 'But perhaps we should get dressed, just in case.'

Nico rolled off the condom, wrapped it in a napkin, wiped himself, then pulled on his boxers and trousers. I dragged my jumper over my head, then got up to look for my skirt.

It wasn't on the sofa. I got up and looked at the side, but it was nowhere to be seen.

'That's strange.' I frowned.

'*Comment*?'

'I can't find my skirt.' And now that my heart rate and body temperature were returning to normal, I really needed it. Despite the heaters still being on, my bum cheeks could feel every gust of wind. Goose pimples were rapidly spreading across my skin.

Nico helped me look around, then I heard him laugh.

I glanced up and saw him leaning over the edge of the terrace.

'*Chérie*.' He grinned. 'I think I find your skirt…'

'Where?' I rushed over, the flaps of the bodysuit blowing in the wind. I quickly did up the buttons. Nico pointed.

OMG.

I looked down, and there it was. My skirt. Caught in the branches of the tree below us. I couldn't believe it.

In the throes of passion, I must have been so eager to get Nico inside of me that I'd tossed it with a little too much gusto…

Imagine if someone was walking along the pavement at that point and saw my skirt flying towards them? Or if a neighbour was staring out the window and saw it sailing down from the sky?

Cringe.

'It is funny, *non*?' Nico chuckled, pulling his shirt over his head.

That skirt had cost a fortune. And how was I going to get it down? I turned to face Nico, whose face was still lit up with amusement, and I couldn't help it. I burst out laughing too.

'Well, I suppose it could've been worse. Someone could've seen us, or I could've tossed a pair of knickers over the edge and it could've landed on someone's head, so yeah. We had a lucky escape!'

I crashed back on the sofa, wrapping the blanket around me, then looked over at the patio doors. I was pretty sure Fabien had closed them both when he left before, but now one was ajar.

Either the wind had blown it open or Fabien had come up for the plates and seen us when Nico was eating me out, or whilst I was giving him a BJ or riding him like a racehorse.

A flashback of when Fabien had been up here filled my head. Yep. He'd definitely closed the doors firmly when he'd left.

Shit.

I'd never be able to look him in the eye again.

CHAPTER TWENTY-SEVEN

Time for breakfast.

I'd deliberately waited until I heard Nico come back from his run before I went downstairs. I didn't fancy facing Fabien alone. God knows how much of our terrace performance he'd seen.

'Morning!' I entered the dining room, putting on my best *nothing to see here* face.

Where was Nico? He must be in the shower in the gym. *Yes.* There was even a shower room in there.

'Good morning, Cassie…' The corner of Fabien's mouth twitched and his eyes danced a little.

Yep. He saw us last night. Awkward.

Oh well. As tempting as the idea was, I couldn't hide under the table with embarrassment. I was sure he'd seen naked bottoms and breasts before. Not mine, admittedly, whilst I was mid-fucking, but hey. *It is what it is.*

'Morning, *chérie.*' Nico walked into the room, buttoning up a crisp white shirt, just as Fabien left to return to the kitchen. Nico kissed me on the cheek. *Mmm-mmm.*

A flashback of his mouth buried between my legs popped into my mind. Even if we'd unwittingly given Fabien a show last night, the morning-after awkwardness was worth it.

'How was your run?'

'*Bien*. Perhaps you would like to come one morning?'

'Ha!' I burst out laughing. 'I didn't realise you were a comedian too!'

'What?'

'Me? Get up and go for a run at six-thirty in the morning? Respect to you for doing that, but I'll pass.' I was *not* a morning person. Rising at seven to get ready for work was hard enough, never mind adding running to the equation.

'You should try. It will make you start the day with more energy. And today will be very long, so I will need it.'

'Oh really?' My heart sank at the prospect that I'd be alone again whilst Nico worked. He had warned me he'd be busy this week, so I knew I shouldn't be sad about it, but I just really enjoyed spending time with him.

'*Oui*. I have a lot of meetings and I know I say before that maybe we will go to the Louvre, but I just remember that this evening, there is an awards ceremony I must attend. You want to come with me?'

'Oh!' My eyes widened. 'Erm, yeah.' I paused, my brain whirring. I pictured myself arriving at some swanky awards with everyone looking glam and me looking like crap.

'What is wrong?'

'It's just that it sounds really posh and I don't have anything to wear, but it's okay, I'll work it out.'

A minute ago I'd been saying to myself how much I hated being away from Nico, so as scary as it sounded, I'd go. It was lovely of him to invite me. I'd just have to go shopping, again. I'd need to do something with my hair too. With the full-on day he had, it wouldn't be fair to ask Nico, but maybe someone in his salon could help me out.

'I'd love to come,' I added. 'Thanks for the invite.'

Nico reached in his pocket, pulled out his wallet, and handed his card to me.

'Go and buy a new dress, shoes, whatever you want. Remember what I tell you before: do not look at the price. If you like it, buy it.'

'I can't…'

'*Really?*' Nico rolled his eyes. 'You want that we do this song and dance again? *Mon Dieu!* I do not think I ever have to persuade someone to spend my money before,' he chuckled.

I smiled weakly, then my face fell. Maybe it was time I explained why I was reluctant to spend his money.

'I really appreciate your kindness and everything, it's just that I… I've had some bad experiences with men paying for things.' I winced. 'So I—that's why I find the whole money thing and you offering me your card a bit awkward.' I glanced down at the floor, then started fiddling with my sleeves.

I'd already used his card to buy clothes at the weekend, then again to buy that lingerie yesterday. Plus, he'd given me cash so I could go sightseeing, get lunch and a few other things. I couldn't ask for more.

Nico lifted my chin, then gazed into my eyes.

'I am sorry. I did not mean to offend you.'

'No, no.' I shook my head. 'You didn't. I know you were being nice.'

'Tell me what happened.'

'Just… stuff.' I waved my hands in the air dismissively. 'Mainly with my ex…' My voice trailed off. I wasn't sure if he'd want to hear about it.

'Tell me,' he repeated, gently stroking my arm.

'Well, it happened a few times, but for example, it was his mum's birthday and we were meeting his parents for lunch. I'd got her a posh body cream that I knew she liked, but when I arrived at his flat, he was still hungover in bed and hadn't even bought her a gift. Even though the cream was fancy, it wasn't enough for a joint present, so I said that whilst he showered, I'd go and buy something nice from him.'

'That was kind,' Nico said. I shrugged my shoulders. It wasn't a big deal.

'Anyway, he reluctantly gave me his credit card and I went to the shops. After carefully checking all the prices and thinking about what she'd like, I chose a bunch of lovely flowers and box of chocolates. But when he saw that the flowers cost twenty-five pounds and the chocolates were fifteen, he was angry and said I shouldn't have spent so much.'

'But that is not a lot. Especially if you have money like him, no?'

'Exactly! At first I thought he was joking. How could someone who splashed out crazy amounts at expensive restaurants complain about spending twenty-five quid on flowers for his own mother? But he was serious. He moaned about it for the whole journey. He made me feel like I'd taken thousands of pounds of his money and squandered it. And I never want to feel like that ever again.'

'Cassie.' Nico took my hand in his. 'I am sorry that he make you feel like this and I understand better now why you find it difficult to take my card, so thank you for explaining this to me. But I trust you. If I say you can buy whatever you want, I mean it. Okay?'

'Okay.' My shoulders loosened and I blew out a huge breath. 'If you insist. But don't come crying to me if I spot a dress that I love that's something crazy like a thousand euros and I buy it.'

'If you find a nice dress for a thousand euros, I will be very surprised. I am certain it will cost much more than that. And before you say anything, that is fine.'

'Message received loud and clear.' I did a mock salute. 'Listen, I know you're already being really generous with getting me a dress, but do you reckon anyone at your salon will be free to help me out with my hair? I can have a go at doing it myself using the products Miriam sent, but I…'

'I am offended.' Nico crossed his arms. 'You ask if someone from my team will do your hair, but you do not ask me?'

'You're too busy! You just said so yourself. I know you very rarely do hair for clients anymore because you're so focused on the business side of things. And I can't afford you.' I smirked.

'You are right. To do your hair, I will have to charge a *lot*.' He leant forward and stroked my cheek.

'Oh yeah?' I teased. 'How much are we talking?'

'Hmmm.' He moved closer, his eyes darkening. 'I think at least one hundred kisses.'

'One hundred?' Our faces were so close that I felt his

sweet breath tickling my chin. 'Oooh. I don't know about that. I'd like to negotiate.'

'Go on.'

'Call it one hundred and *fifty* kisses and we've got a deal.'

'Deal.'

Nico pushed his lips onto mine, and as our tongues collided, my whole body sparked. Even if I'd negotiated a thousand kisses, it wouldn't be enough.

The shrill ring of Nico's phone made us both jump. He glanced at the screen.

'Sorry. We will continue this later, yes?' He stood up.

'Most definitely.' My stomach fluttered at the prospect of locking lips with him again.

'So, I will message to let you know when I will come to do your hair. You take Lucy's number?'

'Yep. Miriam gave it to me.'

'*Bien*. Call and ask her to do your make-up here. And before you start to insist that you pay, forget it. I will go now before you try to change my mind.' He smiled.

The corner of my mouth twisted upwards. He knew me so well. I couldn't help it. I'd always been raised to be independent and not to expect handouts. It wasn't going to be easy to shake off that mindset in just a few days, and anyway, I wasn't sure I wanted to. I liked paying my own way. It was the right thing to do.

'Okay. Thank you.'

Nico gave me a quick peck on the lips, then was out the door.

So, *more* shopping was on the agenda today. This time I wasn't nervous about going to those posh stores. And I wasn't worried about finding something to wear. I knew *exactly* what I wanted. Yep, that stunning blue floor-length gown I'd seen before was about to become mine.

~

After breakfast, I'd gone to the designer shop, strutted through the doors and made a beeline for the dress. I'd tried it on and seriously, it was like it was made for me. The gorgeous material fitted perfectly.

Although Nico had said not to, I couldn't help looking at the price. As expected, it was eye-watering, but I pushed it out of my thoughts. For once, I was going to let someone treat me. I'd even forced myself to try the accessories the helpful sales lady had recommended. A glam clutch bag, a pair of sparkly heels, which looked stunning but felt like sliding my feet into a vice, and a pretty blue scarf that matched the dress.

Before I'd had a chance to change my mind, I'd said I'd take it all. When I'd walked back to the car, I'd seen the huge smile on Maurice's face.

'Very good, Cassie,' he'd said. Nico will be happy.'

Now I was back at the apartment, seated in a chair in Nico's home salon, waiting for him to arrive. It was just like a proper hairdressers'. There were two washbasins at one end of the room and three styling stations with black leather swivel chairs and big mirrors in front. There was also a shelf with several different trophies neatly lined up. It was so cool that I was about to have my hair done by a multi-award-winning hairdresser.

I wondered what he'd suggest with my hair? Recommend that I dye it blonde? Chop it off because my split ends were so bad? He'd definitely recommend I straighten it.

When I was growing up, the hairdressers I'd gone to often hadn't known how to handle my thick curls and they'd always insisted I'd be better off just getting it relaxed, which was basically chemical straightening. But as temperamental as it could be, I liked the texture of my hair. So I'd experimented with different products, styles, and hairdressers until I'd found what worked for me.

Thinking about it, though, maybe tonight would be a good time to wear my hair straight. I could ask Nico to use the Icon irons so I could be a kind of walking example of how good his tools were. It'd be a nice way to show my support.

'Sorry I take so long.' Nico burst through the door.

'No worries! I feel really bad that I'm taking you away from your work to do my hair.'

'Believe me, I am much happier to be here with you.' He leant down and kissed my cheek. 'So.' He pulled the black hairdressing gown that was hanging up off the wall and placed it over me. 'Do you have an idea of what you would like or are you happy for me to tell you what I recommend?'

'Um, well, I was thinking, maybe it would be good to wear it straight, to show how great your irons are at smoothing curly hair like mine?'

'Really?' Nico raised his eyebrow. 'That is kind of you to think of me, but I love your curls.' He ran his fingers through them gently. 'They are beautiful. They are part of you. I do not think we should change that. You have a fringe before?'

'No.' I shook my head.

'I think it will suit you. Frame your face, *non*? I would like to do this and perhaps take a little from the ends…'

'Is that hairdresser-speak for shaving all of my hair off?' I laughed.

I'd once had a hairdresser who'd said they'd take *a little off the ends* and ended up cutting about six inches. And I remembered when Melody had gone to get her shoulder-length hair trimmed and come out with a buzz cut. *Yikes*. I was only joking, though. I knew there were loads of talented hairdressers out there and Nico was definitely one of them.

'How did you guess?' Nico smirked. 'Of course not! And I will give you gloss—some colour to add extra shine. What do you think?'

'You're the expert. I trust you. Go for it!'

'*Bien*. And just for fun, I will cover the mirror.' He smirked, then draped a large black towel over it.

'What? Are you joking?' My thoughts turned to when we'd had our portraits done and how nerve-racking it had been not being able to see what the artist was drawing. But this wasn't a picture. This was my real hair.

'This time I am serious.' Nico commanded the room to play music, and soothing sounds vibrated around the room. No Marvin Gaye this time, but instead Stevie Wonder. 'Like you say a moment ago, just trust me.'

'Okay.' I nodded, feeling like I actually did. 'Work your magic!'

A couple of hours later, I was ready for the big reveal. It had been a weird experience. I was so used to being able to look in the mirror at the salon. To be able to see how much the hairdresser was taking off, watch their movements, their facial expressions—everything.

But this time, I was completely in the dark. I'd felt the colour being applied to my hair, seen my strands falling to the floor as Nico had chopped into my mane, yet I was waiting to see the results. I wasn't nervous, though. I trusted him. You didn't achieve his level of success, or cut hair for the rich and famous, if you didn't know what you were doing.

'*Et voilà!*' He whipped the towel from the mirror and…

Wow.

'Fuck!' I gasped. 'Ooops. Excuse my French. Bloody hell, Nico! I love it!' I blinked, then blinked again. I couldn't believe it was really me. I felt like I was on one of those makeover TV shows.

He was right. The fringe really did frame my face. The colour he'd added was like a reddish brown, and it made my hair look so shiny—like it had been sprinkled with diamonds. And the curls. How had he made them pop like that? It was as if he'd gone through every individual strand and twisted it into a perfect corkscrew.

'You are *good*.' I turned my head to the left, then to the right, admiring myself in the mirror. I couldn't stop grinning. 'I can see why they pay you the big bucks!' I said in a terrible American accent.

'So you like it, then.' Nico held a mirror behind my head so I could see the back.

'I don't like it, I bloody *love* it!'

'*Super!* Okay, *chérie*, I am sorry, but I must return to the office. I will be back in a couple of hours. When will Lucy arrive?'

I looked up at the clock on the wall.

'In about fifteen minutes.'

'*Parfait.* See you later.'

'Yep, and thank you again!' I jumped up and threw my arms around him. I was so happy. And so grateful that he'd taken time out to do my hair.

I had the perfect dress, glamorous hair, and now I was about to get my make-up done. Then I would go to a swanky ceremony with a gorgeous man. Melody was right. I really was living the fairy-tale life.

CHAPTER TWENTY-EIGHT

I stepped into my blue evening gown, then glanced in the mirror. *Wow.* I almost didn't recognise myself.

Lucy had done an outstanding job with my make-up. My eyeliner had a perfect flick at the edges and she'd given me a hint of blush and fiery red lips. Nico had touched up my hair too, so it was flawless. Sounded cheesy, but I felt like a princess. Nico might be the rich one, but right now *I* was the one who felt like a billion dollars.

My suitcase had arrived earlier, and when I'd opened it to check everything was there and all in one piece, I'd spotted the clothes that I'd bought for the trip. Although they were nice, they couldn't compare to what I was wearing tonight. This was the outfit of my dreams.

I sat down on the chaise longue in the dressing room and slid on the high heels. My toes pinched. I didn't think I'd last the night in these, so I'd bring my trainers. The dress was long, so hopefully nobody would notice if I slipped into them later. I needed Nico to zip me up at the back, but other than that I was ready to go.

Of course, I was nervous. I'd never been to an awards ceremony before. Never mind a fancy one in Paris. I was excited, but also kind of dreading it. The whole ceremony would be in French and there were bound to be lots of posh people, so I wouldn't fit in. Saying that, though, at least in this outfit, I looked the part.

Nico strolled into the dressing room and I melted. He was in a dark blue tailored suit that looked like it had been hand-stitched by fairies. He had a blue handkerchief in his pocket that matched my dress.

It was a shame we had to leave for the ceremony because I'd love him to take me right now.

'Cassie, wow. *Chérie*, you look *incroyable*. How do you feel?'

'Amazing! This is a little bit different to how I normally dress.' I smiled at the understatement of the century. 'But I love it. And I *adore* my hair. Thank you again.'

'No thank-you is necessary.' Nico zipped up the back of my dress. The sensation of his warm hands on my skin was like fireworks. 'You are ready?'

'Yep.'

'Let us go.' He held out his arm and I slid mine through his.

As we approached the car, Maurice's eyes popped out of his head.

'*Mademoiselle* Cassie, you look very beautiful this evening.'

'*Merci*,' I said as he opened the car door.

There was a lot of traffic, which gave Nico and me plenty of time to chat.

'So, what are these awards again?'

'It is to celebrate new business innovations in France. A few years ago, they give me an award for the technology we use in the Icon hair irons. And this year my company is one of the sponsors for the event.'

'Oh, cool.'

Nico went on to explain that the evening started with networking, then dinner, and after that the actual ceremony took place. This was going to be even more daunting than I'd thought.

Maurice pulled over and as I looked out the window, I froze. There was an actual red carpet. And photographers. Lots of them.

'You are ready?'

'Um, I didn't realise there'd be photographers?'

'*Oui*. Do not worry. Wait there.' Nico got out of the car, walked around to my side and opened the door. He held out his hand, and I gripped it with so much force I almost crushed it. My heart thudded. I was so nervous.

He led me to the red carpet.

Don't fall over. Don't trip. Focus. Focus.

The photographers clicked away and I was almost blinded by all the flashes. 'Nicolas! Nicolas!' they shouted.

'We will stop for a photo,' he whispered in my ear. 'Do not worry. Just relax and smile.'

Easier said than done.

We paused and I tried my best to steady my racing heart rate whilst the photographers snapped away. Nico gripped my hand tighter, which helped me to relax a little.

I needed all the help I could get. I was rubbish at taking photos. I never knew what to do with myself.

Which way was I supposed to stand? What should I do with my other arm? Put my hand on my hip and try and look cool or put it behind my back? And as for my head, should I turn it to the left or right? Angle my chin up or down? It was a bloody minefield.

'Come,' Nico said as he walked towards the entrance. Once we were through the doors, I breathed a sigh of relief.

We were directed to a grand hall where hundreds of people were gathered in small clusters around the room.

Nico smiled at various guests and to my surprise, rather than turning their noses up at me, they gave me nods of approval. My outfit clearly made them believe that I was part of their world.

It was funny. I'd always wanted to be judged for who I was as a person rather than how I looked. But I had to admit that dressing up like this made me feel more confident. I felt accepted.

But it was all superficial. I knew I was an impostor who'd been given a pass to wealthy-land for the night. If I'd done my own hair and make-up and worn a nice dress from a decent high street store, I bet they'd notice and treat me differently.

A waitress came over, clutching a tray of champagne. Nico took a couple of flutes and passed one to me.

I'd barely taken a sip before two tall stunning women came to greet him, kissing Nico on both cheeks.

Nico introduced them as models he'd worked with recently on a photoshoot. They babbled on in French and the only two words I managed to recognise were *article*, which I assumed meant article, and *magazine*, which, I was going to go out on a limb and guess meant—wait for it: *magazine*. I know, right? My French skills were off the charts. *Ha*. If only.

Thankfully, I spotted a friendly face in the crowd—Lucy. When she'd done my make-up earlier, she'd said that she hoped to make it tonight. *Thank God*. I waved and she came over.

'*Salut!*' She smiled. 'You look amazing!'

'Thanks! So do you.' She was wearing a little black dress with her hair slicked back and beautiful smoky eyes with nude lips.

'*Merci*. So, how are you?'

'I'm okay. No idea what they're saying, though,' I whispered, gesturing towards Nico and the women. Lucy fell silent, clearly listening in.

'They're gushing about the magazine article and saying how hot Nico looked.'

'So they're chatting him up?'

'It's probably just friendly flirting, although I wouldn't put it past them. Since that article came out, he's been the talk of Paris.'

It didn't surprise me. Nico was the human equivalent of a unicorn. Good looks, smart, kind and loaded. They probably thought it was worth trying their luck. It was so shameless for them to do it in front of me, though.

Deep breaths. Deep breaths.

Shortly afterwards, Nico broke away to greet Lucy before she headed off to re-join another client, then he suggested we go and find our table. We only ever walked a few steps before someone would come over and strike up a conversation.

Nico would politely introduce me, but then, under-standably, they'd converse in French. Although I didn't understand a word, I did my best to smile and look inter-ested, but really, I wished the ground would swallow me up. I felt so out of place.

Eventually, we reached the main hall, which was filled with circular tables all covered in crisp white tablecloths. Our table was right at the front of the stage, so we were in prime position.

Nico pulled out a chair beside him. A few moments later, Lucien arrived. He looked at me and frowned.

'Cassie… I did not realise you would be joining us…' He shot daggers at Nico.

Oh, here we go. He's got his arsehole levels turned up to max.

'Of course I would invite Cassie,' Nico said firmly.

'Nico and I have some business to discuss this evening, so perhaps it is better that you sit there.' He pointed to the only empty chair at the table, which was about five seats away from Nico.

'Seriously?' I raised my eyebrow.

'*Non*.' Nico rested his hand on top of mine. 'Cassie will be fine here next to me. I will speak to you later.'

Lucien huffed then stormed over to the seat.

Why did he have to be such a twat? It was like he wanted us to compete for Nico's attention. It was so unnecessary.

As the waiting staff brought out the meals, everyone at the table chatted amongst themselves. People kept coming over to talk to Nico and he couldn't translate everything. I felt so lost. Eventually a woman to my right started speaking to me. In French.

'*Pardon. Je suis anglaise*,' I said, trying to make my accent sound as authentic as possible.

'Ah, English,' she said. 'It is good that you try to speak in French.'

'*Merci.*' I was relieved to receive a compliment for making an effort.

'You enjoy the food? The dinner?'

'*Oui.*' I racked my brain. I was pretty sure I knew how to say I enjoyed it. Aha. Yes. Got it. '*Oui, j'ai joui!*' I said proudly.

The woman's eyes widened with horror. Lucien, who I'd noticed was now towering over me as he waited to talk to Nico, burst into laughter.

'*Pardon.*' I frowned. 'Did I say something wrong?'

'You just told the woman that you have an orgasm!' Lucien announced loudly.

'What?' I shouted. 'No! I said *j'ai joui*, which means I enjoyed!'

Nico excused himself from his conversation and turned to face me.

'*Chérie*,' he whispered. 'That can have different meaning. It can mean to *come*…'

But I thought orgasm was *petite mort*? Clearly there was another way to describe the big O…

I squeezed my eyes shut with horror. I couldn't believe I'd just told the woman I wanted to get my rocks off. Never mind *petite mort*, right now I was *mortified*. This was what I was afraid of. I knew I'd put my foot in it tonight.

'*Pardon, madame.*' I winced. 'I wanted to say I liked the food…'

She scowled, then turned to speak to someone else.

Crikey. How was I supposed to know?

'Do not worry.' Nico squeezed my hand.

'Nico, I need to speak to you,' Lucien snapped.

'I will be back soon, okay?' He got up from the table.

Oh crap. Now I was going to be here alone.

After playing with the tablecloth and scrolling on my phone, I got up. Going to the toilets would help to kill some time. Then hopefully when I returned, Nico would've come back.

As I left the loos, I spotted him pacing up and down the corridor.

'You okay?'

Nico looked up, his thick brows knitted together.

'*Oui*.'

'Come on.' I rubbed his shoulder. I wasn't buying it for a second. Nico always looked so bright and happy. But his shoulders were slumped and his face was crumpled. 'You can tell me.'

He opened his mouth, then closed it again, as if debating whether to open up or not.

'It is nothing. Lucien just tell me that the organiser want that I present a big award.'

'That's great!' I beamed. 'Isn't it? I mean, good exposure for you, as the face of the company?'

'*Oui*, but I must… they want me to read the screen. I do not like this.'

That surprised me. Nico was always so confident. He commanded the room whenever he walked in. He'd even told me he'd performed at hair shows on stage in front of thousands of people, so I'd never have imagined that he'd get worried about giving out an award.

'I'm sure you'll do great!' I added.

'*Merci*, but you do not understand. This will be a problem for me.'

'It's normal to have stage fright sometimes. But if you don't feel like doing it, you're the boss, so ask someone else to. Or get Lucien to go up with you.'

'I already ask that Lucien do it and they say no, which make him angry, but if I am there too, perhaps they will agree.'

'Exactly. They'll get two for the price of one!' I bet Lucien was pissed because he wanted all of the spotlight to himself. He struck me as that kind of guy. As much as I tried, I really didn't like him.

'I will go and speak with them now.' Nico's shoulders relaxed. 'You are okay?'

'Yeah, yeah, I'm fine.' I waved my hands in the air. 'Don't worry about me. Go and do your thing. You'll be great!'

As I headed back to the hall, my feet pinched. I'd tried my best in these heels, but my toes were on fire. I quickly dashed to the entrance and called Maurice to see if I could get my trainers from the car.

Within minutes he'd stepped inside with a bag. I hid around a corner, loosened the colourful laces and slid my feet inside the soft white leather. *Ah. That's better.* The insoles felt like cushions.

My dress covered the trainers perfectly, so no one would be any the wiser. I thanked Maurice as he took my heels and returned to the car.

I wandered back to my table and spotted Lucy. She waved me over to join her.

'How are you coping with the French?'

'Not so well.' I winced. 'I just told a lady I wanted to

orgasm.'

Lucy bent over in a fit of laughter.

'Don't we all, eh?' She threw her head back.

'Yes, but telling a complete stranger that at a posh event probably wasn't the best idea.'

'Is Nico at your table now?'

'No, he's getting ready to go on stage and present an award.'

'Let me come and sit with you, then, until he comes back. I can be your personal translator. And save you from any more faux pas at the table.'

'You don't mind?'

'Not at all. I feel for you. I remember what it was like when I first came to Paris. I bet my French was even worse than yours.'

'Impossible, but thanks for saying that anyway.'

We headed back to the table. The woman from earlier gave me another dirty look. *Seriously?* It was a genuine mistake.

Soon after, the awards started. A glamorous-looking woman came on the stage and started talking.

'She's introducing Nico,' said Lucy. 'She's talking about his article and saying that everyone must have seen it and what a pleasure it is to have Paris's most eligible bachelor here to present the award in person.'

Hearing the word *bachelor* was another stab in my heart. It reminded me that my time with Nico was borrowed. It warned me not to get too attached, because what we had wasn't serious.

Bachelor told the world that he was still single. That he was available, up for grabs. He wasn't mine. I only had him until he moved on to the next woman. I tried to push the thoughts out of my mind.

Nico came on stage with Lucien. I understood him saying good evening to the audience. He then faced Lucien and introduced him. Lucien beamed. His face had looked sour a moment ago when the woman on stage hadn't given him a name check. That was typical of Nico to make sure that Lucien felt included and important. He did that with everyone he met.

Nico looked at the autocue screen.

'He says we are here tonight…' Lucy paused.

Nico was reading very slowly and got a few words mixed up. He was squinting at the screen too. I could tell he was nervous, which was so unlike him. He attempted again.

'…to present…' Lucy paused again.

Nico looked away from the screen and directly at the audience.

'He's just apologised and said they're here to present an award and asked Lucien to do the honours because he's forgotten his glasses and can't read the screen clearly.'

Glasses? I didn't know Nico wore glasses.

'Now Lucien's saying that Nico doesn't wear glasses… that's weird,' said Lucy. 'Why would he say he does if he doesn't?'

Nico looked increasingly uncomfortable and started fidgeting. My heart crumbled. He was really crashing up there. I wished I could run onto the stage and help. Lucien should jump in and save him, but instead he was standing there, smirking.

Lucien said something else and the audience laughed.

'Why are they laughing?' I frowned.

'Lucien's just joked that he'll just let Paris's most eligible bachelor stand and look pretty whilst he does the important work,' said Lucy. 'Ouch! That's a bit bitchy.'

What the hell? I wasn't a fan of Lucien before, but I *definitely* couldn't stand him now. When Nico had got a bit tongue-tied, he'd taken the piss out of him rather than helping out the person that was supposed to be his best friend. *Not cool.*

I watched as Lucien went on to read the text on the autocue and then open the envelope to announce the winner's name.

Nico very graciously handed over the award to the winner, then mopped his damp forehead with the handkerchief, but I could tell from his hunched shoulders that he couldn't wait to get off the stage and crawl into a dark hole. I instantly wanted to run and throw my arms around him and tell him everything was going to be okay.

'Sorry, Lucy, I'm not sure what just happened up there, but I'm going to go and see if Nico's okay.'

'Course. I hope he's alright.'

'Thanks again for the make-up and for helping with the translation.'

'*De rien!*' she replied.

I got up from the table and rushed out of the hall. I looked around to see where I could get access backstage. Just as I turned around I saw Nico and Lucien push through the double doors, arguing. Nico was waving his hands in the air angrily and Lucien was just standing there, with the corners of his mouth twitching. I ran over.

'Nico, are you okay? What happened?'

'Come,' he snapped. 'We are leaving.'

'You cannot leave!' Lucien shouted.

'*Va te faire foutre! Enfoiré!*' Nico hissed at Lucien as he took my hand and led me out towards the doors.

I couldn't be sure, but I thought Nico had just told Lucien to fuck off. Wow. I'd never seen him so furious. Something had happened on stage that was more than just stage fright. Worse still, from what I could gather, rather than help him, Lucien had thrown Nico under the bus in front of everyone. And now we were alone, I was hoping that he'd open up and tell me why.

CHAPTER TWENTY-NINE

'Ready to talk?'

We'd spent the whole car journey home in silence. As soon as we'd both slid into the back seat and I'd tried to talk to Nico, he'd shut down. He'd said he was upset and didn't want to speak about it. So we'd travelled in the lift without saying a word. Now we'd just stepped inside the apartment, Nico tossed his jacket on the sofa, then lay down.

I didn't know what to do. I'd never seen him like this before. Perhaps I should just respect that he didn't want to talk and leave him alone. But I could see he was hurting and I wanted to make it better. Something inside me said I needed to try and help.

I went into the kitchen and opened the cupboard, plucking the packets of chocolate Hobnobs and custard creams that I'd brought over from London off the middle shelf. After I'd checked that my purse and valuables were there, they were the first thing I'd taken out of the suitcase when it had arrived earlier.

Once I filled it with water, I put the kettle on. Fabien said he'd got some English teabags, so they had to be here somewhere. I went from one cupboard to the next until I finally found them.

Whenever there was a problem, I remembered my gran, Dad's mum, always said a cup of tea and a biscuit would help make it better. It was a British tradition. Anyone who'd ever watched TV soaps like *Coronation Street* or *Eastenders* knew that was true. It was a long shot, but I had to try something.

I poured the steaming water into two bowls (yep, still no mugs in this apartment), along with some milk and sugar, popped a pile of biscuits on a plate and carried it in to Nico.

'I know you're not big on drinking it in France, but this is the equivalent of British medicine. A cup of tea is the cure for everything. Personally, I think most of the joy probably comes from the biscuits, but you know, there's sugar in the tea too, so that's got to help.'

Nico turned his head and the corner of his mouth twitched.

'They are the biscuits I eat at Christmas?'

'Yep. I brought them all the way from London, just for you. And if you refuse them, then you know I'm going to have to call you a rude dickhead again and you don't want that.'

The corner of his mouth twitched again.

'Okay, *Mademoiselle Fraise*. I will eat one.'

Nico sat up, swung his feet to the floor, leant forward and took a bite of the biscuit I held in my hand.

As he ate it, his eyes closed with pleasure.

'Better?'

'*Oui.*'

'Told you!' I grinned. 'Now for some tea.' I passed him the bowl. Nico took a sip, then spat it out.

'*Dégueulasse!* That is *not* good.'

'What?' I folded my arms. 'Saying stuff like that will get you arrested in the UK. That's our national drink.'

'I feel very sorry for you. This is worse than the hot wine with fruit you drink for Christmas.' He smirked.

'It's nice to see you smile again.' I sat beside him and rested my hand on his. 'Do you want to tell me what happened earlier?' I softened my voice. 'I wasn't sure if it was stage fright, because I know you've been on stage in front of big crowds before, you know, cutting hair and stuff, and you're such a confident guy. But I suppose stage fright can happen to anyone at any time. Or could you not see the words on the autocue because you didn't have glasses? I didn't know you wore them, but—'

'I do not wear glasses,' Nico interrupted. 'I just say that because... because I am embarrassed.'

'Embarrassed?' I squeezed his hand. 'Why?'

'I...' He avoided my gaze, then looked down at his hands. 'Because I am not good at reading things. I have, how do you say in English? Dyslexia.'

Oh.

I scanned my brain, searching for clues or signs. Maybe that was why there were no books in the apartment? Perhaps that was also why he preferred phone calls and voice notes instead of texts?

Yeah, on the few occasions that he'd texted, there had been spelling mistakes, but I'd thought nothing of it because of the language barrier. I wouldn't even be able to string a sentence together verbally in French, let alone *write* something. And everyone made mistakes when texting. Especially when they were busy like Nico. Nope. I hadn't noticed any signs at all.

'I didn't realise. No wonder you didn't want to go on stage and read out loud in front of everyone. And Lucien knows?'

'*Oui.*' Nico nodded.

'He's out of order!' I snapped. 'He should've read everything. How could he just throw you under the bus like that? That's a total piss-take!'

'Throw me under bus? And what is out of order? I do not understand.'

'Oh God, sorry. *Out of order* means that basically, he's an arsehole. And throwing you under the bus is like throwing you to the wolves—making you suffer deliberately. He took the piss. He's supposed to be your friend.'

'That is why I am angry with him. I know sometimes he like to make joke. We often, I think you call it *banter* in English, *non*? Normally he always helps me and this was not the time to make fun. I think he is upset because they say that they want me to present the award.'

Jealous prick. It wasn't as if Nico had even wanted to go on stage. He had the patience of a saint, though. If my friend had screwed me over like that, I'd be fuming. That was probably why he'd decided to leave. Nico had looked like he wanted to punch Lucien, and having a fist fight in the middle of the awards ceremony wouldn't have gone down well.

'That's no excuse.'

'*Oui.* I will talk to him tomorrow. When I am calmer.'

'So.' I looked up into his eyes, trying to gauge whether

he was ready to open up more. 'Did you always know you were dyslexic?'

'*Non*. When I was at school, it was not something that people talk about. The teachers, they just think I am fool.'

'Oh, Nico.' I stroked his shoulder. 'That must have been awful.'

'It was difficult.' He nodded. 'Every day, I look at the board in the room and did not understand anything. Nothing make sense. So I think they must be right. My teacher tell me that I am useless and I will never do anything good with my life. She say nobody can help me. She throw the—how do you call the thing that delete things from the board?'

'Blackboard rubber?' I frowned, trying to remember the word.

'*Oui*. Every time I make mistake, she throw this at me. I begin to hate school. It make me feel bad. I pretend to be sick when I have exam so I do not have to go.'

Now I understood why he'd changed the subject on Monday night when we'd spoken about school. There I was harping on about the fact that he must have been brilliant at languages and maths. If I'd known, I wouldn't have mentioned it.

'And your parents? Didn't they help?'

'*Non*. My father, he always call me stupid. My mother, she try sometimes, but she did not understand. Finally, I spend as little time at school as possible. Especially when I discover hairdressing.' Nico's face brightened.

'Yeah, how did you get into it?'

'There was a girl… Élisabeth.' He smiled. 'Her mother have a salon and she work there. So one Saturday I go to see the girl. But she was not there. Her mother think I have come for the job, to wash hair. I have done hair for my sister when she was little and I need money and realise that if I work at the salon, I will get to spend more time with the girl, *non*?'

'Smart thinking!' I smiled.

'So I say, okay, I am interested in the job. It is Saturday and Mathilde—her mother—she is very busy. She say she need me to start now. So I work the whole day and I like. I see that when the customer arrive, they look sad. But when they are in the salon, they talk, they laugh, the hairdresser cut their hair and they become a new woman. They leave and they are happy. More confident. I think, *wow*. Hairdresser can create magic! They make people happy. I want to do that. So I ask if she will teach me.'

'That's really cool. And did you find it difficult at first?'

'Not really. Of course, like everything it is a challenge. To be a hairdresser is not easy. Some people think it is something you do if you are not smart, but that is not true. You need to work hard to learn about hair and to cut and colour is a skill that need a lot of practice and study. But when I am in the salon, I start to feel like I am good at something. Mathilde, she push me, but she is kind. And when I do something good, she tell me. You understand how that make me feel? My whole life, everyone say that I am stupid and one day someone I respect say I am good? That I have talent?'

'That must have felt bloody amazing!'

'*Exactement*. So I continue to work there. I spend all the time I can on hair. And when I finish school, I decide I must go to Paris.'

'How old were you then?'

'Sixteen.'

'Sixteen! Weren't you scared? Where did you live? Did you have a job?'

'I *think* I have a job. But when I arrive, they tell me it has gone. At first I was not worried. I have saved money from my job at the salon. But soon the money finish and I cannot afford to pay the hostel. I have two choices: go home or live on the street until I can find a job.'

'So what did you do?'

'I live on the street. I did not want to go home. I need to stay and follow my dream.'

So much started to make sense. That must be one of the reasons why Nico was so keen to help the homeless. Because he'd lived on the streets himself and had first-hand experience of what it was like.

'That must have been tough.'

'*Oui*, but I know if I go home, my father will say he tell me that I was stupid to go to Paris and that hairdresser is job for woman, not man. My father is poison. To go back would be bad for my mental health. So I stay. Many people I meet live on the street for years. They do not have a home to go to at all. But I am lucky. It take only two weeks to find a job. Eventually I go to work at a very nice salon and the owner teach me a lot. We are still friends today.'

'So Mathilde and that boss changed your life.'

'*Absolument*. Without them, today I would not become a success. They show me that there is different type of intelligence. There is a saying: *if you judge a fish by how it can climb a tree, it will always believe that it is stupid*. Just because you are not good at maths or science or language at school, this does not mean that you are fool. It does not mean that you do not have value.'

'That's so true.'

Maybe I should remind myself of that more often. I beat myself up far too much about my academic ability.

'It was only when I start my salon that I discover I have dyslexia. I have to become more involved in business and send more emails and I always make mistakes. Miriam has a friend who does tests for these things. So I go and see her and that is when I find out.'

'Oh wow. So you went through all of your childhood and most of your adult life not knowing why you found things difficult?'

'*Exactement*. I just always think it is because I am stupid. But when the woman explain to me, everything make sense.'

'That must've been such a relief.'

'Yes.'

'Well, I think it's amazing that you've built up such a successful business.'

'My dyslexia make it more challenging, for sure. I am lucky. I surround myself with good people. Miriam help me a lot. She suggest the name Icon for the company. It is Nico with the letters mixed around. Like I do sometimes when I try to write words.'

'Oh yeah! I hadn't noticed that! It's such a great name.'

'*Merci*. Yes, she has good ideas and she always help if I do not understand something. And if I must write some-thing, I can just speak and tell her what I would like to say and she will write it for me. And Lucien. Despite what happen tonight, he help me too.'

And so he bloody should. I was still fuming about what he'd done at the awards ceremony.

'How does he help?'

'With important documents. He check them for me.'

'Like the other night?' I said, remembering when he'd brought something for Nico to sign on my first evening here.

'*Oui.*'

'So you sign the documents if he says they're okay? Don't you ever worry that what he's asking you to sign isn't legit?' I thought about how quickly Nico had scanned the paperwork that evening before adding his signature to the page.

'If it is very important, then I will of course check, but if not, I trust him to take care of it.'

I wished I could be so trusting. Then again, Nate was forever telling us how everyone was out to get us, so I was more paranoid than the average person.

'I know he's your friend, but just be careful with him… sorry.' I shook my head. There I went, sticking my nose in where it wasn't wanted. What did I know? Nico had done just fine without my input. It wasn't my place to give him unsolicited advice. 'I'm sure you know what you're doing. Anyway, I'm glad that you've found a way to manage your dyslexia.'

'Now I am more kind to myself. I believe that everyone is good at something. I am not good at read or write, but I am creative. I am good with my hands. I am good with hair. I am good with people. I give them confidence and make them happy. And I make a good career from this.'

'That's the understatement of the century!' I smiled.

'But why do you hide it? Your dyslexia? You're a *huge* success. You've definitely proved those haters wrong, so why don't you talk about it?'

'I do not know.' Nico shrugged his shoulders. 'You may look at me and believe that I am confident. And I am. Most of the time. But sometimes, when I am in big meetings, I feel like I am impostor. That I do not belong. Remember, I did not go to business school. My passion is hair and to create good products, not business. So even with my success, I am still learning these things.'

'I think everyone is a work in progress,' I said. I was surprised to hear that he felt like he didn't belong. I felt like that every day.

'*Exactement*. I suppose I still believe that if people find out, they will think less of me. I am afraid that if I make a mistake, they will say it is because I am stupid. Because of my dyslexia. I still have my father and the teacher voice in my head. Even today. Even with all of this.' Nico gestured around the apartment.

'I get that. All those years of putting you down have probably scarred you for life.'

It made me so mad. Why didn't people realise the power of their words? Especially when it came to how they spoke to a child. Flippant comments like calling Nico 'stupid' could do so much damage. I wasn't condoning violence, but seriously. If I met his dad or those evil teachers, I'd give them a slap.

'*Oui*. I know I should forget, but it is not easy.'

I threw my arms around him and squeezed him tight. His heart raced. I wished I could do something to make everything better. Nico rested his head on my shoulder and I gently stroked his hair. After holding him for a few minutes and gently rubbing his back, his heartbeat stabilised. I was glad he felt calmer.

'Have you ever thought about, you know, talking to someone about it? Like a therapist?'

Nico pulled away slowly. As our eyes met, I could tell he was turning the thought over in his head.

'Perhaps.'

'It'll be difficult at first, but it might help.'

'Yes. I will think about it, *merci*.'

'Thanks for sharing something so personal with me. It means a lot.'

'I want to share this with you. I do not like that I have to hide it.'

'I can imagine. It must be a huge weight to carry. Maybe you could…' My voice trailed off. 'Never mind.'

'Tell me.' Nico touched my arm.

'Don't worry. It's just an idea I had, but it's too soon. I think you still need time to process everything first.'

'I would like to know. I am a person who is motivated by goals. If you tell me, maybe it can give me another reason to work at this.'

I paused, weighing up whether or not to discuss it. I supposed it was just a suggestion. Nico didn't have to act on it straight away.

'Okay, so I was thinking, in the future, when you feel ready, maybe you could think about turning your dyslexia into something positive?'

'How?'

'By owning it. Openly. Showing people exactly what you said before—that just because you're not a whizz at reading, writing and all the traditional academic stuff doesn't mean you can't make a success of your life. There are so many hugely successful people with dyslexia, like Richard Branson and Jamie Oliver. I think the world should know about Nico Chevalier too.'

'I do not know.' He blew out a breath. 'I realise that I have to do some publicity, for the company, like that article. But that is for the business. I do not like to talk about my personal life. I am a private person.'

'I understand.' I nodded. 'Forget I mentioned it. Like I said, it was just something to think about if and when you feel ready. I only suggested it because somewhere in the world there could be a scared little boy or girl who feels shit about themselves because people are always calling them stupid and they're wondering if they'll ever make something of their lives. Hearing your story could help them.'

'That is true.' Nico sat up straighter.

I knew it wouldn't be something Nico was ready to do right now, but I hoped he'd consider it in the future. He was in such a powerful position. Nico could influence so many people and help remove the stigma of dyslexia. I didn't know a whole lot about it, but I wanted to learn.

'I know your primary focus is the business, but I also know that you want to make a difference in the world. And be known for more than your money and good looks.'

'That is the thing that always interest people. The money.'

'I suppose it's human nature. I'm not into flashy stuff, but even *I* was surprised that you were a billionaire. I mean, I hadn't even got my head around the fact that you were a millionaire, so that article was a bit of a shock,' I chuckled. 'At least give a girl some warning!'

Nico rolled his eyes, then smirked.

'These articles and list of rich people are often exaggerated. They make it sound good to sell magazines. And you know that they write the billion in US dollars, so it make it sound bigger.'

'So you're *not* a billionaire?'

'Perhaps.' He shrugged his shoulders modestly, which I took as confirmation. 'When I first start to make money, I invest in property and several other businesses and apps which have become very successful, so a lot of money comes from these companies, not just my own.'

'Either way, you're loaded and powerful. And what was it that Spider-Man's uncle said? "With great power comes responsibility."' I know you already do a lot to help the homeless. What you did for Maurice, Fabien and Odette is incredible, and I reckon you could change even more people's lives.'

'You make a good point. How do you know about Maurice and the others?' His brow furrowed.

'They told me. I love that you're so humble about this stuff and you never make a big fuss about the good that you do, but actually, I think sometimes there's a benefit to making some of your actions more public. You can reach more people that way.'

'*Entendu*. I will think about this. I do not know you like Spider-Man?'

'Well, yeah. I'm not a mega-fan, but you know, I don't mind a good superhero movie now and again.'

'Good to know. So, you have an opinion on which movie or which actor was the best?'

'Oh God! There have been about a hundred different actors playing that role, haven't there? I can't keep up!'

'I have the most recent movie, but I have not watched

it yet. Would you like to see this with me now?'

'You mean *you* watch Hollywood blockbusters? I thought you'd be all super cultured and only watch high-brow French movies.'

'No, I watch many types of film. Action, Disney movies…'

'Really?'

'*Oui*.'

'I love Disney films too. What's your favourite?'

'Difficult question, but I really like *Ratatouille*.'

'Oh my God, same!' My eyes widened. 'I *love* that film! We should watch that too.'

'I would like that. Did you ever go to Disneyland?'

'No. I always wanted to, but my parents couldn't afford to take us all.'

'It is the same for me. I only go—*pardon*, I only *went*, for the first time a few years ago.'

'*So cool*. I'd like to go one day too,' I said, wishing I could go with him. My heart fluttered. 'I love that you're open-minded about films.'

'If a film is good, that is what is important. Remember I also watch *The Holiday* with you at Christmas?'

'Yes, you did! That's a classic! You watched one of my films with me, so I'll gladly watch *Spider-Man* with you. But I'll need popcorn.'

'Deal.' Nico jumped up. 'I will get the popcorn and something nice to drink.'

'Maybe another cup of tea?' I smirked.

'You have to be joking.'

'I'm not! One day you'll grow to like tea.'

Nico shook his head as a grin spread across his face. 'That will never happen.'

CHAPTER THIRTY

A *www.*
I glanced again at the exquisite roses that Nico had sent earlier this morning. They weren't traditional red roses. These were brighter and more unique, some with beautiful tonal pink shades, others with peach and white. There were at least a hundred of them. Poor Odette had had to split the bouquet into a few different vases because they wouldn't fit in one.

After we'd watched the film, Nico must have thanked me a thousand times for listening. I'd told him that was what people did for those they cared about. And I meant it. About the listening part and caring about him. I cared about him. A *lot*. In fact, the word *caring* wasn't strong enough. Even though I'd been trying really hard not to, I knew the signs. I was falling in love. That definitely wasn't part of the plan.

It wasn't about all the money-related things. You know, the trip to the fancy restaurant in the Eiffel Tower, hiring a private boat, the clothes and these lovely flowers. It was more about how he made me *feel*. And no, I wasn't talking about the multiple *petites morts* I'd had since I was here, (although of course, they were very much appreciated). It was his heart. His kindness. The things he did to help people like Maurice and Fabien. The things we had in common. How comfortable I felt around him. It was so natural. Like breathing.

And there was something about him opening up to me last night too. His vulnerability. He'd thought that telling me about his dyslexia would make me like him less, but if anything, it made me like him more.

For so long I'd put him on a pedestal. I saw my flaws every day and knew I wasn't perfect. Nico, on the other hand, just seemed so flawless. So together. I'd never imagined him being insecure about anything.

I'd assumed that he hadn't opened up about his childhood because he didn't feel that we were close enough. It hadn't occurred to me that he had his own issues and was afraid of me knowing the truth.

But learning that he had insecurities just like me made him feel more human and elevated my feelings to another level. It made me want to be with him even more. And considering I was leaving in four days, that wasn't good.

I couldn't think about that now, though. I had to enjoy the time that I had left with him.

I walked up the stairs to Nico's office. When I arrived, I looked through the glass-panelled walls. There was no one in there with him, but I could see Nico nodding and his lips moving. He must have a call on speaker. *Oh yeah.* He was doing the interview for OnTheDaily.co.uk.

When Nico looked up and saw me, his face broke into a smile, setting off a thousand dancing butterflies in my stomach. He held up both palms as if to say *ten minutes*. I nodded, then gave him the thumbs up.

I didn't mind waiting. It'd give me a bit more time to mull over the ideas I'd been thinking about. I'd just grab a drink from the café a few doors down.

Just as I stepped outside, I saw Lucien smoking. My blood boiled hotter than molten lava. When he spotted me, he screwed up his face like he'd just stepped in dog shit. Arsehole. Who did he think he was?

'Why did you do that to Nico yesterday?' I snapped. 'At the awards? Why didn't you just read the autocue instead of letting him do it?'

The words flew out of my mouth before I could stop them. *Shit.* This was between Nico and Lucien, so I shouldn't get involved. But I couldn't help myself.

'*Putain!*' he hissed. I winced as the strong aroma of cigarette breath engulfed me. Hold on. That was a swear word. He was insulting me. Twat. 'I discuss this with Nico already. This is not your business.'

He went to leave, but now he'd pushed my buttons and I wasn't going to let this go. I hated the way that he spoke to me. The way he looked down at me. I was tired of stuck-up people like him doing that and getting away with it.

'Do you have a problem with me?' I barked. I knew he did, but I wanted to see his reaction.

To my surprise, Lucien took a step forward, stood squarely in front of me and smiled. It wasn't a nice smile. It was an evil one that showed all of his teeth. The kind that I imagined a hungry tiger gave seconds before it devoured its prey.

'No, I do not.' He crossed his arms. 'And do you know why? Because when you return to London, you will be forgotten. Do you think you are the first woman that Nico has met when he travel and invite to Paris?'

I swallowed hard. Yeah, I knew that realistically I couldn't be the first, but Lucien made it sound like Nico was a serial international womaniser. As if there was a conveyor belt of women and Nico added a fresh batch every month. I knew Maurice had said a similar thing about Nico's 'women' when we went shopping, and I'd seen how they'd swarmed around him at the awards last night, but it just didn't ring true somehow. Or maybe I was just naïve.

'Nico's past is not important to me,' I said as if it didn't bother me at all. Of course it did, but I couldn't let Lucien know that. 'Listen.' I stepped forward and stared him straight in the eyes. 'Nico and I have something special,' I added, hoping that was true. 'I know that you're important to him, so for his sake, I think we should try to get along.'

I almost threw up a little in my mouth. Saying those words made me feel physically sick. I mean, who wanted to be friends with the devil? But if that was what it took, I'd do it for Nico.

Lucien looked at me and laughed like I'd just said something ridiculous, like I believed the world was flat.

'There is no point. I told you before. You will not last. What you have with Nico is not *special*. It is an exchange. Nothing more. You are like prostitute. Nico buy you nice clothes and you give him sex. He like to have a new woman to rescue and play with. You are his new exotic toy. But soon he will lose interest. You will see. This is not *Pretty Woman* or how you say? Fifty Shades of *Gris*. This is not a movie. You will not get your fairy-tale ending, Cassie. I can promise you this.'

Before I even had a chance to respond, Lucien walked off. I tried to ignore the sinking feeling in my stomach. I felt like I'd been punched in the gut.

How could he liken what Nico and I had to prostitution? It was more than that, wasn't it? We had a connection. Before I'd come to Paris, I'd been worried that it was just a fling. A holiday romance that would fizzle out. Just like Nate and Mum had said. But now, being here, spending time with Nico, it felt like we had a chance to make this become a real relationship. How exactly, I didn't know. But we could work out the logistics. It would be worth it.

All the things Nico had done for me—arranging the bath, the trip to the Eiffel Tower, what had happened on the boat and the terrace, the way he'd opened up to me last night—surely he hadn't done that for the other women before me?

Then again, Lucien was his best friend. He'd known Nico a lot longer than I had. So perhaps there was an element of truth in what he said. Why would he lie? Maybe in his warped way he was trying to warn me, so I wouldn't look stupid. Then again, I was sure Lucien didn't give a toss about my feelings.

Instead of turning these thoughts over and over in my mind, which would drive me crazy, maybe it was time to do the most obvious, but probably the most nerve-racking thing: ask Nico.

It was time to have *the talk*. The dreaded DTR: the

define-the-relationship conversation. Was this just a fling for Nico, or was he prepared to start a serious relationship with me?

Asking the question outright was the only option. All I could do was hope that I liked the answer.

CHAPTER THIRTY-ONE

I ordered a hot chocolate and perched on one of the stools in the café.

My heart was still hammering with a mixture of anger at Lucien's rudeness and nerves about having *the talk* with Nico.

I pulled out my phone and started typing in the group chat. I needed some moral support.

Me

Just had a run-in with that arsehole Lucien again. He's putting all kinds of thoughts in my head about where things are going with Nico.

Me

Can you believe he likened what we have to a prostitute and her client? I've nothing against a woman doing what she wants with her body, but what me and Nico have is more than a transaction. Isn't it???

. . .

I felt stupid even asking that question. I knew it couldn't be, but I just needed to hear it from someone else.

Melody replied quickly. I'd messaged her earlier to see how her daughter Andrea had got on at her doctor's appointment, so I knew she was off this afternoon.

Melody

What a prick! Of course it isn't like that.

Me

Exactly. I reckon it's time to have the dreaded DTR talk.

Bella

You'll be fine, hon. I really think this can go somewhere.

I hadn't been expecting Bella to reply now. I thought she had lessons. Was good to get her reassurance too, though.

Me

Thanks. Me too. Will let you know how it goes.

Melody

Keep the pics coming! Those flowers earlier were gorge!

Melody

It's like you're living in a fairy tale! Enjoy it.

Melody

Oh, and tell that evil knob Lucien that the baddies never win.

Melody

And if he keeps giving you grief, I'll come over and chop his French sausage off!

. . .

I burst out laughing. I knew chatting to my friends would cheer me up.

Me

I wish I could tell him that.

Melody

You should! I bet he's got a teeny-tiny knob. He probably knows Nico's hung like a donkey and is jealous! I haven't even met him but I can tell he has an inferiority complex. Twit.

Melody

Is he short?

Me

Kinda…

Melody

Knew it! Small-man complex.

Bella

Mel!

Melody

What, Bella-boo? I don't like hearing this git is messing with our girl. Bet he's got small hands too. To match his small dick!

Melody

Next time you see him, check the size of his hands and imagine him naked on stage and everyone laughing at his tiny penis.

Melody

He'll wonder what you're smiling about and it'll drive him nuts! Oops. Pardon the pun, lol! Don't let him get to you, Cass.

Me

I'll try!

Bella

Be careful, hon. Remember, he is still Nico's best friend, so try not to get too involved or rock the boat…

Me

Can't promise… Anyway, ladies, better go. Give my godson a kiss, B.

Bella

Will do. Speak later xxx

I locked my phone, feeling ten tonnes lighter. Where would I be without my besties? I drained the rest of the hot chocolate, then headed back to Nico's office.

As I approached, I could see he was still on the call. After a few moments, he looked up and waved his hand, ushering me in. I quietly opened the door, closed it behind me, then sat down on the sofa.

'*Oui*. It is a very exciting time for Icon. We have many new ideas that are in development, so as you say, watch this space!' Nico smiled as he continued the interview.

'I think that's everything I need,' the female voice boomed from the speaker. 'Thank you so much for your time today, Nicolas.'

'It is my pleasure.'

'The article will be online this Saturday.'

'Saturday?' Nico's eyes widened. 'That is fast.'

'My editor wants to get this story up as quickly as possible. Our readers really love Icon products and, well'—she giggled—'let's just say after a certain article came out earlier this week with all of those lovely photos of you, you've gained an even bigger fan base.'

'*Merci*.' Nico blushed. 'That is kind of you to say. If

you have other questions, please call. You have my direct line.'

'Will do. *Au revoir!*'

'*À bientôt*, Kelly,' Nico replied, then ended the call. He pressed the remote control to shut the blinds, got up from his desk, walked over, then pulled me in for a kiss.

'Mmm,' I said as we came up for breath.

'I have wanted to do that all day.'

'Me too.' I kissed him again. 'So, how did the interview go? Sounds like it went well?'

'*Oui*, I think so.'

'And it's out on Saturday? That's super quick. Is the turnaround always so fast with these articles?'

I *hoped* I was subtle. Ever since that big eligible bachelor article had come out, I'd been dying to know when he'd done the interview. If it had been after Christmas, to me that was a sign that he didn't really see us as more than just a fling. But if it was before…

'*Non*. You are right, this is fast. But it is online, so sometimes it happens quickly. For magazine, like the interview you see this week, sometimes it can take much longer. I do that interview before Christmas, I think in early December, but there was many delays.'

Woo-hoo!

My stomach did a big backflip. He'd done the interview *before* Christmas—weeks before we'd met. This was a good sign. He might have been a bachelor then, but now, hopefully he considered himself a taken man. Off the market. Maybe now was the ideal time to have the talk.

'So, I was wondering…' Before I could finish my sentence, Nico's door flew open.

Lucien. *Great*. Looked like the chat with Nico would have to wait.

He looked straight through me, then said something to Nico in French.

'I do not know where it is. It may be here,' Nico snapped, pointing to a pile of papers on his desk. They might have spoken earlier, but I could tell Nico was still pissed off with Lucien. Didn't blame him. 'I just finish the interview with the British website. Now I go out with Cassie, but have a look and if you cannot find it, ask Miriam. She will be back in half an hour.'

Lucien nodded at Nico then flashed me a dirty look. I looked down at his hands as he sifted through the pile. Melody was right: he did have small hands. I smiled to myself. Lucien looked up and scowled again. Just like she'd predicted, he looked annoyed, as if he wondered what I was grinning about.

If only he knew...

CHAPTER THIRTY-TWO

Whoever said that the simple things in life were the most enjoyable was right. Nico had taken me to a beautiful park called Parc des Buttes-Chaumont (which, of course, he'd said was one of the *biggest* green spaces in Paris), and I loved it.

It wasn't just the pretty manicured lawns, the assortment of trees or watching couples snuggle up on the green benches that brought a smile to my face. It was being here with Nico.

As we walked hand in hand across the concrete path, then up the steep grassy hill so that I could get a better look at the surroundings, warmth radiated through my body. Spending time with Nico made me so happy.

I'd spent so much of my life wishing the time away. Wishing the working day could fly by so I could go home. Counting down the hours until the weekend. But right now, I wished time would stand still. That I could stay with Nico and do simple things like colour and go on walks together, forever.

'So.' Nico turned to face me as we walked along the pea-green lake towards the wooden suspension bridge. 'Do you have some ideas about what we talk about?'

I hadn't planned to mention how he could turn his dyslexia into something more positive again, because I didn't want him to feel pressured. But this morning, he'd suggested I let him know if anything came to mind.

'I have, actually… I have some charitable ideas for the company too.'

'Tell me.' His eyes widened.

'Well, I was thinking, hairdressing saved you, right? It gave you a great life and a career, so maybe you could help other people do the same by opening up a training academy. I don't know the logistics of how it would work, but I think it would be good to nurture and mentor the next generation.'

'I like it.' He smiled. 'It is something I think about many times. I mention this to Lucien last year, but we were too busy to develop it.'

'I can imagine. I was also thinking, maybe it could grow into something even bigger. You could create some sort of charitable foundation. How you helped to transform Maurice, Fabien and Odette's lives is incredible. They all said that without you, they'd still be out on the streets. So what if you did that on a bigger scale, by giving other disadvantaged people a chance to have a fresh start and follow their dreams?'

'I would really love to do that. This is a good idea.'

'And you still cut hair for the homeless, right?' I paused to take a sip from my bottle of water. There was so much I wanted to say that I couldn't get my words out quick enough. Sharing ideas with Nico gave me such a buzz.

'*Oui.*'

'I wondered if you could create some kind of book, featuring photos of some of the people that you help. You know like before and after photos a bit about their story, maybe follow their journey as they try to turn their lives around? Of course, not everyone would feel comfortable doing that, so they'd have to give their permission. You could post some photos on social media or it could be an exhibition or something. And then all the proceeds could go to a homeless charity or help raise money for a shelter or some sort of centre to give them accommodation and food.'

'Wow.' He grinned. 'You really have a lot of great ideas. I agree with everything you suggest.'

Hearing that made my heart dance. It might not be possible for Nico and his team to implement everything, but even if they just did one thing, it would be worthwhile. The thought that they could help turn someone's life around was thrilling.

'I'm glad you like them. I jotted some notes down on my phone, so if you want, I can type them up properly and email them to you or Miriam or whoever you want to look into it, whenever you're ready. Remember, no pressure.'

'That would be *fantastique*. *Merci*. I know that you like to be PA and that is the job you search for in London, but you could take on a different role, *non*? I do not mean that there is something wrong with being a PA. It is a good and very important job, I think that perhaps you can do some-thing that give you more responsibility. More opportunity to be creative.'

It was nice of him to say, but someone like me couldn't just change careers.

'In an ideal world I'd love to, but being a PA is all I know. It's all I'm qualified to do.'

'You do not always need qualifications to get a job. That is what the system teaches you. There are other ways. I prove this.'

I thought back to our conversation last night. I knew that at my age, experience was likely to count for more than having good grades. But that was the thing. I only had experience in one field.

'I hear what you're saying, but it's not the same. You may not have had qualifications when you left school, but you had time to build your experience. And it took years to become a success. I'm too old to start again.'

To get into a more creative field, I'd have to work my way up from the bottom. And with my bills and overheads, I couldn't afford to start interning.

'Too old? At thirty-five? *Mon Dieu!*' He rolled his eyes.

'This year I'll be thirty-six!'

'You are still a baby. There is a saying, I think by Carl Jung. He say "life begin at forty. Until then, you just do research." This mean, Cassie, that you still have four or five years until you become a true adult.' He smiled.

'Ha! I'll have to quote that to my mum the next time she questions my life choices and lack of progress.'

Although it was a good way to look at things, I still didn't think it was that easy to change your career.

I'd had a couple of agencies message me in the last few days with some roles. One was in the city for a big corporate law firm and the other was a PA role for a gambling app. Although the money was decent, neither of them appealed. I was sure there was something better out there for me, so I'd continue my search when I got back.

Ugh. I hated thinking about returning home because it meant leaving Nico. But I was grateful for the time I'd had here. If this all ended tomorrow, at least I'd walk away with good memories that I'd treasure for the rest of my life. And that was the important thing, right? I'd come for an adventure and to enjoy the experience and I'd definitely done that. Anyway, I still had three days left, so I had to try and banish all sad thoughts from my brain until then.

We continued discussing ideas for another hour or so whilst we walked across the suspension bridge over to the Temple de la Sibylle, which was perched at the top of a craggy cliff. As the sun set, we took in the views of Montmartre and the white domes of the Sacré-Coeur. So beautiful.

I shivered as a strong breeze hit my skin.

'You are cold?'

'A little,' I said, pulling my coat across my neck. I'd left my scarf in the car with Maurice.

'Here.' Nico took off his jacket and placed it over my shoulders.

'Thanks, but I can't. Then you'll be cold.'

'Do not worry about me. I want you to be warm. I do not want you to be ill.'

'But…'

'I will not take no for an answer, *Mademoiselle Fraise*.' Nico smirked.

'Okay, okay. If you insist, *dickhead*,' I laughed, tightening his jacket around me and inhaling his gorgeous, comforting scent.

'Come.' Nico took my hand. 'Let us go back to the apartment.'

Once we'd kicked off our shoes, we headed to the sofa and curled up in each other's arms. This was so lovely. So relaxed. So easy. I really could do this, be here with Nico for the rest of my life.

My heart fluttered, then tensed. I was becoming too comfortable. Falling in love when I didn't even know where this was going. Before I got any deeper and started doing crazy things like planning our dream wedding and babies in my head (I know... even mentioning it at this early stage was nuts), I needed to check we were on the same page.

We'd been interrupted earlier, but I had to try again. It was time to woman up. Time to have the talk.

'Can I ask you something?' I said, trying to focus as Nico stroked my leg.

'Of course!'

'What is... *this*? I mean, between us. How do you see us? Is this just, y'know...'

God, this was *so* awkward. No wonder people avoided this when they just started dating someone. Finding the right words was difficult and the fear of rejection was real. My heart thudded. I took a deep breath. *Let's try this again, shall we?*

'What I'm trying to say is, am I just a holiday romance, or do you see this as maybe going somewhere? Y'know, becoming serious?'

Nico bolted up and spun around to face me. His face was more crumpled than a linen shirt.

'I am confused? Of course this is not just a holiday romance. This is not a fling. I tell you in London that I think this could become something special, *non*?'

That was true. We'd both said we felt it could grow into something, but that was *then*. Almost two months ago. When we'd just met. It was Christmas. Like Nate had said, it was the holidays and so for people who loved the festive season, everything probably seemed extra magical. So it was a lot easier to get carried away and caught up with emotions. I couldn't assume that he still felt the same way now.

'Yeah, I know, but obviously at the time, we just said we'd see how things went. It's not like we committed to something officially or anything.'

Things had been great between us this past week that I'd been in Paris, but like I'd said, before that, we'd been apart for several weeks. Although I hadn't dated or seen anyone else, I couldn't be certain that he'd done the same. Lucien had alluded to him hooking up with that model on the yacht and then there were his comments about Nico's women and what Maurice had said too... I didn't know what to think.

'Cassie.' Nico took my hands into his. 'We are together. That is obvious, *non*? You think I just invite woman to stay in my home? To come to my office and meet my staff? I share ideas about my company with you that are private. I almost make love to you in my office. I tell you about my dyslexia. You think I do that with someone who is not important to me? You are my girlfriend.'

OMG.

My stomach flipped with joy. It felt like a million butterflies had decided to throw a rave inside it. I wanted to run around the room, then rush out onto the terrace and shout across the rooftops that this *was* serious. Nico and I were on the same page. We were together! I was his girl-friend. I didn't think I'd ever been so excited about someone calling me their girlfriend since I was seventeen and Dwayne Driver, the guy I'd had a crush on for ages, started dating me.

Nico had never formally introduced me as his girl-friend and we hadn't discussed it, so I didn't want to assume. But now that I thought about it more clearly, I felt stupid for questioning it. Like, *duh*. Of course. Nico's company was precious to him. So him letting me sit in on that brainstorming session and meet his key team members *was* a big deal.

'That's so good to hear.' I beamed.

'You are very special to me. I want us to have a future. Together. Okay?'

'Okay.' I relaxed my shoulders.

It was time to let go of my fears and learn not to jump to conclusions. I could tell from the look in his eyes that he was genuine. I just had to start trusting him more.

Nico was my boyfriend and everything was going to be just fine.

CHAPTER THIRTY-THREE

After asking the English-speaking waiter for directions to the ladies', I went to the loo. I washed my hands, then glanced at myself in the mirror. Normally whenever I looked at my reflection, I'd find a flaw to focus on. I'd tell myself I needed to get my roots done, trim my ends, sort out my eyebrows… there was always something. But not today.

Today I was happy with my hair, happy with how I looked and happy from the inside out. I couldn't stop smiling. If flashing your teeth was a national sport, I'd definitely be bringing home gold.

Nico and I were *official*. Every time I thought about it, my heart beat faster and my stomach fluttered.

Normally, I'd curse myself for acting so soppy and lame, but I'd found a kind, loving, funny, sexy and amazing man who wanted to be with me and was on top of the world. This happened so rarely in my life that I'd decided to just embrace it and feel *all* the feels. Even if I sounded like a lovesick teenager, I didn't care.

This morning I'd headed to the big beauty store Sephora to meet Lucy so I could buy some of the make-up that she'd used on me for the awards. I'd literally skipped down the aisles and every time I caught myself in the mirrors, there was a huge grin spread across my face. Even she'd noticed and had teased me about it.

When I'd mentioned to Lucy that I'd be meeting Nico in Montmartre later this afternoon, she'd insisted that she take me here—to a restaurant in the area that she liked. It was tiny, so we had to wait ages for a table, but the coq au vin was delicious.

'So do you ever miss England?' I asked as we worked our way through a cheese board for dessert.

'Sometimes,' said Lucy. 'It will always be home, but I've made a life here now and I love it. And it's only a couple of hours on the train to London and then about the same to where I used to live in Surrey, so it's not like it's hard to go back whenever I want.'

Lucy explained that she'd grabbed the opportunity to come to Paris to work on a big photoshoot several years ago, because she'd been nursing a broken heart and needed to get away.

Not long after she'd arrived, she'd had a fling (or some *rebound sex* as she called it) and whilst that romance hadn't lasted more than a few weeks, she'd fallen in love with the city. Two months later, Lucy had taken the leap and moved here permanently, and she hadn't looked back.

That struck me as so brave. I didn't think I'd ever be able to up sticks and leave my home so quickly, but it seemed like it had worked out for her.

'We better get going.' Lucy glanced at her watch. 'Don't want you to be late for meeting *lover boy*.' She smirked. 'Look at you!' I was doing it again: grinning like a Cheshire cat that had just been given all the cream.

'I can't help it.'

'Good for you. Enjoy the experience!'

Twenty-four hours ago, I might have got hung up on the word *experience*. It sounded so temporary. I probably would've asked Lucy whether she thought Nico was the type to get serious and want to settle down. But after the talk with Nico, I felt much more assured about the direction of our relationship. It *wasn't* temporary. This had legs. Despite the challenges, we were going to make it go the distance.

'I've still got time, but you can head off now if you want. I don't want you to be late for your job.' Lucy was doing the make-up for one of her wealthy clients.

'If you're sure?' She glanced at her watch again.

'Course! I don't want you to be rushing. You've already been so kind helping me with my make-up.'

'Glad to help,' she smiled. 'Thanks for treating me to lunch.'

'My pleasure.' It was the least I could do. I'd hardly spent any money since I'd been here, so it felt nice to treat someone else for a change.

I'd been racking my brain trying to think of a gift to give Nico. At first it was hard—after all, what do you get a billionaire who already has everything? But then I decided to set up an Audible account for him with a load of audio-book credits. Just because he found reading books challenging didn't mean he couldn't enjoy *listening* to a story. I'd show it to him this evening.

'And if we don't get a chance to catch up before you

leave on Sunday, keep in touch and, you know, let me know if ever you come back to Paris.'

'Definitely,' I said, assured that I would. I'd been thinking about it and until I left my job, Nico and I would probably only be able to see each other at weekends, but we'd make it work.

I gave Lucy a hug and she went on her way.

I wandered through the streets, feeling a lot more confident than I had when I'd first arrived in Paris.

Nico was right. Everything here wasn't as far apart as I'd imagined. Before I knew it, I was back in the area we'd visited on Sunday evening after Sacré-Coeur. I spotted the garden with the I Love You Wall and walked towards it.

My phone vibrated in my pocket. It was a voice note from Nico asking if I was ready to meet. I sent a quick reply to let him know where I was and he said he'd be there soon.

There were also messages from Melody and Bella asking for more details on our talk last night. As I was reading the message, Melody came online, then my phone started ringing.

'Hey!' I said.

'Hiya,' Melody replied. 'Hold on. I'm just going to see if Bella-boo is free.'

Bella came online and joined the call.

'Sooo!' Melody boomed. 'It's official, then!'

'Yep.' I smiled, before filling them in on our talk.

'Told you that you didn't have to worry and that it'd work out!' said Bella.

'Yes, you did. And I'm not even sorry to hear you say *I told you so*. I'm just so happy that it's serious. That we actually have the chance of a proper future together.'

'I'm so chuffed for you, sweetheart. So come on, then. Tell us: where did you guys get busy last night? On top of the Arc de Triomphe? In front of the Louvre?'

I burst out laughing.

'Melody's got a point,' Bella chuckled. 'You guys have been swinging from the chandeliers in all kinds of places this week. A boat, the car, the terrace... where next?'

'I think after the chef saw our last performance, we're putting al fresco fucking on hold for a while.'

'Oh yeah!' said Melody. 'Whatever happened to the skirt? Did you call the fire brigade?'

'The fire brigade? Course not!'

'Well, they rescue cats from trees,' Melody chuckled. 'Why not skirts?'

'I've no idea how or who did it, but Nico found a way to get it down. By the time we got home from the awards ceremony the next night, the skirt was washed, ironed and hanging in the dressing room.'

'I guess when you have money, anything's possible,' Bella said. 'But in all seriousness, I'm just so glad you've found the one, Cass.'

'Me too.'

'Where are you now?' Melody asked.

'Just waiting for Nico at that I Love You Wall.'

'Oooh, how appropriate! You're meeting the man you love at the love wall. Now that you're properly together, are you going to tell him how you feel?'

I swallowed hard. My natural reaction was to immediately deny my feelings. To tell Melody that she was being ridiculous. Insist that I wasn't in love with Nico. Even though I knew that I was.

I could try lying to them, but I couldn't lie to myself. I

was all in. I'd fallen for Nico. *Hard*. I was madly in love with him. In truth, I probably had been for a while. It was crazy, but I'd had strong feelings for him since the night we'd first met. And by the time I'd arrived here, they'd only intensified.

I got off the bench and walked towards the wall. This time I spotted the French for *I love you* immediately.

Je t'aime.

Yep. I was in no doubt. I was one hundred percent in love. Hook, line and sinker. I loved so much about Nico. Not just his looks, the mind-blowing sex or the money. I loved his kindness. He had such a good heart.

I loved the way he made me laugh and my stomach flutter. The way the corners of his eyes crinkled when he flashed his amazing smile. The way his eyes sparkled when he saw me. The softness of his skin. Even the way he dunked his bloody bread in his coffee. Oh man. I had it *bad*.

Knowing I was in love was one thing. But confessing how I felt, saying it out loud, especially to Nico, was another thing entirely. I wasn't sure if I was ready. Although there was a good chance he wouldn't reject me or respond like my exes had, it was best to keep quiet. Just in case.

'Not yet…' I sighed. I looked up and saw Nico striding towards me, his eyes wide. 'Ladies, I better run. Nico's arrived.'

'Happy bonking!' Melody shouted. I chuckled as we said our goodbyes, then ended the call.

'*Salut.*' He kissed me on the lips. How were his lips always so soft? 'I see you find the wall again.'

'Yep!'

'So, did you find the words easier this time?'

'Words?'

'*Je t'aime.*' Nico smiled. My heart flipped. This time I really wished he was saying those words for real.

'Oh, yes! It's right there. See?' I pointed. 'There's the French and down here's the English.'

At that moment, we looked into each other's eyes. The silence stretched between us. I went to open my mouth, then quickly closed it again. If ever there was a time to declare my feelings for him, it was now.

I desperately wanted to say those three big words, but I held back. Maybe it was too soon. Best to wait. At least until he said it. It was safer that way. I didn't want to make a fool of myself again like I had in the past.

I wondered what he was thinking about right now. Whether he was having the same thoughts as me. Then again, Nico didn't overthink half as much as I did, so he was probably thinking about something completely normal, like whether we should eat beef or chicken for dinner.

'So…' Nico broke the silence. 'This evening, my friends invite me for drinks, but I think instead we can just stay at home. Maybe we can colour together? I have a new book which is perfect for two. Or we can watch *Ratatouille*. Is this okay with you?'

Twenty-four hours ago I might have worried that he didn't want me to meet his other friends, but not today. Today I felt secure and happy that Nico wanted to spend time alone with me, doing the things we loved. There was no need to worry.

'Sounds perfect!' I linked my arm in his.

It really did. I was so happy that I didn't mind what we did, as long as we were together. I had two more nights with Nico in this magical city and I was going to enjoy every second.

CHAPTER THIRTY-FOUR

J *ust five more minutes.*

I was dying to go to the loo, but this bed was so comfortable I didn't want to leave. I was knackered. Nico and I had spent hours colouring a huge landscape last night, followed by an epic sex session on the sofa, so I wasn't ready to get up just yet.

I pulled the duvet over my head and crossed my legs, hoping I wouldn't do any permanent damage by holding my wee for a bit longer.

I managed two more minutes before my bladder told me that either I got my bum out of bed pronto or it would release itself. I couldn't bear soiling these pristine sheets, so I quickly hotfooted it to the bathroom.

Nico had gone for a run with Lucien, and Fabien had the weekend off, so I had the place to myself. I should jump in the shower, but I was starving.

I headed down to the kitchen. There was a spread of pastries laid out on the counter, including my favourite *chaussons aux pommes*. After making some coffee, I loaded some treats on a plate and took it to the dining room.

Just as I was about to tuck into a pastry, my phone pinged. It was a text from an unknown number. I opened it. There was no message, just a link. *Strange.*

Before clicking, I examined it carefully. Nate was forever telling us to be careful about scam texts, warning us they could be tricksters trying to get access to our bank accounts to steal all our money.

The link looked legit. It was for On The Daily's website.

Oooh! This must be Nico's interview. The journalist had said it'd be out today.

I clicked the link, excited to read it.

Wow. The first thing that struck me was the photo they'd used of Nico. It was one of my favourites. It was a black-and-white shot of him in a suit with the first few buttons of his shirt undone. *So hot.*

At least this article was in English, so I could read it. I took a sip of my coffee as I scrolled through. They talked a bit about Nico's hairdressing background, his range of tools, and then…

OMG.

There was a photo of *me*. Holy crap. Well, it was a photo of *us* on the red carpet at the awards ceremony.

My stomach fluttered. That must really mean that Nico was serious about me. In the eligible bachelor article, they'd portrayed him as eternally single, but at least in this one my presence was acknowledged, which with any luck would make people realise that he was officially off the market. Woo-hoo!

I read the caption underneath.

Nico photographed with mystery woman at the annual French Business Innovation & Excellence Awards.

Oooh, mystery woman, eh? Made me sound so intriguing. Maybe they'd written that to protect my identity. Although *girlfriend* would've been just fine. I smiled to myself. I couldn't believe this amazing man was all mine. I was one lucky lady.

I continued scrolling down the article.

Hold on.

WTF?

My stomach crashed through the floor.

There, written in black and white in huge letters within large speech marks, were three damning words:

"I am single."

Wait, what?

That wasn't right. Nico *wasn't* single. We were together. He'd told me so himself.

No. There had to be some mistake. My chest tightened and beads of sweat pooled at my hairline.

Calm down. It's fine. Everything's fine.

I took a deep breath.

Before I jumped to any conclusions, I told myself that I needed to read the whole article. Perhaps the text had been taken out of context. I should read it properly. In full. Then I was sure it would make sense.

I read the article, my heart thudding through my chest until I came to the relevant section. The question posed was: *You were recently pictured with a mystery lady at the French Business Innovation & Excellence awards. Is it serious?*

My eyes fixated on Nico's response:

"No. I am dating, but not anyone special right now. If

the right woman comes along in the future, I might consider a serious relationship. Perhaps with someone who is already successful in their own right and understands the business world and my lifestyle. But until then, I am happy to be single."

I dropped my phone on the table.

My heart now raced so fast I was convinced I was on the verge of a heart attack.

My brain whirred, processing and replaying those damning words.

I am dating, but not anyone special.

If the right woman comes along, I might consider a serious relationship.

With someone who is already successful.

I am happy to be single.

I desperately wanted to give him the benefit of the doubt but his answer was clear. The response left zero room for doubt. He'd emphatically said *no*. That we weren't serious.

I was right all along. This *wasn't* special. *I* wasn't special. Nico couldn't see himself with me long-term because we came from two different worlds. I knew it wouldn't work.

But...

The hopeful, romantic side of my brain scrambled around, searching for scraps, explanations or things to disprove what I'd just read in black and white.

Maybe they'd made this all up? There were fake news stories all the time, right?

Then again, this wasn't some tabloid newspaper. This was a professional, respectable website that prided itself on the accuracy and quality of its stories. I'd been reading it for years. They never printed anything salacious. In fact, they were more likely to call out those that did. That was why I'd recommended that Nico do the interview.

I took more deep breaths, trying to calm myself down, still desperately trying to think of an explanation that would help me make sense of all of this.

Okay, so this wasn't the first time that Nico had had an article promoting his single status. There was that other big one too. But that had been done before we'd met, whereas this interview had only taken place this week. Hours before we'd had a conversation where Nico said that we were together.

Hold on. That's right. It had been done a few days ago. And I'd been in the room for part of the interview. I'd heard what Nico said to the journalist. If I could find the part of the article that discussed the things that I'd heard with my own ears, then I'd know how truthful and accurate the whole thing was.

My heart thudded as I scanned the page. I hadn't heard the question the journalist asked, but I remembered Nico's response clearly. *There it is.*

"*Oui. It is a very exciting time for Icon. We have many new ideas that are in development, so as you say, watch this space!*"

That was what he'd said. *Verbatim.* I remembered it word for word, because he'd used that English saying at the end.

So, if they'd published exactly what he'd said for that response, why wouldn't they have done the same for the other questions?

So fucking naïve.

I knew this was too good to be true. I knew that Nico

could never settle with someone like me. Thank God I hadn't declared my love for him last night. Could you imagine? This would've been even worse.

Nate had warned me. Mum had warned me. Maurice, who probably saw everything Nico got up to, had mentioned Nico's *women*. And Lucien had taken great pleasure in telling me I shouldn't hold out for something long-term, but I'd ignored them all. Fell for his charms. Got sucked in. Been blinded by the fancy outings and the great sex.

And now there was an article online, with my bloody photo, basically telling the world that I meant nothing to him. It was humiliating.

Why did I always get it so wrong with men?

I knew Nico had gone for a run, but I needed to speak to him and get to the bottom of this.

I dialled his number. I heard ringing coming from the hallway. Maybe he'd just come back? I went out to check but there was nobody there, just his phone vibrating on the table. He must have left it here by mistake. Or maybe he'd done it deliberately. I didn't know what to think anymore. My head was all over the place.

I heard my mobile ringing, raced back to the dining room and whipped my phone off the table.

'Hello?' I said without even checking who it was.

'Hey.'

'Hi, hon.'

It was Melody and Bella.

'We saw the article,' they said in unison.

Before I could stop them, tears began to fall. And once I'd started sobbing, I couldn't stop.

'Sorry.' I wiped my cheeks with the back of my hand.

'I'm being a big baby. I need to woman up. It's no big deal.'

'Oh, hon. It's okay,' Bella soothed. 'Let it out.'

'Don't worry, Cass. If he doesn't want something serious with you, then fuck him!' Melody snapped. 'I'm sure there's plenty of other loaded fish in the sea.'

'I don't care about his money,' I snapped back. 'Sorry. I'm just upset. None of it makes sense.'

'Have you spoken to him?' Bella said.

'Not yet. He's out. And he's left his phone here.'

'Well, remember what happened last time. When you thought the client that came to his room was his girlfriend and it was a misunderstanding? Maybe this is too.'

'That's a *lot* of misunderstandings.' I raised my eyebrow. Who knows? Maybe he'd lied about that too. I'd given him the benefit of the doubt once, but twice?

'Men are full of shit. Hear him out, but don't let him play you. You deserve better. And by the way, you look fucking hot in that photo. So it's his loss. Just remember that.'

'I'll try.' I heard the key go in the door. 'I think he's back.'

'Keep us posted.' Bella said.

'And don't be afraid to come back home early if you need to,' Melody added. 'We're here if you need anything, okay?'

'Okay, thanks.'

I hung up, then walked out to the hallway, my heart racing.

I needed answers. It was time for Nico to face the music.

CHAPTER THIRTY-FIVE

'What the fuck, Nico?' I waved my phone in the air angrily. 'Why did you say this shit in the interview? You've made me look like a fool.'

'*Comment?*' His face creased with concern as he stepped forward and put his hand on my shoulder. 'What do you mean, *chérie*?

'Don't *chérie* me!' I brushed his hand away. 'The article for OnTheDaily.co.uk. It came out today.'

'Oh. I have not seen it.'

'Well, let me help you out,' I snapped, scrolling to the section which would be engrained in my brain until the end of time. 'To refresh your memory, you said: "I am single. I'm not looking for anything serious." So much for our conversation the other day.'

'I did not say that!' Nico frowned.

'Did you tell them that you're in a relationship?'

'*Non.*'

'Did you say that I'm your girlfriend?'

'*Non*, but…'

'Why not?' Fuck. I hated how I sounded. So bloody desperate. Why the hell should I have to ask or plead with someone to be their girlfriend? I wasn't some thirteen-year-old. I was a grown woman. This was bullshit.

'*Cassie*, this was a business interview. I…'

'Oh, I see! So whatever is good for business always comes first!'

He'd probably thought saying he was single would make him appeal more to his female customer base and help him sell more products. Well, I wasn't going to be his dirty little secret.

'You know what?' I hissed. 'Forget it. I don't know why I ever thought this could work. We're from two different worlds.'

This was humiliating. I couldn't stand here and embarrass myself anymore. Best to leave now, before I lost my last shred of self-respect.

'You should not care what a journalist write or say. It is just an article. It is not important.'

'It is to me! I'd rather you just admitted it. You're rich and powerful and you don't want to limit yourself to just being with someone like me, who doesn't have a big successful career. You enjoy having women throwing themselves at you. The model on the boat, all the women that you give your credit card to.'

I cringed as all of my insecurities came flooding out. Could I really blame him for wanting to be single? Nico could have a different woman every day of the week, so why should I believe that I was special?

'Nothing happen with the model and I have given only three women my card.'

'Knowing I'm the fourth makes me feel *so* special!' I

snapped. I hated feeling this way. So jealous. So out of control. This wasn't healthy. Not if I always felt like I was never good enough. Like I didn't deserve him.

'It is not like that!' Nico shouted.

'Look, there's no point prolonging this. It's obvious we think differently and this isn't going anywhere.'

I stormed upstairs and grabbed my passport and suitcase. Thankfully, I didn't have to pack. I'd never got round to properly unpacking since it had been returned. The only things I'd taken out were my purse and the biscuits. I'd been using the toiletries that were already in the bathroom when I arrived and wearing the clothes that Nico had paid for. I wouldn't be taking any of that. He could keep his fancy shit.

I dragged my case down the stairs.

'Where are you going?' Nico frowned.

'Back to London.'

'But, Cassie! You are overreacting, *non*? Stay. Let us talk about it.'

What else was there to say? I could've left as soon as I'd read the article. I could've run straight away like I had at Christmas without confronting him first. But this time I'd done the adult thing. Had a conversation. I'd heard him out and he'd confirmed my fears. He hadn't told the journalist that I was his girlfriend. He'd said that things weren't serious between us. But I wanted something serious, so there was nothing else to discuss.

If I was important to Nico, he wouldn't have broadcast to the whole world that he was single and ready to mingle. I got the message loud and clear. I wasn't going to stick around any longer to be humiliated anymore.

'No. And don't bother trying to follow me. Thanks for

your hospitality. I've left all the clothes you paid for upstairs. Enjoy your happy single life.'

I slammed the door and the tears began to fall. It was over. My perfect Paris romance had come crashing down around me.

Just as I'd feared from the beginning, I wasn't going to have my happily ever after.

CHAPTER THIRTY-SIX

I rushed out to the street, then started running. If I knew Nico, he'd come chasing after me, but I didn't want that. I didn't want to see him. Or anyone. Thank goodness Maurice wasn't working today. If he had been, I was sure he'd have given me an *I did try to tell you* look.

I felt drops of water on my forehead. It'd started to rain. I'd heard that Paris rained just as much as London, but apart from the odd few showers, it'd been dry for most of the week. I was glad it was raining. At least no one would realise the dampness on my cheeks was my tears.

I dabbed a tissue underneath my eyes, then quickly took a left and then a right. I needed to get to the Metro. I was sure it was this way. Dammit. *See?* This was what happened when you got ideas above your station and started getting used to being chauffeured every day.

Who did I think I was? One week of living the high life and I'd already forgotten how to find a tube station like a normal person. It was a good thing I was going home before I got so snooty I disappeared up my own backside.

I took my phone out of my bag to pull up Google Maps. There were already three missed calls from Nico. Dickhead.

'Cassie?' I heard someone call my name.

I spun around and saw Lucy. As happy as I was to see a friendly face, my first thought was whether she'd seen the article too.

'Hey.' I strained a smile.

'Where are you off to?'

'Home. London.'

'Already? I thought you weren't going back until tomorrow. Is everything okay?' She looked genuinely concerned. Before I had a chance to think it through, I ended up spilling my guts about the article.

'And so yeah, I'm on my way to Gare du Nord now to get the Eurostar back.' At least one of the perks of going in fancy class was that you could change your ticket at any time without paying extra.

My head started to feel a bit fuzzy and everything went blurry. Suddenly my knees buckled.

'Cassie!' Lucy grabbed my arm.

'I'm fine,' I said, coming back to my senses. I wasn't sure what had just happened. I must've blacked out for a second.

'Have you eaten?'

'Yeah, I had…' I was about to say that I'd eaten a whole plate of pastries. Then I remembered that the text had come through before I'd got the chance, so all I'd had was a sip of coffee. 'Actually, no. Not since last night.'

'That's not good. And you don't have an umbrella or coat.' They were in my suitcase. Unsurprisingly, right now, they weren't at the top of my priority list. 'Come on, I'm housesitting a friend's place just around the corner. I only came out to get some bread.' She waved the baguette in the air. 'I'll make you breakfast.'

'Thanks, but I'm fine. Once I get on the Eurostar there'll be breakfast, so I can eat then.'

'No way. No offence, but you don't look good. You already had a disaster on the way to Paris. Do you really want to risk fainting on the tube or the train on the way back? Come and have some breakfast and *then* get the Eurostar back.'

My phone started ringing. It was Nico again. I pressed the cancel button, then switched it off. He was the last person I wanted to speak to.

'Okay,' I said. 'Let's go.'

It was now Sunday afternoon and I was back at home in London and still in bed. I sniffed my armpits. *Whoa.* I really needed a shower, but I couldn't find the motivation to drag myself to the bathroom. Normally I'd wash straight after a long train journey, but last night I hadn't been in the mood.

I'd got back around nine. I'd only intended to go with Lucy for breakfast and then head straight for the station to catch the train. But after eating and reliving the whole thing with her, I'd been shattered, so she'd suggested I have a nap. I thought I'd sleep for an hour. Two max. But when I woke up it was after three in the afternoon.

By the time I'd had a coffee, taken the Metro to Gare du Nord and waited for the next train it was after 5.30. Because of the time difference, we'd arrived in London after eight, and of course there were engineering works on the tube, so I had to get the bus all the way home, which took ages.

Still, at least the journey was peaceful. No suitcase or food incidents.

I supposed I should switch my phone back on. I'd turned it on briefly last night to let Bella and Melody know I was back in London safely.

The phone lit up with notifications. Nico had sent more messages. I'd seen that there were a load of voice notes yesterday, but I couldn't bring myself to listen to them.

My mobile started ringing. I half expected it to be Nico, but it was Lily.

She'd messaged last night too, but I'd been too tired to reply, so promised myself I would call her today. She'd beaten me to it.

'Hey, you.'

'Hey, sis,' Lily said softly. 'You okay? I saw the article…'

Shit. I'd forgotten that Lily liked that website too. I hoped my parents and Nate hadn't seen it. What was I saying? If Nate *had* seen it, he'd be at my front door right now, demanding Nico's address.

'Yeah.' There wasn't much else to say. I didn't want to relive it.

'Men are dogs,' she hissed. A few days ago, I would've disagreed and told her that they weren't all the same, but I could hardly stick up for the male species now, after recent events. 'If you want to talk about it, I'm here. God knows I've bent your ear enough about River, so it's the least I can do.'

'Did you sort things out with him?'

'No. Not yet. He's away at some work thing. *Apparently*,' she huffed. 'Anyway, I wasn't calling about, *y'know*... I phoned last night because Mum summoned me to help clear out the loft. Anyway, there was a box of papers which is yours, so I was going to say I could drop it off to you tomorrow lunchtime and then we could grab a sandwich so you could tell me all about Paris. But I'm not sure now if you'd want to?'

Oh yeah. I'd stored a load of stuff there last year when I was decorating. I'd been taking a bit home every time I visited and now had one last box to collect.

Even though I wasn't in the mood for socialising, I was absolutely dreading going back to work tomorrow, so seeing a friendly face at lunchtime would help break up the day.

'Yeah, okay.' I said. 'It's not too heavy, though, is it?'

'Nah, it's fine. I've got a big bag I can put it in so it's easier for you to carry.'

'Thanks.' My phone chimed. It was another message from Nico.

'I better go. I'll message in the morning about timings and stuff. See you tomorrow.'

'Laters.' I ended the call and blew out a breath. I supposed I should start going through Nico's voice notes.

I skimmed through them. The first few were variations of *Where are you?* Then I think the fourth or fifth one said he was at Gare du Nord, looking for me.

My traitorous heart flipped. Even though I'd told him not to follow me, he had. That meant that he cared. Or that he felt guilty.

I skimmed to the next few.

'I do not understand where you are. I wait at the station for two hours, but you are not here. Miriam check with her contact and they tell her that the ticket has not been used. You have not taken the train. Are you still in Paris? Tell me, *chérie*. If you are in London, I will come and see you. I understand why you are upset and I want to talk about it. I want to fix this.'

Oh my God. My heart betrayed me again and fluttered. He'd waited hours for me. I hadn't known. I'd been fast asleep, with my phone off.

He sounded worried. I should message him. Let him know I was okay. *No.* What would be the point? It wouldn't change anything. He'd hurt me. It was a little late for him to be concerned about my well-being. If he was really bothered about my feelings, he wouldn't have publicly humiliated me.

I listened to the next message from last night.

'Cassie, *s'il te plaît*. There is so much I want to talk to you about. Do not let this article ruin something good with us. You worry that we do not have a future, but I was going to talk to you about a job. I want you to come and work at my company. Please. It is better that we speak face to face. Message and tell me if you are in London.'

What the hell?

So now he thinks he can buy me by offering me a job?

Well, I wasn't falling for it. I wasn't going to push Miriam out of her position just so he could ease his guilt.

Rich people. They think they can buy their way out of everything. Just throw money at a situation and it will magically go away.

It was a ridiculous idea anyway. One, my French was shit, so there was no way I could do my job as a PA competently when I only knew how to say *bonjour, oui, au revoir, chausson aux pommes, s'il vous plaît* and a handful of other words.

Two, there was no way I'd work for someone I'd been romantically involved with. It would be too awkward given recent events, and I didn't want to rely on him for my salary.

And three… well, I couldn't think of point number three, but I was sure something logical would come to me to emphasise why the idea was pants.

I listened to the last message. The one he'd left ten minutes ago.

'I can see you are in London now and you listen to my messages, so at least you are safe. Tell me when you are ready to talk and I will come and tell you the truth. It is not what you think. You must believe me.'

He sounded sincere. Could I have got it wrong? I didn't see how, though. This time I hadn't run. Well, not straight away. I'd asked him. I'd listened to him. And he'd told me that he hadn't put the journalist straight about us, so what more was there to it?

Still, I had to admit, I was curious to hear what he had to say. Having regrets wasn't good, so if this really was the end of us (if there ever really had been an *us* to begin with), maybe I should hear him out one last time.

My gut had told me he was good. When we were together, he genuinely seemed to be into me. But maybe I'd only seen what I'd wanted to. Maybe that was part of his charm. Women were duped by charming, handsome men every day and most of them never saw it coming. So why did I think I was any different?

No. It was over. I needed to focus on my future.

Continue looking for a job. A real job. Not some pity PA role Nico wanted to give me.

First, though, I had to shower, eat and then start preparing myself mentally for returning to the office tomorrow. Oh. Happy. Day.

CHAPTER THIRTY-SEVEN

I yawned loudly. Even though I'd gone to bed extra early, hoping that I'd wake up refreshed, I felt like I'd slept for about five minutes.

Of course it wasn't because I'd spent the whole night thinking about Nico. I'd barely even thought about how much I missed the heat of his body next to mine or the sensation of his heart beating against me when I was wrapped in his big arms. *No.* It wasn't that. I was just having trouble readjusting to the sleeping conditions. After spending the past week on a bed that felt like it had been crafted by angels, it was to be expected that trying to get a good night's rest on my cheap mattress wasn't going to measure up. That was all it was.

After hitting the snooze button for the sixth time, I dragged my bum out of bed. Then, after showering and dressing, I walked to the station.

Surprisingly, the journey to work was better than I'd feared. The tube came quickly and no one gave me any funny looks. I was in the clear.

I'd probably overreacted about the reach of the article. Yeah, the website was popular, but these days, with all the weekend newspapers, magazines, Twitter, Facebook, Instagram, Snapchat, TikTok and gazillions of other websites, there was so much news to consume.

Plus, people did stuff at the weekend. Saw their friends, stayed at home and watched Netflix, read books... it was stupid to assume that they'd even get the time to see Nico's article, and if they did, I was sure they'd pay zero attention to some random woman on his arm.

The only person who was bothered about the article was me. There was nothing I could do about it now. I just had to find a way to live with it.

So what if Nico said he was single, then told me we were together a few hours later? People lied all the time.

He'd said before that these articles were good for business, so that was probably why he'd done it. Rather than announcing he was off the market, like I'd said before, it was better for Nico's image if he was single. A bit like back in the day, when boy band members and actors were told to say they were unattached by their managers to appeal to a larger female fanbase.

I'd thought about it a bit—okay, a *lot*—and I'd come to the conclusion that when I'd asked Nico to define the relationship, I'd put him on the spot, so he'd just said we were a couple because he hadn't wanted to hurt my feelings.

This was just one of the perils of modern dating. I wasn't the first woman to experience this and I wouldn't be the last. I just had to move on.

I'd be fine. I was okay.

Well, maybe I wasn't completely okay right now, but I

would be. I had good friends, family, a home—I had a lot to be thankful for.

It might take some time, but I'd get over Nico.

Eventually.

Somehow.

Actually, as much as I'd been dreading returning to work, maybe it would do me some good. Help keep my mind off things.

'Hello, Cassie,' said Ronan, the security guard at reception, as I walked through the doors. 'Nice holiday?'

'Yes, thanks,' I said politely. He didn't need to hear about my personal drama.

As I stepped out of the lift, my stomach tightened. The last thing I wanted to deal with right now was Spencer, but I needed this job and the money, so I had to suck it up. Just five and a half more weeks. I'd call the recruitment agencies again later.

'Hey!' said Brian, one of the directors. 'Nice time in Paris?' He raised an eyebrow. *How did he…? Uh-oh.*

'Hi!' said Eunice, who worked in marketing. 'Saw that article. Aren't men just the worst? Sorry it didn't work out. Must have been fun, though. Going to all those fancy parties with a guy like that. He is *lush*.'

Fuck. They knew. They'd seen the article.

I opened my mouth to speak, then closed it again. I didn't even know what to say. Thankfully, Eunice filled the silence.

'Actually, do you think you could get me a pair of his straightening irons? I've always wanted them, but they're a bit pricey for me.'

'No, I… I don't think so,' I stuttered. 'Anyway, I better get to work. First day back and all that.' I plastered on a smile and darted to my desk. I wished I had curtains going all the way around it so I could shut myself away from everyone, but no such luck.

'*Ah!*' Spencer's voice boomed from his office. 'You're back. Get in here.'

Would it have hurt him to put a *please* at the end of that sentence?

I dropped my bag on the floor and trudged over to him.

'So…' He smirked. 'Did you enjoy your holiday?' I couldn't gauge whether he was being genuine or if he knew about the article, but I doubted he cared either way.

'Fine, thanks,' I said robotically. I just wanted him to tell me what he needed so I could get back to hiding behind my desk.

'I was wondering if you could take a look at this.' He swivelled his computer screen around to face me. The blood immediately drained from my face. It was the article. He'd zoomed in so that the photo of me and Nico covered the screen completely. 'Is this *you*? It says a *mystery woman*, but we've all been debating over the weekend, and we reckon it is.'

Who exactly were *we*?

'I…' Screw it. It was obvious. There was no point in denying it. 'Yeah, it's me. *And*?'

'Oh, nothing. I know you're not the brightest tool in the toolbox, but even *you* have to be smart enough to know that France's most eligible bachelor wouldn't want to date someone like *you*, surely? I mean, don't get me wrong, his —what do the kids call it? His *glam squad* have done a decent job of tarting you up for the photo, but you're still an ordinary girl. Let me give you some advice, sweetheart: stay in your lane.' He winked.

It took every ounce of self-control not to climb on that desk and punch him. I'd only been here five minutes and he'd pushed more buttons than a telephone operator. Clearly, Spencer was still pissed that his dad had granted me the holiday and this was another pathetic attempt at revenge. He wanted to get to me, but I wasn't going to let him.

'Was there anything else, *work-related*, that you needed?' I crossed my arms. 'If not, I'm going to start going through my emails.'

'That's all for now.' He leant back in his chair, irritated that I hadn't run out of the office crying.

'Good,' I huffed and returned to my desk.

How had my career come to this? Spencer spoke to me like I was a piece of shit on the bottom of his designer shoes.

I deserved better.

Before I'd gone to Paris, him saying that I wasn't 'the brightest tool in the toolbox' would've been something I'd have taken to heart, because I'd believed it. I'd been insecure about my abilities. I hadn't thought I was worthy of anything better. I would've bought into what Mum always told us: *beggars can't be choosers*. But now, I saw things differently.

Whatever I'd had with Nico was over, but what he'd said when opening up about his dyslexia was true: there were many types of intelligence. Just because I hadn't done well at school and wasn't smart in a traditional academic way didn't mean I couldn't do more with my career. It *wasn't* too late. I was almost thirty-six, not eighty-six. I still had time to change my career path.

I wasn't going to let Spencer make me feel like I

wasn't good enough anymore. Despite what he thought of me, *I* knew I was worth more than this job.

Right then, I decided: I wasn't going to stick around working in this toxic environment for another five and a half weeks. Someway, somehow, I'd leave sooner. I'd find a job that I loved. Where my hard work and commitment was valued. Where I would get the respect I deserved.

I'd gone through most of my emails by the time Lily messaged to say she was downstairs. Lunch couldn't come quick enough. I grabbed my bag and went to meet her.

We found a quiet table in a nearby coffee shop. After I'd given her the ABC version of events in Paris, Lily pulled out the box.

'Thanks for this.' I rifled through the papers. 'It's actually handy you bringing them here, because I can shred anything I don't need at work.'

'Smart thinking. You should just coast. Do as little as possible until you leave.'

'Damn right.' I continued flicking. 'I'm going to spend the afternoon job-hunting and I'm not serving out my notice period either. That's bullshit. I'll take the first decent temp job the agency offers and get out of there ASAP.'

'Good for you, sis!' Lily bit into her sandwich. 'So… have you heard anything more from Nico?'

'Nope. Not since his message yesterday. I'm still thinking about whether or not to speak to him.'

'Can't be easy. Especially with tomorrow and everything.'

'Tomorrow?'

'Yeah, you know—Valentine's Day.'

'God, I'd completely forgotten about that.' Or maybe

I'd chosen to block it out. Nico flashed in my head for about the millionth time. It would have been lovely to spend that day with him, but it wasn't meant to be.

Tomorrow was definitely going to be hard. Seeing all the romantic window displays and the big bouquets being delivered to the office. My mind turned to Nico again and the roses he'd sent me the morning after the awards. I'd been so happy. That felt like a lifetime ago now.

'The timing isn't the best...,' I added, then paused, fixating on the document in my hands.

It was my employment contract. The hard copy I'd signed. HR hadn't got back to me after I'd requested a duplicate, so I was supposed to collect my original copy from my parents before I'd gone to Paris, but I hadn't got the chance because I'd gone shopping instead.

I flicked through it and landed on the termination notice page.

WTF.

'I knew it!' I shouted.

'What?' Lily frowned.

'I knew it! I knew the contract I signed didn't say I had to give one month's notice plus an extra week for every year of service!'

'What? But what does it say, then?'

'It says one month's notice. The bastard lied.' I checked the date on the contract again just to be sure. Yep. This was the most recent version. 'Sorry, Lily, I've got to go. I'm tired of men fucking with me. I'm going to sort out this Spencer shit, once and for all.'

I ran to the office and took a copy of the contract as a precaution. After going to HR and insisting that I check the contract they had on file immediately, I had all the proof I needed. I pressed record on my mobile, slipped it into my pocket, then stormed into Spencer's office.

'I told you to knock before coming in!' He quickly zipped up his trousers, eyes bulging. *God. Not again.* This man was seriously depraved. I threw my contract on the desk.

'You lied! My notice period *is* one month. Look!' I pointed to the page.

The blood drained from Spencer's face.

'This… you're—no! I think you'll find…,' he stuttered. He hadn't expected to be caught out. 'You saw the contract I showed you…'

'That was bollocks!' I snapped. 'I've already checked with HR and the contract I have here is the one they have on file. You must have doctored the one that was on your screen.'

'That's ridiculous! I wouldn't…'

'Do you know what? I don't give a fuck anymore. I'm sick to death of the way you treat me. The way you talk to me, your unreasonable demands, your lack of morals, your rudeness. I don't have to put up with this shit. I'm better than this. I can do better than working for someone like you. I quit.'

'You can't!' Spencer jumped up from his desk, his mouth on the floor.

'I just have. What you've done is unethical, and no doubt illegal. So let me go, quietly—otherwise I *will* take it further.' I strutted towards the door, then paused. 'And let me give *you* some advice,' I added, replicating the condescending tone and words he'd used when he'd spoken to me earlier. 'Pull up your flies properly and stop wanking at your desk. It's disgusting.'

I slammed the door, loaded all my stuff into the bag Lily had given me, then headed to the lift.

I exhaled. I'd done it. I'd left my job.

I'd said earlier this morning that I'd find a way to leave sooner. I hadn't been expecting it to happen so quickly, but as pissed as I was that he'd lied, at the same time, I was relieved. No more Spencer. I was finally free.

I didn't care that I wouldn't get a reference or that I hadn't served my notice period. Although I had no idea how I'd pay my bills once the money I had ran out, I deserved better. I refused to continue to be treated like shit anymore.

The lift doors opened.

'Hey, Cassie!' Sally, Spencer's mistress, stepped out.

I scowled at her, then pressed the button for the ground floor firmly to close the doors. Now I no longer worked for Spencer, I didn't have to pretend to be civil or hide my disapproval of their affair.

Just as I approached the exit, I saw Priscilla, Spencer's wife, walk inside. She was about to go up to his office, but Sally was already there.

Shit.

Before, even though I didn't condone his actions, I would've felt compelled to cover for Spencer, but not anymore. It wasn't my problem.

'Hello, Cassie.' Priscilla smiled.

'Hi.' I nodded in acknowledgement and continued walking. Just as I reached the door, I stopped.

I couldn't do it. Even though their situation had nothing to do with me, I had a heart. I didn't care about Spencer, but no wife deserved to walk in on her husband doing God knows what with another woman. She might not thank me, but I had to at least warn her. I had to try and do the right thing.

'Priscilla,' I called out. 'Before you go upstairs, I think you should prepare yourself to see something you might not like…'

Priscilla turned on her heel and walked back towards me.

'It's okay.' She rested her hand on my shoulder. 'I know. That's why I'm here. But I appreciate you thinking of me. Rest assured that Spencer will get what he deserves.' She strode towards the lift, her head held high.

Well, I wasn't expecting *that*. I was relieved that Priscilla had a handle on the situation and would make Spencer pay. Maybe karma was real.

I exited the building. As the cold air hit my cheeks, the reality of my situation struck me.

A few days ago, I'd been employed and had what I thought was a great man. Now I had no job and was single. But at least I had my self-respect.

I'd call the recruitment agencies and tell them I was available straight away. Something was bound to come up soon.

I'd taken control of my destiny and I was one step closer to getting my career back on track.

If only the same could be said for my love life.

CHAPTER THIRTY-EIGHT

That sounded promising.

I'd just been speaking to a recruitment agency. They might have a few days' admin work for me next week at a law firm in the city. Although the role sounded about as exciting as watching paint dry, it would give me some money in my pocket whilst I looked for something better.

As well as calling the agencies, I'd also fired off an email to Reg. After he'd spoken to Spencer about signing off on my holiday, he'd said to contact him if ever I needed anything, and I'd decided to call in the favour.

I'd thought about it, and why should I leave without a reference after the shit Spencer had pulled? And why should I be out of pocket? That was why, in my message, I'd asked if he'd give me a reference and pay me at least until the end of the month.

I could've asked for more, or threatened to take action, especially as I had the recording of Spencer on my phone. But Reg had always been good to me. I didn't see why he or the company should suffer because of Spencer's behaviour. Hopefully he'd do the decent thing and help me out. Maybe he'd address Spencer's management style too, but that was up to him. It wasn't my problem anymore.

I continued walking along the South Bank, watching the waves of the river Thames rippling as a boat sailed along it.

My thoughts immediately turned to Nico and our time on the Seine. How he had been genuinely concerned about me and arranged the ginger tea, just in case I threw up. And how he'd *relaxed* me. I remembered how beautiful Paris had looked from the river and how romantic the evening had been.

Then I thought about how we'd walked here hand in hand at this very spot on Christmas Day and how much fun we'd had with our snowball fight.

I took my phone and scrolled through the photos we'd taken together in Paris. I'd even taken a pic of the portrait the artist had done. My heart fluttered.

I zoomed in. Despite what had happened, I still adored this drawing. It was very true to life: a genuine reflection of the two of us.

Nico obviously looked amazing. He always did. But what surprised me most was that now I realised that I looked okay too. In fact, I actually looked nice.

And that portrait had been drawn when my hair was in its natural state—*before* it'd been cut and coloured. When I'd only had on a bit of mascara and lip gloss. As for my clothes, well, you could only see my top in the portrait, but that day I'd worn jeans and trainers. Yet, despite not having a fancy outfit or wearing professional make-up, I was glowing.

All this time I'd thought it was being glammed up that had made me look pretty at the awards. But it was the happiness I felt *inside* that made me glow on the outside.

Like I'd said in that brainstorming session, there was more than one type of beauty. But for too long, I'd allowed myself to feel like I wasn't enough for Nico. I'd believed that I couldn't offer him anything.

Yeah, I wasn't a supermodel, but just like every woman, I was beautiful in my own way. And I *did* have something to offer him. I was kind and loyal and I had a good heart. I'd met enough arseholes in my life to know that those qualities were rare. Nico had always seen that. But somehow, I hadn't fully believed it. I hadn't realised I was worthy of true love. Until now.

I scrolled through the photos we'd taken at the I Love You Wall and it was the same. In fact, in every picture I'd taken with Nico, something about me was different. My eyes were bright. My smile was wide. And *that* was what made me look nice. Being with him made me happy, which was reflected in my face. Nico helped me radiate with happiness.

Although I'd tried so hard not to, I had to be honest with myself. The truth was, I missed him.

There. I'd said it.

Despite having my 'be strong and forget about Nico' pep talk playing on repeat in my head, it hadn't made any difference. In the battle of head over heart, heart was kicking head's arse.

I clutched the left side of my chest. There was an ache in my heart. It was a feeling of emptiness.

A few days ago, my heart had been full. It had been bursting with excitement, happiness and joy. But now, it was as if someone had slashed it up with a machete, then fed the pieces to a hungry pack of wolves. I felt hollow. Lost. Like an important part of me was missing.

Since I'd walked out of the office a couple of hours ago, I'd reached for my phone about fifty times, desperate to tell Nico my news. Just like when I'd resigned last month, he was the first person I wanted to speak to.

I knew how happy he'd be. He'd say, 'I am so proud of you, *chérie*,' in his gorgeous accent, and he'd totally mean it.

Nico would have loads of encouraging words and advice. He'd hold me in his big strong arms and shower me with congratulatory kisses. He'd make me feel like the most special woman in the world.

That was the thing. When I was with him, I *did* feel like the most treasured woman in the world. Yes, he was charming and he had a way of making everyone close to him feel that way, but it was different with me. The way he looked at me was different. I saw the emotion in his eyes. When he told me I was special, I felt it in my bones. When he told me we were together, he meant it. I didn't know how I knew, but I just did.

In fact, the more I thought about that article, the more things just didn't make sense.

For example, who had sent the text with the link in the first place? I'd known straight away that it hadn't been Nico, because he hadn't had his phone with him.

It had come from someone in France, but apart from Maurice, Miriam and Lucy, who I'd already saved as contacts, no one else had my number.

And if I really was just a plaything to Nico, why would he wait at the station for hours? Why would he care? He could just move on to the next woman. There'd be a line longer than the queue to visit the Eiffel Tower. Especially after that eligible bachelor article. And even if he'd given his card to three women before me, did it matter? That was before we were together.

Thirdly, why would he offer me a job? If I really meant nothing to him and he didn't see me as a long-term prospect, surely it'd be awkward to have me work for him all day.

Also, I remembered that when that big article had come out, Nico had said he was a private person and didn't like talking about his personal life. So why would he go into great detail about how little I meant to him and proclaim so publicly that he was single? Especially when he knew I was such a fan of this website, and was bound to read it?

No. Something wasn't right.

I managed to catch Bella and Melody on the phone and they both agreed that there must be more to it. I was determined to find out.

After making my way to Waterloo Station, I headed home. As soon as I'd kicked off my shoes, hung up my coat and chucked my bag on the sofa, I went to the kitchen. I needed a cup of tea.

I flicked on the kettle, then tipped some chocolate Hobnobs onto a plate. I felt the corner of my mouth twitch as I remembered when I'd brought Nico tea and biscuits to help cheer him up after the awards. Then I chuckled as I recalled how he'd spat the tea out because he thought it was disgusting.

I poured the water into the mug and smiled again as I

pictured the bowls we'd had to drink out of every morning and how Nico dipped his bread in his coffee.

Was I really not going to see or speak to him ever again? I took the plate and mug into the living room, then got my phone out of my handbag.

No messages. Maybe he'd given up. Then again, he'd followed me to the station. Waited for hours, sent loads of messages. Those were the actions of someone who wanted me to know they cared.

The problem was, I more than cared. I *loved* him. Despite what had happened this weekend, I knew it would be hard to find someone else who made me laugh like he did. Who made my stomach flit and my heart flutter.

But as much as I wanted him, I couldn't bear to put my heart on the line again and see it get crushed. It had been hard before with my other exes, but my feelings for Nico were stronger than anything I'd ever known. The pain would be multiplied by a million and the humiliation would be public. Just like the article. I didn't think I was strong enough to handle that.

But equally, I wasn't sure if I could handle this feeling of emptiness and loss anymore either. Now that I wasn't working, I'd have even more time to think about him.

I had to speak to Nico. Clear some things up. I reached for my phone and dialled his number. The phone rang out. Even if he didn't want to speak to me, I'd try again later. I couldn't give up.

After changing into my onesie, I curled up on the sofa. My phone pinged. I picked it up, hoping it was Nico. It wasn't.

Lily

I'm outside River's house. He messaged earlier to say

he wasn't well, so wouldn't be able to see me tomorrow—on Valentine's Day. I didn't believe him and I was right not to!

Given what she'd told me about him, that did sound like a red flag. I quickly typed out a reply.

Me

Why? What did you find out?

Lily

It's not good, Cass. It's definitely over between us.

Me

What happened?

Lily

typing…

Typing flashing repeatedly, but no text came through. My eyes stayed glued to the screen for at least a minute before Lily went offline.

Me

Are you okay?

I was desperate to find out what was going on. Five minutes later, my phone pinged.

Lily

No, I'm not, but can't talk now.

Me

Sorry to hear that… Text me when you're home so I know you're back safely, okay?

Lily

Will do.

She went offline again. Poor Lily. What had River done? I'd just have to wait until she was ready to explain.

I glanced at the time. It was half six. I should start making dinner soon. Once I'd eaten, I'd try Nico again.

Just as I reached for my colouring book, there was a knock at the door. Must be my neighbour, Shelley, asking to borrow something.

I opened the door and nearly fainted.

What the…

'*Salut.*' Nico flashed his grin and I nearly melted into a puddle.

'What are you… when did you…?' My brain scrambled and I lost the ability to string a sentence together.

'I arrive in London this afternoon. Can I come in? You will not answer my messages, so I decide I will come to you.'

'I just tried calling you!' I said, still recovering from the shock that he was actually here. Right in front of me. My stomach flipped.

'You did? I am sorry. I did not hear it. Anyway, I tell you I will find out what happen with the interview. Why they say those things. And now I do.' He stepped inside the flat. 'Cassie, it was not me who tell the website that I am single and you mean nothing to me. It was someone else.'

'Who?' I frowned.

'Lucien.'

Holy shit.

CHAPTER THIRTY-NINE

'Lucien?' I flopped down on the sofa, my face looking more crumpled than a pug's forehead. 'Seriously?'

I'd known the guy was an arsehole, but surely not even *he* would stoop *that* low.

'But he wasn't even in the interview with you.' I frowned.

My guard flew up again. Although I was happy to see Nico and I really wanted to see if we could work things out, at the same time I didn't want to be made a fool of. I needed to make sure he was being honest.

'I know! But it is true. That is why I take so long to get here. I want to come yesterday, but first I need to get proof.'

Nico pulled out his phone and played a recording. There were two people speaking. I recognised the female as the journalist I'd heard interviewing Nico, but the man's voice wasn't Nico's. I gasped.

It *was* Lucien!

The journalist explained that her editor had just given

her a few more questions to ask—ones of a more personal nature—and asked 'Nico' if he'd be happy to answer them. Lucien, like the squirmy prick he was, said, 'Of course.'

The first question was the one I'd read, mentioning that Nico had been spotted with me at an awards ceremony and asking if it was serious. Lucien then went on to give the exact response that was printed in the article.

'What an arsehole!' I shouted. 'How did you find out?'

'As soon as I read the article on Saturday, I contact the journalist that do the interview, but she is on holiday, so she did not call until this morning. But she tell me that she write exactly what I say. I tell her I did not say that. Then she explain that she call back fifteen minutes after the first interview finish and speak to me again. That was when I know. Remember after the interview, Lucien come into my office to look for some documents?'

'Yeah, yeah, that's right.' I scanned my brain. 'Miriam was away from her desk and we went for a walk, so we left him there. Alone.'

'*Exactement*. So he hear the phone ring, she tell him she is from the website and ask for me and he tell her that *he* is Nico. She think that we sound alike, with the French accent, and so she believe him.'

'What a deceitful prick! But why would he do that?' I asked, then immediately answered my own question in my head.

That was the same afternoon that Lucien and I had had that run-in outside. When he'd told me that he guaranteed that I wouldn't get my happy ending with Nico. Looked like he'd seen an opportunity to make good on his promise by sabotaging my relationship prospects with Nico, and he'd grabbed it.

'He never liked me. I could tell from the beginning. He told me that you normally date models and actresses and basically that I wasn't good enough for you. Made out that I was just some sort of passing fetish.'

'You are serious? *Putain!* I wish that you tell me this, Cassie. That is not acceptable. I was angry when he try and say I do something with the model in front of you, but I did not know he say other things.'

'I'd rather not know about who you've been with...' I waved my hand away. 'I realise that we'd been apart for a while and you had needs.'

'*Non!* It is important that you know. I have not been with any woman since you, at Christmas. I am a grown man—not a teenage boy. I can control myself. If I have needs, I can use these.' He raised his hands.

'Oh.' I had to admit, that was a relief. Quite literally... 'In case it wasn't clear, I haven't been with anyone either,' I said.

'And I tell you before, you are *more* than good enough for me. You are so smart and strong. You are kind and caring. And beautiful.' He reached out and stroked my cheek. My skin warmed from his touch and the sweet words he'd used to describe me. 'But I do not think that is the reason Lucien did this. You remember I tell you we did not speak for many years?'

'Yeah?'

'When we were young, I think about twenty-one, Lucien move to Paris. He have a girlfriend. He loved her very much. He was ready to do everything with her. Get married, have children.'

'Wow, at twenty-one?'

'Yes. It was very serious. She was friendly. I enjoy

conversations with her. She ask me a lot of advice. She say she want to become a hairdresser, so I introduce her to my boss and he give her a job at the salon. But Lucien become jealous, because we spend a lot of time together. Not *together*, we just work at the same salon. Anyway, Lucien decide to propose to her, but she say no, because she is in love with me…'

'What the hell?' My mouth dropped open. 'Did you know?'

'Not at all. I just think she is friendly. She is the girl-friend of my best friend. I would not do that. But Lucien, he blame me. He say that I must do something with her to make this happen. He tell me that I make him lose the one woman that he ever love.'

'Didn't she explain to him?'

'She try, but he does not listen. After that we did not speak again until recently.'

'What, when he found out you were rich?' I rolled my eyes.

'Maybe. But at this point, the company is growing very fast and I need more people around me that I trust. And without what happen with the girlfriend, Lucien is a good friend. We talk, he apologise and say that before we are young and stupid and ask for me to forgive him.'

'So you're saying he did this—he deliberately sabo-taged the interview as some kind of payback?'

God, Lucien must have really wanted me out of the picture. What he'd done was so stupid, though. Surely he must have realised he would get found out at some point? I supposed he'd just seen an opportunity to get rid of me and taken it without thinking it through. Shithead.

'*Oui*. He see that I…' Nico paused and looked into my

eyes as his face broke into a smile. 'He can see that I am in love with you and he want revenge.'

'Wait, *what*?' I paused, then frowned as I tried to process what he'd just said. 'You're *in love* with me?' My heart thudded as I held my breath.

'Of course,' Nico replied.

Oh.

He hadn't said a definitive *yes*, he'd said *of course*. I'd heard those words before. My gaze dropped to the floor and my shoulders slumped.

Nico lifted my chin and looked me straight in the eyes.

'Cassie, *chérie*, I love you with all of my heart. I realise that I did not make my commitment clear enough before. I just assumed that you knew. But I want to tell you now that I never feel about a woman the way I feel about you.'

Nico's eyes were smiling. Wide. Happy. Kind of how I imagined my eyes looked when a waiter brought me a big chocolate dessert, but multiplied by a billion. His were filled with emotion. Filled with... love.

He loves me.

Nico just said he loves me.

Holy shit.

It felt like I'd swallowed a million butterflies. My stomach fluttered with happiness.

OMG. This was *crazy*. In the best possible way. This was the best news. *The greatest.*

I wanted to do a cartwheel and multiple backflips in my living room. Better not, though—I'd probably end up with my foot in the TV.

Instead, I threw my arms around his neck and kissed him. It was slow, gentle and heartfelt.

We came up for air and I stared into Nico's hypnotic eyes, thinking I'd be happy to just look at him all day.

'You see? *This*. What we are feeling now, that is what Lucien see,' Nico said as I tried to take it all in. 'This is the reason he try to come between us. Cassie, I want to wake up with you every morning. I want you to fall asleep in my arms every night. I want to travel the world with you. I want us to discover things, together. Create amazing things, *together*. You think that I am not serious, but the opposite is true. I want to share my life with you. That is why I say I want you to come to Paris. To live with me. To work with me. I love your ideas. I would like you to bring them to life. I need you. Help me start the foundation. What do you think?'

About the fact that you love me? My head screamed with joy. *I think it's fucking fantastic.*

I came to my senses. He wasn't asking about that. He'd asked me about… wait. I'd been so caught up with the fact that he'd just declared his love for me that I'd just realised the second part of what he'd said. He wanted me to move to Paris and set up the foundation for him?

Whoa.

'*That* was the job that you were talking about in your message?'

'*Oui.*'

'Oh!' My eyes widened. 'I thought you wanted me to be your PA.'

'*Non.*' Nico shook his head. 'I tell you before that I think you can do something different. Something bigger.'

Bloody hell.

My heart flipped for about the tenth time in the last ten seconds. That was *amazing*. Incredible. But also terrifying.

I mean, the plus sides were obvious: a life with Nico, living in a new city, getting to do work that I really enjoyed, having new challenges. I'd always said I wanted to do more meaningful work, and I was unemployed now, with no exciting career prospects on the horizon, so this would be a brilliant opportunity. But then there were other, more challenging things to consider, like the language barrier and leaving my home, my family and friends.

Plus, and this was a biggie, I'd be working *for* Nico. I'd be reliant on him to pay my wages. *Hmmm*. That didn't sit right with me. I'd always been independent. I wasn't sure I liked the idea of having all of my eggs in one basket and relying on a man for everything. That would put me in a vulnerable position. If it didn't work, then I'd be out of a job. It was risky.

But you'd have a life with Nico…, my brain screamed again. *Surely that would make everything else worthwhile?*

Good point.

I considered telling Nico that I needed time to think about it. It was a big decision. But I also felt like I'd been waiting my whole life for someone like him. Why waste any more time?

And what did I have to lose? I could keep my flat here for a few months and, worst-case scenario, if it all went tits up in Paris, I could come back home to London.

'Will you be my boss?' I rested my finger on my chin.

'*Non*. This will be your vision. We will be equal. I will arrange a contract in both French and English with everything in writing, to make you feel more comfortable. And of course I can wait until you leave your job.'

'No need. I quit this afternoon.'

'Wow!' Nico's eyes widened. '*Chérie!* That is amazing!' He threw his arms around me and lifted me off the ground. 'I am so proud of you.'

I knew he'd be happy for me. *I knew* he'd be supportive. Nico always was.

And it was at that moment that I realised he always would be.

I knew Nico was *the one*.

Before I had gone to Paris, I'd listened too much to the wrong people. Instead of believing the positive things voiced by my besties and Nico, I'd believed the negative things people had told me throughout my life instead. That I wasn't worthy of the good things in life. That I shouldn't wish for true love and happiness.

I'd let other people's opinions get into my head. I'd let Nate's fears and overprotectiveness and Mum's beliefs that I shouldn't expect too much from life fuel my insecurities. And then when I'd arrived, I'd allowed Lucien's toxic comments to get to me. But they were all wrong. They didn't know what I had with Nico and how he felt about me. From now on, I'd trust my instincts. And my gut told me that this was the real deal.

I didn't know the finer details like the salary or responsibilities, but we could discuss that—and work out the logistics of how and when I could make the move there— properly later. I trusted Nico. More importantly, I loved him. From the bottom of my heart. I couldn't let this opportunity for happiness slip through my fingers.

'I'm in!'

'*Fantastique!*' Nico spun me around the room. 'You have your passport here, yes?'

'Yeah, why?'

'Come, let us go.'

'Where?'

'It is Valentine's Day tomorrow, *non*? So we go to the most romantic city in the world to celebrate.'

'Erm, I think you'll find that we're already in London.' I folded my arms in mock protest and raised my eyebrow.

'You are funny! You know I talk about Paris. There is a Eurostar leaving in one hour. If we go now, we can be in Paris in time for a pre-Valentine's dinner.'

'But I need to get changed!' I gestured at my Minnie Mouse onesie. I'd forgotten I was wearing that. It was *so* comfortable.

'You look *adorable*!' Nico smirked.

'Seriously?' I raised my eyebrow.

'*Oui!* What you are wearing does not matter.'

This time I believed him. Now that I thought about it, onesies were the perfect travel outfit. Who cared if people gave me funny looks?

'I haven't packed or anything!'

'We have clothes in Paris.' Nico rolled his eyes. 'And you already have a closet in our apartment with things to wear.'

Our apartment.

That sounded so lovely.

True. I'd survived without a suitcase once, so I could do it again.

'If there is something else you need, we can buy it there. You can use my card. And before you argue or think that you are just another woman I do this with, I want to tell you that when I say before that I only ever give three women my card: one was my mother, the second was my sister and the third was an ex on her birthday. But I did not give her the black card that I give to you. If I did, I would be bankrupt!' he laughed.

'It doesn't matter.' I smiled. It was nice of him to explain, but it wasn't important anymore. 'That was in the past.'

'This is true. And now *you* are my future.' Nico pulled me in for a kiss.

It was as if all of our emotions were transported through our lips. Every fear or worry I'd ever had about our relationship evaporated under the heat of his tongue.

'Come on.' I pulled him into the hallway. 'Let's continue snogging on the way there. We've got a train to catch.' I grabbed my passport, coat and bag and took Nico's hand, and we headed out the door.

CHAPTER FORTY

B *loody hell.*
My mouth fell open as I spotted a silver Rolls-Royce waiting outside my building. The driver jumped out and opened the passenger door for us.

'This is fancy!' I raised my eyebrow.

'Only the best for my *girlfriend*.' Nico smiled as he slid onto the cream leather seat next to me. 'I prefer something more subtle, but this is the car Miriam organise for me, so…'

'Well, I was going to suggest we get the tube or an Uber, but I suppose I can suffer this luxury,' I chuckled.

'You are so selfless.'

'I know.'

Nico strapped into his seat belt.

'So, what happened to Lucien? Not that I care about the arsehole, but out of curiosity.'

'I speak to him. Our friendship is over. And he will not return to the business. It is difficult to fire people in

France, but my lawyers will take care of it. Especially because he steal from the company.'

Nico explained that Lucien had been getting him to sign off on product orders, which Lucien would then intercept; he'd sell the products to unauthorised retailers online and then pocket the money for himself. In fact, the document he'd got Nico to sign that first night I'd arrived was one of them.

'I knew it!' I gasped.

'You were right. I trust and rely on him too much. Normally I am a good judge of character, but with Lucien I make a mistake. I have worries about some things that he do, but I ignore them, because I believe it will be harder to run the business without him and I think I need his help because of my dyslexia. But I am not afraid to talk about this anymore. I run the business without him before, so I will do it again. Thank you.'

'For what?'

'If you do not mention your concerns, it will take me longer to discover his lies. To, how you say, smell the coffee?'

'The saying is *to wake up and smell the coffee*. Although really, in the UK it should be to smell the tea— your favourite drink!' I laughed.

'Tea? Ugh, *dégueulasse*.' Nico winced, then grinned. 'Anyway, *merci*. You help open my eyes to the truth. I tell you that you are good for me.' Nico stroked my cheek and my whole body lit up.

'I'm glad you found out, but I'm also so sorry. I know it must be hard to be betrayed by someone close to you.'

Before I'd thought Lucien didn't like me because in his

eyes I didn't deserve Nico. But now I reckoned he'd been more worried about me seeing through his lies.

'*Oui*. It is hard to lose someone I believe is a friend, but it is life.' He shrugged his shoulders. 'Like I say before, in business, you must not have weak links and I do not keep toxic people around me. Also, the journalist remove Lucien's lies from the article.' Nico reached for his phone and tapped on the screen. My mobile pinged. 'They edit the article. I just sent you a link.'

I reached in my bag, pulled out my phone, then clicked the link. The photo of us was still in the article, but…

OMG.

I read the caption underneath. Instead of Nico with the 'mystery woman', it read: "*Nico with the special lady in his life, Cassie.*"

My heart.

I scanned down to read the rest of the article. They'd removed the big quote about him being single, which was good. I spotted the question where 'Nico' was asked if it was serious between us. This time, the real Nico's response was:

"Very. For me this is a serious relationship. I am very happy."

My whole body zinged with joy.

'Wow. I…' I stuttered, trying to find the words. 'I'm surprised they changed it but also really, really happy to read that. Thank you. That was a risk for you, though. What if I didn't want to see you again?' The corner of my mouth twitched.

'The risk is worth it. And I know you feel what I do. I mean what I say, Cassie. You are special to me.' Nico took my hand in his and squeezed it.

'And they were happy to change it. Like you tell me, they are a very authentic website. They do not want to have lies in their stories. And when I tell the journalist how I feel about you, she want to help me fix it. I also tell her that maybe we will have a story for her about my dyslexia.'

'You've decided to talk about it?' My eyes widened.

'*Oui*. If I can help other people feel better than I did and help them see that it is possible to be successful even if you do not get good results at school, it will be worth it. I am glad you encourage me to do it and not to hide this anymore. Thank you.'

'That's brilliant.' I threw my arms around him. 'We're going to do so much good work with the foundation. I can just feel it.'

For the first time in forever, I felt excited about my career prospects. I didn't want this to be like the poncy charity work that some rich people did just for show. I wanted this to make a *real* difference. To create *real* opportunities, scholarships and training programmes for disadvantaged people.

I'd like us to help those who didn't do well in school because their skills weren't suited to the traditional academic measures of success—people like Nico and me—make something of themselves.

I couldn't wait to get started on this new venture and, of course, continue my romantic adventures with my amazing Nico.

An hour ago, if you'd told me that I'd be on my way to St Pancras to catch the Eurostar with him, I wouldn't have believed you. And tonight of all nights. I thought tomorrow was going to be another Valentine's Day by myself, with just a pizza and a tub of Häagen-Dazs for company.

'So you came to get your *girlfriend* to whisk her away for Valentine's Day, eh? I have to say, even though you're romantic, I didn't think you'd be into that.'

'Well, you are right. On one hand, I believe that every day should be like Valentine's Day, *non*? If you show your partner that you love them only on this day, that is not good. But I also believe that there is not enough love in the world, so if this day makes people share their feelings more, that is not a bad thing.'

'True.'

'I will also sleep better with you beside me. Since you left, it has been difficult, but the audiobook you get me help. *Merci.*'

'You listened to one?'

'*Oui.* I like.' That warmed my heart. 'But it will be great to have you back in our bed, especially tonight. Now this day will always have a very special meaning.'

'Why?'

'Because we will remember that the night before Valentine's was the day that we both tell each other that we are in love for the first time.'

'I didn't say I loved you.' I smirked.

'Ah.' Nico nodded. 'This is true. But it is okay. You do not have to. I *feel* it.' He took my hand and placed it on his heart.

He was right. I was truly, madly, completely and utterly in love with Nico. And it was time that I told him so.

Telling someone you loved them didn't mean you were weak; it meant you were strong. Strong enough to put your heart on the line. No risk, no reward, right? I turned to face him.

'I love you, Nico.'

There. I'd said it. And it wasn't so bad. I didn't feel nervous or vulnerable. It didn't seem scary. In fact, it felt so right. Now I wished I'd told Nico sooner. I leant over and gave him another long, slow kiss. I couldn't get enough of this man.

'I love you, Cassie.'

'And I love you too,' I repeated. Telling him once wasn't enough.

'And Paris?' he said when we eventually pulled apart.

'Hmmm.' I put my finger on my chin. 'Of course I do! I *love* Paris!'

'And you want to be there more than London?'

'If you'd asked me before, I would've said not to push your luck. But now, I've changed my mind. And do you know why?' I stroked his cheek.

'Why?'

'Because in English we have a saying: *home is where the heart is*. You have my heart, Nico. You are my home. So, if the man I love is in Paris, then there's nowhere else I'd rather be.'

EPILOGUE

Two months later...

There was a knock at the door.

'*Entrer*,' I said in my best French accent, inviting them to come in.

I still couldn't believe I had my own office. And it wasn't a little broom cupboard either. It was a big, light and airy room with a tall ceiling and brilliant white walls. Plus, the huge double windows had sweeping views of Paris. I didn't think I'd ever tire of looking at this beautiful city.

I looked up and my whole body bubbled with excitement.

'*Salut, chérie!*' Nico leant against the door frame, looking as gorgeous as ever. He was dressed in dark trousers and a crisp white shirt with the sleeves rolled up to his elbows, exposing his muscular forearms. *So hot.*

Nico beamed as he strode towards me, stepped behind my chrome and glass desk, then pressed his lips on mine.

'Mmm,' I groaned with pleasure as I stood up, wrapped my arms around his waist and pulled him in closer. 'I missed you this morning. How was your meeting?'

'*Bien*. I missed you too.' He took my hand and led me to the sofa. 'But I have no more early meetings this week, so we can stay in bed and hold each other for longer.'

'Perfect!' I said, snuggling up beside him. That was always the best part of the morning. Being wrapped in Nico's arms: my favourite place in the world.

'Well, except on Sunday, of course, when we will go for our run…'

'Don't worry, I haven't forgotten. I'll be ready!'

Hard to believe, but I'd been running with Nico at least one morning a week. He used to go with Lucien, but now that arsehole was out of his life for good, I knew Nico missed having a running partner, so I'd volunteered. Last time we went at 6 a.m. Six! *If that isn't love, I don't know what is.*

'You've been working hard on the foundation, so today, you deserve a break.'

I'd officially started working at Icon about a week after our epic Valentine's Day in Paris two months ago and it had been full-on ever since.

With the help of one of his trusted business advisors, Nico and I had created a solid plan for the foundation, which had been so satisfying.

Every morning I woke up excited to go to work. I even found myself scribbling down ideas in the middle of the night when I should be sleeping. We were on track to launch it in a few weeks and I couldn't wait. I really believed we were going to make a big difference.

'Sounds good. Want to go for a coffee?'

'*Non*. I would like to take you for lunch.'

'Cool! What time?'

'Now.'

'But it's only half past ten!'

'I know. I will take you to a nice restaurant in Versailles and then we can visit the château and the gardens. What time is your dinner?'

'Around half seven.'

'*Parfait*. We will be back by then.'

Nico and I walked hand in hand to the car where Maurice was waiting.

'*Salut!*' I smiled as he opened the door. '*Ça va?*'

'*Bien, merci, et toi?*'

'*Je vais bien, merci*,' I replied, letting him know all was well. Last month I'd started taking French lessons at a language school, and although it was still very early days, my confidence was growing.

'Are you looking forward to your dinner tonight?' Nico asked as he slid onto the back seat next to me.

'Definitely!' I was meeting Lucy for a catch-up. Ever since I'd moved to Paris, we'd met at least once a week.

'I am very happy that you have a friend here.'

'Me too! Speaking of dinner, Mum texted earlier to ask when you're coming round again. You were a big hit with my family.'

I'd finally taken Nico to meet them at my parents' house last weekend. Mum had been inviting us constantly since the day after Valentine's Day, when I'd arranged a family group video call and dropped the bombshell that I was in Paris and was going to live here. Permanently.

Of course, Mum, Dad and Nate had freaked out, but I'd told them point-blank that I was in love with Nico, I'd made up my mind, and whilst I appreciated that their concerns were well-intentioned, there was nothing they could do or say to stop me. Eventually, they'd come around to the idea and wished me well.

I could've taken Nico to meet them sooner, but I wanted us to have time to settle into our new life without any judgement or negativity.

I needn't have worried. Nico went down a storm. Within half an hour of his arrival, Flo and Lily dragged me into the bathroom, squealing with delight at how amazing he was and how perfect we were for each other.

Dad quickly bonded with Nico over a mutual love of football, and as for Mum—well, I'd never seen her so in awe. She hung on Nico's every word and gushed about his lovely accent. Plus, Mum gave Nico the biggest roast potatoes, which was a sure sign that she adored him.

Even Nate pulled me aside after dessert to apologise for being so harsh during Lily's birthday dinner. 'I hold my hands up, Cheeks,' he'd said. 'I was wrong about this one and you were right: Nico's a keeper. I can see now that he's a good guy. I'm happy for you, sis.' Hearing those words made my heart dance.

'That is very nice of your mother to invite me. Tell her I would be happy to visit again, or perhaps she would prefer to visit us in Paris?'

'Are you joking?' My eyes widened. 'She'd be on the first Eurostar out here!'

'Then it is settled. Find out when your family would like to come, and Miriam will organise the tickets. It will be good for them to see where you are living. It will help them worry less.'

I threw my arms around Nico. He was always so thoughtful. I'd give Mum a call later. She'd be so excited.

Bella and Melody were also trying to sort out dates so that they could come over. We were still in constant contact with group video calls and texts, but it wasn't the same as seeing them in the flesh. I couldn't wait for them to experience Paris.

'So this evening, when you are out with Lucy, I will have another session with Violette.'

'That's brilliant!' I squeezed his hand. Violette was Nico's therapist. He'd been having sessions twice a week and although he'd found opening up to a stranger hard at first, he'd stuck with it. 'I'm so proud of you.'

'*Merci*. It is helping. I am glad that you suggest this. I think soon I will be ready to talk about my dyslexia more publicly too.'

'Great! But remember, there's no rush.'

I was so happy we were both making progress. Nico with his therapy and me with my new life in this wonderful city.

All that I needed now was my visa. As the UK was no longer part of the EU, moving here was more complicated. However, Nico's hotshot lawyer assured me that he'd find a way to make my stay permanent.

I'd rented out my flat in London, so my mortgage was all covered. For once, I didn't have to worry about money, but not because of Nico's billions. The salary we'd agreed on for my new role was fantastic, plus Reg had offered me a generous payout and I would've been crazy not to take it.

He'd called me the day after I'd emailed, and I'd told him all of the despicable things Spencer had done—and I mean *everything*. Although I hadn't actually seen him with his dick out, in my eyes, suspecting that he was pleasuring himself in the office was cause enough to at least report it. The last thing I wanted was for someone else to witness that. Who knew what trauma it could cause?

Reg had apologised repeatedly for Spencer's behaviour and sacked him soon afterwards.

I lowered the car window and the cool breeze hit my skin as I watched us leave the city behind. I'd always wanted to go to Versailles. I loved how Nico did spontaneous things like this. Surprising me for Valentine's Day, organising a picnic in the park or suggesting we go for a romantic walk by the Seine *just because.*

My phone chimed. It was Lily. She was still getting over her break-up with River, but was considering taking a sabbatical and going travelling around Spain, which I totally supported. Look what had happened when I'd gone to Paris. I had a feeling that she had exciting adventures ahead of her. I hoped she'd find the same happiness I had.

I tucked my phone away, then rested my head on Nico's shoulder, breathing in his delicious scent. As he gently stroked my back, warmth flooded through me.

For the first time in my life, I felt complete. I was fulfilled in every area: work, home and love. Every day felt like I was living in a fairy tale. I'd had to kiss a lot of frogs to find my Prince Charming, but Nico had been worth the wait.

It was crazy that because of the distance and his money, I used to think that Nico and I could never be more than a fling. But now I knew that when you found *the one*, no obstacles were big enough to keep you apart. You'd find a way to be together—even if it meant moving to another country.

'Do you know what?'

'Tell me, Cassie.' He stroked my cheek.

'I really love you.'

His face broke into a huge grin.

'*Je t'aime beaucoup, chérie. Pour toujours. T'as compris*?'

'*Oui*,' I said. A flutter of excitement filled my chest. My heart was so full it could burst. Nico had been speaking to me more in French to help me learn the lingo faster, and right now I was so glad that I'd understood every word that had just fallen from his lips. 'You said you love me a lot, forever.'

He smiled proudly, then kissed me softly, causing my whole body to zing with happiness.

Yep. The more time I spent with Nico, the more I knew that our relationship wasn't fleeting. My Paris romance was the kind of deep, all-encompassing, heartfelt, meaningful love which would last a lifetime.

Want More?

Would you like to know how Cassie and Nico spent Valentine's Day? Join the Olivia Spring VIP Club and **receive the *My Paris Romance* Bonus Chapters for FREE! Start reading now:** https://BookHip.com/CSSAGKW

Read Book 4 Now!

After her break-up with River, will Lily find love with Nate's best friend, Carlos, in Spain? **Order the steamy brother's-best-friend romcom novel *My Spanish Romance* from Amazon now!**

ENJOYED THIS BOOK? YOU CAN MAKE A BIG DIFFERENCE.

If you've enjoyed *My Paris Romance*, **I'd be so very grateful if you could spare two minutes to leave a review on Amazon, Goodreads and BookBub**. It doesn't have to be long (unless you'd like it to be!). Every review – even if it's just a sentence – would make a *huge* difference.

By leaving an honest review, you'll be helping to bring my books to the attention of other readers and hearing your thoughts will make them more likely to give my novels a try. As a result, it will help me to build my career, which means I'll get to write more books!

Thank you SO much. As well as making a big difference, you've also just made my day!

Olivia x

ALL BOOKS BY OLIVIA SPRING:
AVAILABLE ON AMAZON

ALSO BY OLIVIA SPRING

The Middle-Aged Virgin

Have you read my debut novel *The Middle-Aged Virgin*? It includes Bella from *My Paris Romance* too! Here's what it's about:

Newly Single And Seeking Spine-Tingles...

Sophia seems to have it all: a high-flying job running London's coolest beauty PR agency, a long-term boyfriend and a dressing room filled with designer shoes. But money can't buy everything...

When tragedy strikes, Sophia realises she's actually an unhappy workaholic in a relationship that's about as exciting as a bikini wax. And as for her sex life, it's been so long since Sophia's had any action, her bestie has started calling her a *Middle-Aged Virgin*.

Determined to get a life and *get lucky*, Sophia hatches a plan to work less and live more. She ends her relationship and jets off on a cooking holiday in Tuscany, where she meets mysterious chef Lorenzo. Tall, dark and very handsome, this Italian stallion might be just what Sophia needs to spice things up in the bedroom...

But the dating scene has changed since Sophia was last single, and although she'd score an A+ for her career, when it comes to men, she's completely out of her comfort zone. How will Sophia, a self-confessed control freak, handle the unpredictable world of dating? And how much will she sacrifice for love?

Join Sophia today on her laugh-out-loud adventures as she

searches for happiness, enjoys passion between the sheets and experiences OMG moments along the way!

Here's what readers are saying about it:

"I couldn't put the book down. It's **one of the best romantic comedies I've read**." Amazon reader

"Life-affirming and empowering." Chicklit Club

"Perfect holiday read." Saira Khan, TV presenter & newspaper columnist

"Olivia has an innate knack for the sex scenes, which are very hot. **This book was steamy**, but with such a huge element of humour in it that when you read it **you will certainly giggle throughout at the escapades**." Book Mad Jo

"Absolutely hilarious! A diverse, wise and poignant novel." The Writing Garnet

Buy *The Middle-Aged Virgin* on Amazon today!

AN EXTRACT FROM THE MIDDLE-AGED VIRGIN

Prologue

'It's over.'

I did it.

I said it.

Fuck.

I'd rehearsed those two words approximately ten million times in my head—whilst I was in the shower, in front of the mirror, on my way to and from work…probably even in my sleep. But saying them out loud was far more difficult than I'd imagined.

'What the fuck, Sophia?' snapped Rich, nostrils flaring. 'What do you mean, it's over?'

As I stared into his hazel eyes, I started to ask myself the same question.

How could I be ending the fifteen-year relationship with the guy I'd always considered to be the one?

I felt the beads of sweat forming on my powdered forehead and warm, salty tears trickling down my rouged cheeks, which now felt like they were on fire. This was serious. This was actually happening.

Shit. I said I'd be strong.

'Earth to Sophia!' screamed Rich, stomping his feet.

I snapped out of my thoughts. Now would probably be a good time to start explaining myself. Not least because the veins currently throbbing on Rich's forehead appeared to indicate that he was on the verge of spontaneous combustion. Easier said than done, though, as with every second that passed, I realised the enormity of what I was doing.

The man standing in front of me wasn't just a guy that came in pretty packaging. Rich was kind, intelligent, successful, financially secure, and faithful. He was a great listener and had been there for me through thick and thin. Qualities that, after numerous failed Tinder dates, my single friends had repeatedly vented, appeared to be rare in men these days.

Most women would have given their right and probably their left arm too for a man like him. So why the hell was I suddenly about to throw it all away?

Want to find out what happens next? Buy *The Middle-Aged Virgin* on Amazon today!

ACKNOWLEDGEMENTS

I can't quite believe this is my ninth acknowledgements page! I have so many people to thank for helping me to bring *My Paris Romance* to life.

First up: Mum and Jas. Thanks for looking at the very early drafts of this book and for supporting me from day one. Knowing you always have my back means more than you know.

Shout-out to my brilliant beta readers. Emma: I absolutely loved your enthusiasm for this book and, of course, for Cassie and Nico! I'm so grateful for your invaluable input throughout this journey. You're a true diamond.

Marianne: *merci beaucoup* for checking my French and for reading over the book so diligently. Your attention to detail and fantastic suggestions really helped to strengthen my novel. I can't thank you enough!

Loz, aka laser eyes. I was always excited to receive your messages whilst you were reading, because I loved how you picked up on the little but important details that could easily be missed. Thanks a million.

To my exceptional editor, Eliza, super-talented cover designer, Rachel, and fab web designer, Dawn. Thanks for helping to make this book shine.

Amazing Matt: thanks for giving me an insight into dyslexia and showing that it needn't be a barrier to success. You're an inspiration.

To my real-life Nico: thank you for your continued encouragement and for showing me what true love and happiness means. It's definitely been helpful when writing books about romance! *Je t'aime*.

Sending big virtual hugs to the wonderful bloggers and ARC readers who took the time to read this book and write lovely reviews. Thank you sooo very much for helping to spread the word about *My Paris Romance*! Your support makes such a difference!

And as always, the biggest thank-you is reserved for *you*, dear reader. Just like the I Love You Wall mentioned in this book, if I could, I'd create my own gratitude wall to thank you in hundreds of languages. I really appreciate you buying and reading my novels, recommending them to your friends and sending me kind messages that always make my heart sing. You're the best!

Lots of love

Olivia x

ABOUT THE AUTHOR

Olivia Spring lives in London, England. When she's not making regular trips to Spain and Italy to indulge in paella, pasta, pizza and gelato, she can be found at her desk, writing new sexy romantic comedies.

If you'd like to say hi, email olivia@oliviaspring.com or connect on social media.

TikTok: www.tiktok.com/@oliviaspringauthor

 facebook.com/ospringauthor
twitter.com/ospringauthor
 instagram.com/ospringauthor

Printed in Great Britain
by Amazon

31654393R00223